The Great Celt

Published by
Glen Kelty Books
a division of Corrxan Inc.
1135 Hunterston Road NW
Calgary, Alberta, Canada
T2K 4M9

ISBN # 978-09948242-4-0

Publisher's Note
This book is a work of fiction. Names, characters, places and incidents either are the product of the author's imagination or are used fictionally, as with the use of actual historical figures and events. Any resemblance to actual persons, living or dead, business establishments, events or locales is entirely coincidental. The publisher does not have control over and does not assume any responsibility for author or third party web sites or their content.

www.glenkeltybooks.com

Uneasy lies the head that wears the crown.

Shakespeare
King Henry IV, Act III, Scene I, Line 31.

1

Moscow
October 12, 2007

Evgenia slowly climbed the stairs to her fifth-floor apartment. On each floor, she passed the doors of the broken elevator, sitting idle for two years now. For her, it was a sign of democracy. Back when the government owned everything, elevators got fixed. Now, with private enterprise, the building's owner didn't want to spend the money and no one could force him to. *Let's hear it for freedom*, she thought to herself.

She reached her floor and flung open the stairwell door. The hallway was thick with smells from the tenants cooking their dinners. As she passed each door, she could tell what everyone was having. The Popovs, a cabbage stew. The Katins, some sort of ham dish. As she reached her door, she could smell her mother-in-law's favorite borsht. Sasha's parents were here. She smiled. Now she wouldn't have to make dinner.

Turning her key in the lock, she swung open the door to be greeted by her four-year-old son, Andrei, who ran down the hallway and wrapped his arms around her legs.

"Hi Mama," Andrey said.

"Hello my little *mal'chik*. Are Baba and Ded here?"

"Yes. Papa is home, too."

She smiled down at him and rubbed his hair. "Well, let me in the house so I can go see them."

Andrey spun around and ran back down the hallway. Evgenia took off her knapsack and coat, then closed the door behind her. She took a second to straighten her hair before moving down the hall.

She found her husband and his father sitting at the table, each with a glass of vodka. "You're home early, Sasha. Is crime at an all-time low?"

Sasha worked for the FSB as a junior detective. His father was a district captain. "No. Papa came by the office today and said he needed a detective for a short project. Apparently, it involves drinking vodka at home."

Evgenia looked at her father-in-law. "Dmitri, Sasha's colleagues already look on him with suspicion because of you. This kind of thing makes it worse."

Dmitri Raynykov shifted his weight in the chair uncomfortably. Evgenia suppressed a smile. She could never quite figure out why a man like Dmitri could be so intimidating and dangerous in the streets of Moscow, but still seemed uncomfortable around his little daughter-in-law.

"Evie, did the DNA results come in?" Sacha asked. She caught a note of anxiety in his voice, too.

She sat down across from her husband. "Is that why the two of you skipped out of work?" They had both shown considerable interest in the DNA work her lab had been doing. The project was a very old but very famous crime. The subjects were ninety-year-old human remains suspected to be members of the last tsar's family. "OK, the results are conclusive. The male remains are those of Alexis Romanov. The female remains are either Maria or

Anastasia. They were too close in age to figure one from the other without a direct independent DNA sample to compare the results with."

"It's Anastasia," Dmitri said.

Evgenia looked at her father-in-law. "You sound pretty definite about that considering they died almost forty years before you were born."

Sasha and Dmitri looked at each other. Evgenia didn't like the look they were giving each other, as if there was a dangerous secret she was unaware of. "What?" she asked.

"We should tell her," said Sasha.

"Tell me what?" asked Evgenia.

"I don't know," Dmitri said.

"You blurted out Anastasia," Sasha replied.

There was a moment of silence before Evgenia spoke. "Is this part of your secret family history?"

Dmitri scowled at Sasha. "What have you been telling her?"

"Nothing," said Sasha. "When we talk about the past, I don't bring up much past your history, which I don't know much about, either. But she's family now. I know we can trust her with the story."

Dmitri looked over at Evgenia. With her eyes, she tried her best to intimidate him into talking. "You know I like history," she said. "If your... our family has a link to the last tsar of Russia, I'd love to know."

Another moment passed before Dmitri nodded. "Very well, but it cannot get out about our family link."

"Really? After almost a hundred years, would anyone important really care?"

Dmitri's face went blank. "You would be surprised."

Evgenia felt a chill go up her spine. She couldn't imagine what dangers such information could bring upon her family, but Dmitri ran in very dangerous company. Although he was officially just a district captain in the FSB, she knew his real job was much darker. She spoke in a near whisper. "Agreed."

Dmitri leaned back in his chair, the look on his face unchanged. He let the silence hang for a moment before beginning. "In the old Russia before the revolution, our family were aristocrats. My great-grandfather, Vasili Ivanovich, was the last Count Raynykov. Our ancestral lands were just north of Zelenograd. He had the ear of the tsar at one time, but as the war continued to go badly, Nicholas was rather deaf to anyone past Rasputin. It was during the Second Fatherland War, or what western Europeans called the Great War.

"Conditions were so terrible that even Vasili could tell that the tsar had to go, but not to his death. Vasili supported the Bolsheviks because they wanted to get Russia out of the war; it was causing wide spread famine and destroying the Russian army. When the Bolsheviks took over, Vasili tried to get control of the royal family's custody. But he was considered too close to them. The best he could do was to take over command of a regiment and be assigned to duty close to the family in Yekaterinburg. He was able to place one of his men, a Yakov Yurovsky, as the chief jailor."

"Yurovsky worked for your great-grandfather?" Evgenia asked.

Dmitri smiled. "Yes, but no one else knew. Even to this day. Things began to unravel when Vasili couldn't convince the regional Soviets to just let the Czech Legion leave Russia. The results were the Legion took over vast regions of Siberia, including Yekaterinburg."

Dmitri sighed before continuing. "As the Czechs were approaching, the order came to assassinate the royal family. Yurovsky's second-in-command received the order while Yurovsky was out on business. By the time news of the order became known to him, the royal family had already been assembled in the basement of the Ipatiev House. Rushing to the house, my great-grandfather was only able to save Alexis and Anastasia. Both of them had been wounded. While Yurovsky reported the entire family as killed, Vasili smuggled the two royals to safety."

"But their remains were found near the others," Evgenia said. "If they survived, how did they end up there?"

The kitchen door burst open and Baba Raynykova burst in with a huge pot of borsht. "Dinner is ready," she said, placing the pot in the middle of the table. She scowled at her husband. "Why is the table not set? You had one job, and there were two of you." She slapped the back of her son's head. "Get. Get."

Evgenia grinned. Baba Raynykova was the only person Dmitri was definitely afraid of. As Dmitri and Sasha started to grab plates, Evgenia asked, "So what happened next?"

Baba put her hand on Evgenia's shoulder. "Is he telling you the story of his great-grandfather or of the Great Celt?"

"The great who?"

"Bah," Baba said. "The Great Celt was the founder of the Raynykov family. Apparently he showed up again five hundred years later to help Alexis Romanov escape."

"No," Dmitri answered. "It wasn't *the* Great Celt. It was his ancestor with the ancient sword."

"Wait a minute," Evgenia exclaimed. "What do a 500-year-old Raynykov and a sword have to do with royal Romanovs in 1918?"

Baba shook her head, looking at her husband. "We eat first, then you can tell the story."

Evgenia had a feeling it was going to be a long night.

2

Constantinople
May 29, 1453

Connor Rainey watched with relief as the Anatolian infantry finally retreated into the darkness away from the ramparts of what was left of the Theodosian Wall. His breathing was heavy; his arms felt like great weights were pushing them down. He glanced over the makeshift stockade filling the breach in the walls to see his commander, Giovanni Giustiniani Longo, looking back at him. The shiny gleam on his armour was gone. Still prominent, though, was the hole in his breastplate where a stone chip from a cannon blast had almost killed him twenty-four hours earlier. They both smiled.

Rainey looked back out at the darkness, wondering what he was doing there. When he had joined Giustiniani and his merry band of Genoese mercenaries sailing to Constantinople's defense of back in January, he thought it would be a worthy and fairly successful enterprise. It had to be more important than the city-state wars that were consuming in Italy at the time. Besides, he had heard about how wonderful the City was, full of Byzantine splendor. When he arrived, however, he found a large defensive wall surrounding what was now little more than a group of villages. The City had been decaying for over two hundred years, ever since the Fourth Crusade had spent much of its time sacking the place instead of crusading in the Holy Lands.

But the Wall was intact. For a thousand years, it had defended the City from all sieges, twenty-three in all, not counting this current one. It had never been breached. But this siege was different. The young sultan, Mehmet, had brought modern weaponry to bear. When he marched his mighty army to lay siege to the great city, large cannon were a major part of his force. Over the last fifty-three days, his cannon had punched nine opening into the Wall around the Lycus Valley. Giustiniani had ingeniously built stockades in the breaches with dirt, wood, broken stone from the Wall, and anything else that was available. The stockades were topped with barrels filled with stone for his soldiers to fight behind.

Which was exactly what they had been doing for the past four hours in the dark of night. First, Mehmet sent in his fodder. Azaps, mobs of untrained and ill-equipped soldiers, stormed the stockades. They were easily repelled by the skilled soldiers defending against them. But this took two hours. After only ten minutes for the defenders to rest, the Anatolian infantry attacked. These men were much better trained and armed. After a great effort, they made it up to the barrels and engaged in hand to hand combat. Rainey had drawn his sword and thrown his arquebus weapon over his shoulder onto his back, because he knew he would have no time to reload it. The battle was vicious. Even with their own men in the way, Turkish cannons continued to fire. One large ball finally smashed through the stockade beside Rainey. The

Anatolians began to flow through, but the hole wasn't very large. After an hour, the defenders had killed or pushed back all the Turks who had made it through. That was the last gasp of the Anatolian attack.

As Rainey saw the remnants of the Anatolians disappear into the dark, he noticed other movement out beyond the ditch. Giustiniani saw it, too. "We're not done yet, men," he called out.

Rainey scanned the battlements to his left. About fifty yards from him, he could see Constantine XI, the emperor of the City, lit up by some of the fires burning down behind the stockades. He had shed his royal cloak. He had announced that he would fight to the death and Rainey knew he meant it. To make sure everyone else would know this, all the gates through the inner wall behind the defenders had been locked. It wasn't quite what Rainey had in mind for himself, but his honor told him to continue the fight until nothing remained to fight for. Then it would be time to leave.

Giustiniani had given Rainey a command of thirty men to defend one point of the stockade. Now he had less than twenty men left. Some of the dead lay below the barrels, some on the rampart's down slope. It was customary to carry away the dead after a fight, but the Turks were not going to give the defenders time to do much but catch their breaths. The attack's next wave was forming up. In the light from the fires, Rainey could see a well-dressed Turk on a horse behind his men exhorting them to glory.

"That's Mehmet," Giustiniani mumbled, barely heard over the noise of the cannons. He turned to his men. "We stop them this time, we win. He has his personal bodyguard lined up now. He's running out of able soldiers."

Rainey grimaced. Mehmet may have been on his last troops, but there were still a lot more of them than there were defenders. And this next wave of troops was the dreaded Janissaries. They were fresh and skilled. Rainey and the defenders had been at it for four hours. It was time for the miracle that all the religious types in the City kept praying for.

He turned back to the Turkish army forming up in front of him. A mighty roar emanated from the mass of men as they surged forward into battle. Rainey brought his arquebus up to his shoulder, loaded and ready to fire. As the approaching enemy got within fifty yards of the Wall, Giustiniani yelled for the archers to start shooting. At thirty yards, the crossbows let lose. Rainey continued to wait.

Giustiniani turned. "FIRE!" The combined fire of numerous arquebuses crackled with devastating impact on the attacking force. It had a strong effect on the attackers' morale as well. The stones knocked the lead attackers back, slowing the movement of those behind, allowing time for the soldiers to reload their arquebuses. As the first Janissaries reached the gap in the stockade, Giustiniani yelled again.

"FIRE!"

Rainey squeezed the lever on his arquebus. Several others fired at the same time. Through the smoke, Rainey saw the Janissaries falling back onto their fellows. But that was it. Sliding the arquebus over his shoulder on its strap again, he drew his sword and charged for the opening in the stockade. His men followed him.

* * *

Rainey had no sense of the time, but he began to see the enemy more clearly, indicating that the dawn was coming. He and his men had been up against the Janissaries now for at least an hour, maybe more. The sultan's elite troops had made it through the breach at least twice, only to be thrown back each time. But the number of defenders was dwindling. He was down to ten men as they slashed and stabbed and cut everything they could find in front of them. His position brought him right up beside his commander.

Then things changed. Rainey heard the sound of a projectile hitting metal beside him. With a quick glance, he saw Giustiniani falling back. Rainey reached over and caught him as he fell, slowly pulling him back from the line. Three other Genoese soldiers came to their commander's aid.

"Get me out of here," Giustiniani said breathlessly. His spirit for the fight was visibly gone.

Rainey looked up at the other three soldiers. He recognized Paolo, Victori and Giacomo. Nodding to them, he said "I'll go get the emperor."

He jumped up and ran to his left where he had seen the Emperor standing before the Janissary attack began. It took him only a minute to run between the inner and outer walls to where he found Constantine commanding his men.

"My emperor," Rainey began. "Giustiniani has fallen. We need to get him to his ship."

Exhaustion lined Constantine's face. Upon hearing Rainey's words, it was like a cloud descended over his entire body. Rainey could see his fighting spirit was hanging on only by the thinnest thread.

"Take me to him."

Rainey led the way back to Giustiniani, who was propped up against the inner wall next to one of the locked gates. Constantine knelt beside the stricken Genoese.

"My dear friend," Constantine said. "The Janissaries are losing their spirit. A little longer and we will win. Please, you must stay just a little while longer until the danger is past."

Giustiniani spit up some blood. "I am sorry, but I must leave to get fixed up on my ship. I will return when I can. Paolo and Giacomo will take command until then."

"I can send for my surgeon."

"No! I must leave . . ." Giustiniani spit up more blood, as if to make his point.

Constantine stood up slowly. "Very well." He reached for a set of keys under his belt and unlocked the gate. As it swung open, four men lifted Giustiniani and carried him through.

Before the gate could be closed as Constantine ordered, several Genoese followed their commander. Fighting on without their commander had proved too much for them. All Rainey could do was watch as they ran past him and the emperor and into the city.

Constantine peered over at Rainey. "Aren't you leaving, too?"

"I'm not Genoese," he replied. "And as you said, the Janissaries are faltering. Don't want to miss that."

Constantine laughed. Rainey could see some of the emperor's earlier spirit returning. "Then you best get back up to your post. I'll send over some men."

They nodded to each other and headed off in opposite directions. Constantine never relocked the gate.

* * *

Another band of Janissaries charged up the ramparts. One was a giant, slashing and hacking with a sword in one hand and planting his Turkish flag with the other. He stood his ground and fended off all attacks until Rainey put a group of men together to charge him. As five men kept his attention high, Rainey and two other men came in below and slashed at his legs with their swords. Rainey's sharp blade severed the giant's foot, making him topple over. The rest of the men stabbed him repeatedly. Standing again, Rainey looked around to see Janissaries passing through the stockade into the enclosure between the two walls. Rainey spun to get a look down the ramparts. More Janissaries were moving up towards him.

"The City is taken!" came a cry to the north. Rainey looked up and saw Turkish flags on the tower by the Blachernae Palace. Up there was only a single wall. That meant the Turks were in the City. Though the fighting went on, the cry continued, too. Panic began to spread among the defenders. A mad dash began to the open gate through which Giustiniani had been taken, but there were too many men. No one could get through. Rainey scanned the area for a sense of where to go next. Up on the rampart to his south, he saw Constantine fighting off Janissaries who had also penetrated the outer wall.

As good a place as any. Slashing at the Turks around him, Rainey launched himself along the stockade towards Constantine. He arrived in time to hack the arm off a Turk about to swing his sword at the emperor's head. Rainey fell in line between Constantine and John Dalmata.

"You still here?" Constantine asked.

"Nowhere else to go," Rainey responded.

And together with Theophilus Palaiologos and Don Francisco, they fought a tough retreat into a tower. They forced the door closed behind them before they could relax for a moment. In the room were also seven or eight of Constantine's elite guards.

Above the pounding on the door, Constantine said what everyone was thinking. "We have lost the City."

After a pause, Dalmata said, "We will die with you, my emperor." Everyone else nodded in agreement except Rainey. Constantine was watching him from across the room.

"Tell me who you are?"

Rainey looked up, noticing everyone's eyes were on him. He let out his breath and began. "My name is Conner Rainey. I am a mercenary in the pay of Giovanni Giustiniani."

"You fight without armor, yet somehow you do not seem to have any wounds. How is that?"

Rainey glanced down at his leather tunic, trousers and boots. "Armor slows you down. I'm quicker than regular warriors so I can avoid getting hit."

Constantine nodded. "You stayed behind when your commander left. You have fought extremely well. But we are all going to our deaths today. I do not wish to live on as the emperor who lost Constantinople."

"I understand," Rainey said.

Rainey didn't know what else to say. He glanced down at his sword. The Asian blade had been in the family for 150 years. It had never been lost in battle. He had no intention of letting it be lost here. He wasn't about to announce it to the room, but now was time to leave.

He reached behind him and grabbed his arquebus. "Let's say we get on with it, then." He began loading the gun.

When he finished, he stepped back from the door and aimed. Dalmata went for the door, checked to make sure everyone was ready, and released the latch.

The door exploded inward. The first Turk through the door took Rainey's shot straight to the chest, almost lifting him off his feet. As he fell back, Constantine and Don Francisco charged forward and pushed the mass of men out of the doorway. Dalmata followed them out, with Rainey right behind him. At the door, Rainey jumped to the right to engage a Turk. A small pocket opened up by the door, allowing Constantine's guard to leave the room. The fight was on.

Rainey slipped his back to the wall to sidestep his opponent, slicing the man's throat. He then jumped and spun to get an angle on another Turks' head, bringing his blade across the man's face. Landing, he went into a crouch to avoid another's sword and thrust his blade up into the man's gut. As that man fell away, Rainey saw the open space below, between the walls. Most of the Turks were not fighting. They were looking for a way over the inner wall. Any plunder to be had would be on its inner side.

If he stayed with the emperor, he would surely die. But getting past the attackers at the tower door presented Rainey with a survival option. Fighting for Constantinople might have been a noble cause, but dying for it was another matter.

Ladders were going up along the inner wall, giving him an escape route from the death trap. Launching himself forward, he took a second to scoop up a Turkish helmet and plopped it onto his head. Then he made for one of the ladders.

3

He ran through the streets among the advancing Turks. No one took notice of his clothes. The helmet was enough to fool the Turks, with their minds so focussed on pillage. They were all heading for Hagia Sophia, the center of the Byzantine world, rumored to contain great riches. It was easy for Rainey to keep sidestepping across fields and into streets, running towards the Golden Horn without being noticed. However, by the time he was within reach of the sea walls, Turkish sailors were flowing over them like rats, not wanting to be left behind in the search for booty.

He had to hide. Passing by a row of buildings, he spotted a Turk standing in a doorway looking in. A mass of Turks surged toward him. Rainey had to get off the street. As he crept toward the open doorway, he heard tables being overturned and other sounds of rummaging. A Turk inside said, *"Buraya gel küçük."*

Rainey thrust his sword through the back of the man in the doorway. Pushing the body forward, it slammed into a second Turk, knocking him to the floor. With a quick jerk, he pulled his sword free and took a look at what he had walked into.

Two more Turks had turned to face him, swords at the ready. In the far corner, a small child was curled up under a table. The furniture had been cleared out of the way, leaving an open space in which the Turks could attack him. A plan quickly formed in Rainey's mind and his instinct and training took over.

He bolted to his right so he had to engage only one of the Turks at first. Blocking the downward thrust from a scimitar, he spun quickly behind the Turk and, in a single motion, slashed open the man's back. Without stopping, he leapt onto the table with the little child under it, ready to engage the next man. As expected, this man raised his sword to block a downward thrust. Rainey, however, thrust his sword downward then quickly raised it as he came off the table. The Turk tried to compensate, but it was too late. The swords clanged together, both going upward as Rainey slammed into the man, driving him down onto the floor. The Turk's scimitar flew out of his hand, leaving him open to Rainey's sword swiping down into his face.

The fourth Turk had by now regained his footing after pushing away his dead comrade's body. He was rushing towards Rainey, who rolled to his left and came up on his feet, sword at the ready. The Turk hesitated slightly, taking a second to view Rainey's handiwork. With rage in his face, he charged with a yell, scimitar rising. It would sweep down across Rainey's body from left shoulder to right hip.

Rainey ducked left under the scimitar as it passed and brought his sword into the man's mid-section. He heard a grunt as he drew his sword across, opening up the man's bowels. A slow exhalation was the only sound as the man collapsed to the floor.

Rainey threw off his stolen helmet and closed the door. He turned back to the child, looking at him blankly.

"It's safe now," Rainey said in Greek.

The child didn't move. Rainey took in the creature huddled under the table. Long dark hair all in a tangle, one piece of rough cloth as clothing down to the knees, feet bare. It was a little girl, her eyes a deep dark brown with no trace of fear, just distrust. Rainey tried again. "I'm not a Turk. I'm looking for a place to hide. Can you help me?"

The girl still didn't move. *Maybe the child doesn't know Greek.* But then, her eyes flickered as she made a decision. Quickly crawling out from under the table, she stood and beckoned Rainey to follow. Leading him into a back room, the child pointed at a piece of slate on the floor. "Lift that." She did speak Greek.

Rainey looked down and saw that all the dirt had been dug out from around the slate. He knelt and pushed his fingers to the edges of the slab, trying to get a grip. It was very heavy, No wonder the little girl hadn't moved it herself. The slab began to move. As he got it up just a bit, the girl grabbed a dagger from behind her and shoved it into the gap. Rainey let the slab go, the dagger taking its weight.

"I'll need a short pole now," Rainey said. From behind a curtain, she pulled out a pole as long as she was tall. "Perfect." He wedged the pole in beside the dagger and heaved. The slab moved significantly, the dagger falling into what appeared to be a cavern underneath. He muscled the slab sideways until the hole was fully exposed. A rope hung in the opening. The child immediately crawled down, grabbed the rope and began descending into the dark.

Rainey saw a foothold partway down. He figured it was used to put the slab back into place from below. Looking around, he found a rug and pulled it over the slab, climbed into the hole and manhandled the slab back over the opening. After it slipped back into its proper spot, Rainey grabbed the rope and lowered himself. At the bottom, he found himself in a cave.

From one side, a glimmer of light came into the cave. The sound of water dripping echoed off the stone walls. The smell of sewage was strong, but that was a good thing. Turks would figure no booty would be found down here, making it the perfect place to hide. Rainey could live with the smell.

He settled down onto a stone slab and leaned against the wall. It was only then that he realized how exhausted he was after what he estimated had been eight hours of virtually continuous battle. His eyes closed almost instantly, his ears shutting out the distant screams from the city above.

He had no knowledge of how long he had been asleep, but his eyes fluttered open to see more light than he had expected and warm air on his face. He rose up to look around and saw a small fire burning on a dry piece of rock, the girl stoking it with a stick.

"Where did you get the wood?" he asked.

She didn't answer. Lowering the stick, she picked something up and walked over to Rainey. She held out a chunk of bread.

"Thank you," Rainey said, taking the bread. She turned and went back to the fire. Rainey bit off a piece while the girl picked up more food for herself. She ate silently.

Rainey watched the smoke rise from the small flames to see where it was going. It drifted up, then along the ceiling of the cave out towards where some light made its way in. There didn't seem to be enough smoke to worry about being detected, regardless of where it ended up.

"We should keep the fire small or put it out," Rainey said. "Don't want anyone up there to see the smoke."

The girl just shrugged and kept poking the fire.

"You can speak," Rainey said. The child turned her head and just nodded. "Then how about telling me your name."

"What's your name?" she asked in a tiny voice.

Rainey smiled. "Connor Rainey."

After a pause, she said, "Aunshaunie."

"That's an unusual name. It doesn't sound Greek. Where are you from?"

Aunshaunie continued watching the flames. "I don't know. I just know it's very far away."

"Was the place above us your family's home?"

She spat at the flames. "My master's."

"You are a slave."

"My master left five days ago and never came back."

"Then you're free now."

"To do what? I'm only a child."

Rainey looked around, seeing a fair amount of food and firewood piled on another ledge. "You seem to have set yourself up well here."

"It wasn't for me."

Rainey turned his eyes toward the dim light in the distance and realized he was gazing down a tunnel. Estimating the arrangement of the house above and the direction he was looking, he figured the tunnel emptied out into the Golden Horn to the city's north. It would be the right direction to go when it was time to leave.

As if reading his mind, Aunshaunie said, "We can't stay down here forever. We need to go soon."

"Three days," Rainey replied.

"Why three days?"

Rainey looked down the tunnel again. "Tradition is that Mehmet will allow looting for three days. Then his army will leave the city. They will likely all leave by the gates through the west walls. We can head out while they're leaving and find a boat. If we leave before then, we're more likely to be seen."

Aunshaunie turned back to the fire. Rainey watched her for a moment, wondering what he was going to do with a child in tow. He couldn't just leave her behind. That was not in his nature. In his mind, he could hear his father saying, *We always help the innocent.*

Where to go next also had to be decided. His original plan was that after saving Constantinople he would sail off to another adventure with Giustiniani. But the city had fallen, Giustiniani was gone, and he was hiding in a tunnel with a child. He hadn't been paid, either.

He looked himself over, taking stock of what he had. No armor. Rainey wasn't very big, so he had always relied on speed and agility. Armor got in the way of his fighting style. His leather tunic bore signs of blades that had gotten pretty close. A large split across his shoulder was the worst damage, received almost a week ago.

He reached back and pulled his sword from its scabbard. He went to a cask for water to clean the blade of the blood that had stained it since the attack's first wave the night before.

"Where did you get your sword?" Aunshaunie asked.

Rainey brought the dripping steel close to his face and examined it. Taking a cloth from his tunic, he slowly dried the blade.

"It's been in my family for generations. It comes from far away to the east."

"You don't look like you are from the east."

Rainey smiled, remembering the story of Angus Rainey and his travels to what seemed like the end of the world. "My ancestor went there over 150 years ago."

Aunshaunie went back to poking the fire, adding a little more wood. Rainey returned his sword to its scabbard and returned to where he had been sitting. He double checked the flow of smoke from the fire.

Three days. He could definitely use the rest, but he also had to figure out where to go from here.

4

1460

Rainey had been on the road for days. Riding east for the Grand Principality of Muscovy had seemed like a good idea when he decided it was time to leave Kiev, but no one had told him how far it was. Each day, he rode on by himself, living off the land, his mind staying blank. But this day, his thoughts began to return to what had brought him to this point in time, on this journey to— where? Hell? Even he wasn't sure to where.

The escape from Constantinople was anti-climactic. With all the Turks filing out through the west gates at Mehmet's command, Rainey and Aunshaunie emerged from the tunnel into the bright sunlight to find the Golden Horn full of ships of all sizes and no one in sight along the shore. Stealing a small boat, they sailed north, as that was the way the wind was blowing. Night had fallen when they passed between the twin Turkish fortresses of Anadolu Hisarı and Rumeli Hisari, seeing nobody on the walls keeping watch. Out into the Black Sea, they hugged the coast, putting in at the town of Ahtopol. There, they were able to sell the boat, bartering for two horses and provisions. They continued their journey north out onto the Rus steppe until arriving in Kiev. By then, winter was setting in.

They survived that first winter by Rainey renting his sword, the phrase he used to describe his service as a mercenary. First, he was hired by the city's merchants to keep their wares safe. His reputation grew and the following spring one of the local princes took him on as a body guard. It was easy work and paid fairly well, enough to hire servants who could care for Aunshaunie. It was nice, for a change, to be in a land not at war.

However, it wasn't long before a war had found him again. By August of 1454, Casimir, the Polish king, had gone to war with the Teutonic Knights over something called the Prussian Confederation. Rainey didn't care about a squabble between strangers hundreds of miles away, but the prince sent him off with a small army of farmers, as his duty to his king required. Rainey tried to train these peasant warriors as best he could while they travelled north, but when they reached the town the Prussians called Konitz, they were far from ready to face the battle-hardened Teutonic Knights.

Konitz was a disaster for the Poles and their allies from Kievan Rus. Rainey had warned about the possibility that the knights besieged in the town of Chojnice could charge into the rear of the Polish army. But King Casimir had been advised that this was highly unlikely. But the knights did charge out, right into the rear of the Polish lines, just as victory had seemed assured. The hastily armed farmers didn't stand a chance.

The war dragged on for years. Each spring, Rainey would head out with another batch of peasants and every fall, come back with far fewer than he had left with. Each winter, he worked to train the peasants in warfare, but there were never enough of them to make a difference. As she grew in strength and stature, Aunshaunie participated in the training as well. Rainey had decided that since he wasn't around very much, she had best learn to take care of herself. She turned out to be one of his best students.

By the end of 1459, Rainey was tired of war. The Polish king was still fighting with farmers, far outnumbering their enemy but without the skills needed to win. Aunshaunie had grown into a beautiful and capable young woman. She had caught the eye of a younger brother of the prince who employed Rainey. Believing that she was safe, Rainey made the decision that he would no longer lead hapless peasants into battles they had no reason to fight. As the next call-up was made in the spring of 1460, he said farewell to Aunshaunie, saddled his horse and disappeared into the night, leaving everything and everyone behind.

He had only one direction to take. North or west would have been back toward the wars he wanted no more part of. South was back towards Mehmet and the Turks. That left only east.

He had heard stories of Muscovy. After years of civil war, it had become a powerful princedom with a strong ruler and army. It didn't fight wars, it fought decisive battles. And those battles were few and far between, as everyone was frightened of the Muscovite army. For Rainey, it was the place to go. He could try for a position as a *bogatyr*, what a knight was called in the land of the Rus. He would also look into engaging in a business of some sort. After all, the principality's great city, Moscow, was also a major trading center.

His recollections were interrupted by the clang of swords coming through the forest. Curious, he spurred his horse forward towards the sound. In a clearing, he saw a man on a horse, sitting with his back to him. The clanging was coming from further on.

Suddenly aware of Rainey's presence, the man spun in his saddle. Rainey raised his hand in greeting, only to be met by the man wheeling his horse around, pulling out his sword and charging. All Rainey could do was to pull out his sword and charge forward as well.

The attacker swung his sword in a sweeping motion, attempting to cut Rainey across the chest. He was ready for that. He brought up his sword at an angle that deflected the other man's blade towards him. Then leaning into the attack as they passed each other, Rainey flicked his blade up to cut deeply into the man's shoulder. The other man grunted a guttural curse as he dropped his sword, galloping away down the road from which Rainey had just come.

Rainey watched the man disappear into the trees before returning his attention to the clanging of swords. Riding to where the other man had been, it was an opening into a meadow. There, one very young man with a sword in each hand was fending off two others while a fourth man stood and watched. Several bodies lay about the meadow, signs of what looked like an ambush.

That doesn't look very fair, Rainey thought. He guided his horse down a small incline to make himself visible to the combatants. He was first spotted by one of the two attackers, who stopped and stepped back. The observer turned to see him as well. The duel fell silent as everyone watched Rainey and his horse slowly plodding towards them.

The observer spoke first. "This is none of your concern. Leave us or else."

It was a different Slavic dialect than what he'd learned in Kiev, but he could understand its meaning. "Or else what?" he replied. He stopped his horse and slid off to the ground.

The observer drew his sword. "He's a Pole," the man said under his breath. Looking over his shoulder, he said, "I will take care of this one." He marched menacingly towards Rainey, raising his sword to strike.

Rainey still had his sword in his hand, walking calmly forward, observing his opponent's approach. As the heavy sword swept down towards him, Rainey suddenly spun to his right. The force of his missed strike forced his opponent to fall forward. Rainey completed his spin and sliced open the man's exposed back. The man fell heavily to the ground and lay still.

Rainey looked up and saw his opponent's cohorts staring at him. The man with the two swords took the opening given him and attacked the man on his left, cutting him down before he could even raise his sword. The last attacker, now finding himself alone, turned to run. Rainey watched as two swords fell to the ground and in a single motion, a knife was thrown square into the fleeing man's back.

That left just the two of them. The stranger quickly picked up his two swords and turned towards Rainey. "Who are you?"

Rainey turned his blade down and placed its tip into the soft ground, a non-threatening gesture. "I am the man who just saved you,"

"You are a Pole," the man replied.

Rainey smiled. "I learned Slav in Kiev and Warsaw. So I sound like a Pole, but I'm not one."

The two stood, watching each other for a moment. Then the man lowered his blades a little. "You don't look like a Pole, either. Where are you from?"

"I was born in Scotland."

The man frowned. "You are a long way from home. Why are you here?"

"Tired of fighting wars for Casimir."

The swords came back up. "You are a soldier for the Polish king?"

Rainey held up his hand. "Was. I had had enough. It was time to move on." Rainey was kicking himself for forgetting the politics in this part of the world. Muscovy and Poland didn't get along.

The man finally made a decision, lowering the swords and moving towards the dead men scattered about the meadow. He came to one lying face up, a crossbow bolt sticking out of his chest. He knelt beside him, closing the corpse's eyes. "I am sorry, Piotr Andreyvich." He got up and went to fetch some horses that had been quietly grazing nearby. When he returned, he looked at Rainey. "Help me put him up on this horse."

* * *

The two men rode east in silence. Rainey had introduced himself and asked if the road they were on went to Moscow. The man answered in the affirmative, but didn't give his name. He never spoke again, not even when they reached the city gates. As they rode through the streets, Rainey noticed the looks the man was getting from the people. It was part curiosity and part fear; they bowed to him. Rainey was getting the impression the man he had saved was a very important person indeed. His impression was confirmed when they arrived at the city's center, where stood a kremlin. Behind its walls rose a palace with domed towers.

Silently, the two men rode through the gate, unchallenged. As they came into the fortress's courtyard, men ran forward to take the man's reins.

"Take Piotr Andreyvich into the hall," he commanded, slipping off his horse and purposefully striding towards a large pair of doors. He stopped in the porchway and turned. "Are you coming?"

Rainey dismounted and followed his new potential friend into what appeared to be a palace of some sort.

"Gunter!"

A large man hurried out of an adjoining room. "Yes, my prince."

"See to our visitor. He has a story to tell which will require actions by you." And then the prince was gone.

Rainey stood in the hall, taking in the high ceilings and noting the lack of any art on the walls. Gunter came up beside him. "And who might you be?"

"Connor Rainey. And you?" bowing slightly.

Gunter returned the bow. "Gunter von Markenburg. I am the chancellor to the grand prince of Muscovy."

"So that would mean . . ." Rainey said, pointing in the direction where his new friend had exited.

"That was Grand Prince Ivan Vasilyevich. If you would follow me."

They walked through the palace corridors, Rainey telling Von Markenburg of the day's events, from the man on the horse to the grand prince's killing of the last attackers. Von Markenburg asked Rainey to describe the man on the horse, he no doubt being the instigator of the ambush that almost took the grand prince's life.

Once finished, Rainey got the impression Von Markenburg knew exactly who the man was.

"I believe he is a boyar," Von Markenburg began. "He controls territory for the grand prince about twenty miles from here along the river to the west. But I do not see a reason why he would betray the grand prince. So I find it hard to believe it was him."

"The proof will be the deep gash I gave him on the back of his right shoulder."

Von Markenburg nodded. "Then we will have to find him and see for ourselves. Did you tell this to the grand prince?"

"He was silent all the way here."

"Very well. I will see what else I can find out before I speak with him in the morning. In the meantime, would you like some refreshment before I show you to your room?"

"That would be appreciated," Rainey replied.

As they moved down a hallway, Rainey asked, "How does the grand prince of Muscovy come by a German chancellor?"

"Ah, that is a story for another time. You can then tell me the story behind that unusual coin on your sword's hilt. It's Templar, isn't it?"

Rainey nodded. "You have a good eye. My ancestor was a Templar."

"As was mine," Von Markenburg replied. "When the order fell, he joined the Teutonic Knights. I believe we will have many stories we can trade." He stopped at a door. "This will be your room while you are here." He opened the door.

The room was opulent, much finer than anywhere he had stayed before. The princes of Muscovy had grown rich over the years. It was their good fortune to control a major trade route into the Rus lands' vast interior.

"Do you have some time to speak with me?" Rainey asked. "This is a new land for me and I'd like to gain an understanding of how things work here."

Von Markenburg crossed the room and sat in a chair. "Certainly. I could use some fresh information on how things are in the west. Where have you traveled?"

"I fought in Casimir's war with the Teutonics. Had enough of that, so came here. I'd be glad to tell you what I know."

"Teutonics. I was one of them once, but became tired of killing Casimir's farmers. No challenge in that."

Rainey shifted uncomfortably in his chair. "I spent six years leading a small band of those farmers."

Von Markenburg raised his hand. "So you left for the same reason. Understandable. It was a terrible war with no end in sight. I saw that two years in and left then. What can you tell me about the situation now? We don't hear very much way out here."

And so information was passed between them. Rainey asked Von Markenburg about the city's history, about its rulers. He learned that Ivan was co-ruler of Muscovy, along with his father Vasily, also a grand prince. He asked who the princes might or might not be vassals to. Rainey wanted the lay of the land if he was going to spend time here. Von Markenburg in turn asked about the martial skills and the politics between the several combatants in the endless Teutonic war, searching for possible advantages for Muscovy.

Muscovy, Von Markenburg explained, was still considered a vassal to the khanate of the Great Horde to the south, and paid tribute yearly. The Great Horde was what was left of the Golden

Horde after it broke up into individual Tartar khanates. By paying tribute to Mahmud of the Great Horde, Muscovy maintained relative peace with the main khanate. The leader of the Crimean khanate, Giray, seemed to have more interest in fighting the Great Horde than in conflict with Muscovy. The southern borders of Muscovy were, therefore, reasonably secure. To the east, however, the Kazan khanate remained a concern.

The Kazans were repeat raiders into Muscovy territory, sometimes with a large force. Over the last few years, Vasily and Ivan had been building up their army to put an end to the raiding, but to do so effectively required security in the west. This is where Von Markenburg centered his inquiries.

"Casimir will not be in a position to do anything to his east until the Teutonic wars are over," Rainey told him. "The Lithuanians are more of a concern, but they really can't do anything serious in this direction without Casimir's permission. I know they have their eye on Novgorod, but that's about the extent of their current interest."

"Novgorod can be more of a concern on its own," Von Markenburg said.

"They're a vassal to Muscovy, aren't they?"

"They are an independent republic. They choose their own prince and archbishop, but those must be approved by Muscovy. Their archbishop is consecrated by the metropolitan here. Also, any dictates of the Veche, their governing assembly, must carry the seal of our grand prince to be official. Other than that, they rule themselves. They have been playing Muscovy and Lithuania off each other for years, keeping their freedom in the process."

"Well, good for them," Rainey retorted. "I take it they don't have an army capable of bothering Muscovy?"

"Not that we are aware of. And I would know."

"Then, I'd say Muscovy's western frontier is fractured enough to require watching, but not to hold up the army from operating elsewhere."

"The grand princes will be happy to hear this." Von Markenburg stood up. "It is always a pleasure to speak with someone from the west. You have a strong command of the situation there. I thank you. Now I must retire. We have our current problem of a missing assassin still to deal with."

Rainey stood and clasped Von Markenburg's hand. "I thank you and your grand princes for your hospitality. I hope I can be of further service to them in the future."

* * *

It was late into the night when Rainey finally fell asleep, only to be awakened by a rustling sound moving towards his bed. As his eyes opened, he saw a flash of light off steel moving swiftly towards him. He rolled away as the blade whacked into the mattress. The first thing he could find in the dark was his arquebus. It was loaded, but he had no flame. He turned to the fireplace and spotted embers glowing dully. Seeing the sword again coming at him, he rolled away towards the fire. He thrust in his hand, ignoring the pain. The shadow and sword were almost upon him as he raised the weapon and slapped the embers onto the firing hole.

The attacker's face was exposed for a second as the arquebus roared. Rainey saw that it was the man from the ambush. The determined look on his face was the same as Rainey remembered from the road. Then it was gone. At such a close range, the stones that blasted from the weapon's muzzle flung the man back onto the bed, where he lay still. Rainey got to his feet and rubbed his burnt hand hard on his leg. He then immediately started reloading the arquebus. A flurry of noise came down the hallway. The door crashed open. The first to enter was Grand Prince Ivan, torch in hand, followed by several other men.

"What was that noise?" he demanded.

Rainey raised the arquebus, fully loaded again. "It's a hand held weapon. Like a small cannon."

Ivan looked at the dead man on the bed. "You killed him with that?"

Rainey nodded. Von Markenburg entered through the crowd, a hint of worry on his face.

"Why would this man want to kill you?" Ivan asked.

"I don't know anyone here, but that's the man on the horse who was watching your ambush today. Probably didn't like the fact that I know what he looks like."

Ivan stepped towards the bed and pulled back the hood from the dead man's face. "Kolchin?" He spun on Von Markenburg. "Why was I not informed of this?"

Von Markenburg took a step back. "I was gathering more information so I could report fully to you in the morning. I wanted Kolchin found and confirmed before accusing one of your more loyal boyars."

"He doesn't look too loyal now. You will report fully to me before I retire again." Ivan turned to Rainey. "I want to see your little cannon in the morning as well. Igor, get that corpse out of here."

After they had left him alone again, Rainey got back into bed. His arquebus, a lit candle and his sword were all within easy reach.

5

"So you have everything in the barrel, just like a cannon. You've lit the cloth on the lever. Now aim the barrel at the rock and squeeze the lever."

Ivan raised the arquebus to his shoulder, looked down the barrel and squeezed the lever as Rainey had instructed. The arquebus roared, sending its load flying at the rock. The rock exploded into pieces.

Ivan lowered the arquebus from his shoulder. "Very impressive. And you used this during the Siege of Constantinople?"

"Held off Mehmet for fifty-three days," Rainey replied. "The Genoans and the Venetians make use of such weapons to build their trading empires. They also use them against each other."

"And the barrel is cast just like cannon, only smaller?"

"Yes. The rest of it is wood."

Ivan turned to an old blind man sitting behind him. "What do you think, father?"

Old Vasily took the arquebus in his hands, feeling the shape of all its parts. "I believe we can make these in the armory. And if it has impressed you, my son, we should start making them now."

"You have an armory?" Rainey asked.

Ivan grinned. "We make our own cannon. That is why everyone is afraid of us." He turned to Vasily. "Can we take you back in now, Father?"

"No. I am enjoying the sun on my face. But you have other matters to attend to. Go."

Ivan and Rainey left the old man in the courtyard. "That is your father?" Rainey asked.

"Yes."

"And he's the grand prince."

"Yes."

"And so are you."

Ivan nodded. "He made me his heir and grand prince so I could rule with him. It securely establishes me as heir to the throne. When my father dies, there won't be a fight over power."

"If you don't mind me asking, how did a blind man become grand prince in the first place?"

Ivan sighed. "He wasn't always blind. He was usurped by my uncle, who had him blinded as a safeguard for my uncle's rule. But even blind, my father was able to take back the throne. He is a wise and deceptive old man. I have learned much from him about how to rule."

"And someone doesn't want to give you the chance to rule alone."

"I am sure there is more than one, but only Kolchin has shown such boldness. He has always shown his loyalty to my father and to me. He helped regain the throne for my father. I did not know he could be so deceptive. Gunter is surprised as well and he sees things as they are much better than I do." Ivan stopped walking. "Tomorrow, you and my chancellor will ride out to his town."

Rainey hesitated. "I don't want to get involved in the politics of Muscovy."

Ivan laughed. "You already are involved, my friend. When you saved me and then when you were attacked last night. Besides, you have much to teach me, both about your little cannon and how you fight with your sword. But first, would you like to see our armory?"

* * *

Ludmilla Kolchina was having a regular day. In the morning, she had gone into the town for thread so she could repair her finest dress. In a few days' time, she was to meet her betrothed, arranged by her father and a boyar from Vladimir. The idea of marriage at the age of 15 did not really appeal to her, but there wasn't much she could do. It was her duty to her family and would form a business bond for her father. Even if she was ambivalent about the whole thing, she could at least look her best for the poor boy, a third son who would most likely inherit little. Hopefully, she could grow to love the boy, much the same way her mother had grown to love her father. And maybe Vladimir would be a more exciting place to live than Zenoplata was.

As she was sewing, she heard the clop of hooves coming through the courtyard gate. She moved to the window and swung open the wooden shutter to take a look. She recognized Von Markenburg right away, having met the chancellor a few times during trips to Moscow with her family. She didn't know any of the other men. Most wore all black, which was how Von Markenburg's personal guard always dressed. They were called the black knights. But one man looked out of place. He wasn't dressed in black. His leather tunic and leggings were brown, as were his boots. And he carried a very strange sword strapped to his back.

Ludmilla's mother and younger brother went out into the courtyard to meet their guests.

"Welcome, Chancellor. What brings you to our town?" her mother asked pleasantly.

"Is your husband home, madam?" Von Markenburg said curtly.

"No. He is due back late tonight."

"Is your oldest son here?"

"Andrey is out with the fur trappers. I expect him back in three days. What is this about?"

"Where is your daughter?"

Fear began to creep into Ludmilla's mind. Von Markenburg sounded impatient and dangerous. She heard her mother again, confusion apparent in her voice. "She's up in her room. Why?"

What happened next shocked her to the core. Two men brought out crossbows and shot her mother and brother. They crumpled to the ground, holding each other's hands. Von Markenburg then signaled two other men towards the house. They got off their horses, drew their swords and headed for the door. Ludmilla could hear the servants' screams as they ran out of the two men's path. The clump of boots told her they were coming up the stairs for her.

Panic set in. She looked about her room, searching for any kind of weapon she could defend herself with. But what chance would she have against two soldiers of Muscovy? Her eyes fell on the open window. She had to escape.

She scrambled out onto the ledge and was climbing up onto the roof as she heard her door come crashing in. In the courtyard, she saw, the men on horseback were looking up at her. They raised crossbows, aimed at her. Two bolts whizzed past her head as she scrambled along the roof. Behind her, a man was clambering through the window onto the roof.

She was aiming for the stable at the far end of the house. There, she could get a horse and leave by the back gate. She never gave a thought to where she would go. She just had to go. Reaching the end of the roof, she looked down. It was a big jump. Behind her, the man on the roof crawled cautiously towards her. There was nothing to do but jump.

She landed hard. Pain shot up her legs as she crashed through the thatch onto a large pile of straw. She lay there for a moment, eyes closed. When she opened them, she could see the man looking down on her through the hole she had made in the roof. The anger in his face galvanized her. She rolled out of the straw and onto her feet. Turning towards the horses, she stepped right into the arms of the stranger with the strange sword. He held the sword's blade up under her arm. He grabbed her, pulled her close and whispered in her ear.

"When I let you go, fall down and pretend to be dead."

The hand on her back came around and slapped her on the stomach. Then he let go of her. She looked down and saw blood on her dress where he had slapped her.

He stabbed me. He has killed me. The thought drove her mind towards darkness. And then there was nothing.

* * *

The voices were quiet at first, getting louder as her mind slowly climbed out of the darkness. She began to understand what they were saying.

"But what happens when the boyar comes back? How can we explain this to him?"

"We have a new boyar now. He can explain it. All we have to do is keep quiet and be loyal to whoever wins."

"We will still be punished."

"What could we have done against Muscovy guards? We would be out there ourselves, dead on the ground. If there is punishment, at least we will still be alive."

Ludmilla began to recognize the voices. They were Orina and Grigori, the house servants. Ludmilla opened her eyes to find herself on her bed looking up at the ceiling.

"Orina?"

Orina came over to her. "Oh, my lady. How are you feeling?"

"What happened?"

Orina glanced over at Grigori. Ludmilla propped herself up on her elbows. "What happened, Orina?" she said forcefully.

"The new boyar saved you by pretending to kill you. You fainted."

"New boyar? He's still here?"

Orina nodded nervously. Ludmilla looked down at her dress, the blood stain dried. She brushed at it to find it was only reddish dirt. "Get me a new dress."

Orina hurried to a chest in the corner. Grigori stepped forward. "He seems like a nice man."

Ludmilla's face flash with anger, "He was part of killing my entire family. That is not very nice."

Grigori shrugged. "He didn't kill you."

She looked around the room, thinking about what she should do next, wondering what she didn't know about how things were outside this room. "How many men stayed with him?"

"None," Grigori answered. "They all left with the chancellor."

At least she didn't have to keep playing dead. Orina came back with a dress. She shooed Grigori out and proceeded to help Ludmilla into it. Now she was ready to go meet this new boyar. The new ruler of her house. It was then that her mind remembered her mother and little brother, crumpled in the courtyard. She sagged and reached for a chair to steady herself.

"They are dead," she said to no one in particular. Orina and Grigori stood silently, waiting for orders from their lady. She looked up at them. "Where are they now?"

Grigori answered. "The boyar placed them in your mother's room. The priest is with them now."

Tears formed in Ludmilla's eyes. "I am alone," she said. At the door, she turned towards her mother's room. There, she saw Father Kirill standing over the bed that held her mother and brother, mumbling prayers. She gasped, her hand covering her mouth. She let out a cry and fell to her knees, weeping. She slumped onto the floor and curled up. She could hardly breathe through the sobs.

How much time passed, she didn't know. She didn't care. But finally the sobbing ceased. She could sense Orina and Grigori sitting on the bench behind her, but it was a strange voice she heard first.

"I'm sorry."

She tilted her head towards the voice. The man dressed in brown stood in the doorway, looking down on her. Sadness in his face. Then the anger came back.

"What are you sorry about? That my father and brother are still out there?"

"No. That your mother and your younger brother are dead."

"You'll be more sorry when they come home."

"They won't come home. The grand prince is looking for them."

Ludmilla struggled to pick herself up off the floor. "The grand prince doesn't frighten them. And neither will you." She stormed past him into the hallway. "Enjoy your short time in my home." She moved towards her room and its door, which she could bar against the man's hateful presence.

The man spoke again. "We can have a funeral tomorrow. I am not familiar with your customs . . ."

"And you won't have to be."

Ludmilla waved Orina and Grigori into her room and pulled the door shut behind her. "What room will he be sleeping in?"

They both looked confused. "What room?" Grigori asked.

Ludmilla sighed. "Yes. What room will he be in later tonight?"

"He chose the guest room," Orina answered.

The guest room. Why would he pick the guest room? Her father's room was much larger, with a better bed. She shook her head. It didn't matter.

"Orina, I need you to bring me a big knife from the kitchen after he's gone to sleep."

Orina now looked worried. "What do you need . . ." The realization showed in her face.

"That is very dangerous, my lady," Grigori warned. "You should not give him a reason to regret not killing you today."

Ludmilla stared down Grigori. "He is an intruder into our home. He must be dealt with."

Grigori stayed silent. Ludmilla continued. "I need you to bring in a pitchfork from the stable. In case I don't cut him enough, you will come in and help."

Grigori was shaking his head. "No, no, no."

Ludmilla grabbed him by the arms. "You have to help me, Grigori. For our home."

Grigori was still shaking his head, but the motion slowly came to a stop. Then he nodded.

* * *

Ludmilla waited until well into the night. She kept picking up and putting down the carving knife Orina had brought to her hours before. She paced. She lay on her bed. She paced again. This was all new to her. She had never plotted anyone's death before. Where she had once been convinced it had to be done, as she got closer to the actual act, doubt and fear had taken over. Could she get close enough to the man to stab him? Once he was within her reach, could she actually do it? She knew Grigori would be more than happy to leave the pitchfork outside the main door.

She finally pushed down all the doubt and fear, remembering her mother and brother and how it was her job to avenge their deaths in the absence of Andrey and her father. Again, she had convinced herself that it had to be done. She picked up the knife one final time and went to her door.

Slowly passing into the hallway, she made her way to the top of the stairs. Below, on a bench by the door, Grigori sat with his head down. She tapped the railing with the knife, gaining his attention. He got up, opened the door and brought in the pitchfork. His face showed resignation as he slowly and quietly climbed the stairs.

Orina was sitting on the floor outside the stranger's door. She got up as Ludmilla reached for the latch. Ludmilla paused for a moment to push the fear down again, then lifted the latch. The door began to swing open, the iron hinges creaking every now and then. On the bed, under the blankets, she saw a lump. Slowly stepping into the room, she moved alongside the bed, raised the knife and held it there.

This was it. Vengeance. Her mind spiralled back to the scene in the courtyard. The crossbows. Her family crumpling to the ground. Her escape out the window, falling through the stable roof. And ending up in the arms of this man who had come with the killers.

But he didn't do any killing. He didn't kill her. He wasn't one of the crossbowmen. He didn't order anyone in the courtyard. Was this vengeance being perpetrated against the wrong man? She heard a voice telling her something, but it wasn't the answer she sought.

"Are you going to stab my pillows or not?"

She turned towards the door. Her gaze was met Orina's and Grigori's, shock on their faces, before the door slammed shut. Slouching in a chair behind the door was the man, his strange sword in his hand, watching her. And he was smiling.

A rage grew quickly in her heart. A deep guttural scream rose from deep inside her. She threw herself across the room, knife held high. Just as she reached him to plunge the knife into his heart, a flash of steel passed before her eyes. The knife was gone. Her momentum carried her onto this man she hated so fiercely, her empty hand slapping his chest, right where she had been aiming the knife. Their faces were inches apart. She stared into his eyes. What she saw stole her rage away. Her breathing slowing down, she felt the flush on her face melting away.

It was his eyes. They looked calm. Tired. Like they had seen too much evil that had eaten at his soul. Then the moment was gone. She pushed herself away from him, but he got up with her, holding her tight. He opened the door.

Orina and Grigori still stood there, the same dismayed expression on their faces that Ludmilla had seen before the door closed. The man threw her out of the room at them.

"Lock her in her room for the night," he said. "And Grigori, put the pitchfork back in the stable." He closed the door.

6

The sun had risen, warming the room. Ludmilla had not slept for one minute all night. Conflicting emotions filled her soul. Who was this man who had watched as her family was slaughtered, yet had saved her from the same fate? And when he stopped her from killing him, he just walked away. She had never met a man like that before. Granted, she hadn't met a lot of men in her young life, but the ones she had would never have let her actions from last night go unpunished.

But he was still part of the group that had come to kill her family.

Although the man had instructed Orina and Grigori to lock her in her room, she knew they would never dare actually do it. Regardless, she had stayed in her room. Now with the sun up, she was in no hurry to face the man again or deal with the awful task of burying her family.

She opened the shutters to look out over the courtyard. Grigori was in the midst of his morning chores, carrying a bucket of water from the well to the stables. She called down to him.

"Grigori, where is the new boyar?" The term made her cringe as she said it. She realized she had no idea what the man's name was.

"He's gone into town, my lady, to fetch the priest."

A shiver went down her spine. She remembered her lifeless loved ones down the hall. She had to get out of the house. "Saddle Mischka. I will go for a ride when I come down." She closed the shutters and got dressed.

After stopping in the kitchen where Orina had set out some kielbasa and cheese, Ludmilla went out the front door to find Grigori holding Mischka's reins. He helped her up into the saddle and spread her dress across the horse's back.

She glanced over to the spot where her mother and brother were killed. Blood stains were still visible on the ground. She fought down the emotion, wishing Andrey would be back soon. He would know what to do about this stranger.

Ludmilla looked down at Grigori. "Do you know his name?"

Grigori nodded. "Kona R-ray-nee. It's a funny name."

She frowned. "He sounds Polish, but that doesn't sound Polish at all."

"Maybe he learned Polish?"

Ludmilla nodded. "It's not a mystery we will have to solve. Once Andrey or Father are back, he will go away. I'll be back by noon." She urged Mischka forward and rode quickly out of the gate.

She rode hard through the town and out into the fields, heading for a forest where she knew she could be alone. Her total focus was forward, driving Mischka to go as fast as he could. As they reached the forest, Mischka let up on his own and no amount of effort by Ludmilla could get him going again. They trotted through the trees on the main path. Without having to focus on driving Mischka, Ludmilla's mind began to drift towards yesterday's terrible events. She began sobbing, lowering her face into Mischka's mane and wrapping her arms around the horse's neck. Mischka stopped, sensing her grief. To Ludmilla, Mischka had become her only friend in the world; a shoulder to cry on, sort of, and express her grief to.

She cried for a while, then went silent. She let the horse stand there for what seemed like hours until Mischka decided it was time to move towards some grass so he could graze. As he lowered his head, Ludmilla had to let go or else slide down the horse's neck. She sat up in the saddle and wiped her eyes.

"Thank you, Mischka," she said. "Have some grass and then we will head home." She sniffled and brushed her long hair back from her face.

* * *

Riding through the gate, Ludmilla could see several townsfolk in the courtyard. A cart containing two coffins sat on the cobblestones, the contents of which she was all too aware. Grigori ran to take the reins as Ludmilla dismounted Mischka. The town elder strode up to meet her.

"My lady, we are all shocked to hear about what happened yesterday," he said. "We do not understand why the grand prince would order such a thing."

"Thank you, Anton. I don't understand myself."

"Is the new boyar staying on or just until the boyar comes home?"

Ludmilla glared at him. Anton wanted to know who to be loyal to. "You should know better than to ask that question."

Anton backed away with a bow. "I apologize, my lady. The townspeople will want to know."

"They should also know where their loyalty belongs." Ludmilla stormed away towards the house. At the door, Rainey was waiting for her.

"What lies have you been telling the townspeople?" she demanded.

Rainey didn't move. "Just that I was here from Moscow taking care of things, primarily the funerals. I haven't told them anything about what happened."

"They can guess. They know what the chancellor looks like. They want to know if you're here to be the new boyar."

"I can't be held responsible for what they assume. I haven't even talked to you yet about what this all means, which I believe I should do before any official announcement to the town. But first, we should bury your family. I'm told you have a private space in the church yard."

The thought of burying her family brought tears back to her eyes. She lowered her head to hide this from Rainey and pushed past him into the house. Rushing up to her room, she heard Orina following her.

"I have laid out your black dress, my lady," Orina said as Ludmilla threw herself on the bed, in tears once again. After a moment, she felt Orina's weight on the bed as she sat and stroked her back. "I know, little one. It is a big shock, but I know you are strong and you must show that to the town now. Let them know that the family Kolchin still demands their loyalty."

Ludmilla rolled over and looked up at Orina. Her tears had stopped. "Why are you still loyal to my family? My mother was always cruel to you."

Orina grimaced. "She wasn't well liked in the town either. But I stay loyal for you."

Ludmilla understood. Orina had been more of a parent to her than her own parents while she was growing up. Although she loved her mother, there hadn't been much warmth between them. Her mother had focussed on her older brother Andrey, the heir. Her father only looked at her as a tool to marry off to some other boyar for political advantage, and spent virtually no time with her at all. Orina may have been loyal all these years out of fear, but now her loyalty was true.

Ludmilla reached up and hugged Orina. "What am I going to do?" she cried.

"Oh, my little *malyshka*. There is only one thing you can do. It is what we all do. You must do whatever it takes to survive."

Ludmilla looked up into Orina's eyes. "I don't know how."

Orina grabbed her by the shoulders and looked at her sternly. "Yes you do. You must make peace with the new boyar. Then in three days, Topoff comes to marry you to off to his third son. You will be off to Vladimir and the new boyar will no longer be your concern."

"But what about you and Grigori?"

"We will be fine. The new boyar seems to be a good man. The fact that you are still alive after trying to kill him is a very good sign."

Ludmilla shook her head. "I wish you were going to Vladimir, too. I don't understand why you were not allowed to go with me."

"I wanted to, but it was not my place to ask. Perhaps the new boyar will allow it. You could ask him."

Ludmilla got up from the bed. "Yes, I will. If he says he's the new boyar, maybe he knows why my father didn't come home last night."

* * *

Father Kirill conducted the ceremony at the grave site. There was no sound save for his voice and the rustling of the leaves on the trees that surrounded the cemetery. Ludmilla was flanked by Orina and Grigori, across the graves from Rainey and all of the villagers. She scanned the crowd quickly, knowing that they were all there out of fear rather than sorrow. There was no crying, no tears. Her eyes settled across the graves at Rainey, who looked up and then away several times. Finally he raised his head and stared back at her, his eyes never wavering. A small pang of fear rose in her throat, but she pushed it back down. She willed herself not to look away, no matter how much she wanted to.

Then he smiled. His head tilted to the right, followed by his eyes moving back to Father Kirill. Ludmilla could feel her cheeks flush. He was dismissing her. She wanted to scream at him, but she held her tongue. This was not the place.

As the mourners returned to the house, Rainey broke off and headed for the stable. Ludmilla followed him there, Orina and Grigori in tow.

"So, you say you are the new boyar of Zenoplata," she said as she entered the stable.

Rainey was bringing hay and water to his horse. He did not reply. That infuriated her even more. She glanced behind her at Orina and Grigori, waving them to leave.

"I am talking to you, sir," she said sternly.

Rainey didn't turn, but spoke so quietly that she almost didn't hear him. "We have much to talk about. Me being boyar is not important."

Ludmilla stepped farther into the stable. "How is that not important? It is an open challenge to my father's authority."

"Your father's dead."

Ludmilla felt like she had been punched in the gut. All air was expelled from her lungs as that sentence's import impressed itself in her mind. Rainey turned towards her. She struggled to speak, but only a weak sound came out. "How?"

Rainey didn't move. A sadness came over his face, as if he knew what he would say next would be even worse. "I killed him while he was trying to kill me."

Ludmilla let out a cry from deep within her soul before Rainey had finished his sentence. Rage surged up through her. Turning to her right, she saw the pitchfork. She snatched it with a scream and lunged for Rainey. But he was gone.

Something pulled hard on the pitchfork from behind her, wrenching it from her hands. She spun around to find the prongs right in front of her face.

"We are going to have to do something about that temper of yours," Rainey said.

Ludmilla fought to control her breathing, slowly calming down before she spoke. "Why did you kill him?"

"I told you. He was trying to kill me."

"Why would he want to kill you?"

"Because I saw him while he was leading a plot to kill Grand Prince Ivan."

That made no sense to Ludmilla. "My father is loyal to the grand prince. He would never do that."

"At some point, his loyalties changed."

She took a step back from the prongs, thinking about the implications. Perhaps this man was lying, but her father was missing. However, the deaths of her mother and brother, along with the attempt to kill her, began to now have reason.

"My father committed treason."

"Yes." Rainey leaned the pitchfork back up against a pillar.

"And the grand prince made you boyar of the village."

Rainey shifted uncomfortably. "That I didn't know until the chancellor was leaving. I'm also to await your older brother's return and kill him. But perhaps we'll talk first."

Another thought came to her. "And I am supposed to be dead, too. How are you going to explain that?"

Rainey smiled and shrugged. "I don't know yet."

"And a boyar from Vladimir will know."

Rainey's smile disappeared. "What are you talking about?"

"I'm supposed to wed a boyar's son in two days."

The look on Rainey's face sent a shiver down her spine. He was going to have to kill her now. But the question he asked was not what she expected.

"Do you want to marry the boy?"

"I don't understand."

Rainey sighed. "It's a simple question. Do you want to marry the boy? Do you love him?"

Ludmilla shook her head. "I've never met him."

"So, you don't want to marry him."

"There was never want. I am doing my duty for my family."

"Never mind your duty. The decision is now in your hands. I will agree to whatever you want to do in this matter. But consider the fact that you can disappear into this boyar's family. You'll be safer than if you stayed here."

Ludmilla's head was spinning. This man was going to let her decide? This was new. Every decision about her life and future had always been made by her parents.

"I don't know," she said weakly.

"Then you have two days to decide. If you want to stay here, we will hide you when the boyar arrives. If you want to go through with the marriage, I will pretend your father is still alive and I'm his representative. Once in Vladimir, you can have lots of children and forget you are a Kolchin." He moved back towards his horse.

Ludmilla left the stable in a daze. Orina was waiting for her.

"Come, child. You need to eat."

7

Those two days passed quickly, too quickly for Ludmilla. She did ask if Orina could go with her to Vladimir. Rainey agreed if Orina agreed. She asked for Grigori as well, but Grigori refused, not willing to leave the only home he ever knew. He also seemed to be taking a shine to the new boyar.

Rainey had spent much of those two days in the village getting to know the merchants and meeting up with her father's overseer for the farmers. Krepsky wasn't well liked as the overseer, having taken advantage of his position with the knowledge that the old boyar didn't care what happened to his farmers. As long as they paid what was due, Krepsky could take whatever extra he wanted. No doubt he presented himself to the new boyar in the best light. Rainey, however, seemed to see through his bravado.

Ludmilla still hadn't decided about the marriage by the day the Topoffs were due to arrive. She was still pondering her dilemma when she heard the sound of horses entering the courtyard. She went to her window to see if she could get a good look at the Topoff boy. Perhaps that would help her make her decision. But from the window, it wasn't the Topoffs she saw.

It was her brother.

With all that had happened over the last few days, she had totally forgotten about Andrey. He had been due to return from Novgorod by today to see her off to Vladimir. The six men who rode in with him stayed on their horses while Andrey dismounted and headed for the door. Ludmilla ran to the stairs.

She reached the top in time to see him enter. "Andrey!" she shouted.

But Andrey didn't respond to her; he was looking into the room to his left. "Who are you?" he demanded.

Rainey stepped to the doorway and into Ludmilla's view, "I live here now. Who are you?"

Ludmilla bolted down the stairs and grabbed her brother's arm. "Andrey, I must talk with you."

Andrey shook her hand off his arm. "I am Andrey Alexandrovich Kolchin. I will expect more respect in the future from a hired hand. When did my father hire you?"

"Andrey . . ." Ludmilla pleaded.

Rainey spread his hands and walked out the door into the courtyard. Turning, he backed toward the horsemen who had made a semicircle behind him. "Your father is dead. Made the mistake of trying to kill me."

"What?" Andrey shouted. "And you thought you could just live here?"

"Oh, no. The grand prince gave it to me. Your father committed treason."

Ludmilla saw Andrey stiffen. *He knew father was planning on killing the grand prince*, she thought. She moved towards the two men. "Andrey . . ."

But Andrey was pulling out his sword. Rainey reached back and did the same, moving to one side as the six men dismounted.

"Ludmilla, go back inside," Rainey called. Orina took her by the shoulders and pulled her back to the doorway. She held her hands out and clutched the wooden doorjamb.

Everything after that happened so fast she could barely follow it. The first of Andrey's men attacked Rainey, who spun out of the way and went after the man on the end, slicing his chest open. One quick sidestep and he was on the second man before he could turn to face the attack. That man fell as well. Now the first man had recovered and stepped towards Rainey, who spun around him and stroked the man's back. Continuing his spin, Rainey's sword clanged against the blade of the next man in line. He shifted his weight and ran his sword down the other one's edge, flicking it at the end. The man screamed and fell to the ground, clutching his handless wrist.

The last two men standing quickly backed up, swords at the ready to protect Andrey. Rainey raised his sword slowly, standing very still. "How much is Andrey paying you?"

The two men looked at each other, then back at Rainey. "Not enough," one of them said, and both bolted for their horses. Rainey let them go.

"Damn," he said. "I was going to offer to hire them."

Ludmilla broke away from Orina and launched herself between Rainey and Andrey. "Please, spare him. Let me speak with him first. He will see reason."

The sound of more horses coming towards the courtyard made everyone turn. It was the Topoffs. They stopped suddenly at the gate, shocked at the bloody scene.

"What is going on here?" demanded the older gentleman in the group.

Rainey looked at Ludmilla. "Your chosen's family, I presume? This will be hard to explain, but the decision is made now. You are going to Vladimir." He lowered his sword and walked towards the horsemen.

Ludmilla turned to Andrey, pounding her fist on his chest. "You idiot. You needed to talk to me first about what is going on here. That man, as you now know, is dangerous. You can't just kill him outright. Besides, the grand prince wants us dead and this man is the only reason I'm alive."

Andrey's face had fallen. "Father failed. All is lost. Where is Mother? And little Anton?"

She put her hand on his arm. "They are dead, by order of the grand prince. The same order condemns us as well."

* * *

Rainey reached the gate, glancing at a large man leaning against the gatepost eating a chunk of bread. He looked familiar, but Rainey couldn't place him. He looked back at the newest arrivals.

"Good afternoon," Rainey began. "Welcome to Zenoplata. Come join me inside where we can discuss the arrangement."

The older gentleman spoke. "Where is Alexander Kolchin?"

Rainey shrugged. "He has not returned as of yet. I will be his representative for these discussions"

Topoff scoffed. "You are a Pole. Kolchin would never trust a Pole."

I really have to do something about this accent, Rainey thought. "I'm not a Pole. I'm a Celt."

The old man didn't have an answer to that, so he looked over at Andrey and Ludmilla. "Are not those his children?"

Rainey looked over his shoulder. "Yes."

"What was going on here?"

Rainey's mind had been working out a detailed response for that very question. "The son was unaware of my position. I had to defend myself. Come. I have refreshments set out. Take your horses over to the stable where my man will take care of them. Meet me inside."

After a slight hesitation, the old man signaled his party forward. Rainey stepped over to the man at the gate. "Igor, right?" It was the man who had taken Kolchin's body away back in Moscow.

The man smiled and bowed. "Igor Fedorovich Krasenoff, at your service."

"What are you doing here?"

"The grand prince sent me to watch your back."

Rainey looked over the three dead men in the courtyard. The man with the severed hand was twitching on the ground, surrounded by a large red stain. "You didn't do a very good job."

Krasenoff shrugged. "They were all in front of you."

Rainey broke out laughing. "I think I'm going to like you. Keep an eye on the Kolchins while I go in and deal with the Topoffs."

"Are they not supposed to be dead?"

Rainey grabbed him by the shoulder. "As far as you are concerned, they are. We will speak later."

* * *

The conversation with the Topoffs was brief, but illuminating. Rainey craftily steered the conversation so the Topoffs revealed the extent of their arrangement with Kolchin. After ensuring that Alexander Kolchin would honour the deal made there, with dowry and inheritance rights for Ludmilla according to Rus law, Topoff agreed. Her dowry turned out to be commission rights for furs from Novgorod in exchange for access to a silk trade Topoff could control from Vladimir.

A branch of the Silk Road ran down through territories the Ottomans controlled. Demand in Europe required a new route, which Rainey now discovered ran up the Volga River and over to Vladimir. From there, the silk traders made their way to the northern German ports to sell their exotic wares throughout Europe. According to the Topoffs, the route would go through Vladimir and onto the Moskva River right here at Zenoplata. Kolchin was to have exclusive rights to sell the silk into Novgorod. In the back of Rainey's mind, he found it interesting that the arrangement involved Novgorod. Combined with Andrey's return from there, he wondered if somewhere the grand prince's death had been required to complete whatever plan Alexander Kolchin had in the works.

As Rainey and Topoff got up to shake hands, they both noticed Topoff's son, Pyotr, gazing out the window at Ludmilla. They could see Ludmilla looking back.

"Perhaps our arrangement isn't necessary for the marriage," Topoff said with a wink.

"One never knows," Rainey replied. "Ludmilla Kolchina will be a challenge for him. I suggest he not cross her."

Topoff waved Rainey off. "A woman knows her place. Come, Pyotr. Let us meet your new wife."

Pyotr Topoff smiled. Rainey figured he couldn't be more than about 17 years of age. He stepped over to the boy and whispered in his ear. "If you hurt her, I'll know. And I'll cut off your head."

The boy stiffened. Rainey stepped back to let him pass. *Should be an interesting wedding*, he thought.

* * *

Ludmilla and Orina left with the Topoffs an hour later. Old man Topoff wanted to reach the next town before nightfall. Ludmilla looked around the courtyard as the party made for the gate. To Rainey, she looked sad. He remembered that Aunshaunie had never smiled until they had been about a month in Kiev. Not knowing one's future was a sad burden to carry. At least Ludmilla would be safe in Vladimir where she could disappear into the Topoff family. He headed for the kitchen where the young Andrey Kolchin was seated at the table, hands clasped in front of him. Krasenoff stood behind him, playing with a dagger.

"Would you leave us?" Rainey asked Krasenoff, who frowned. "He'll be in front of me the whole time." Krasenoff sighed and left the room.

"You came from Novgorod," Rainey said. Andrey didn't answer. "Do you have friends and connections there?" Andrey still didn't answer.

Rainey sat down across from him. "Let me state your situation. I spared your sister, leaving the grand prince's chancellor thinking I had killed her. Now she's safely off to Vladimir, out of sight of the grand prince and with a new name. You must disappear as well. Go to Novgorod. Meet up with your friends and change your name. I now have a business venture in Novgorod, one I have no idea how to manage or have the contacts to initiate. I believe you do."

He shifted in his chair. Andrey had not said a word or changed his expression. Rainey continued. "The silk trade is yours."

That got a reaction. Andrey's eyebrows lifted. The silk trade was a very lucrative and would quickly set him up for life. "Why would you do that?" he asked.

Rainey leaned back from the table. "Because I'm new here and don't think suddenly having business in Novgorod would be in my best interest with the grand prince. Having your sister disappear and this deal distanced from me suits me. Money is not that important to me. I have more than enough and I have Zenoplata to concentrate on."

"And I can just walk away?"

Rainey grinned. "It is a little more complicated. First, you must relinquish, in writing, any claim to Zenoplata. I don't need your progeny coming back and trying to reclaim the village. I'm sure you'll make much more money trading silk than any transit fees you could collect here. Second, you must change your name. I think you'll find the name Kolchin will be dangerous to keep. And third, you must keep quiet about this arrangement." Rainey paused for effect. "If you think you can use this against me in the future, I should tell you that I am going to tell the grand prince you never came back. Exposing this deal will lead to exposing yourself to the grand prince's wrath. Not to mention that I will come to Novgorod and kill you."

Andrey thought quietly for a moment, then put out his hand. Rainey took it. The deal was done. He pulled a scroll from his coat.

"Sign this and be on your way tonight." Rainey got up to fetch a quill and inkwell from another table. Andrey glanced at the document briefly, then signed.

As Andrey got up to get his horse, Krasenoff passed him in the kitchen doorway.

"If you are giving away a silk trade, I would have taken it."

Rainey was rolling up the scroll. "The grand prince would cut your head off if you owned that."

"There's a growing trade in silk in Moscow. How does Vladimir figure in that?

"I don't know. Perhaps there is another supplier with another route."

Krasenoff grunted. "It would have been easier to kill him and bury him beside his family."

"You will find that that is not my way."

"Your way could get you killed."

Rainey smiled. "Many have tried, as you have seen just today."

Krasenoff grunted again. "The grand prince hasn't wanted you dead yet."

* * *

Andrey Kolchin arrived at the gates of Novgorod with mixed feelings. He was happy to be alive and given the rights to the silk trade between Vladimir and Novgorod. But now he was totally alone and beholden to a man he didn't know. He didn't trust this new boyar back in Zenoplata, but for the life of him, he couldn't figure out what sort of plot the man was hatching to secure Zenoplata's boyarship. Leaving Andrey and Ludmilla alive made no sense. Something more had to be at play.

He arrived at his friend's house right around dinner time and knocked on the door. It was opened by his friend's sister, Natalia.

"Andrey," she exclaimed, throwing her arms around his neck. "We did not expect you back so soon. Mika, Andrey Alexandrovich is back."

Mikhail Shermenskoff appeared in the hall. "That was very quick. So, we have the silk trade?" Andrey nodded. "Then why are you looking so sad?"

Andrey didn't know how much to tell his friend, but the less, the better. "My family has died. I am the only one left. I am selling off my lands to come work here with you."

"Oh, I am so sorry," Natalia said. "Come in and have some food. You have family here."

"It is a sad day for the Kolchin family," Shermenskoff said.

Andrey remembered what Rainey had told him. Word would eventually get around about his father's treason. He had to change his name.

"I have also decided that I need to change my name. To make a break with the past. My name now is Andrey Alexandrovich Kolochoff."

8

1462

The swords clanged together loudly as Grand Prince Ivan and Rainey swung at each other. Ivan made a spin to his right, his sword sliding down Rainey's to the hilt, then swinging around and hitting Rainey in the back with the flat of the blade. They stopped in those positions.

"Very good," Rainey said. "Even with that big heavy sword of yours, that was fairly fast."

"I have been asking you to let my sword makers make another one like yours, but you keep refusing," Ivan replied.

"I have to keep some advantage," Rainey said. "Besides, I know they will want to melt some part of it down. That would never do." He circled Ivan and spun his blade. "Again, this time to the left."

The training had begun shortly after his first trip back to Moscow. It was less than a day's ride from Zenoplata and Ivan asked for him a lot. Krasenoff had become his constant companion and close confidant. He had not once brought up

Andrey or Ludmilla and had stood by him on many of their adventures.

Ivan finished his spin and brought the flat of his blade up against Rainey's back, only to run into Rainey's blade with a loud clang. He stepped back.

"We're planning a major excursion into Kazan territory from some of our northern cities for this summer."

Rainey nodded. "With no serious threat from your other borders, it is a good time. Are you going to keep it cautious as I suggested?"

"They will advance, raid, pillage. At the first sign of a major Kazan force coming to meet them, they will retreat."

"Good. You'll get a feel for how fast they respond and how they would deal with a full invasion. It will be good information for future forays. Who do you have leading it?" Rainey swung his sword forward and across, meeting Ivan's sword with a clang. He quickly twisted his sword down and back up, Ivan countering and blocking the swing. They stepped back.

"Boris Kozhanov and Boris Slepoy," Ivan said. "I was thinking of sending Kasim with them, but . . ."

"No benefit in risking him getting killed," Rainey replied. Kasim was the Kazan Khan Ibrahim's older brother, rejected because of Kasim's friendship with Ivan. If Ivan could put him on the throne, Kazan would be an ally, not a threat.

"It's not the right time," Ivan said. "I don't think he has enough support to usurp Ibrahim yet."

Rainey nodded. "He's been waiting around for quite a while for that time. He is an heir to Kazan, but I know the Tartars don't necessarily go with the oldest son. Kasim deserting to your father sixteen years ago doesn't help his cause."

Ivan's consort, Maria, entered the hall. "Are you two at it again? Really. You would think that you would be out of things to teach each other." She pointed to the hallway above them. "No doubt he's learning early." Four-year-old Ivan Ivanovich, the Molodoy, stood there stock still, watching through the railing.

"It will do him well to learn to fight," Ivan said. "The world is a dangerous place."

Maria moved effortlessly across the room and kissed Rainey on the cheek. "Hello, Connor. What brings you back to Moscow? I'm sure it wasn't so you two could swing swords at each other."

Rainey glanced at Ivan. "You'll have to ask your husband. He summons, I come."

"The problem with the silk and fur trade? Connor can help you with that."

Rainey nodded, but inside, he tensed up. The deal he had brokered with the Topoffs and Andrey Kolchin might be coming back to haunt him.

Maria looked around. "And where is that rogue who follows you around everywhere?"

"You know Igor Fedorovich. No doubt drinking and trying to get the attention of the women of Moscow."

Maria turned to Ivan. "Should I tell the kitchen that we have guests?" Ivan nodded. "Good. I will send word to Anna Tripenskaya to come by for dinner." She winked at Rainey. He rolled his eyes. Maria had been placing Anna and Rainey in the same room whenever possible for over a year now. She didn't think Rainey should stay unmarried out in Zenoplata alone and Anna, being a friend and a widow, seemed particularly interested in him.

"I thought you preferred two swords, Husband," she said as she glided out the door.

Ivan grinned and picked up a second sword, swinging them in unison and eyeing Rainey. Rainey grinned back. "You know, two swords do slow you down," Rainey said.

"Yes, but it does keep you from spinning behind me." Ivan surged forward and the clanging of swords continued.

* * *

The road to Novgorod was long and tiresome. To pass the time, Ludmilla gazed out the carriage window into the wilderness. The land was still white with snow; the long Rus winter had not relinquished its grip to spring. There was nothing interesting to grab her attention.

It had been hard on her for almost two years in Vladimir. It started out well. Pyotr was a good husband then. Every time he'd gotten angry with her, he seemed to pause and then leave the room. She had seen him hit servants and townsfolk, men and women both. But for some reason, he never hit her.

That changed after six months had passed and Ludmilla was still not pregnant. It wasn't from a lack of trying. She dearly wanted to have a child with Pyotr. It would raise her status in the family, adding to her security, even if it was the third son's child. She had no idea what was wrong.

The first time Pyotr hit her, it was for dropping one of his boots. His blow was hard, like he had been waiting for any excuse. Her life changed dramatically that day. Pyotr no longer slept in their bed. Later, she discovered he had started sleeping around with other women. Then, as the first year of her marriage came to a close, he sent Orina away. No word came about where she had been sent. Ludmilla had heard nothing from her since.

She was moved to smaller quarters in the house and left without a maid or servant. She was all alone. The only good thing was that Pyotr never bothered to come by and hit her anymore.

With no other recourse, Ludmilla decided that she must escape. She thought perhaps she could just walk out the door, get on a horse and ride away. She didn't think about where she would go, only that the Topoffs didn't seem to care whether she was there or not. But when she tried it one day, she found herself beaten senseless and locked in her room for three days without food or water. The wife of a Topoff, no matter how worthless, was not free to leave.

So it was a blessing of sorts when she was ordered to go to Novgorod with Pyotr. She was told emphatically to be on her best behaviour when she met the silk traders there. Having her on Pyotr's arm would raise his stature among them. But she had other ideas. Outside of Vladimir for the first time in two years, this was her best chance to escape. The best place would have been when they passed through Zenoplata, but for some reason Pyotr had the carriage bypass the town.

They rolled through the gates of Novgorod and stopped in front of a grand house in the middle of the town's market square. The front doors flew open and a large man descended the stairs.

"Pyotr Yuryevich. Welcome to Novgorod. I hope your travels have been comfortable?"

"Good evening, Mikhail Illych," Pyotr said as he stepped down from the carriage. "Yes, they were. It is good to be back in Novgorod. May I present my wife, Ludmilla Topova."

Ludmilla was getting herself down from the carriage. Pyotr didn't offer her his hand. Mikhail strode up and gave her a big bear hug.

"It is wonderful to finally meet you, my dear. And so lovely. I can see why Pyotr keeps you hidden away in Vladimir. I am Mikhail Illych Shermenskoff."

Ludmilla put on a smile, but glanced over at Pyotr to see his reaction. He showed none.

"Come in," Shermenskoff said, guiding them to the steps. "My sister Natalia will look after your lovely wife. We have some vodka to drink and tales to tell before getting down to business."

"Will Kolochoff be joining us tonight?' Pyotr asked. "I would like to finally meet this mysterious agent for the Celt."

Ludmilla's attention was heightened, but she did not react. There couldn't be that many Celts in the Rus. They climbed the stairs to be met by a woman.

"Welcome. I am Natalia Kolochova. You must be Ludmilla. Come. I have refreshments put out for you in the kitchen."

Ludmilla followed Natalia away from the men. All was going well so far, but she knew that she would have to sleep with Pyotr tonight and had no idea how that was going to work. The plan was to escape. She didn't know anyone she could trust and with the land still in the grip of winter, she couldn't just run away. She had to have help.

"Sit," Natalia said. "Eat and tell me about yourself." She wore a knowing smile.

Ludmilla was more interested in gathering information. "Who is the Celt?"

Natalia's expression changed drastically. "We do not talk about him."

"Is he the boyar of Zenoplata?"

Ludmilla was shocked by the look of worry that crossed Natalia's face. "He is a very dangerous man," Natalia answered.

"My husband does not discuss him and you should not ask questions."

"But your husband is the mysterious agent for this man?"

Natalia abruptly got up and walked to the cupboard, taking down a plate. "You ask too many questions." She put sausage, a small loaf of bread and a kasha pastry on the plate and placed it at the head of the table where no one was sitting.

"Who is that for?" Ludmilla inquired.

A shadow moved in the darkness, coming forward in the shape of a man. When the light reached his face, Ludmilla gasped.

"Andrey!"

Natalia reached over and grabbed her wrist. "Quiet, child. Your husband will hear you." Andrey sat down and began eating. Ludmilla stared at him, her mind full of joy—and foreboding.

"His name is now Andrey Alexandrovich Kolochoff," Natalia said. "Remember that. He is my husband, but not to be known as your brother. Your husband might recognize him, so he must stay hidden."

"Andrey Kolchin must remain dead," Andrey said. "I am the agent for the Celt."

Ludmilla understood. "The Celt is the boyar of Zenoplata."

Andrey nodded. "But I am only an agent in name. He has nothing to do with the silk business other than collecting a toll for it as it passes through Zenoplata. He gave it to me, but he and I must keep up appearances for the Topoffs. When one of them comes to Novgorod who was there that day two years ago, I must stay hidden."

"Why would Rainey do this?"

"I have asked myself that question every day. I still do not have an answer. But tell me about you. How is life in Vladimir?"

Ludmilla's face fell, thinking back to her current state in life.

"I don't think it is going very well, is it dear?" Natalia said. She turned to Andrey. "Pyotr disrespected her in front of the house."

Ludmilla could feel tears starting to run down her face. All the emotion she kept bottled up for two years suddenly came pouring out. "He hates me. I can't give him a son, so he beats me and ignores me. I must get away, but I'm his wife. He can find me. I don't know anyone in Vladimir and I have nowhere to go."

Andrey moved next to his sister and wrapped his arms around her. "I'm sorry I couldn't be there for you. I know I never paid that much attention to you myself, but you are family. Natalia and I will take you in."

Ludmilla looked up at him. "But how? I am his wife. You do not have the right to protect me from him. He will destroy your business."

"Let me worry about that," Andrey replied. He looked at Natalia. "Keep her here. I think it is time for Pyotr to meet his mysterious agent."

"No," Natalia said. "It is too dangerous."

"Don't worry. Pyotr Topoff is also going to have an unfortunate accident tonight."

* * *

Shermenskoff suggested that they go out for a drink. Pyotr agreed and followed his host to a tavern. Pyotr spent his time eyeing up the service staff while drinking his vodka. Shermenskoff finally got up and went out the front door. Andrey was waiting there.

"He's pretty drunk. Are you sure you want to go through with this? I have to wonder how our business might suffer. And then there is the Topoffs' retribution."

Andrey was twirling a knife in his hand. "They will just send another son. This will be another story of robbery in Novgorod, or perhaps a feud between pro-Muscovy and pro-Lithuania boyars. You know which street to take him down?"

Shermenskoff shrugged. "I never liked the little shit anyway. I will have him there in five minutes."

Andrey moved off to the place for his ambush. Standing in a dark corner, he waited for Shermenskoff and Pyotr to stumble into the street. When they appeared, Shermenskoff started to trail off and Pyotr continued down the street. Andrey stepped into the light.

"So, you wanted to meet the mysterious agent," he said in a low growl.

Pyotr's eyes widened. "You. You . . . you are Ludmilla's brother. I thought you were dead."

"So you were meant to believe. I hear you have been mistreating my sister." He raised the knife. "You will now regret I am still alive."

Terror flashed across Pyotr's face, but he was looking past Andrey. "No," he said. "How could you know?"

Confused, Andrey turned and saw Rainey standing behind him. A shiver ran down his spine. "What are you doing here? I've kept to our agreement." He struggled to hold down his own fear.

"Don't worry, I'm not here to kill you," Rainey replied. "What is this about?"

Pyotr began to back up and tripped himself, landing in a heap. "I'm sorry," he babbled. "I will treat her better. I promise."

Rainey glanced at Pyotr and back to Andrey. "What is he babbling about?"

"I want to know why he is more afraid of you than me," Andrey replied.

Rainey smiled. "Everyone is afraid of me. You should know that."

He took a step forward towards Pyotr, who let out a cry, bringing his hands up to protect himself. A smell rose up telling them he had soiled himself.

"He was beating Ludmilla, wasn't he," Rainey said.

"Yes, and now he will pay." Andrey raised the knife, but Rainey stopped him.

"Go, I'll take care of this."

"This is my duty to my family. What is it to you?"

"I made this shit a promise. I'd like to honor it."

Andrey was stunned. "You want to spare him?"

Rainey shook his head. "No, I promised I'd cut his head off if he hurt Ludmilla."

Andrey stepped back and lowered his knife. "May I help?"

"You have a family to protect. Best you not be directly involved."

How did he know about my family? Andrey thought for a minute about Natalia and little Alexey. Natalia had hinted that she might be pregnant again. He nodded. "Very well. Can you not make it quick?"

Rainey pulled out his sword, eliciting another cry from Pyotr. "I don't think I can scare him any more than I already have. Go home. I'll meet with you and Mikhail tomorrow about why I'm here."

Andrey trotted down the street, not stopping when he heard a scream cut short by the swish of a sword.

* * *

Natalia led Ludmilla into her house's entry hallway and up to a comfortable room. A bright fire warmed the room, making Ludmilla feel safer than she had for almost two years. Natalia brought in little seven-month-old Alexey to meet his aunt before sending him off to bed with his nursemaid. They chatted about Andrey's life after Zenoplata. Together with Natalia's brother, they had made the business flourish. Natalia and Andrey had married within six months of his arrival. Her brother said it made good business, but she adored Andrey and considered the business a bonus.

Andrey arrived after a few hours. He was tired and sent everyone to bed. Before leaving Ludmilla, he leaned down and kissed her on the forehead.

"You're safe now," he whispered. "Tomorrow, you can tell me about our Celt friend and why he made a promise about you."

"He made no promise to me."

Andrey smiled. "No, he made one to Pyotr, one he kept tonight."

"What . . .?"

"Shhh. Go to sleep. We'll talk in the morning."

Andrey silently left the room, closing the door behind him. Ludmilla lay there, wide awake, feeling safe and confused at the same time.

9

They met in a tavern that had a back room for privacy. Rainey waited quietly while Shermenskoff and Andrey sat down with a vodka bottle. They toasted the day, then discussed business.

"I've been sent by Grand Prince Ivan Vasilyevich to find out why the supply of furs to Moscow is petering out," Rainey began. "The silk traders don't come to Moscow anymore because there are not enough furs to trade silk for. I couldn't very well tell him that I knew why, or that I never knew the trade went through Moscow in the first place, so I traveled here to make a new arrangement. The furs passing through Zenoplata must now go to Moscow. I know that was not the deal I made, but perhaps it's time to cut the Topoffs out of the business."

Shermenskoff and Andrey looked at each other, then back to Rainey. "I don't see how that is any of your business," Shermenskoff said.

"It will be if the grand prince decides to march over here with his army to find out for himself," replied Rainey. "Do the Topoffs have an army that can protect you? Does Novgorod?"

Andrey stayed silent. Shermenskoff hesitated a moment but then assumed a brave face. "Our army can meet and defeat the grand prince."

Rainey smiled. "And how did that go in the past? Not well, from what I hear. Do I have to mention his cannons?"

The room became silent. The two men could see their enterprise being destroyed by fate. Rainey tapped the table. "There is a way out of this. Return the fur trade to Moscow and the silks will continue to flow to you here. Your profits will be lower because now I will be at risk and must take a percentage for arranging the trading in Moscow. The grand prince isn't too fond of Novgorod since the city fails to behave properly, but he isn't likely to care where I sell the silk. Right now, he is focussed more on Vladimir, which is more under his control. He actually thinks I'm there. If I bring your fur trade back to Moscow, he'll be happy. I would like to avoid any war. Wars tend to be messy and unpredictable."

"Why would you do that for us?" Shermenskoff asked.

"The same reason why I gave Andrey the business in the first place. I had other things to do. Now, it seems I can't avoid being part of it. You know the business here. It makes sense for me to keep you part of it."

Andrey knew the danger if the grand prince followed the trail himself. He turned to Shermenskoff. "With Pyotr dead, it will take a while for the Topoffs to organize their caravan back to Vladimir. We could ship the furs to Moscow this once and see how the Topoffs respond."

Shermenskoff was coming around. "I didn't know the Topoffs were cutting all the trade away from Moscow. I would have not been so enthusiastic about it if I knew."

"Good," Rainey said. "Can you have your furs ready to move in two days?"

"They are ready now," replied Andrey. "The Topoffs' caravan is expected to pick them up tomorrow. I'm sure that can be delayed with Pyotr's death."

Rainey grinned. "At least he had some worth by dying. But don't mention his death. Best if he just goes missing. They won't find him. I have a caravan coming in. They will pick up the furs and head out as quickly as possible. Thank you, gentlemen." He threw a bag of gold pieces on the table. "This should cover the furs. Now, I would like to speak with Andrey. Alone."

Shermenskoff hesitated, but with a nod from Andrey, he got up and left the room. Andrey looked nervously over at Rainey.

"How's Ludmilla?" Rainey asked.

'She is well. I am trying to find a way for her not to return to Vladimir. I'm hoping they just don't want her back."

Rainey shook his head. "I've met several people like the Topoffs. They don't give up what they think they own, even if it's the wife of a missing third son. If he was beating her, I'm surprised she didn't kill him herself."

"Ludmilla would never do that. It's not in her nature."

Rainey laughed. "You really don't know her very well, do you? She tried to kill me the first night I stayed in Zenoplata."

Andrey shook his head. "I don't believe that."

"Ask her yourself. She was defending your family's honor, just like you tried to do when you arrived. The reason she's still alive after that is I understood her motivation. I'm sure she wasn't part of whatever scheme your father was up to." Rainey shifted in his seat. "Which brings up the matter I want to discuss. Routing fur and silk trade around Moscow must have been something he thought would have long-term benefits if the grand prince was dead. The throne would be weak, looking at Ivan's baby son and his brothers still being young. But I don't think your father would have tried to kill the grand prince just as part of a business deal. There is something bigger involved."

Andrey shook his head, trying to look convincing. "I was not privy to anything else. We made friends of other boyars in Novgorod and Vladimir, all for business. Even I was unaware of how much business would be cut away from Moscow at the time." He wasn't lying. He knew that his father had attempted to assassinate Ivan, but past the business part, he didn't understand why. "Can you keep the knowledge of our business from the grand prince?"

Rainey nodded. "I have to. Besides, I have a special relationship with him. Don't want to disturb that." He pulled out his arquebus. "He has a lot of these, thanks to me."

Andrey scowled. "You are making him too powerful."

"About time someone was. The Rus Lands have a long history of being overrun by invaders. Perhaps it's time they could defend themselves."

"He will use them to conquer."

"You may be right, but continuing in his father's footsteps and uniting the Rus Lands would be a good thing. These petty raiding wars between principalities would come to an end, for one."

Andrey leaned forward, placing his hands on the table. "But why Ivan? There are other princes."

Rainey shook his head. "After meeting several princes over my lifetime, I have only met one who has the intelligence, character and skill to rule all the land. And that's Ivan. Extraordinary for a man his age. Other princes are all too deep in their petty bickering.

Reminds me too much of Italy with their constant wars. You show me a better prince than Ivan, I'll support him. I very much doubt you can."

Andrey had to agree. There was no other prince with more force or presence than the grand prince of Muscovy.

"And some advice for you and Mikhail," Rainey said. "Do not associate with anyone who is leaning towards Lithuania for support against Muscovy. Someday they will find themselves dangerously on the wrong side of politics."

"Mikhail and I stay as much out of politics as we can. We don't need the trouble."

"Good. What are you going to do about Ludmilla?" Rainey asked.

Andrey stayed silent. He really didn't know what to do. If the Topoffs came looking for her, how could he protect her without exposing who he was?

"May I make a suggestion?" Rainey said.

* * *

The Topoff group were in a quandary trying find out what happened to Pyotr. There was no sign of him anywhere. Shermenskoff told them that Pyotr had insisted on walking back to his lodging alone after their night at the tavern, and that was the last he had seen of him. Ludmilla was missing as well, but that was a minor concern for the caravan's leader. They spent days searching, but Rainey had hidden the body very well.

The caravan from Zenoplata arrived on time, Krasenoff leading it into the city. Rainey met them at the warehouse where they loaded up the furs as quickly as possible.

"So, where are you going to say these furs came from?" Krasenoff asked offhandedly.

"Vladimir," Rainey replied with a grin.

Krasenoff shook his head. "I have never met anyone who could lie to the grand prince and get away with it like you do. He usually has the chancellor follow up on people."

"He likes me. And I never lie about anything he needs to know about. I'm getting his trade back without the need for a war. He doesn't need to know the details."

"Things will be different now." Krasenoff's voice became grave. "I received word that Grand Prince Vasily has died. All Muscovy is in mourning. I don't know if they will still be mourning when we arrive, but you will go see the grand prince immediately upon our arrival. He sent the chancellor personally out to fetch you as we were assembling our caravan. That was not good."

Rainey grimaced. He knew the grand prince had a close bond with his father. He wished he could be there now for his friend. But he had another concern. Rainey was on good terms with the chancellor, but the chancellor's job was to be the eyes and ears for the grand prince throughout all his territories. Apart from being a soldier, Rainey had found Von Markenburg to be a skilled politician who traded in information. With Rainey being such a confidant of the grand prince, he didn't want Von Markenburg gathering information about him that could ruin his reputation.

"You told him you were going to Vladimir?"

"Of course, and then we had to head northeast because he didn't leave right away. Backtracked west and north to get back heading west. You're lucky we still made it here on time."

"Many thanks, my friend. Now there is just one more thing you need to know." Rainey turned and waved his hand.

Shermenskoff came in, with a hooded figure at his side. As they reached Rainey, the hood was pulled back.

"No, no, no . . ." Krasenoff grabbed Rainey's arm. "She can't come back. You know that. It puts you at risk."

"Igor, my friend," Rainey said. "It's been almost two years. Everyone in Zenoplata has known the whole time. Chances are the chancellor knows as well by now."

"He'll be saving that information for the right time."

"So, whether she's in Zenoplata or not, what's the difference? And since I never plan on becoming a threat to the grand prince, Gunter will have no need to use it."

"How about you becoming a threat to Gunter?"

Rainey shook his head. "That's politics. Gunter is well aware that I have no designs in that arena."

Krasenoff looked over at Ludmilla, standing there, fear etched on her face. "You better be worth it, girl." He turned and walked away.

"He worries about me," Rainey said, trying to break the tension. He looked over Ludmilla's shoulder. "Is Orina still in Vladimir?"

Ludmilla started to cry. Rainey put his arms around her. "Now, now. I will go get her for you after we are finished in Moscow."

"I don't know where she is," she sobbed. "They sent her away months ago."

Rainey could feel the anger rising in him. He hadn't liked the Topoffs when they first met, but he had not given them much thought since. Now here was this young woman they had beaten, isolated and deprived of her only friend. He was going to find Orina for her, but it wasn't going to be easy.

"I'll see if I can bring her home," Rainey said soothingly. "I'm hoping she can stop Grigori from sulking around the house all day. He misses her, too." He released Ludmilla and held her by the arms, looking directly into her eyes.

"Where is that woman who was brave enough to come at me with a knife?"

Ludmilla smiled in spite of herself.

10

The mourning for Grand Prince Vasily was still going on when Rainey and Krasenoff arrived in Moscow. Most of the foreign princes and their entourages had already come and gone, so no crowds remained in the streets. But the solemnity of the city was palpable. Shops and taverns were quiet. It was like the whole city was collectively sad.

"He was well liked," Krasenoff explained. "Muscovy has grown into this powerful principality due to Grand Prince Vasily. He will be sorely missed."

"It is in good hands with his son," Rainey replied. "Is there any protocol I don't know about now that our friend is the sole ruler?"

"Yes, but none you probably have to worry about, being his pet and all."

Rainey reached over and punched Krasenoff in the shoulder. "I want to show respect."

"All right." Krasenoff looked up at the sky while he thought. "They've been co-rulers for four years. They have been received by the same protocols all that time. So, perhaps just bow lower."

"You're a big help."

They rode past the palace and approached the Cathedral of the Annunciation, where they were told Grand Prince Ivan was spending much of his time in mourning. They entered to find him prostrate at the altar, silent and still. As they approached, Ivan began to rise and turned to face them.

"My two best friends in all the world," he exclaimed, running down the steps and embracing them together. Rainey glanced at Krasenoff, who was looking back uncomfortably. So much for protocol.

After what seemed an eternity, Ivan stepped back. Tears were in his eyes. "I no longer feel alone. You are here."

"Wasn't Gunter keeping you company?" Rainey joked.

Maybe it was too early for a joke like that, but after staring at Rainey for a moment, Ivan broke out laughing.

Krasenoff leaned over to Rainey's ear. "My God, you live dangerously."

Ivan slapped Krasenoff on the shoulder. "No, my friend, he just knew I needed a good laugh. Gunter, keeping me company. Ha! I'd be in the grave with my father if I listened to him for too long."

Rainey took the opportunity to bow. Krasenoff bowed lower, and Rainey followed until they were both almost touching the floor with their heads.

"What are you two doing?" Ivan asked. Rainey noticed Krasenoff was wearing a huge grin. Both came up quickly.

Sadness began to creep into Ivan's face again, but he sighed. "I feel lost without him. I don't know what I should do. What is it like out in the city?"

"Very much the same as it is in here," Krasenoff answered.

Rainey put his hand on Ivan's shoulder. "You have been co-ruler with him for four years. You know what his legacy is. You know how to continue that legacy. You are young, strong, and smart, and Igor and I are here to support you in everything you choose to do."

They three stood there silently, not hearing the metropolitan as he arrived at the altar.

"My grand prince, should I put out more candles?"

"No, Theodosius," Ivan replied. "My loyal friends are here now. It is time I went back out into the world." He led them down the aisle. "So, what did you find out about my missing fur trade?"

* * *

Ludmilla settled back into her old room in Zenoplata, feeling safe for the first time in two years. The townspeople appeared glad to see her. She had always been their favorite Kolchin. She began to learn how the town had changed under Rainey. Gone was her father's overseer. The new overseer was a man she knew was both kind and good with figures. She was also surprised to learn that Rainey regularly visited throughout the town, something her parents had never done. Everyone seemed to like him.

"Even the grand prince came to visit once," one shopkeeper told her. "It was a very exciting day. We know we are safe with Boyar Rainey here. Do you know when he is coming back?"

Ludmilla had spent the last two years thinking of Rainey as her family's destroyer. She had hated him. Feared him. But who was this man, she wondered, who made everyone in town happy?

She had to admit she didn't really know the man. Just four days with him two years ago, and then the trip from Novgorod where he never spoke a word to her after they left the city's gates. And then off to Moscow he went. Just about everything she knew about him was second hand. She decided she would spend the time to find out directly how he had transformed Zenoplata into what it had become.

She stepped through the gates into the town, having decided to pick up some new furs to make Rainey a new coat, one befitting a grand boyar. It would be a way to approach him, show that she could be trusted not to try to kill him again. She was passing a table with some exquisite jewelry on it. The seller saw her interest and stepped forward.

"From the far-off lands to the east. The green stones are called jade. Very rare."

Ludmilla picked up a ring with a large jade piece in it. She couldn't recall if Rainey wore any jewels at all. If he did, they weren't very noticeable. The only thing she could think of that was fancy about him was his sword. She put down the ring and picked up a plain smooth jade stone. *Maybe this would look good on his sword . . . .*

The force that snapped her head back made her shout. Arching her eyes to see who had done such a thing suddenly filled her heart with dread. She saw a face she had hoped never to see again.

Pyotr's older brother, Ilya.

"I knew you would be hiding here," he sneered. "You seem not to have learned that you belong to us. Where is Pyotr?"

With her back arched, she couldn't move. "I don't know."

Ilya brought his face right up beside hers. "So why are you here and he is not? That little snot cost us a shipment of furs from Novgorod. Our father wants an explanation."

"I told you I don't know where he is."

Ilya stood her up, spun her around and threw her into the arms of one of the men standing with him. "Doesn't matter. You are coming back to Vladimir with us. I think a scullery maid might be a good job for you."

Ilya's men dragged her to their horses, with her struggling all the way. The man pulling her stopped for a moment to slap her across the face so she would stop fighting him. He pulled her up and threw her across the front of his saddle. Ludmilla looked around for help, any help. What she saw she did not expect.

Standing in the road, blocking the horses' path, was Grigori. He was holding a pitchfork.

Ilya spun his horse around. "Get out of my way, old man." But Grigori didn't move. Ilya turned to one of his men. "Shoot him."

The crossbow came up. "NO!" shouted Ludmilla. Her voice was drowned out by a large bang.

The noise surprised her as much as everyone else. An explosive sound. The man with the crossbow pitched backwards off his horse. His bolt shot high and lodged itself in the wooden wall of a building behind where Grigori stood. Ludmilla craned her neck to see where the sound had come from. She saw the blacksmith laying down a hand cannon and picking up another one.

The silence was filled with the sounds of doors opening and closing as Zenoplata's townspeople, men and women both, rushed into the street. They carried cleavers, scythes, knives, clubs. All started to form a wall behind Grigori.

"You are not allowed to come here and take," Grigori said in a low growl. Ludmilla had never heard him sound like that before.

Ilya was defiant. "She is my brother's wife. I am only taking what rightfully belongs to my family. Let us pass!"

Ludmilla squirmed, but that only made the man holding her tighten his grip. She twisted to get a look at him. That's when she saw his knife. She reached out, her fingers wrapping around the handle. With a quick yank, it came free of his belt. Before he could react, she thrust it into his thigh.

The man howled in pain and released his grip. She slipped backwards off the horse and stepped clear. She turned around, only to find Ilya and his men between her and the townspeople. She turned and ran for her house.

"Get her!" Ilya screamed, wheeling his horse around and charging after her. A roar rose from the crowd as it surged forward after the horsemen. She reached the gate and sprinted across the courtyard towards the stable. The turn slowed the horses down, giving her time to get into the stable and slam the door behind her. She pulled the bolt to lock it and backed away.

"Get out here, you little . . ." Ilya's snarl was cut off by the roar of the crowd as it surged into the courtyard. She heard swords drawn, metal hitting metal. Then the crowd sound died away. She heard crunching noises. Boots. Someone walking up to the door. She backed up a little more.

There was a polite knock. "My lady, you can come out now." It was Grigori.

Slowly, Ludmilla crept up to the door, peering through gaps between the boards. Her faithful servant's trusty pitchfork was still in his hand. He was smiling. She drew the bolt back, ran out and hugged him. A cheer went up from the crowd.

"Thank you, Grigori," she cried. "You saved me."

"The town did," he replied.

She let him go and looked over the crowd of smiling faces. In the middle of the courtyard, Ilya and his men were lying on their faces, tied up and gagged.

"What are you going to do with them?" Ludmilla asked.

"Nothing," Grigori said. "We must wait for Boyar Rainey to return."

"That could be days."

"Then these men better have eaten recently."

She looked into Grigori's eyes. She saw none of the nervousness that she always remembered as part of his character. No fear.

Zenoplata really has changed, she thought.

* * *

Rainey and Krasenoff returned three days later. Ludmilla would not let the Topoff men starve, and brought them food herself to the back of the stable where they were kept under guard. Ilya, however, was tied up and locked in a root cellar. Ludmilla remembered her imprisonment without food and water when she had tried to leave Vladimir. It was Ilya who had enforced it.

As they rode through town, Rainey and Krasenoff noticed the townspeople seemed especially happy, like they knew of some nice surprise awaiting the two of them. When they took their horses to the stable, they saw four men sitting on the floor, tied to posts. One had a bandage on his leg.

"Wonder what we missed," Krasenoff mumbled.

Grigori entered the stable. "Welcome home, Boyar Rainey."

"Who are these men?" Rainey asked casually.

Grigori shook his head. "I promised the Lady Ludmilla that she could tell you. She's in the house. But I can tell you, the one with the leg wound? She did that." He took the reins and led the horses to their stalls.

Rainey glanced at Krasenoff. "Whatever we missed, it sounds like it'll be a good story."

They found Ludmilla in the great room, doing some sewing. When they entered, she calmly put down her work and got up, bowing slightly.

"Boyar Rainey, it's so nice to see you have returned." She glanced at Krasenoff. "Igor."

Rainey took off his cloak and coat and put them over a chair. "I hear you had some excitement in town recently." He moved to the big padded chair and sat. Krasenoff remained at the door.

"Oh, it was nothing," Ludmilla said airily. "Ilya Topoff came to take me back to Vladimir. He failed."

Krasenoff stepped into the room. "Topoff?"

Rainey put up his hand. "Is he the one in the stable with the wound in his leg?"

Ludmilla sat back down and picked up her sewing. "I don't know who that is."

Rainey leaned forward. "Ludmilla. Where is Ilya?"

She went back to sewing. "He's at the baker's."

"Why is he at the baker's?"

"The baker has a root cellar."

Rainey looked up and nodded to Krasenoff, who promptly left, off to the baker's house.

Rainey turned back to Ludmilla. "Grigori tells me you stabbed the man in the leg with his own knife."

She lowered her sewing again and smiled knowingly at Rainey. "I found the girl who came at you with one."

* * *

Krasenoff dragged Ilya Topoff into the kitchen and put him down in a chair opposite Rainey. He was still tied and gagged. Krasenoff removed the gag and the ropes around his wrists.

"How dare you let your peasants treat me this way," were the first words out of his mouth. "Do you know who I am?"

"Yes," Rainey replied casually. Grigori came over and loudly dropped a plate of food in front of Ilya.

Ilya looked down at the plate and back up at Rainey. "Am I to be poisoned now?"

Rainey reached over and shoved the plate away. "Fine. Starve. But if I wanted you dead, you wouldn't have made it out of that cellar."

They sat there staring at each other, but Rainey could see Ilya's eyes shifting back to the plate of food. Finally, he reached over, grabbed the plate and began eating in what could be described as desperation.

"Grigori, some wine for our guest," Rainey said.

For a moment, he didn't think Grigori was going to get it, but wine was poured and brought to the table. Ilya slurped it eagerly and went back to the plate.

When he was finished, he pushed the plate away and downed the last of the wine. "So, what do you want?" he asked.

"That's better," Rainey responded. "It's really very simple. I want Ludmilla's maid back." Out of the corner of his eye, Rainey saw Grigori stop and look at him.

Ilya spat. "All this for a maid?"

"You came here uninvited and tried to take someone who is not yours to take. I am within my rights to hang you."

Ilya got up to lean across the table, but Krasenoff shoved him back into his seat. Ilya looked down a moment before giving

Rainey a withering look. "I am within my rights. The woman belongs to the Topoff family. For taking her from us, I am within my rights to hang you."

"But you can't, can you?" Rainey leaned back. "You are in my house. My rules apply. The only recourse you have is to take your grievance to the grand prince in Moscow. Are you sure you want to do that?"

Krasenoff shifted behind Ilya, a flicker in his eyes betraying his nervousness. *Oh, relax, Igor*, Rainey thought. *I know what I'm doing.*

Ilya remained silent. Rainey smiled. He had him. "All I want is the maid."

"And what do I get in return?"

Krasenoff snorted, pulled his knife and leaned into Ilya's ear. "You get to walk out of here alive." He drew the flat of the blade across Ilya's neck and then tapped him on the shoulder with it.

"Do we have a deal?" Rainey asked.

"My father is expecting me to come back with the girl."

"Tell him you didn't find her."

"But my men work for my father."

"They won't be going home with you."

"How can I explain that?"

Rainey laughed. "I'm sure you'll think of something. The Rus is a dangerous place."

"What about Pyotr?"

Rainey knew this was likely to come up in the conversation. "What about him?"

"Where is he?"

"How should I know?"

"You have his wife living in your house."

Rainey had a plausible answer ready. "When Pyotr abandoned her in Novgorod, she joined a caravan back to Vladimir. When she reached here, her ancestral home, I invited her to stay. Apparently, she was not too interested in returning to Vladimir."

"She should have returned with our caravan."

"The one you route around Moscow?"

Ilya paused for a moment. "The one that you were part of creating."

"Can you prove that?"

Ilya was at a loss for words. Rainey knew he had no proof, one of the benefits of passing the deal off to Ludmilla's brother in the first place. The fur caravan passed through Zenoplata, but then so did many others. They were on the main river route for cargo through Muscovy to the northwestern Rus.

Rainey got up. "You're from a minor boyar family living in an insignificant town that happens to be a bit off the Oka River. Easy for you to divert silk caravans off the Oka and away from Moscow if you have a supply of furs that Moscow doesn't. Those furs will no longer be going to Vladimir."

Ilya's jaw dropped, but no sound came out.

"Can I kill him now?" Krasenoff asked.

"Yes. Yes," Ilya said quickly. "I will find your maid."

Rainey nodded. "Igor will accompany you home. If you do not produce the maid two days after that, you might just disappear like your younger brother did."

Ilya's eyes widened. "You . . ."

"No, do not assume I had anything to do with your brother's fate. I'm just suggesting you might fall victim to a similar one. You leave in an hour."

11

Krasenoff and his party returned nine days later, with Orina. Rainey enjoyed watching her reunion with Ludmilla. They both seemed so happy. Grigori came out to meet them as well. It had been a long time since he'd seen Grigori smile like this.

Krasenoff, however, wore a scowl. "Don't ever ask me to go to Vladimir again unless it's to burn it down."

"That bad?"

Krasenoff got off his horse. "The Topoffs got rich with the silk trade, but never spent a kopek on the town. It's spring, and everything is covered in mud, including the people. We had to find the maid among the workhouses. She had been bought and sold about three times. Which reminds me. I had to pay for her."

"I'll pay you back."

"I know you will. But it's something else. Vladimir is using different coins. I had to change mine and that was expensive."

Rainey was confused. "Vladimir is in Muscovy territory, right?"

"Yes, but the merchants there wouldn't accept Muscovy coins. I don't know what they think they are doing over there. Besides, where did they get the silver to make their own coins?"

"Silver?" That was alarming. If Vladimir was making its own silver coins, someone was supplying the silver. And the only reason you would make your own coins is if you were planning on . . .

"They want to break away from Muscovy."

"They can't do that."

"If they get rich with the silk trade and Moscow gets poorer, they can buy themselves an army while the grand prince loses his to poor revenues. Then they can try. But to make it work . . ."

Krasenoff finished his thought. "You can't have a prince like Ivan on the throne."

* * *

"You failed me," Yury Topoff spat. "And to make it worse, you let that Celt take away our key source of power. How am I ever going to get the other boyars to follow you if you cannot do a simple thing like bring home your brother's wife?"

"Father, he gave me no choice," Ilya pleaded.

"You always have a choice. Did I not teach you that?" Topoff slowly got out of his chair and moved to his desk. "I now have two shipments of silk with no buyers. I can't take them into Moscow this far down the path we have taken. You will take them all to Novgorod and force Shermenskoff and Kolochoff to give you furs for them. Do not come back without those furs."

"Yes, father."

"And when you pass Zenoplata, kill the girl."

* * *

"What are we doing here?" Ludmilla asked anxiously. Rainey had asked her to go riding with him. After a pleasant trot into the woods, they emerged into a meadow. He stopped and got off his horse.

"Come on down. I want to show you something."

Ludmilla stayed on her horse. Rainey continued walking toward the center of the meadow. He turned to see her still on her horse.

"Ludmilla, get off your horse and come over here."

"What are you going to do to me?"

"What am I . . ." Rainey shook his head. "No. Nothing like that. I think of you as my daughter. I want to teach you how to defend yourself."

"Why do I need to know that?"

"Because the Topoffs are not going to go away."

Ludmilla looked around. Her fears had not subsided. Quite the contrary. The name Topoff always gave her a chill now. She got down from her horse and went to join Rainey.

"Now, the first thing to learn is balance. You need to spread your feet apart."

"Like this?" She moved her left foot to the side. Rainey stepped forward and pushed her. She gave a yelp as she fell backward into the grass.

"No, like this." He placed his right foot both to the side and back. "This stance gives you balance. And with your right foot back, you can put more power into a punch by stepping into it, like this." He stepped forward, throwing his fist forward as he did.

Ludmilla looked up at him from the ground. "You didn't have to push me."

"I find people learn better from experience. You now know for certain that the stance you took is wrong." He held out his hand. "Come on up and I'll demonstrate."

She took his hand and he pulled. She felt like she flew up. She ended up against his chest. She looked up into his eyes. A strange feeling came over her. She felt warm. She didn't want to step back. But Rainey did.

"Now, stand like I did." Ludmilla didn't move. "Ludmilla." She moved her right foot back. Rainey stepped up and pushed her again. She was able to resist. He pushed her harder. Still, she was standing. "That was much harder than when I pushed you the first time."

She was looking at his face, the lines around his eyes, the shape of his chin, the color of his eyes. She wanted to understand this man who was becoming such a big part of her life and stirring feelings in her she didn't understand.

"Ludmilla, where are you?"

I'm right here, with you, she thought. Then she realized Rainey had actually said that.

"I'm sorry. Yes. I feel less likely to fall."

Rainey stood there, a slight grin on his face. "Now punch me." She reached over and gingerly thrust her fist against his chest. "Ludmilla, come on. Step into your punch like I showed you." She threw a second punch, stepping into it, but moved slowly.

Rainey's fist shot out and clipped her shoulder. "Ow," she cried. "What was that for?"

"I didn't step into that one and it hurt, didn't it? Imagine if I'd stepped into that punch. Where would you be?"

A flash of rage sparked in her brain and she lashed out. Stepping into the punch, she aimed with all her might at Rainey's chin. But his chin was gone. With nothing to stop her fist, she started to fall forward, but caught herself in time with her left foot.

"Much better," Rainey said from behind her.

Ludmilla turned around. "How did you . . ."

"Now, I will teach you the spin."

* * *

Every morning as the weather grew warmer, Rainey and Ludmilla rode out to the meadow and continued training. After learning moves and stances, he showed her what to look for in an attack, how to counter it with what she had learned so far and where to hit people with the most effect.

"I can't kick a man there," she protested. "It's hardly fair."

"The man is trying to kill you. What has fair got to do with it? You do what you have to do to win and live."

"Kicking in a dress is not easy."

"Maybe you should start wearing leggings and boots."

Ludmilla giggled. "Father Kirill would be scandalized." She saw Rainey smile. She liked it when he smiled at her. "Have you met women who wear leggings and boots?"

"A few."

"Tell me about them."

Rainey's smile dropped. "There was one young lady. I trained her, too, because I knew that one day, I wouldn't be around to protect her."

Ludmilla's curiosity heightened. "Was she your wife?"

"No. I've never been married."

"Then what was she to you?" She was surprised to feel anger welling up inside her.

Rainey sat down in the grass. He patted the ground beside him. Ludmilla sat down.

"Her name is Aunshaunie. She was ten years old when I met her. It was the day Constantinople fell to Mehmet."

"You were at Constantinople? What was it like?"

"It was so decayed, we all wondered why Mehmet wanted it. It was more a gathering of villages behind the wall than a great city. I found Aunshaunie trying to avoid a Turk's grip. We escaped together and ended up in Kiev. She grew up into a fine young woman, much like you. I trained her to take care of herself while I was spending every spring and summer fighting Teutonic Knights for King Casimir. Finally, two years ago, when she was betrothed to a fine young son of a prince, I took the opportunity to leave Casimir's wars behind and head east."

"But you are a warrior. You live to fight."

Rainey sighed. "Even warriors get tired of all the death. I came east to settle down. And I was given Zenoplata for saving the grand prince's life."

"That was when you met my father."

"Didn't exactly meet him. First time, we swung swords at each other. The second time, I shot him in my bed chamber as he tried to kill me." Rainey looked over at Ludmilla. She did not care now that he had killed her father. After all she had been through, she was going to live in the present. And the present had her sitting beside Rainey, a man who had saved her life twice.

"I'm not your daughter," she cooed and leaned towards him. But his face turned away from her. The look on his face made her concerned.

"Get to your horse," he said quickly. He got up, grabbing her hand to lift her up too.

"What is it?"

As they began running, she heard something flying past her head. She saw the crossbow bolt hit the ground few yards in front of her. Panic rose in her throat. Someone was trying to kill them.

When they reached the horses, Rainey pulled out his sword and arquebus. "Get on your horse and get to town. Don't stop for anyone."

"I'm not leaving you."

Dropping his weapons, he grabbed her around her waist and threw her across the saddle. "Yes, you are." He slapped the horse and it galloped off. Ludmilla struggled to get herself up in the saddle and regain control of the horse. She heard the arquebus fire as she seated herself and reined in the horse, only to find herself confronted by three men standing in the path.

One of them was Ilya Topoff.

"There you are, you little witch," he said scornfully. He turned to the other men. "Go and make sure the Celt is dead. I will take care of this one." He drew his sword.

Ludmilla's fear was strong, but mixed with anger now as well. "I'm tired of being afraid of you." She pulled a knife from her saddle and charged her horse at him, taking him by surprise. He couldn't get out of the way and the horse knocked him down hard. His sword flew from his hand. Ludmilla jumped down quickly and kicked him hard between the legs.

Ilya cried out in pain. He was helpless in front of her. There was no fear left. Her anger swelled into rage. She fell to her knees and with both hands thrust the knife as hard as she could into his chest. Ilya's back arched, his eyes bulged out. He hung on her blade for a second. Then air exploded out of his mouth and he sank to the ground. His dead eyes glared at Ludmilla.

She knelt there, both hands on the knife, not daring to move in case Ilya got up and killed her. Then she remembered Rainey, who she thought must be fighting men with crossbows. She tried to pull the knife free, but it wouldn't come out. She left it and ran back to her horse.

As she reached the clearing, she saw one man standing among several bodies scattered on the ground. It was Rainey. She jumped down off her horse and ran to him.

"Ludmilla!" Rainey yelled.

The force of the bolt slamming into the back of her shoulder knocked her down, face first in the dirt. Her mind began to close down. *I'm dead*, she thought. The last thing she saw was Rainey running past her.

12

She heard voices. One sounded like Father Kirill, praying. Another was Orina, telling someone to get out.

Several times, Ludmilla drifted in and out of consciousness. Each time the pain was too great, her mind not willing to deal with it and putting her back under. In the darkness, her dreams were violent. In one, Ilya Topoff took the knife imbedded in his chest and thrust it into hers while Pyotr stood by and laughed. In another, Rainey looked down on her sadly and said *you were not ready*. She would look down and see his Asian sword sunk to its hilt in her stomach. These dreams made her fight against the darkness, but it was too strong. She didn't know how many times she almost made it up to the light, but she finally got angry about this vicious cycle and fought hard against drifting back down. The pain and darkness fought back, but she prevailed, slowly seeing light as her eyes crept open.

It took her a minute to adjust, but she found herself in her room, on her bed. A wave of relief washed over her. It was over. She was alive. She tilted her head towards the door and saw Orina in a chair, sewing.

"Orina." It was almost a whisper. She barely heard it herself, but Orina did. She put down her sewing and came to the bedside.

"Good, you are awake, *malyshka*. How do you feel?"

Ludmilla didn't move. "It hurts."

Orina shook her head. "You are one difficult young woman to take care of. People kidnapping you, shooting arrows at you. It's all I can do to keep you alive." A small smile creased her face as she spoke.

From the stairs came a loud clatter of several footsteps muddled together. Orina made for the door as it burst open. Krasenoff was the first one there, but Orina was already pushing him back, and the crowd behind him.

"I get out of my chair and you all come running? I could have been going for a shit. Get out. I will call you when you can see her."

Krasenoff resisted, looking seeing Ludmilla long enough to know she was awake. He smiled at her. It was the first time he had ever smiled at her.

Orina had grabbed a broom. She hit Krasenoff over the head with the handle. "I said, get out." The crowd retreated and Orina slammed and locked the door. The exertion made her huff as she put the broom back in the corner.

"Was Connor there?" Ludmilla asked weakly.

"Yes, he was," Orina replied. "Don't you worry about him. He's fine."

"I know. No one can kill him."

"That's right. And may all of the Rus know that and leave us alone." Orina sat back down with her sewing. "You rest. There will be plenty of time for those men downstairs to see you later."

Ludmilla didn't dare close her eyes. She didn't want to give the darkness any chance to take her back. She focused on listening to what was going on in the house. She could make out voices from downstairs, but not what they were saying.

One voice stuck out. It was a woman's voice. At first she thought it was one of the townspeople, but no. Her speech was too refined. Too noble.

"Is there a noble woman visiting?" she asked

"She's from Moscow. Came to visit Boyar Rainey. She has that look of a woman seeking a man."

A woman? After Connor? The same feeling she'd had when Rainey first mentioned Aunshaunie rushed over her again. She had to do something. But she hadn't the strength to get up.

"Orina, I want to see Connor now."

"You need your rest."

"Now, Orina."

Orina put down her sewing again and went to the door. "Boyar Rainey," she yelled down the hall. "My lady wants to see you. NOW!" She left the door open, went back to her chair and resumed sewing.

Ludmilla heard Rainey coming up the stairs. She smiled as he came through the door, but her smile dropped when a woman followed him into the room.

"It's good to see you awake," Rainey said.

Ludmilla frowned. "My shoulder hurts."

"I know. It will heal."

Ludmilla glared at the woman. "Who's she?"

The woman smiled, but Ludmilla didn't feel any warmth in it, whether it was genuine or not. "This is Anna Tripenskaya," Rainey said. "She's a friend from Moscow."

"It is a pleasure to meet such a brave young girl," Anna said.

"I wasn't brave," Ludmilla said coldly. "I was trained."

She noticed an odd look on Rainey's face as he looked at her, but ignored it. "How long are you planning on staying?"

Anna seemed to take her tone in stride. "I haven't decided yet. Perhaps Boyar Rainey can convince me to stay forever." She gave him a loving look.

Ludmilla watched Rainey for a reaction. She saw confusion, his eyes shifting from Anna to her.

"We should let you rest," he said abruptly. He offered his arm to Anna and directed her to the door.

"Connor!" Rainey spun around, surprised. "I want to talk to you. Alone."

Rainey glanced at Anna, who narrowed her eyes at Ludmilla. "I'll just be a few minutes," he said. "Orina, could you take Anna downstairs?" Orina stood and escorted Anna out. Just before Anna went out the door, she slapped Rainey on the arm and scowled at him.

Rainey closed the door. "All right, young . . ."

Ludmilla cut him off. "Who is she?"

"I told you. She's Anna Tripenskaya from Moscow."

"Why is she here?"

"Visiting."

"People don't 'visit' Zenoplata."

"She's a friend."

"She thinks she's more than that."

Rainey smiled. "I know she does. Are you jealous?"

Ludmilla pouted. "No."

"I think she wants me to propose to her. What do you think I should do?" he teased.

Ludmilla could feel her face flush. She looked up at Rainey's grinning face, then turned her head away. "You can do what you want. She looks like she can give you many children."

Rainey's laugh stung the worst. "Maybe. But shouldn't I be in love with her first?"

"You need an heir. For Zenoplata. Love is secondary."

Rainey's face went serious. "Did your father teach you that?" Ludmilla stayed silent. "You should know by now I don't think like that. Rest now. We'll talk again later." He leaned down and placed beside her the knife she had used to kill Ilya. "Thought you'd like this back. And no, you are not my daughter." He turned and strode out the door, closing it behind him.

As that last comment sank in, Ludmilla beamed.

* * *

Ludmilla was up the next day. There was no way she would languish in her room while that Tripenskaya woman in the house. Although she was unable to do anything with her arm in a sling, just staying close to Rainey was enough to make sure that other woman didn't get any ideas. Rainey seemed to think it was all rather entertaining, while Krasenoff and Grigori found any reason to be somewhere else.

Anna knew what she was doing. That was obvious. The way Anna glanced at her; found ways to make it look like Ludmilla was not even there; was always suggesting that Rainey take her out riding where she knew Ludmilla could not follow. This went on for four days until one of Von Markenburg's black knights came requesting Rainey's presence in Moscow.

"I want to go with you," Ludmilla pleaded.

"You're not fit to ride yet," Rainey responded. "Besides, although it is probably a well-known secret, you're supposed to have died two years ago. I don't think anyone is quite ready for you to return from the dead."

"But you'll be alone with . . ." she cut herself off.

Rainey hugged her gently. "Don't worry your little head. I will not come back married."

"Why do you like her?"

Rainey let her go. "She's nice, friendly, and she's a friend of Maria of Tver."

Ludmilla was surprised. "The grand prince's consort?"

"Yes."

"I see. So, that is why you pretend to like her."

Rainey chuckled. "You just won't give up, will you?"

"Never." She threw her good arm around him.

* * *

"She is an intriguing child, but a child none the less."

Anna was riding in the carriage while Rainey rode alongside.

"She's hardly a child. She was married for two years."

"I was married when I was fourteen. I admit I was still a child at the time. But I am a woman now."

Rainey looked up the road, hoping she wouldn't see his eyes rolling. Although he liked Anna, he found her very unsubtle when it came to affairs of the heart.

They had been introduced to one another a year earlier by Maria of Tver. No one seemed to know where Anna came from, but she had endeared herself to Maria. Stories about her origins circulated in court. That her husband was a boyar who was murdered in Pskov. That she had escaped from the khan's harem. That she was a spy from Novgorod. All the stories seemed rather farfetched to Rainey, but even to him, the truth stayed hidden. He even approached Von Markenburg, who was supposed to know everything about everyone. He just shrugged his shoulders.

Anna never talked about herself. The fact that she had been fourteen when she was married was one of the very few personal things Rainey now knew about her, assuming she had told him the truth. Whenever he asked her a personal question, she deflected it. She did inquiry constantly about him, however. He found the one-sidedness of the information flow a little disturbing.

She was most alluring. Beautiful and educated. She could converse on a number of topics, from philosophy and religion to history and government, very unusual for a Rus woman. He did enjoy her company. At first, the relationship was friendly, but as time passed, Anna started to become a little obsessed about Rainey, at least in his eyes. Coming out to Zenoplata for the first time, unannounced, definitely displayed her intentions. But Rainey needed to know more about her. It was time to be direct.

"Married when you were fourteen. Not unusual. Who were you married to?"

"He's dead now. He's not important."

Rainey became more forceful. "Who was he?"

Anna lowered her eyes. "Why do you want to know?"

"Because I know virtually nothing about you. If your intentions are what you have been showing me as of late, I need to know who you are."

Anna recoiled, a small tear visible on her cheek. Rainey shook his head and urged his horse forward. He moved over to ride beside Krasenoff.

"Trouble with the lady?" Krasenoff asked.

"I believe that woman could cry on demand," Rainey said. "I don't know anything about her and she won't tell me anything."

"Who can understand women?"

"Hell, if her past is so bad, she could make something up. And she should know me well enough by now that unless she's a murderous witch, I can handle her past, whatever it might be."

"Maybe she is a murderous witch."

Rainey spat. "You know, Igor, sometimes you are absolutely no help at all." He spurred his horse into a trot and moved ahead to ride alone.

They arrived in Moscow late. After bidding good night to Anna, Rainey and Krasenoff went into the palace, where they were met by Von Markenburg.

"Pleasant journey, I hope," the chancellor said.

Krasenoff elbowed Rainey. "Depends on your point of view. For me, I didn't get rained on."

"Always the simple pleasures for you, Igor," Von Markenburg said. "Boyar Rainey, breakfast will be served at dawn. Afterwards, you are requested in the Great Hall. You know which rooms are yours, so I'll leave you until tomorrow." With a great turn that sent his cloak flowing behind him, Von Markenburg exited.

"See you in the morning," Rainey mumbled. He headed off to his room.

Exhausted from the trip, Rainey washed and got right into bed. Thoughts of Anna kept him awake. He truly did enjoy her company, but trust was a definite issue. Keeping her past secret may have had a certain mysterious allure to it, initially, but they should have been past that by now. He knew she wanted to marry him. Telling him more about herself was a given, in his mind, if she wanted him to agree.

Then there was Ludmilla. He could sense the feelings she had for him, especially during their training sessions. She went that extra mile just to impress him. And he had to admit, he had become particularly fond of her, too. He liked her fiery spirit, undaunted after two years of suppression by the Topoffs. If he was to marry Anna, he wasn't sure what Ludmilla would do. The one thing the girl wasn't was subtle.

First, he sensed it. Someone was in the room, moving very slowly towards the bed, trying not to make a sound. When he felt that the person was next to the bed, his hand shot out, gripping his sword. Rolling quickly, he swung the sword upwards, stopping it right next to Anna's neck.

She gasped, mouth open, eyes wide with fear. Her hands were on the bed as if she had been trying to climb up.

He lowered the sword. "Anna, how did you get in here?"

Anna said nothing, moving back from the bed. She stood there in her sleeping gown, looking sad in the dim light that filtered through the window. He repeated his first question, emphasizing each word.

"How did you get in here?"

Very quiet and meek, Anna said, "Maria let me in."

"Why?"

She swallowed hard. "I want to tell you about me."

They stared at each other for a moment. Then Rainey nodded. Anna's hands went up to her shoulders. Her gown fell to the floor. Pulling back the covers, she crawled in beside Rainey and pressed her body against his, kissing him deeply.

"I was born in Strausberg," she began, "a small town outside of Berlin."

* * *

Two hours before dawn, Anna padded barefoot down the hall from Rainey's room. Turning left, she came up to the man she knew would be waiting. Von Markenburg.

"Well?"

Anna smiled. "It went very well. You were right for me to tell him my true story. It is a sad tale."

"But you left out the part about when I sent for you to come to Moscow?"

"Of course. The only connection he can make between us is that we're both German."

"So, he'll marry you now?"

Anna rubbed her belly. "He didn't ask. But there should be an added incentive soon. I'm fertile. He is a man who will feel guilt. He will agree to marry me."

Von Markenburg nodded. "And then you can keep a closer eye on him for me in Zenoplata."

"Is he that close to the grand prince that he could be a threat?"

"No way to tell. We possess different talents that the grand prince makes effective use of. But there may come a time when we could become rivals. Best you find information I can use when that time comes."

"What about the girl? She may be a problem for me."

Von Markenburg put his hand on Anna's cheek. "Really, my dear. You can't deal with a young girl who is supposed to be dead? That's not the Anna Egger I know."

13

Rainey and Krasenoff stood together by the throne in the Great Hall waiting for the grand prince to arrive.

"You look happy," Krasenoff said. "Happier than usual."

Rainey was smiling, in spite of himself. "Anna told me everything. Where she was born, her life before coming to Muscovy, everything."

"When did she tell you all that?"

"Last night."

Krasenoff's eyebrows raised. "Last night? Did anything else happen last night?"

"Yes," Rainey answered smugly.

"Are you sure she wasn't just telling you a story to get into your bed?"

"Since when do women need to tell me stories to get into my bed?"

Krasenoff shrugged. "I haven't seen any women in your bed since I've known you."

Rainey was about to reply when the grand prince entered with Von Markenburg and his black knights. Ivan looked very serious as he plopped himself down on his throne.

"The two of you brought me information, which I had Gunter check, about the new coins in Vladimir. This is a serious breach of the laws of Muscovy. You are here to witness the application of those laws." He turned to Von Markenburg. "Let them in."

With a wave, Von Markenburg signalled two of his knights to open the big doors at the hall's far end. As they swung open, the old Yury Topoff and his only surviving son, Arkady, entered the hall. Upon seeing Rainey, Yury Topoff scowled, but quickly recovered as he approached the throne.

He bowed deeply. "My prince. You have summoned us and we are here. How may the Family Topoff be of service?"

Ivan shifted in his throne. "I understand you have been making coins."

Topoff hesitated for only a moment. "Yes. Just small batches to take the strain off your royal treasury. We do not get a supply of coins in Vladimir very often, so to help with our town's expanded commerce, we began making our own."

"I see," responded Ivan. "What sort of expanded commerce is Vladimir involved in?"

"Oh, nothing important. Mostly internal buying and selling. The coins do not leave Vladimir."

"And why is that?"

"No one else would put a value on them."

Ivan flung his hand out and several silver coins bounced at Topoff's feet. "If they were made of silver, they would. Is that your face I see on these coins? And where does Vladimir get a supply of silver?"

"I . . . I . . ."

"Answer me!" Ivan demanded.

Topoff fell silent. Arkady took a very slow step back from his father.

"Could it be this is the supply of silver that you have been using to cut off the silk caravans from coming to Moscow? And then selling the silk to Novgorod? Is the silver from Novgorod?"

Rainey glanced over at Krasenoff. So, there was more than furs for silk. Silver was involved as well. He would have to ask Andrey about that.

Topoff pointed at Rainey. "It was his deal. He married that witch off to my son to route the silk and fur trade around Moscow."

Ivan looked at Rainey and smiled. Rainey didn't know what the smile meant.

Turning back to Topoff, Ivan leaned forward. "But there is no evidence of any of that. Believe me, we have looked. And I do not recall any witch Rainey would be marrying off to anyone."

"The Kolchin girl. She's out at Zenoplata right now. She married my son, Pyotr, who went missing recently in . . ." He stopped himself.

"Let me guess." Ivan leaned even farther off his throne. "Novgorod?" Topoff seemed to melt away.

Ivan leaned back in his chair and nodded. One of the black knights stepped up with a knife and slit Topoff's throat. Arkady was turning to run when a second knight impaled him with a sword.

"Gunter, find me some respectable boyars to take over the Topoff family's duties and properties." He got up off the throne. "You two, follow me."

Rainey got a bad sense of foreboding. He started counting the black knights in the room, wondering if he could fight his way out.

They retired to a small room off to the side of the Great Hall. Ivan turned to face them, but said nothing.

After a moment of silence, Krasenoff spoke first. "I was just there watching his back, as ordered."

Ivan raised his hand. "It's all right, Igor. Connor, I know what the story is, but I need some questions answered. When did you decide to let the Kolchin children live?"

Rainey was very uneasy. Ivan had said *children*, so he knew about Andrey as well as Ludmilla.

"Did you order the chancellor to execute Alexander Kolchin's entire family?"

"No," Ivan replied. "He was to go with you and officially place you there as boyar. Gunter knows the Rus ways. There should be no Kolchins left to defy you.

Von Markenburg could have said something on the ride over. "I saw no reason to kill Ludmilla," Rainey stated. "I'm sure, as a girl, she had no knowledge of any plot to assassinate you and no reason to be a threat to me. In order to send Ludmilla to a safer place, I had to make the deal with the Topoffs to make the marriage happen. And then I had to keep Andrey around to manage that deal in Novgorod. I had no idea the plan was to route silk around Moscow."

"But when you did find out, why didn't you tell me?"

"Honestly, I was worried about how you would react. I really wasn't directly involved in it. The Topoff caravans came through Zenoplata much like all other caravans. I never asked if they bypassed Moscow. I have had no contact with Andrey Kolchin for two years. I set the deal up and walked away. The first sign it was a problem was when you sent me to Vladimir to investigate why no silk was coming through Moscow. I was hoping to fix it without you needing to know everything."

"But you went to Novgorod."

Rainey wasn't surprised. "Yes, because that is where Andrey is. And that is how the furs are now coming back to Moscow. You're very well informed."

Ivan smiled. "Come now, Connor. Gunter always knows everything. That's why I keep him and his black knights around. He is a valuable talent to me."

"You should tell him that."

Ivan was silent for a moment. "Topoff only brought one son with him. Where are the other two?"

"Dead."

Ivan stepped away, turning his back on Rainey. "Just out of curiosity, did you kill them?"

"Pyotr. In Novgorod. Ilya was killed by Ludmilla."

Ivan spun around. "The girl?"

"Yes. Thrust the knife into his chest right up to the hilt."

"So, you're training her."

"Best way to protect her is to make it so she can protect herself."

Ivan nodded slowly, then turned back around to face a small altar on the wall. "That is all. You may leave."

Rainey and Krasenoff hesitated. There was still Von Markenburg and several black knights out in the Great Hall.

Ivan continued. "You are safe. I don't need the black knights bleeding all over the floor of my hall."

* * *

The tavern was full. A small band of musicians played in the corner. Serving girls circulated around the tables keeping glasses filled with beer and vodka. Rainey and Krasenoff had been there for several hours, drinking. Krasenoff kept his eyes on the serving girls, a silly grin on his face. Rainey stewed in his chair, angry with himself for getting into a position that he might lose the grand prince's faith in him. He was surprised that Ivan had let them leave. He had learned Rus ways since Constantinople, but in Muscovy, they were a little bit more extreme.

Von Markenburg found them there. "Greetings. May I join you?"

Krasenoff sneered. "The chancellor stooping to grace this hovel of a place with his presence? Things must really be different in Moscow these days."

"You're drunk and there are many boyars here. It is hardly a hovel."

Krasenoff looked around. "Oh, I was thinking of another place." Then his head went down with a thump on the table.

Von Markenburg addressed Rainey. "Are you about to go to sleep as well?"

"What do you want, Gunter?"

Von Markenburg sat down. "I want to give you some clarification about what happened today."

Rainey snorted. "Pretty obvious. The Topoffs are dead because of the silver coinage, a sure sign they were planning on setting up their own principality. Me, I should be at least in prison for whatever part I took in the grand plan Topoff had going."

"You have a fair grasp on Muscovy law."

"The law is whatever the grand prince decides it is that day."

"And you are drunk and know better than that."

Rainey lowered his head. "Yes, I know."

"He knows you were not being malicious when you made the deal with the Topoffs. I made sure of that."

"Why would you do that?"

"Because he needs you like he needs me in these times. He needs us for different reasons and skills and I believe we both understand that."

Rainey looked up at Von Markenburg. "When did you know about Ludmilla?"

Von Markenburg chuckled. "That day, actually. The look on your face and the way you ran to the stable. You were not going there to kill her."

"Very astute."

"Where did you get the blood?"

"It was mud. From the color of her dress, it didn't need to be red to look good from a distance."

Von Markenburg nodded. "Interesting trick." He leaned in to Rainey. "You know, when I first came to Muscovy, I thought the Rus ways were rather barbaric. Over time, you too will see that, in many cases, the grand prince does not have any choice, as his power stems from the boyars. They pledge allegiance to him, but they can also remove him for one of his siblings if it suits them."

"I didn't know that."

"So, he must always have a strong hand. His father went through many trials, including his blinding, to stay on the throne of Muscovy. In the end, the boyars preferred him to his opponents."

"How did you end up in Muscovy?"

"I was first hired in 1446 to put Vasily back on the throne permanently. I've seen Ivan grow into the fine man he is today."

"He should treat you better."

Von Markenburg shook his head. "He has a distaste for my talents, even as he uses them to stay ahead of his enemies."

"Where did you come from?"

"Malbork."

Rainey rose up in his chair. "Ah yes. I remember. You were a Teutonic knight."

"As were my black knights."

"Why aren't you still part of the order? Fighting Casimir's farmers couldn't be the only reason."

Von Markenburg shrugged. "Politics."

"Really? I thought you were very adept at politics."

"I am. That is how I recognized that the Teutonic Order's time was past. Its reason to exist didn't exist anymore. There were no more pagans to convert. We became cruel overlords to people who hated us. It was not what many of us signed up for. When Casimir started the war against the Order, we were recalled to Prussia. We could have fought forever against those farmers Casimir kept sending out. But after two years, it was too depressing. When Vasily asked us come back, we took the opportunity to leave the war behind." He glanced at Rainey. "You were leading those farmers for a time. Perhaps we met in battle somewhere."

Rainey smiled. "If we had, you wouldn't be here right now."

"Indeed. You do have a very good talent for killing."

"Only when attacked."

Von Markenburg paused. "I would like to broach another subject, if I may?"

"Go ahead."

"What would be Ludmilla's status with you?"

Rainey was confused. "I don't understand."

Von Markenburg shifted in his chair. "Well, you married her off to the Topoff boy, so I assumed you are considering yourself her guardian. In that capacity, do you have any plans for the girl?"

"Plans? No, she can do what she likes."

"Actually, she can't. I'm only saying this because strong alliances can be established through marriages. As you have no children of your own . . ."

Rainey put his hand on Von Markenburg's shoulder. "I am not going to marry Ludmilla off for political gain. She is not my possession to do with as I please."

"I see. You are a rare man in this world."

"I know. Sometimes it's hard to stay that way."

"Perhaps you, yourself, could use a wife. I understand that the Lady Tripenskaya has shown an interest in you."

Rainey smiled, remembering the night before. "Nothing gets by you, does it, Gunter?"

Von Markenburg smiled back and tapped the side of his nose. "It is my job to know."

Krasenoff's head popped up. "Where are you going, you beautiful wench?"

Von Markenburg got up from his chair. "I will leave you to your . . ." He looked at Krasenoff. "Dreaming? Until next time."

I like him, Rainey thought to himself as he watched Von Markenburg leave the tavern. *Ivan is lucky to have him around.*

14

Spring turned into summer. The sun warmed the fields and the crops were looking green. Anna Tripenskaya rode the boat up the river to Zenoplata, glancing down at the small bump her belly made under the fabric of her dress. She had not seen Rainey in two months; it was time to announce her condition to him and subtly press for marriage.

As the boat rounded a bend, the sound of wood banging together echoed from the shore. She saw two figures swinging and spinning in a dangerous dance. One figure she recognized as Rainey, but the other was a slight figure in boots, pantaloons and a shirt. Anna noticed waist-length hair tied back behind the figure's head. As the boat got closer, she realized she was looking at a woman.

It was Ludmilla.

Anna stepped behind a stack of crates and watched the two fight. Every now and then, they would stop. Rainey looked like he was giving instructions. Then the dance would start again. As the boat passed around the next bend, Anna began to worry about her prospects. She didn't know why Rainey was training the girl to fight or if he still looked upon her as a daughter, as he had originally told her.

This was not going to be as easy as she had hoped. She was going to have get rid of Ludmilla and she had no plan to do this.

At the Zenoplata wharf, Anna disembarked. Her two servants gathered her baggage onto a handcart and they walked towards the boyar's house. They found Grigori in the courtyard carrying water from the well.

"Good day to you, Grigori," Anna said. "I see Boyar Rainey was out by the river with Ludmilla. Do you know if they will be long?"

Grigori stood stiffly, his glance moving from her face to her midsection and back. "I'm sorry, my lady. When they go out like that, there's no telling when they will be back."

"Then get a horse and cart. You will take me out to see them." Grigori didn't move. "Now, Grigori."

As Grigori left for the stable, Anna's servants started to move her baggage into the house. Orina opened the door, standing there in shocked silence.

"Hello Orina," Anna said. "I'll be going out to see the boyar. Please help my servants set up my room. I shouldn't be long."

Orina beckoned the servants in. Grigori brought out a horse cart and helped Anna into it. She stared forward as he climbed up and took the reins.

It took fifteen minutes for the ride to the clearing where Anna had seen Rainey and Ludmilla. She found them still swinging wooden swords at each other, weaving and spinning, thrusting and blocking. Grigori stopped the cart twenty paces away from them.

Rainey stepped back as he saw his visitor arrive. Ludmilla lowered her sword and turned around. She was breathing heavily, but her look of contempt for Anna was unmistakable. Grigori jumped off the cart and helped Anna down.

"Lady Tripenskaya," Rainey said. "We weren't expect . . ." His words tailed off as he noticed her shape.

Anna smiled. She had gotten the desired effect. Walking towards him with the step of a woman much more pregnant than she was, she said, "Good day to you, Connor. I see you are well."

Connor didn't reply. However, Ludmilla did.

"I will leave you two alone," Ludmilla said, throwing down her wooden sword and striding purposely to her horse. Swinging herself into the saddle, she snatched up the reins and rode off.

Rainey and Anna were left there, silently looking at each other. Grigori broke the silence. "The lady asked me to bring her here."

Rainey broke his trance. "It's all right, Grigori. Take my horse. I'll bring the cart back."

Waiting until Grigori had left, Anna said, "Are you not happy to see me?"

Rainey said only one word. "When?"

Anna pouted. "Have you already forgotten our night together?"

"No, I haven't," Rainey said curtly. He paused for a moment before continuing. "What are you expecting from me?"

Anna hesitated before answering. She had to play this just right. "I am a woman. It is not my right to expect anything."

Rainey lowered his head. One corner of Anna's mouth curled up ever so slightly. She knew she couldn't demand anything. That was not the way of the Rus. But she knew Rainey well enough now to know the way of the Rus would never be part of his nature. Although Anna couldn't demand anything, she knew Rainey would offer. After all, it was his child.

"Who else knows?"

"The grand prince's consort, of course." She knew that mentioning Maria of Tver would tell Rainey that everyone at court knows, including the grand prince himself.

Rainey was nodding now. "I see." He stepped forward and took Anna by the arm. "We should get back to the house." He helped her up into the cart.

Anna grabbed his hand as he went to pull away. "I do love you." She looked deep into his eyes, trying to see some sign that she was winning; that he was submitting to what she wanted. But he just nodded again and went around to climb up beside her.

They rode back to the house in silence. Every now and then, Anna stole a glance at Rainey, but she never caught him looking back. They were almost to the gate when he finally spoke.

"I'm settled down now, so I suppose I should be thinking about marriage."

Anna felt a surge of anticipation rise in her. This was it. He was going to ask her to marry him. Von Markenburg would be so pleased.

"But I had never considered you before."

Anna's heart sank as fast as her anticipation had risen. She thought she was going to be ill. Had she totally misjudged Rainey's character? Would he actually reject a child that was his?

"I suppose I should consider you now."

The up and down of emotions made Anna feel faint. She steadied herself on the cart's rough seat and looked straight ahead, trying to breathe steadily. Her mind whirled, trying to calculate what to do next. The game was still on, but it wasn't going to be as easy as she had hoped.

The cart pulled into the courtyard. Grigori ran forward to collect the reins from Rainey. Ludmilla stood in the doorway of the house, arms crossed, staring at Anna.

First things first, Anna thought. *That little bitch has to go.*

* * *

Rainey went about the business of being boyar as if nothing had changed, but his trips out of the village with Ludmilla for training were reduced to the point that Ludmilla began asking about them. He spent most of his time the first week trying to avoid Anna, which was hard, as she spent most of her time trying to be near him. At the beginning of the second week, he got on his horse and rode out of the courtyard without telling anyone where he was going. He headed north, following the river. He drove his horse hard for the first twenty minutes, then settled down into a trot. The whole time, he let his mind go blank. He found he could think more clearly if he just shut everything out for a while.

As he emerged from the forest, he found a familiar small knoll at a bend in the river. It was a place he had found a year ago that offered a clear view down the river as it turned to the west. He had come here several times to think about where he was in his life and where he wanted to go. There were times he missed the adventure of being a mercenary. He had conceded that, although being a boyar had its advantages, it consisted of a different kind of warfare. Politics were the weapons used. Innuendo, gossip, having to keep an eye on the other boyars. Rainey was a favorite of the grand prince, which made him a target. But all he wanted was to be left alone.

Today, his thoughts centered on emotion. Anna Tripenskaya showing up pregnant with his child was something he had not expected. He liked Anna, but past that he wasn't sure about his feelings. Then there were the feelings for Ludmilla that had been stirring in his heart over the last few months. He knew she was feeling them too, but didn't know if he should act on them. Considering his position over her, he felt he would be taking advantage. It was all so confusing to him.

He rode past the last trees to find a horse standing on the knoll. A man was sitting on the ground, facing the grand view Rainey liked so much. As he rode up, he recognized the seated figure.

"You sure take your time riding along the river," the man said.

"Igor, what are you doing here?"

Krasenoff looked over his shoulder. "The way you have been behaving lately, I figured one day you would ride out here to think."

Rainey got off his horse. "How do you know I come here?"

Krasenoff shrugged. "Remember, I'm here to watch your back."

"And perhaps spy a little?"

"Not anymore. I hope you know that."

Rainey sat down beside his friend. They sat there in silence.

"So, what is on your mind today? Like I couldn't guess," Krasenoff finally said.

Rainey looked at him. "Oh, Igor, what am I to do?"

"I could tell you the Rus way. The Tripenskaya women has no claim on you. If she's a problem for you, just behead her."

Raney scowled. "That's the Rus way?"

"Yes, as you are well aware. She's a woman. She is nothing more than a possession, one that seems to want to be owned by you. If you don't want her, send her away or drown her in the river. Your choice. Although I know that is not your way."

"I can't imagine you drowning a woman just because you don't want her anymore."

Igor nodded. "No. But Rus women know better than to assume they can bend a man to their will. This Tripenskaya woman is not of the Rus and she knows you don't follow Rus ways. You have to decide if you want to let her manipulate you."

"She isn't manipulating me."

Krasenoff raised an eyebrow. "Even Lady Ludmilla would agree with me on that."

Ludmilla. The other part of the triangle. Rainey wanted to ask Krasenoff's opinion about Ludmilla's feelings for him, but he was afraid of what would be said. His friend wasn't exactly the place to go for advice on love. He sat silently for a moment, contemplating what kind of reason Anna would have to insert herself into his life. She was a confident of Maria of Tver, living at the court in Moscow. What could possibly make her want to give that up to move to a small town like Zenoplata?

In the end, that was what bothered him. Having his child would not change her status at court. Yes, she may very well love him, but leaving court did not seem to Rainey like something Anna would do.

"What do you know about Anna?"

Igor shrugged. "Not much. The same rumors you know of from around court. I never paid that much attention to her. I thought she told you everything about herself."

"When did she first show up in Moscow?"

"I don't know. A couple of years before you did."

"Where from?"

"Didn't she tell you?"

Rainey thought back to that night in the Kremlin. "She's German, you know. Said she married a Rus from Pskov. When he died, she came to Moscow."

"Sounds about right," Igor said. "Like I said. I didn't pay too much attention to her."

"A beautiful woman shows up at court and you didn't pay her any attention?"

"Fine. I tried my charms on her. She wasn't interested. I was just a lowly bogatyr."

"And that's not the Rus way," Rainey said. "Who else showed an interest that made you decide it was too much trouble?"

"She joined Maria of Tver's court. I was not considered high-bred enough for her then."

Rainey grabbed Krasenoff by the shoulder. "That never stopped you from pursuing Olga for three months."

Krasenoff looked uneasy. "It was different with Anna. Maria herself told me to forget her."

Rainey let him go. They sat silently for a moment.

"I know people in Pskov," Krasenoff said.

Rainey turned his head to face him. "Like who?"

"I know their prince. We became friendly during a visit the grand prince made to Pskov when he was much younger. I could go to Pskov and find out about this Tripensky that Anna was married to."

"You want to see if her story is true?"

"Don't you want to know? Before you marry her?"

Rainey sighed. He thought he could get a more comprehensive answer to the mysteries of Anna if he asked Von Markenburg to investigate. However, this was not something you took to the chancellor of Muscovy.

"All right. Go to Pskov. See what you can find out."

As they rode back to Zenoplata, Rainey wondered what Krasenoff would discover in Pskov and whether he really wanted to know anything more about Anna than he already knew.

* * *

With Krasenoff away to Pskov, Rainey decided that he couldn't just ignore Anna any longer. He began to use his time with Anna and Ludmilla to get them to like each other. He couldn't just order them to like each other, so a slow process began with pushing conversations over meals and walking through town with both of them. As time wore on, it seemed to be working.

Then came the morning when Anna started the next phase of her seduction. While sitting at breakfast, she said, "Connor, you should start to consider finding a good match for Ludmilla."

"What?" Rainey exclaimed. Ludmilla dropped her knife.

"Well, she's still young. She would make a fine wife. And there are political alliances that could be made."

"She just became a widow this year."

Anna tilted her head. "Is Pyotr Topoff dead?"

Rainey cringed inside. He hadn't meant for that to slip out. "He might as well be. He hasn't shown up here for months to reclaim his wife." He glanced at Ludmilla. She had picked up her knife and was holding it like he had showed her to defend herself with.

Anna pressed ahead. "From what I have gathered, Ludmilla didn't like him very much. I'm sure we can find her a more suitable match at court."

Ludmilla was staring at Rainey as if to say *stop her*. With this topic of conversation, he could see all the work he had put in over the last few days to get the two women to at least tolerate each other going for naught. He had to try to end it quickly.

"I made an agreement with Ludmilla that she can choose who she wants to marry. She chose to marry the Topoff boy."

Anna looked over at Ludmilla. "That only shows her lack of judgment. I'm sure I can help find her a much better choice and she will approve. I have a short list of eligible men in mind."

Ludmilla was still staring silently at Rainey.

He broke the silence. "Why don't we just marry her off to Igor?" he asked, smiling.

The knife whizzed past Rainey's head and stuck in the wall behind him. Ludmilla got up and stormed out of the room. "I was joking," Rainey said, but she kept going.

"That was rude," Anna declared.

"I deserved it."

"Women have been executed for less."

Rainey leaned towards her. "And so have women who have assumed a pregnancy entitles them to a marriage. You know we don't live by all Rus ways here."

Anna's smug expression evaporated, replaced with fear. Rainey held back a smile. No matter what happened, he could always maintain some control over her. He leaned back in his chair.

"This is Ludmilla's home. If she doesn't want to leave, she doesn't have to."

"What about me?" Anna pleaded. "She obviously dislikes me very much. How can I live here with her?"

Rainey smiled. Perhaps it was time Anna did some of the work Rainey had been doing. "You're going to have to make her like you."

Anna looked perplexed. Rainey knew Ludmilla would be a huge challenge, even for Anna. But if she could win over Ludmilla, it would make his life so much easier. And perhaps Anna might even turn out to be worth marrying.

15

The summer marked a continuing parade of the sons of boyars from across Muscovy coming to Zenoplata to meet Ludmilla. Although Anna behaved as pleasantly as she could with her, the parade of suitors made clear that her goal was getting Ludmilla out of the house. Ludmilla, however, was not having any of it.

The first few suitors arrived with the attitude that they were there to buy something. They checked Ludmilla over like she was a horse. After a couple had been slapped and one cut on the arm, Anna began to coach the boys in how to approach the fiery young Kolchin girl. Rainey found it all rather amusing, especially when he rode into the courtyard and found one suitor hanging from Ludmilla's window, Ludmilla banging at his hands with a broom handle. Apparently, the boy had made the mistake of thinking manhandling her was the way to go.

As the summer faded into autumn, the line of suitors for Ludmilla's hand petered out. Her reputation, politely called "difficult," had become the talk of the court. Anna was exasperated with her failures, but out of it all a faint bond had formed between the two women. Rainey had stayed clear of the whole enterprise, but he had noticed that some of their conversations did not appear to be arguments. When he was told that they had begun taking walks in the village together without him, he had to agree that they were getting along.

The day a black knight arrived with a letter from the grand prince marked a change in what Rainey had come to call the "March of the Suitors." He was out in the village when he saw the knight riding towards the courtyard. He knew all of the knights by name; this one was Gerhard. He had been part of the party that had killed Ludmilla's family before her eyes. Rainey quickly settled his discussion with the village blacksmith and hurried back to the house.

When he arrived, Gerhard had dismounted and was standing by the door. Orina was talking with him, but Rainey spied Ludmilla over behind the stable door, staying out of the knight's sight.

Orina pointed at Rainey as he approached the house. Gerhard turned and strode towards him, helmet in the crook of his left arm.

"Boyar Rainey. I have a message from the grand prince." He handed Rainey a small scroll.

Rainey opened it. It was a summons to Moscow. He looked up at the sky. It was getting late. As the scroll did not mention any urgency, there was no point beginning the journey before tomorrow morning. "It is late, sir. May we offer you the hospitality of our home for the night and leave at dawn?"

Gerhard nodded. "Thank you, Boyar."

"Come in and rest. Orina, get us some ale and food."

Grigori already had a fire going in the hearth against the night chill creeping in. Rainey helped the knight out of some of his armor and sat him down in a comfortable chair. "How are things in Moscow?" he asked

"Fine," Gerhard replied. The black knights were not known for their conversational skills.

"Anything new and exceptional come in with any caravans lately? I'd like to pick something up for the women while I'm there."

Gerhard rubbed his close-shaved head. "No."

The black knights had always kept to themselves. But after years in Muscovy, Rainey would have expected some sort of assimilation to take place. They were all Teutonic knights to the core, with absolute loyalty only to Von Markenburg.

"Have you been in Muscovy since Gunter came here?"

Gerhard's head slowly pivoted towards him, a blank look on his face. "We all have been."

Ivan had told Rainey the story of the Teutonics and their history in Muscovy. In 1446, Von Markenburg had arrived with his knights to help Ivan's father regain the throne of Muscovy from Dmitry Shemyaka. Once securing Vasily on the throne by the early 1450's, they headed back to Malbork to rejoin the Teutonics, just in time for the war with Casimir of Poland in which Rainey had fought. By 1456, they received word that Vasily wanted them back permanently, offering Von Markenburg the title of chancellor as an incentive.

From Rainey's experience, the Teutonics' mantle of warrior monks was very thin. Soon after their beginnings in the 1200's, they were sent on a crusade to the Baltic lands. That crusade spilled over to target Eastern Orthodox Christians as well as the pagans who had been the original enemy. By the time the knights started the first war with Poland, another Catholic nation, in 1326, the Teutonics had become mostly just another feudal overlord in a region where choosing enemies had very little to do with religion. Many of the knights turned to mercenary work, being renowned as able warriors. This was the tradition that Von Markenburg and his black knights followed.

"Been in any battles lately?" Rainey asked.

"Have you heard of any?" Gerhard replied sarcastically.

Rainey bit back a smile. Although the black knights were still a formidable group of warriors and very intimidating in their black armor, they were getting up in age. No one really knew how good they would be in a battle; they hadn't fought one in at least five years.

Orina entered with a platter of food and a jug of ale. Rainey got up from his chair. "I have some duties to attend to. Enjoy the food. Grigori will show you to your lodgings when you are ready."

Rainey passed down the hallway to the dining room where he found Anna and Ludmilla huddled together at the table.

"If he was here to kill anyone, he would have done it by now," Anna said. "The black knights do not play games."

Rainey sat down across from them. The fear was apparent in Ludmilla's expression. "I know," he said. "He was here when your mother died."

"He was the one chasing me across the roof," Ludmilla replied.

Rainey didn't remember who had been on the roof with her. "Oh. But, how does that matter? You are a different person now. He's big and slow. So what do you do?"

Ludmilla looked confused. "I don't understand."

Rainey placed his hands flat on the table. "What does your training tell you?"

"As he approaches, spin out of his way, get in close and knee him in the . . ."

"Ludmilla!" Anna exclaimed. "That is not being a lady."

Rainey smiled. "Of course it isn't, but she'd be alive afterwards."

Ludmilla gave him a weak smile. Anna frowned at him. "Why is he here?" Anna asked.

"I've been summoned to Moscow."

Anna nodded. "It is that time of the year. I should have suspected."

"What time of the year?"

"Don't you know? The tribute is taken to the khan. The grand prince chooses from his boyars to lead the caravan. He must be choosing you this year."

Rainey leaned back in his chair. "I don't know anything about delivering tribute. Doesn't the grand prince do that himself?"

"Vasily never went because he was blind. It became a tradition for a boyar to go. It is a great honor. He must trust you very much."

Rainey wasn't so sure. When he and Krasenoff last left the Kremlin, it was after the Topoffs had been executed. The grand prince hadn't been too pleased about the Silk Affair and Rainey's role in it.

"Then I guess I will be gone for a while. Can I trust you two to behave yourselves while I'm away?"

"We will be fine," Anna declared.

Rainey turned to Ludmilla, who just nodded. He smiled. "And no getting married until after I return."

Ludmilla scowled. Anna laughed.

* * *

The caravan was ready to go by the time Rainey arrived in Moscow. There was no rest for him. At the front of the procession, the grand prince sat waiting on his horse.

"You must learn to travel to Moscow faster," Ivan said. "You will ride up with me."

"This is the tribute caravan to Sarai?" Rainey asked.

"Yes."

"I didn't know you were going with us."

"I have some particular business to deal with."

"So why am I required?"

Ivan turned to Rainey, a very serious look on his face. "We also have much to discuss. Where is Igor?"

"He hadn't returned from a task I sent him on when I left Zenoplata."

Ivan continued to stare at him for a moment, then prodded his horse forward.

This is not going to be a boring trip, Rainey thought.

* * *

Krasenoff arrived back at Zenoplata a week after Rainey left. Opening the door, he called out for Rainey. Ludmilla appeared at the top of the stairs.

"He's gone," she said.

"Where?"

"With the tribute caravan."

Krasenoff seemed to be confused. Ludmilla came down the stairs to meet him.

"He will be gone for a while."

Krasenoff shrugged. "I guess he will. Where is the Tripenskaya woman?"

"Her name is Anna," Ludmilla said forcefully.

Krasenoff looked surprised. "So you are her friend now? I was wondering if she'd still be alive by the time I got back."

Ludmilla slapped his chest. "She is with child. I have been helping. You, however, have been gone for months. Where have you been?"

Krasenoff seemed to want to tell her something, but instead stepped past her to the stairs. "None of your concern."

Ludmilla watched him climb the stairs to his room. He had been gone since shortly after Anna had arrived. She climbed the stairs and went to see Anna.

"Igor is back," she said as she entered the room.

Anna was sitting up in bed at an angle that her large belly would allow. "I heard him calling for Connor when he came in. Where has he been all this time?"

"He wouldn't tell me."

"Well, it is of no consequence. With Connor gone, it will be good to have Igor here." She looked at Ludmilla with curiosity. "What do you think of Igor?"

Ludmilla knew instantly where this was going. "I'm not marrying Igor."

Anna waved her hands. "No, No. Although it might be worth taking a look."

"He visits prostitutes."

Anna nodded. "Perhaps not. But you know him better than I do. What's he like, other than the prostitute obsession?"

"He is a kind man. He is well liked in the village. As you know, he is rather imposing, but he is not a threat unless you give him a reason to be. His loyalty to Connor is absolute. Connor thinks of him as a friend, but their bond is much stronger than that. More like brothers."

"I see. And through Connor, his loyalty to the grand prince is also absolute."

"I suppose."

Anna nodded again. "Thank you, Ludmilla. I must get to know the members of this household better if I am to be staying here permanently."

Inside, Ludmilla cringed. Even though she had accepted Anna's presence, its permanency was still an issue for her. It would lead to Anna becoming Connor's wife. She'd come to the conclusion that Anna would make a fine wife for Connor where she was still too young and possibly couldn't give him children. But although her passionate feelings for Connor had faded, deep in her heart she still felt a desire for him.

"If I were to marry Igor, I would be staying here," Ludmilla said.

Anna remained silent for a moment before responding. "I will admit, at first, trying to find you a husband was my way of sending you away. Later, I thought it would be good for you to be at court in Moscow. You proved to me to be a fine young lady who could blossom among the boyars. But, I have to admit, I have grown accustom to having you here. I miss the court myself somewhat. You are a very pleasant substitute."

Ludmilla smiled. "Perhaps, after the baby is born, you could take me to court. I am curious about what it's like."

"You already have a reputation there. Many of the boyars would like to meet the young Kolchin girl who has put the run on all their sons."

"And they deserved it," Ludmilla said defiantly.

"Did you like any of them?"

Ludmilla crossed the room and sat on the edge of the bed. "There was Demyan. He was nice and showed an interest in what I thought. But the smell."

Anna giggled. "Yes, I remember him. His family has hogs. I think they have him cleaning out the pens."

"And I don't think there would be any way to clean that smell off him."

They both laughed. Then there was silence. Anna reached up and gripped Ludmilla's arm, bending forward in pain.

Ludmilla reached out to her. "Are you all right?"

Anna nodded. "Just some pain. I get some every now and then. Orina tells me it's normal. But that one hurt a lot.

"The bed is wet."

They looked at each other, both knowing what that meant. "I'll get Orina," Ludmilla said and bolted for the door, getting just into the hallway before bellowing "ORINA!!"

From behind her, Anna let out a scream.

* * *

It had been two days of travelling south down the Moskva and Oka rivers to the Volga, and another two days before Ivan spoke with Rainey.

"Have you figured out why you are here?" he asked.

"Not really. I figure you want me to meet the khan, but that doesn't explain your silence during this journey."

"How much silk have you seen in our caravan?"

So that was it. "You usually have a lot more."

"Yes. I'm not sure how the khan will react, but I want you there to see it firsthand."

A lesson. Rainey didn't think he needed a lesson on low silk supply, but Ivan obviously wanted to give one. "I understand."

"No, I don't think you do. We live a precarious existence here in the Rus. The khan, at any time, can order me off my throne for any excuse. I have Kazans to the east continually raiding my lands. Novgorod keeps giving me indigestion with their connections to the Lithuanians. I have traitors in my own court, ready and willing to tell the khan of some transgression. Giving you Zenoplata did not come without cost. Alexander Kolchin was a well-respected boyar on a very important trade route.

"Finding him dead on my bed with a sword in his hand must have helped."

Ivan glowered at Rainey. "This is not a laughing matter. Even executing the Topoffs had a price, although there were many who would have gladly done that for me."

"Then why did you not have me killed when you knew I had a connection to the silk trade?"

"Because you saved my life when most men would not have gotten involved. You have never told me why you did get involved."

"It wasn't a fair fight."

"That can't be the only reason."

Rainey was silent for a moment. "I don't really know. It's just in my nature. I knew it was an ambush when Kolchin came at me with a sword. Perhaps I wanted to know what it was all about."

"Curiosity kills most men."

"Most."

Ivan smiled. "You are an interesting man, Connor. I am glad to be able to call you a friend."

"If the khan gets upset with the lack of silk, you want my sword there, don't you?"

Ivan laughed. "You know me so well. But there is also the journey. Gunter only gave me four of his black knights for protection."

Rainey looked over his shoulder, seeing the four knights riding together in the middle of the column of wagons. "Does he usually assign more?"

"The boyar I send to lead arranges for protection. He would usually go to Gunter, who gives him a large contingent of his knights. As you are the official boyar leading this caravan, the lack of protection is your fault. You didn't even bring Igor."

Rainey smiled. "My apologies, my grand prince. I assumed since I am worth ten men and you yourself are worth six . . ."

"Six?"

"I'm still training you. In another year, you'll be worth ten."

"I see. Then, ten for you, six for me, and four knights . . ."

"Come now, they are worth at least two men each."

Ivan chuckled. "Then we have . . . twenty-four men to protect the caravan. Yes, I can see how that is plenty."

"Why doesn't the khan buy his own silk? Don't the caravans go by Sarai on their way up the Volga?"

Ivan looked at him like he was a child. "Why buy what he gets from me for free?" He paused to change the subject. "So, tell me how you and Anna Tripenskaya are doing. According to the gossip at court, she should be giving you a child soon."

16

The flurry of activity at the house seemed chaotic to Ludmilla. Grigori was sent into town for the midwife. Krasenoff sat sullenly in the kitchen, eating a piece of bread Orina gave him to keep him out of the way. Ludmilla had never seen him like this before, realizing that he hated being useless in any time of crisis. But it wasn't like he could deliver the baby.

Orina and Ludmilla tried their best to keep Anna comfortable, but her pain was constant. Orina sensed something was wrong. When the midwife arrived, the worst was known. The baby was backwards, coming out feet first.

Ludmilla was regularly sent for more water as the birth took hours. Each time she passed through the kitchen, she would see Krasenoff sitting at the table, never moving. Every so often, she would see tears on his face. When she was in the room with Anna, she stayed back by the door, moving only when instructed to. Anna screamed throughout her labor. Ludmilla couldn't imagine what she was feeling.

Finally, Anna's screams stopped, replaced by the sound of a small baby crying. As Orina and the midwife backed away from the bed with the child, Ludmilla gasped at the scene. So much blood, everywhere. Anna's face was white and damp. She was breathing unevenly. Her eyes locked onto Ludmilla, filled with fear. Then she stopped breathing.

"Orina," Ludmilla said in panic.

Orina glanced over her shoulder and sagged in resignation. "She's gone. It was all we could do to save the child."

Ludmilla tentatively approached the bed, sitting beside Anna. She reached out and closed Anna's blank eyes. The tears started to flow. She lowered her head onto Anna's shoulder and wept.

She felt ashamed of how she had treated Anna when she had first arrived. But in spite of that, a friendship had eventually grown between them. She had become closer to Anna than she had been to her own mother, but she had always kept some of her feelings hidden. Now, that seemed cruel and a betrayal of their friendship.

Ludmilla didn't know how long she had been there before a firm hand gripped her shoulder. She looked up to see Krasenoff gazing sadly down on her.

"Come, little one," he said. "You must be hungry."

Ludmilla sniffed and nodded. She gave one more look to Anna, then got up. As she followed Igor out of the room, Orina moved to clean up around Anna's body. The midwife, seated in a corner, was feeding the baby from her own breast.

Once back in the kitchen, Ludmilla saw that Krasenoff had been busy putting together a small feast for everyone. Grigori was sitting across the table, waiting. Ludmilla and Krasenoff joined him and ate silently, pondering the day's events. Her mind was numb, buried in sadness. Suddenly, a very distinct question popped into her mind. She looked up at Krasenoff.

"What happens to the child?"

Krasenoff shrugged, casting a glance at Grigori, who noticed their attention on him. "It will need a nursemaid. Perhaps it will be given to a family in town to raise."

"It's the boyar's child," Krasenoff said. "You can't just give it away without telling him."

Ludmilla noted the child was referred to as *it*. She realized no one at the table, including herself, knew if it was a boy or a girl. In their grief, no one asked. She got up from the table and returned to the stairs. She met Orina coming down with the baby bundled in her arms.

"Is the child a boy or a girl?"

Orina smiled. "Come back into the kitchen. I can announce it there."

Krasenoff and Grigori both rose as Orina entered. She passed the bundle to Ludmilla and crossed to the table, grabbing some meat off a platter. She tossed a piece into her mouth and stood looking at them all while she chewed.

Krasenoff was the most impatient. "Well? Or do I have to go check myself?"

Orina swallowed and smiled. "It's a boy. Healthy. All his parts are there. Grigori, go see the baker. The baby will need a nursemaid and the baker's wife has mentioned that she would be honored if called upon."

Grigori reached for more meat, got up and left the kitchen.

"It has been a long day, Igor," Orina said as she plopped herself down in a chair. "Can you be so kind as to get me some ale?"

* * *

As dusk descended on the barges carrying the caravan, Rainey found Ivan up by the bow staring south. He came up beside him.

"You look deep in thought," Rainey said. "Anything I can help with?"

Ivan shook his head. "Just thinking about the state of my lands and what dangers to them will emerge in the future."

"Being a grand prince isn't easy."

"No, it isn't. I have a great army, but it is not enough to fend off invaders. Lithuania and Poland are joined now and can field an immense army. The Ottomans can advance north with impunity. The Kazans are always a concern. And the khan in Sarai can also threaten all of the Rus lands. All my army is good for is in little wars against other principalities. I keep the khan pleased by collecting some of his tribute for him."

"Well, the khan will likely protect you since you're so valuable a vassal."

"But will he? The Horde is in decline. The other Rus princes are worried about how my power is growing."

Rainey snorted. "What can they possibly do about that?"

"Make alliances with Lithuania."

Rainey shook his head. "The politics over there would make any alliances null and void. Casimir is both the king of Poland and the duke of Lithuania and yet the Lithuanians wouldn't let him use their army against the Teutonics. All the other principalities could hope for is a defensive pact, and only as long as the Teutonic war continues. That means you don't have to go marching over there because there's no threat. You keep peace with the khan, there's no threat from the south. You really have only one concern, and that's the Kazans. Concentrate your army there. Use ambassadors to keep everyone else strong enough to cause you harm looking somewhere else. You don't need allies. You just need to keep the other players worried about each other."

"Diplomacy. I don't know if I can trust it to keep Muscovy safe," Ivan said.

"When I was in Italy," Rainey said, "the city-states were always at war with one another. Alliances shifted all the time, but the smart princes only attacked when they had the right alliances in place first, and that meant they were stronger than their opponent. It was tricky work keeping track of who was talking to whom, but the best princes set the board before moving. Often enough, their army would march across and never have to fight. Just showing up at another city's walls was enough for the defenders to sue for peace. Right now, the threats from your west aren't well organized. Use diplomacy to keep it that way."

Ivan nodded. "You know, you're right. It'd just be nice to have a bigger army."

Rainey smiled. "I have an idea about that. You know, you rule because your boyars support you."

Ivan gave him the same look as when Rainey suggested that the khan buy his own silk. "You think I don't know that?"

"My point is, what if you had more boyars? You'd have a bigger army."

"And how do I get more boyars? I can't just make them."

"From other principalities."

Ivan looked at Rainey, confusion knitting his brows. "I don't follow."

"Those princes rule because their boyars let them, just the same as you. If you could get them to support you, then you would slowly absorb their lands into your lands."

Ivan thought about that for a minute. "I still don't see how I would get their support."

"You carry out raids into their lands?"

"Yes, as they do into mine."

"Perhaps instead of another set of raids, you can send an envoy and give the boyars a choice. Protection within your lands and no more raids, or destruction. My experience tells me a boyar's self-interest will always win the day and he won't worry too much who his prince is as long as he can profit. That's why your boyars support you."

Ivan nodded. "Interesting idea. But my brothers will want a share of any new lands. They could even challenge me for the throne. You may not be aware of the challenges our father faced from his brothers over the years that they fought over the throne."

Rainey placed his hand on Ivan's shoulder. "Your father didn't do you any favors by splitting up Muscovy lands up among his sons. And by leaving them free to do as they wish."

"That is tradition. It is the law."

"And that's why the Golden Horde was able to run over the Rus two hundred years ago. No one got big enough to challenge them properly because of your succession rules. Your brothers' lands go to their descendants, correct?"

"Yes."

"And that splits up your power even more. I understand how these rules can keep anyone from getting too strong, but it leaves everyone vulnerable to outside forces. Back in Europe, a king has the power to replace anyone in his court who refuses to supply armed men for the king's wars. With the Ottomans, a dead sultan's brothers have to fight it out to see who gets the throne next. Then the winner takes the entire army under his control. But here, your brothers can just say no and you have to fight without them. That has to stop. You need to gather all the military power into your own hands."

"That won't be easy."

"Nothing worth doing ever is. But with support from more and more boyars, your throne becomes much more secure. Treat the boyars right, you solidify that support. That point I believe you know already. You have great support from most of the boyars now because of the freedoms they have. Offer that freedom to boyars of other princes and you can get control of their military power. Their princes will become your direct vassals, honor bound to support any war you undertake for their benefit."

"Taking in all that military power will mean we have to take in the administrative power, as well."

"Yes. That is how it's done in Europe. But if you leave enterprise to the boyars and don't overtax them, they will stay loyal. And they'll make their princes stay loyal, too."

Ivan turned to Rainey. He stood silently for a moment before speaking again. "I like the way you think. You would be a good match for Gunter."

Rainey shook his head. "I may have good ideas, but I am no match for Gunter in carrying out those ideas."

"Still, you come across as friendly and honest. That would work much better in the other principalities than Gunter's intimidating ways. I think you will put your idea to work, and I know exactly where to start. Have you ever been to Yaroslavl?"

"No."

"When you get back, I will send you there. If you get me those boyars without having to use my army, I can feel safe launching a campaign against the Kazans."

* * *

The barges nosed up against the shore where several tents had been set up. Rainey scanned the steppe where he noticed several horses grazing. Ivan came up beside him.

"Come. I want you to meet someone."

They disembarked with the black knights and walked towards the tents. A man in Tartar clothing came out flanked by several others, all looking stern. Rainey's reached for his sword, but Ivan pulled his hand down. "There will be no need for that."

An older man, smiling, emerged from the tent, stepping in front of his men. "Ivan Vasilyevich. You are a day early. The river must be running fast these days."

"Hello, Haci," Ivan replied. "It's good to see you too." The two men embraced.

Rainey immediately knew who this was. Haci Giray, khan of the Crimean Khanate. Ivan was not a vassal to Haci, but to the Great Horde Khanate at Sarai. Haci had broken away after a long war to form his own khanate, something Rainey had learned when he was traveling to Kiev with Aunshaunie. He didn't know Ivan had any relations with this khan, considering his vassal status with a rival khanate.

"How are things in your domain?" Ivan asked.

Haci winked. "I have things well under control. It has been rather peaceful this year." He glanced at the barges. "Is all that for Mahmud or is some of it for me?"

Ivan laughed. "You brought me horses. Of course, I plan to pay for them. Come on board and make your selections."

Haci looked at Rainey and the black knights. "Is this your boyar for the journey? He doesn't look like a Rus."

Ivan stepped over to Rainey and placed a hand on his shoulder. "That's because he is a Celt. He's my Great Celt."

Haci looked skeptical. "Can't say I ever met a Celt before. What's so great about him?"

Ivan stepped away from Rainey. "Who's your best warrior?"

Haci smiled. "Kamil! We have a challenger for you."

A very large man stepped out of another tent. His huge hand rose to his sword hilt, a long, curved blade at least a foot longer than Rainey's. He walked slowly towards Rainey, menace in every movement.

Rainey gave Ivan a long look. "Is this your idea of diplomacy?" He reached back and pulled his sword free of its scabbard.

Ivan just smiled at him and backed away some more.

Rainey's Tartar language skills were not the best, but he knew enough to get an idea of the rules. "To first blood?"

"Death," Kamil said.

Rainey sighed. He hated these kinds of sport. He brought up his sword and stood firm, waiting for Kamil to make the first move. The two stared at each other for what seemed to be an eternity. Kamil finally broke forward, swung his sword first up and then around into a downward movement. Rainey raised his sword to block and began his spin to the right. But Kamil's power took Rainey's sword down too far, slowing his spin. He also pivoted right along with Rainey, never turning his back on his opponent. The big sword came up quickly, riding up Rainey's sword and towards his head. Rainey jumped back and disengaged. There was no smile on Kamil's face as they again sized up each other.

Rainey calculated quickly. Kamil was surprisingly fast for such a large man. But Rainey was still faster. A cut and slash dual would be long and wearying. A plan emerged. It was risky, but it should allow him to get inside Kamil's sword swing.

He charged forward behind his sword's point. As Kamil's sword came up to deflect it, Rainey swung it slightly down to the right. Kamil's sword missed contact, his swing taking his sword up to Rainey's left. Rainey continued forward and aimed for Kamil's ankle. As he was delivering his blow, though, Kamil's left arm swung, knocking Rainey off his course and to the ground. He went into the roll and came up ready. He saw Kamil looking at his foot, blood visible on his boot.

He looked up into the big Tartar's eyes. "End?"

Kamil took a step with his wounded leg and stumbled. Putting his weight on his good foot, he swung his sword defiantly. Rainey looked over at Ivan. "I don't want to kill him."

"That is not your choice," came the reply.

He glanced around the crowd that had gathered to watch. They all stood silently. He didn't know if that was tradition or they were dumbfounded that their champion might actually be bested by this foreigner. His eyes stopped on Haci.

"He can heal," Rainey said. "He doesn't have to die."

Haci didn't reply.

Kamil stood there, waiting. Sword at the ready. Rainey knew he couldn't try that move again and he couldn't just block the man's powerful swing. There had to be another way to get inside that long sword's reach.

He jumped forward and then back, getting a reaction out of Kamil. Rainey had thrust his sword forward in a stabbing motion. He did it again and got the same response. He saw his opening. Jumping forward on his left foot, he immediately pitched to the right. Kamil's sword came out and past him. He was inside. Kamil was also sideways, his left hand and arm back. When he saw his thrust had missed hitting Rainey, he started to bring his left arm forward.

But it was too late. Rainey's sword cut across his stomach, cutting deep. Rainey followed through by ducking, but Kamil's forearm still caught him at the temple. He hit the ground hard, slightly dazed. He looked up and saw Kamil on his knees. Rainey slowly got up, also on his knees, and brought his sword up to thrust into Kamil's back. It was unnecessary.

Kamil fell over on his side, a low growl coming from his throat before he lay still. Rainey dropped his sword and fell over as well, the world spinning from the blow he took to the head. He saw Ivan running towards him.

"That took longer than I thought it would," Ivan said. "You must be getting old." He helped Rainey up.

Rainey rubbed his head, getting his balance back. "I don't understand what the point of this was."

"Respect," Ivan replied. "Haci and I have an understanding, but every now and then, I need to show that attacking my caravan can have very bad consequences. We may have similar interests when it comes to Mahmud in Sarai, but interests change."

"Did you know my opponent would be so large?"

Ivan smiled. "Why do you think you were fighting him instead of me?"

* * *

The trading took place over a meal. Haci had made some nice choices among the contents of the caravan while Ivan received one hundred steppe ponies for his army. Smaller than Rainey's horse, they were ideal for archers on the steppe. A significant amount of silver was traded to Haci as well. From the conversation, Rainey was able to discern that the Ottomans were exerting pressure on the nascent Crimean Khanate. The silver was to keep the Turks at bay for another year. Rainey wondered how far Mehmet had advanced his empire since conquering Constantinople.

The next morning as the Muscovy contingent prepared to continue their journey to Sarai, Rainey found Ivan and an escort mounted and ready to head back north. Rainey ran over to see what was going on.

"My Prince, are you deserting us?"

Ivan scowled down at him. "That was a poor choice of words, Connor. This is as far as I was ever planning to go. You will continue on to Sarai as leader of the caravan."

"You could have told me this before now."

"I suppose I could have, but I chose not to. Try and get back to Moscow before it snows. It gets very cold out here in winter."

Ivan pointed his horse north and headed off, followed by twenty men and the hundred ponies he'd bought from Haci. Rainey turned around and found the Tartar tents quickly coming down. There was no sign of Haci Giray. Soon, there would be no sign that anyone had met here at all.

Rainey stepped up onto the lead barge and found himself facing the four black knights, the stern, blank looks on their faces disguising any of their thoughts.

"Gentlemen," Rainey began, "Let's go to Sarai."

17

Rainey didn't know what to expect upon arriving in Sarai. The capital of the Great Horde could be anything. It could be a great metropolis in the image of European or Muslim cities. It could be a dirt settlement reminiscent of Mongol encampments. Turned out to be a bit of both. The city's walls were indeed made of dirt, sloped with wooden barricades along the top. He wondered how Mehmet's cannon would fare against these walls. Probably the crude barriers would just absorb the cannon fire. But inside the walls, stone buildings were abundant, intermixed with Mongol tents. A large market filled the middle of the city. The barges came ashore right in front of the city's gates. The guards looked them over before letting a number of slaves out the gates to unload. The tribute was carried to the palace with Rainey and the Muscovy contingent following behind. At the palace, they were told to find lodgings and come back in three days. In Europe, that would be an insult and a reason for war. But here, the khan was all-powerful. You did what he told you.

It was during those three days that Rainey began to feel that perhaps the khan's power was slipping. He was shadowed wherever he went. In the market, he detected a feeling of unease from the merchants and peddlers. Although he didn't speak the language, he regularly came across a name spoken in fear. Ahmed. Eventually, he discerned that Ahmed was a challenger to Khan Mahmud's leadership of the Great Horde. Considering that Haci Giray had already defected and Ahmed was now looking like a serious threat, Mahmud must be under a lot of stress, seeing danger in all corners of his realm.

On the third day, as ordered, Rainy led the Muscovy contingent into the palace. As they came up and bowed to Khan Mahmud, Rainey got a sense of how troubled the khanate really was. He was confident that his shadow would have reported back to the khan about what Rainey had been up to over the last three days, who he had talked to, what he may have bought, and anything else that might have been considered useful information. Rainey had made sure to have been positively boring, which would assuage Mahmud's fears about someone new in his court—or accentuate them. There was no middle ground.

Mahmud sat on his throne trying to look bored, but his eyes continued to shift all around. The throne was backed right up against a stone wall. The guards around him continually scanned the room. For an all-powerful khanate, what Rainey saw looked like a lot of fear emanating from the throne.

Rainey bowed low. "Great Khan, I bring you greetings from the Grand Prince Ivan Vasilyevich of Muscovy."

Mahmud sat silently. His great flowing silk robes fluttered a bit with a breeze that flowed the length of the throne room. Rainey didn't know what else to say. He supposed he would get some questions to answer.

A man sidled up to the throne and whispered into Mahmud's ear. Mahmud waved him away, looked hard at Rainey and then waved him away, too. Rainey bowed deeply again and began to back out of the throne room. Getting no questions about the lack of silks in the tribute was good, but it also gave another strong signal that all was not well in the khanate.

As the Muscovy delegation gathered outside the palace, everyone looked at Rainey for what to do next. Everyone seemed uneasy. Even the black knights gave a sense of wanting to get out of Sarai. Obviously, this was not the usual way an audience with the khan went.

"Let's go home," Rainey said.

* * *

It was snowing lightly as Rainey rode into Zenoplata. The journey home from Sarai had taken much longer than the journey there, going against the current of the Volga River. After a brief stay in Moscow to report to the grand prince, he carried on home on horseback. He knew Anna would have delivered her baby; he was anxious see her.

Before he left the capital, his report to Ivan was accepted gladly. Ivan had heard rumor that there was a struggle for the Great Horde's throne. With the Crimean khanate being relatively friendly towards Muscovy, a distracted Horde meant Ivan would face no threats from the south. Rainey suggested that Muscovy could get involved in perpetuating the dispute between Mahmud and Ahmed, extending an offer of help to both to keep each from being able to conquer the other. Von Markenburg would be very useful in how to accomplish that.

Rainey was thinking about all this as he rode slowly into town but suddenly was pulled back into the present. He immediately sensed something wasn't right. Many people waved at him as he rode through town, but the smiles he usually got were lacking.

Beginning to wonder what was wrong, he hurried his horse towards the courtyard.

Grigori came out of the house upon hearing the horse's hooves on the courtyard stones. Rainey swiftly dismounted and made for the doorway without acknowledging Grigori at all. He entered and followed the sound of the fire blazing in the great room. He found Ludmilla sitting by the fireplace with a bundle in her arms. She was quietly singing a Rus folk song.

> *Mice are dancing in a round,*
> *On a bench a cat is sleeping.*
> *"Hush, you mice, don't make such noise*
> *Or you'll wake up Vaska Cat*
> *Vaska Cat will jump and leap*
> *And will spoil and break your round"*

She looked up when Rainey entered.

"Where's Anna?" Rainey asked. Ludmilla's face went very sad. "What happened?" Rainey asked softly.

Ludmilla sniffed. "The baby came out backwards. It took hours. Anna died right after the birth." She wiped a tear off her cheek.

A familiar hand landed on Rainey's shoulder. "I'm sorry, my friend," Krasenoff said. "There was nothing anyone could do."

"When?" Rainey asked, almost in a whisper.

"It was over a month ago," Krasenoff replied. He lightly pushed Rainey farther into the room. "Go meet your son."

Rainey took a few tentative steps forward and then found a reserve of strength to stride the rest of the way to Ludmilla. He knelt down by the chair as she pulled back the wrappings around the baby's face.

"He looks like you," she said.

He gently stroked the baby's face. A small hand reached out and lightly gripped his finger. He smiled and the baby seemed to smile back. Then the baby threw up. Ludmilla grabbed a cloth and wiped the little bit of mess from the baby's face.

"I guess I have to name him," Rainey said. "What is a good Rus name?"

"I thought you would name him after the grand prince."

Rainey chuckled. "After what he put me through, I'd be more inclined to name my horse after him."

Krasenoff had come up behind them. "That would be treason."

"Only if I didn't like my horse. I like mine."

Ludmilla began rocking the child as it began to fuss. "I have always liked the story of Ruslan and Ludmilla. It's about a brave prince as he goes out and saves a princess from a wizard. I've been calling him my little Ruslan for a while now."

Rainey nodded. "Ruslan. I like it. Ruslan Connoryevich Rainey."

"He will need a Rus family name," Krasenoff said, "for the baptism."

"Father Kirill is waiting to baptize him," Ludmilla said. "I insisted that we wait until you returned."

"And not a moment too soon," Krasenoff added. "The father was going to come here and do it in the next day or two regardless if you were back or not."

"And he still wants to know when you will convert," Ludmilla said. "He can bless you with a Rus name at that time."

Rainey shook his head. He had never been religious. He had been baptized as a Catholic, but that was pretty much the end of his direct relationship with the church in Rome. His father had not had much respect for priests. Although he liked Father Kirill, he had yet to set foot into his little church in town.

"We will get the baby baptized. I will assume I will not burst into flames if I attend. And I didn't know he *needed* a Rus family name."

"So do you," Ludmilla said.

"No, I don't. And I don't care what Father Kirill has to say about it, either."

There were no flames two days later when the baptism took place. Rainey stood up at the front of the town church with Ludmilla and little Ruslan. Father Kirill seemed a little upset that Rainey was in the holy space without a conversion ceremony planned, but he had learned to live with the boyar and his non-religious ways. The moment was for the baby, a new and important addition to his church family.

"What is the name of this child?" Kirill asked.

Ludmilla and Rainey looked at each other. Rainey nodded, giving the honor to Ludmilla. She did, after all, name the child.

Ludmilla smiled and turned back to Father Kirill. "Ruslan Connoryevich Raynykov."

18

1463

After Rainey had reached Moscow on his return from Sarai, he spent a few days reporting to Ivan about his impressions of Khan Mahmud. Ivan was pleased to know that trouble from the Great Horde was unlikely for the next few years. This also allowed for the continuation of expeditions into the Kazan. Ivan also broached another subject, Rainey's idea of enticing the boyars from the small independent principalities in and around Muscovy to support his takeover of those lands. Yaroslavl, in particular, was to be Ivan's first target. Conquering with an army would not produce loyal boyars for him. It would also provoke challenges from other princes, leaving them to run to the Lithuanians for protection.

Yaroslavl was a particular thorn in Muscovy's side. Ruled by Aleksandr Fedorovich Brukhati, it was known for continually raiding into Muscovy. Ivan retaliated with counter raids, some of them extremely brutal. But such raids had been going on for years without any resolution. Rainey's plan to try to separate Yaroslavl's boyars from their prince could put an end to the conflict altogether.

Through the winter months, Rainey began travelling among Yaroslavl's rural boyars, accompanied by only a small group of horsemen to keep any sense of threat low. At first, he was received tentatively, but as the weeks passed, he found the boyars were anticipating his visits. Many of them could see the advantage of giving their allegiance to Ivan. Brukhati was known for being cruel and vain and for overtaxing his subjects. By mid-February, Rainey had visited Yaroslavl itself where he met with many boyars who wanted to change allegiance, but didn't know how. They were afraid to challenge Brukhati directly. Rainey assured them they could stay loyal to Brukhati until the time was right and then could count on full support from Muscovy to back them up.

It was during his departure from Yaroslavl that things got interesting. Word of what Rainey was up to in the city had reached Prince Brukhati. At the city's open gates, he and his entourage were confronted by some of Brukhati's personal guard.

"You do not have permission to leave," the lead guard said to Rainey.

"On whose authority?" Rainey asked.

"The prince," was the reply.

So they sat quietly on their horses. Rainey wished that he had Krasenoff along for this trip, but his bogatyr had been needed in Zenoplata. He could sense his companions' anxiety. Something didn't feel right to him, either. He began scanning the buildings around him for anything that signalled danger. He moved his arquebus into his lap and checked the firing cloth for heat.

That's when he saw it.

A window was slowly opening across from the gate. As it opened fully, it exposed the tip of a crossbow. Rainey quickly raised the arquebus, aimed at the window and fired. Some of the stones smacked up against the shutters, but most of them passed through the window. The crossbow disappeared.

The sound of the arquebus froze everyone. "GO!" Rainey yelled to his men. They spurred their horses forward as the guards rushed to close the gates. Rainey shifted the arquebus to his left hand so he could reach his sword with his right. He felt more than heard a crossbow bolt whiz by his head as he charged for the gate. He leaned to his right to swing his sword at the guards trying to close the gate. They jumped back, giving him and his entourage the opening they needed to get through. But they still had the portion of the city outside the walls to make it through.

Rainey glanced back to see if all of his men had made it out. They had, all leaning down behind their horses' heads to avoid being an easy target for more crossbows. He looked back to find a group of horsemen gathering on the main road in front of them. Pumping his sword twice to his right, he pointed at a street coming up on that side. Leaning to the left, he did the same. His men had all been trained in his signalling: *two down the right street, two to the left.* That left him with three riders. At the sound of swords being drawn behind him, he let out a yell and urged his horse to charge.

The opposing horsemen were caught flatfooted. It was a surprise to them for four men to charge twenty. All they could do was get out of the way as Rainey and his men blew through them, swords swinging. When they regained their wits, they went into pursuit. Which is what Rainey had hoped for.

He and his companions broke out into the open fields at a full gallop. Rainey glanced back to see his pursuers—and his four flanking horsemen coming up behind them. He smiled. *This shouldn't take long.*

The pursuers were totally focussed on catching up to the lead riders. They were riding in a bunch, which allowed Rainey's trailing swordsmen to start thinning the group out from behind. It only took a few minutes before Rainey began reining in his horse and turned. The pursuers galloped past him. Rainey and his men quickly moved out of the way and deflected the sword swings. The pursuers reined in their mounts and turned to make another charge. What they saw made them pause.

Rainey lined up with his seven men. Along the road back to Yaroslavl, riderless horses milled around a scattering of men lying motionless in the dirt. As the remaining pursuers glanced at each other, they realized only three of them were left. And the entire chase had taken place within view of the walls of Yaroslavl.

"Go back to your prince," Rainey said. "Tell him what happened here and that I will be back. I will expect an audience with him when I do."

He waved his sword from side to side and his men formed along each side of the road. After a little hesitation, the pursers became the defeated and slowly made their way back to the city gates.

Rainey glanced back and forth amongst his men. "And that's what happens when you are better trained than your opponents."

The men chuckled lightly, all nodding in agreement.

"Let's go home," Rainey said.

It may be known to Brukhati what Rainey had been up to the last few months, but how much did he really know? Rainey figured the man would either strike back or capitulate. Which option he took became clear fairly quickly.

* * *

Rainey had only arrived back in Zenoplata a few days before word came that the farms farthest from the town were being attacked. It was very concerning. It had been a long time since the last raid had taken place on Zenoplata land. In the old days, a gang of ten men or more would carry out a raid on a farm house. Boyar Kolchin had never bothered to do anything to protect his peasants' farms, but Rainey had trained the farmers in how to protect themselves. He also began sending out roving bands of horsemen over two years ago with the aim of stopping the raids. These tactics proved successful; it became apparent to the leaders of the raiders that they raided Zenoplata land at their own peril. Although raids were very rare during the winter, Rainey kept up the patrols. They kept his farmers feeling safe, knowing their boyar cared. It was from such a patrol that a rider charged into the courtyard that frosty day.

"Boyar!"

Rainey came out of the house to meet the horseman. He was fairly young, probably out on one of his first patrols. "What is it, boy?"

"A very large raiding party is heading for the town."

Rainey frowned. "Who is your commander?"

"Bogatyr Krasenoff."

Rainey nodded. He knew what Igor would do. He would be gathering the men from any other patrols that were already out and leading them back to town. He looked up at the boy. "Go find the blacksmith; tell him to meet me at the east road. Then tell everyone you meet that town defense is required. Spread the word!"

The boy nodded earnestly, spun his horse and charged out of the courtyard. Rainey trotted back to the house.

Ludmilla was at the top of the stairs with Ruslan in her arms. "What's happening?"

"We are having a rather large number of unwanted guests. Give Ruslan to Orina and start closing up all ways into the courtyard and house."

"What are you going to do?"

"Defend the town." He picked up his arquebus and headed out the door. Grigori was at the gate as he headed out on foot.

"How many are coming, Boyar?" Grigori asked.

"No idea," Rainey replied. "Lock this gate behind me and go around to check all the doors. I have Ludmilla doing the same. I don't want any entrance missed."

Grigori nodded. Rainey put his hand on his shoulder. "You know Ludmilla can take care of herself. It's up to you to protect everyone else in the house."

Grigori smiled. "I know."

"Good man." Rainey strode out into the street.

He reached the east road to find the blacksmith and several other men and women building a barricade across the entrance to the village. Rainey stopped them.

"No. I want this built 30 yards down the road into the town. Between the bakery and the meat house. I want to funnel them into this street so they can't flank us. It will also allow us to close in behind them."

"You want to let them into town?"

"Only that far. With small raids, we can discourage attackers by barricading here where they can see us. From what I've heard is coming, there will be a fight and I want the most advantage we can get. They will think we don't know they're coming and ride right into this street where we can pack them in with nowhere to go. Have a group make something that can be thrown into the street here to stop them retreating."

The blacksmith nodded and ran off to give instructions. Rainey moved up the road and looked over the field between the town and the forest. There was no way the raiders could sneak up on them. A lone horseman galloped out of the trees, heading right for him. It was another man from one of his patrols. He was breathless from riding hard.

"Bogatyr Krasenoff will be coming up from the south. I'm to tell you that the raiding party is very large. Two hundred men or more. Bogatyr Krasenoff only has forty-five men."

Rainey nodded. "Thank you for getting here." He looked south to the forest's edge. He turned and assessed the preparations going on behind him. Two hundred men coming in on the east road wouldn't fit between the buildings. Many would spill around outside, giving them many access points into the town that couldn't be covered.

"Go back to your commander. Tell him to set up in the forest to the south and stay hidden. When the raiding party gets here, some will run along the south side of town. Your group is to engage them. I'll take care of the ones that come into town."

As the rider sped off, Rainey returned to the preparations. The primary barricade was in place, with a table behind it. On it lay an assortment of crossbows, longbows and arquebuses along with various collections of ammunition for each type of weapon. He nodded his approval. He turned and looked up at the roofs on each side of the road. He remembered the siege lessons he had learned from Giustiniani. *When defending a position, always draw the attackers into a pocket so you can hit them from more than one side; from above being the most ideal.* He got the blacksmith's attention.

"Take the crossbows up onto the roofs. Arquebuses stay here. Longbows set up on either side of the table."

The blacksmith was a smart man, respected by everyone in town. Still, Rainey could never pronounce his complicated name right. He hid that fact by never actually using it in public. Everyone knew this and it became a regularly used point of humor for the townsfolk, although never within the boyar's earshot. As part of the joke, they also never spoke the blacksmith's name around Rainey. Orina had once tried to teach him how to say the man's name, but all he could get was that it started with an 'S' and had seven syllables. The man did have a flair for military matters under Rainey's tutelage, so he became the town's general when it required defending.

Preparations were complete as the sun set behind the townspeople. Food was distributed as no one knew how long it would be before the raiding party arrived. Women sat on stools behind the main barricade with powder and ammunition for the arquebuses. It would be their job to reload them and keep the firing cloths lit while the men fired them. Men with crossbows sat at the doors of the two buildings whose roofs they would use as shooting platforms. Other archery teams were assigned to various places around the town to fight in the streets if the barricade did not stop all the raiders. Rainey stood out in front of the barricade, watching the distant forest for any signs the raiders were there. A piece of bread was held out in front of him. He took it and turned to the person who gave it to him.

"What are you doing here? You're to stay in at the house."

Ludmilla was chewing on her own piece of bread, clothed in her heavy fur coat, fur hat down over her ears. "Grigori has everything there prepared. Orina is with little Ruslan. And I don't plan on cowering behind the courtyard wall when everything that's going to happen will happen here." She raised her sword, a straight, thin, double-edged blade two feet long, with a curved hand guard, a hilt designed for both her hands to grip it like she had been taught by Rainey, and a balancing pommel up against her wrist. "See what our town's general made for me?"

She handed it to Rainey. He looked it over, admiring the workmanship the blacksmith had put into it. The sword was a fine weapon for someone like Ludmilla. Light, strong, balanced, and built for the speed of the movements he had taught her. He handed it back.

"They're going to be on horseback," Rainey explained, "which puts all of us at a disadvantage in hand-to-hand combat. With any luck, you and I won't have to use our swords."

Ludmilla stared out at the darkening forest. "Why is the barricade so far back?"

"We want some of them in among the buildings. Easier to kill them when they're trapped, and they won't see the barricade until they are trapped."

Ludmilla nodded. "You will have to teach me how to defend the town in case you are not here next time."

Rainey smiled. "We have the town general for that."

"And people die all the time."

He turned to her. She stood there like a professional soldier. No fear in her eyes. He had to remind himself that she had yet to reach her eighteenth birthday. But she had grown up so much since their first encounter over two and a half years before. When she had returned from Vladimir, she still seemed to be a frightened little girl. That girl was gone now. Before him stood Lady Ludmilla of Zenoplata. Strong, fearless and willing to die defending what she believed in. She turned and caught him staring at her.

"What?" she asked.

Rainey turned away. "Nothing. Stay here and take the first watch. I'll come back and relieve you in an hour."

19

It was almost pitch black when the hour neared its close. Ludmilla had taken to pacing to kill time, stopping regularly to take a hard look at the forest. All had been still, until now. As she watched, a light came out of the forest. Then another, and another. She could make out the torches held by men on horseback. The raiders were here.

She turned and strode purposefully towards the barricade. "They're here. Where is Connor?"

The blacksmith stood up and began to rouse the rest of the townsfolk snoozing behind the barricade. Crossbowmen climbed into position. The women began a quick check of the firing cloths to make sure the coals on them were sufficient. The men began double-checking the arquebuses. A runner headed into town to find Rainey.

Ludmilla turned back towards the forest. A large group of horsemen was forming up on its edge. Fire quickly spread from man to man as unlit torches touched those already aflame. The field between the trees and the town began to light up like it was day. Ludmilla got her first look at how many horsemen were there. Fear built up in her gut. *There are so many.*

"Ludmilla, get behind the barricade." Rainey was running up from the center of town. She whirled around and moved to him.

"There are too many," she blurted, panic in her voice. "They'll surround the whole town."

"Go back to the house," Rainey said.

The words sounded like a dismissal to her. With help from a spark of anger, she regained her courage. "No. I will fight. But we are going to have to deal with some of them going around us."

Rainey smiled at her. "That's true. But what they don't know is that Igor is waiting for them."

Her eyes widened. "Igor is back?"

Rainey nodded. "He's in the trees with all the patrols to our south."

Igor is back. Suddenly, the coming fight didn't seem so desperate to her. She turned back towards the forest. "Then let them come," she declared with confidence.

As if they heard her, the raiders started moving towards the town, slowly at first and then faster until they entered the main street at a full gallop, torches held high and ready for throwing. They never got the chance.

The leading horses stuttered to a halt as they became aware of the barricade in the darkness ahead of them. The horses coming in from behind stacked up tight, quickly congealing into a swelling mass of horse and man, stationary. Ludmilla thought this was the time they could kill them all very quickly.

"FIRE!!" yelled Rainey beside Ludmilla, as if he had read her mind.

The roar from the arquebuses startled the horses. Men were hit and falling backwards. The lead horses, scared and with nowhere to go, reared up and began dumping other men onto the ground. The crossbows opened up from the roofs. Ludmilla could see bowmen were targeting riders at the rear of the packed-in horses. Without riders, these horses turned and galloped out of the killing zone. As they passed beyond the town's last buildings, two wagons full of hay were rolled across the entrance. The trap was closed.

The next wave of arquebuses roared. Ludmilla looked back to see the first wave being reloaded by women behind the row of men, each of them now picking up a third arquebus. Some of the raiders were struggling to their feet among the horses. The arquebuses were aimed at them.

"FIRE AT WILL!!" Rainey screamed. Each of the unhorsed raiders was targeted and hit at the close range, falling in a heap.

"ARCHERS!" Beside Ludmilla, the bowmen stepped up, bows drawn, arrows at the ready. They targeted men in the middle of the pack. Each arrow found its mark across the short distance from bow to man. Another hail of arrows flew and each horse was now empty of men.

"HOLD FIRE!!"

It had all taken less than a minute. The first arquebuses were reloaded and held at the read, aimed out at the heaving mass of horses. Several horses were lying down, squealing in pain. Men were screaming, trying to get up, others trapped under their dead horses. Most of the lit torches were smoldering in the snow where they had fallen. Others flickered dangerously close to the buildings. Townsfolk moved out quickly from the barricade to stamp them out. As the sound of wounded horse and man began to dissipate and their battle came to an end, Ludmilla could hear swords clanging behind her. Rainey appeared by her side.

"I'm heading back into town. Can I leave you and the general to clean up here?"

Ludmilla nodded. "How do we do that?"

"Start by bringing the horses through the barricade. Have someone take the uninjured ones to the courtyard. Take any injured ones back out to the field."

"What about the raiders?"

Rainey shrugged. "I want one kept alive if possible. Other than that, it's up to the town to dispense justice." He turned and headed into town.

Ludmilla turned back to the carnage in the street. There was still movement among the horses as the townsfolk were already moving among the mass of flesh. She moved through to the first horse. She stroked its nose and it responded to her touch.

"Check the horses. Wounded ones to the field. Unwounded, take to the courtyard. Be careful. Some of the raiders will still be dangerous." As she said it, she saw a woman with a pitchfolk stab a man on the ground. There was grunt. She pulled the pitchfork free and moved carefully towards the next man. Ludmilla was now aware of what dispensing justice meant for the townsfolk of Zenoplata when faced with raiders.

She moved through the horses, her sword in her hand. There were no more sounds of battle. She looked around, seeing some townsfolk checking horses, some checking the raiders. Every now and then, she heard a groan as another half-dead raider was impaled.

Something grabbed her by the ankle. She whipped her sword around and found a boy, lying on his back, a crossbow bolt and an arrow sticking out of his chest. He was shaking and breathing unevenly, fear beaming from his face. He looked so innocent.

Ludmilla guessed he was probably younger than she was. She lowered her sword and knelt beside him.

"Where did you come from?" she asked softly, brushing his hair away from his face. The boy didn't answer, so she brought her sword up to his throat. Putting more menace in her voice, she asked again. "Where did you come from?"

"Yaroslavl," he croaked. His breathing was labored. His body suddenly spasmed. He took a big intake of air and as he expelled it, his whole body went limp.

Ludmilla was reminded of that day last spring when she had thrust her knife into Ilya Topoff's chest. He died the same way this boy did. But here, she felt no rage. This was just a boy, likely out on his first raid. He would have had no idea what it involved. Now he was dead. A life ended before its time. She felt no rage. No anger. Just sorrow. She reached down and closed his dead eyes.

* * *

Igor did manage to capture one raider with only a minor leg wound. All the rest of those that had split off around the town's southern edge were dead. Igor's charge from the trees had caught them off guard. Only about ten made it into the town, only to be killed by armed townsfolk. It turned out to be a very one sided battle. Two of Igor's horsemen were wounded and a woman by the town well took a slash from a sword to her arm as she impaled the rider with a pitchfork.

Rainey found Ludmilla at the house, warming herself before the main hall's fireplace. She was staring into the flames as he came up behind her.

"Is everything cleared away on the east road?" he asked. Ludmilla just nodded. "How many horses did we acquire?"

Ludmilla looked up at him. "All those men dead and all you care about is how many horses?"

Rainey shrugged. "They attacked us and paid for it. I don't like killing, but they really didn't give us a choice. Just wish I knew where they came from."

Ludmilla turned back to the flames. "Yaroslavl."

"How do you know that?"

"A young boy died in front of me. Before he died, I asked him."

Yaroslavl. Rainey suspected as much. Brukhati would naturally have been pressured to respond to Rainey's escape. Rainey was just surprised his response had come so quickly. But now he was down more than two hundred men. Forcing him to sign over his succession to Ivan could happen much sooner than Rainey and Ivan had planned.

"Why did Yaroslavl attack us?" Ludmilla asked.

Rainey didn't know how to reply. He wasn't sure she should be told of Ivan's plans to establish his dynasty. But then, she would find out soon enough.

"The grand prince is consolidating Rus lands. Yaroslavl's boyars are being offered positions at court and access to our trade. The idea was to accept the boyars' loyalty; that meant Prince Brukhati would have to leave or become a loyal boyar himself."

"Is that what you have been doing these last few months? Wandering around looking for more land for the grand prince to steal?"

"He's not stealing it. He's . . ." Rainey thought for a moment about how to best describe the process. "He's taking control of it."

"How is that different from stealing?"

Rainey sat down beside her. "He's trying to make the Rus strong. Right now, the Rus is nothing but a crowd of princes who fight and raid each other. Separate, they are weak against any invader. What the grand prince is trying to do is unify the Rus so it can govern itself."

"You mean he can govern it."

"Someone has to. Looking at the other choices, I'd pick Ivan over someone like Brukhati."

"And you have been trying to talk his boyars into abandoning the prince in Yaroslavl."

"Yes, and it hasn't been hard."

Ludmilla turned to face him. "So, this attack was caused by you."

Rainey stared back into her face, strangely calm to his eyes. He could see hints of anger, though, accented by the flickering colors the fire cast onto her face.

"How many of our people died as they burned their way across our lands to town?" Ludmilla continued. "Did you even think of the risk to little Ruslan?"

Rainey couldn't hold back a smile. A flash of anger crossed her face. "You think this is amusing?"

"Ludmilla," Rainey said. "No farmers died out there. They all got away and are now here in town being taken care of. In the spring, we will help them rebuild their homes, even giving each of them the gift of a horse or two. As for Ruslan, he was in no danger. The raid was doomed to fail because we were prepared." Another thought occurred to him. "I'm glad to hear that you are so concerned with his well-being."

Ludmilla's features softened. She turned back to the fire. "Why is the world so cruel?"

"That's a question for Father Kirill. I can tell you this; it is and always has been. All we can do is be prepared when cruelty finds its way to our door." Rainey got up to leave.

"Will you be staying home now?"

Rainey shook his head. "No. With Prince Brukhati short his little army, the time to force his hand is now. I'm going back to Yaroslavl to gather his boyars together and force him out."

Ludmilla stood and floated around the chair to Rainey. She kissed him on the cheek. "Then hurry back."

* * *

Ludmilla rose the next morning to a bright and sunny wintry day. She crossed her room to the crib where little Ruslan slept soundly. He was almost seven months old now and growing in strength every day. Orina said he was going to be a big man when he grew up. Leaning into the crib, Ludmilla strained to pick him up. He was getting heavy. Taking him to the rocking chair by the window, she sat down and began rocking and humming the Rus folk melody, *Knight of Light and Kindness*. Orina had taught her the song when she was young. Ruslan opened his eyes and smiled at her before closing them again and dozing off.

Ludmilla had decided months ago that having a child of her own would be just like having Ruslan with her. She loved the little boy with all her being. If she could not have any children of her own, then Ruslan would be her son. How to get Rainey to agree to that would be the challenge. Marrying him was not part of any plan she could think of.

A soft knock on the door preceded Rainey entering the room. He placed his hand on his sleeping son's head. Ludmilla smiled up at him.

"I'll be leaving in a few minutes," Rainey said. "Just wanted to say good-bye."

"Sit with me for a minute?" Ludmilla asked.

Rainey sat at her feet. Ludmilla continued to rock back and forth.

"Did you love Anna Tripenskaya?"

Rainey rubbed his cheek. "What brought this on?"

"I was wondering if you had ever planned to marry her."

"Kind of a moot point now."

"But it wasn't while she was here."

Rainey looked down at his feet. "I don't know. I was fond of her, but wasn't sure of her motivations."

"She was pregnant. I think her motivations were quite clear."

Rainey looked up, a very serious look on his face. "I think there was more to it than that."

"Like what?"

"I don't know. I just had a feeling that maybe . . . . But it isn't important any longer. She's gone." Rainey got up to leave.

"I'm sorry. I liked her, too."

Rainey glanced back at Ludmilla. "I'm glad. Ruslan is your responsibility now and I trust you to take that very seriously."

She smiled. *So, it would not be that much of a challenge after all.* "He is your son and I will treat him as if he is mine as well."

20

Snow still lay on the ground as Rainey and Krasenoff found themselves only ten miles from the gates of Yaroslavl. With them rode several boyars who had willingly transferred their allegiance to Muscovy. A rider had been sent ahead. When he reported back, they learned that several more boyars who no longer were supporting Brukhati would be found in the city. A couple of important boyars who supported the prince had died in the ill-fated attack on Zenoplata.

Rainey had grown quiet over the last day. His mind had been drifting to thoughts of Anna. He was torn between wanting to know what Krasenoff had learned in Pskov and not wanting to spoil the image of Anna he had formed in his mind's eye. Krasenoff had kept his findings to himself all this time and Rainey had never asked him.

"You look miles away, my friend," Krasenoff said.

"I've been thinking about Anna," Rainey answered.

"Ah. A tragedy."

"Yes. But did I really know her that well?"

"You'll have to ask Ludmilla about that. I wasn't there much."

"I know. You were in Pskov."

Krasenoff didn't answer. They rode silently for a minute.

"Do you want to know what I found out?"

"I don't know," Rainey said. "I don't know if it matters now."

"Then why did you bring up Pskov?"

Rainey shook his head. Krasenoff knew the hint when he heard it. Now it was out there. Rainey would have to know about Anna and Pskov or never bring it up again. He turned to Krasenoff. "Fine. What did you find out?"

Krasenoff exhaled loudly. Rainey knew right then that he wasn't going to like what he heard.

"There is no record of a boyar or anyone else named Tripensky in Pskov. There is also no record of Anna ever being there. However, I did hear a story about our chancellor, who passed through Pskov many years ago on his way to Moscow. It was quite the parade with him and his black knights. But there was also a young girl with him who spoke German. She was described as having blond hair and dark blue eyes. She looked quite distinctive, well dressed; she was very pleasant with those she met, which is why people remembered her. The chancellor's knights were not so pleasant."

"You think the girl was Anna?"

"She would have been about the right age. And the way some people talked about her eyes, I'm sure it was her."

Anna came to Muscovy with Von Markenburg. Rainey now wondered if Anna had actually loved him, or was she just a spy for the chancellor? Rainey had thought his relationship with Von Markenburg was better than that. Would Von Markenburg go as far as to have Anna become pregnant just to keep an eye on him because he was close to the grand prince? Their paths were the same. They were both devoted to Ivan. It disturbed Rainey to think that he could be considered a threat to the Muscovy throne. Now, any illusion of Anna being in love with him had been destroyed and he wondered if his relationship with little Ruslan would change. Or his relationship with Ludmilla.

"You are not to speak of any of this to Ludmilla," he told Krasenoff.

"I have never intended to do so without your explicit blessings," Krasenoff replied. "That is between you and her."

Rainey nodded. "You're a good friend, Igor."

Krasenoff smirked. "I'm just here to watch your back. Speaking of which, what are we going to do when we get to Yaroslavl?"

"Have a paper signed."

As they reached the gates of Yaroslavl, they were readily invited in by the court boyars. All support for Brukhati had evaporated. He was locked up in his throne room with a small entourage. Rainey and Krasenoff were escorted to the room. Brukhati sat sullenly on his throne as they entered.

"So, you are here to kill me?" he asked. It was more like a statement.

The prince of Yaroslavl was an old man. He'd been on the throne for over forty years, slowly watching his principality fade away. Rainey wasn't surprised that the old man had sent his small army out to Zenoplata in a last-ditch effort to keep his inheritance together. But, as Ivan had told Rainey, those efforts were becoming very irritating to his neighbors.

"What would be the point of killing you?" Rainey said. "We'd just be stuck dealing with your sons and their poor judgment. No, we have a more permanent solution." He pulled a scroll from his shoulder bag. "The grand prince of Muscovy gave me this scroll last October, telling me if the opportunity arose, I was to get you to sign it. After you wasted two hundred men trying to attack my town, I'd say that opportunity has arrived."

"What is it?"

"You are to sign your succession over to the grand prince of Muscovy, including all your lands and privileges, and you will swear allegiance to him and to Muscovy."

Brukhati's face turned red. "This is an outrage. I will do no such thing."

One of the Yaroslavl boyars stepped forward. "Yes, you will. We have all sworn our allegiance to Ivan, grand prince of Muscovy. You no long hold any power here. If you fail to sign, we will kill you and all your family so as to ensure no further claims can be made to the throne of Yaroslavl."

"You wouldn't dare."

The boyar raised his hand. The doors opened and a number of soldiers brought in three men. Rainey guessed that they were Brukhati's sons, swords at their throats.

Rainey spoke up. "In exchange for you signing this scroll, you will keep your rank as a prince until your death. You will be given good lands to the south. We will be here for three days, after which you will sign. Word of your inept attack on Zenoplata has been sent to Muscovy. A delegation from there is likely coming this very minute."

Rainey bowed to the prince as a sign of respect. No one else did. A sure sign of the prince's powerlessness. Rainey began to back towards the door. Krasenoff followed him out.

"I'd like to hear what's being said in there right now," Krasenoff said, straight-faced.

* * *

Brukhati took all three days to make his decision. Rainey and Krasenoff met regularly with the Yaroslavl boyars to continue assuring them that backing Muscovy was the right move. Rainey had a list of freedoms and advantages that the grand prince had agreed to and he stuck to them religiously, even when he thought a small modification might be better. Ivan had proven himself adept at this type of diplomacy, so Rainey wasn't taking any chances of creating another problem like the silk trade episode.

Late on the second day, an armed group of forty riders arrived from Moscow, led by Von Markenburg himself and several of his black knights. Rainey was surprised to see him, never having known the chancellor to actually travel this far away from the city. He always thought Von Markenburg was afraid of what might happen or what he might miss if he was gone too long from Ivan's court.

"Gunter, I didn't expect you. Things too quiet in Moscow?"

Von Markenburg ignored the jibe. "It's winter. Everything's quiet everywhere. What are you doing here?"

Rainey smiled. "Following the grand prince's orders. If it looked like Yaroslavl could be pushed to allegiance with Muscovy, I was to get Prince Brukhati to sign a succession document."

Von Markenburg shook his head. "I wish our prince would tell me these things. When we got word of your complete victory over Brukhati's attack, he sent me here to put an ultimatum to him."

"That's been done already. He has to decide by tomorrow."

"What terms did the grand prince give you?"

Rainey took out a copy of the scroll given to Brukhati. Von Markenburg opened and read it through.

"This covers most of what is required. We also need them to agree that all trade must now go through Moscow."

"The boyars won't go for that. Paying tribute and taxes to Muscovy is one thing, but not having the freedom to trade with whom they want could very well send them back to supporting Brukhati."

"That's the arrangement. The alternative is the grand prince coming up here with his army in the spring."

Rainey grimaced. All the work he had done to take over Yaroslavl peacefully with the support of its boyars could be so easily undone by such a move. This was counter to what Rainey and Ivan had discussed. It sounded more like Von Markenburg and the Muscovy court boyars were taking a shot at stealing Yaroslavl's economy.

"The document is for succession. There is no need to put the commerce of Yaroslavl into it. That can be discussed later."

"It will be told to them now."

Rainey glanced behind Von Markenburg. The black knights had all placed their hands on their swords. Krasenoff had stepped up beside Rainey, his hand on his sword.

Rainey leaned forward, glaring at Von Markenburg. "You don't want to do this. I'm placing Yaroslavl in the grand prince's hands with the city gladly agreeing to it. Your way will bring war and bloodshed and a city that will regard Muscovy with hatred."

"No, they will regard Muscovy with fear. Now take me to the boyars or face the consequences."

A smile slowly appeared on Rainey's face. The chancellor's betrayal with Anna gave him permission to be bold here. "You think you brought enough black knights to handle me and Igor? I suggest you think again."

"Take us to the boyars or face treason."

"Gladly. Let's go to Moscow right after my document is signed and ask our grand prince what his wishes really are."

Von Markenburg's face never changed, but after a moment, he shifted his stance. Rainey could see the black knights relaxing, but their hands stayed on their swords.

"I thought so," Rainey said. "I don't blame you for trying, but this is my arrangement. I am no threat to you if you give me no reason to be. I wish you'd learn that."

"You're asking me to trust someone other than my loyal knights. That is not in my nature."

"So, you're saying you don't trust our grand prince?"

"Do you?" Von Markenburg retorted. He turned and left, his knights following.

"That was uncomfortable," Krasenoff said.

Rainey looked up at his friend. Doubt filled his mind. When it came down to it, trust was fleeting when it concerned ruling princes or dukes or kings. He had known from past experience that loyalty and friendship was not enough if it was more expedient for a ruler to have you killed. He had learned something important about Von Markenburg that day and understood why the chancellor was so good at what he did.

"What would you do if Ivan ordered you to kill me?"

Krasenoff snorted. "I would think he wants me dead to send me up against you. I have seen you fight."

Rainey relaxed. "Yes, that would probably be how he'd have you killed. Me, it would be with poison or something."

Krasenoff shook Rainey. "Stop with this talk. The chancellor has gotten into your head. Let's go get some ales and talk about the women here in Yaroslavl."

Rainey laughed. "Whatever you do, Igor, never change."

* * *

Brukhati signed the document. Von Markenburg being there made it official by placing the Seal of Muscovy in wax next to the Seal of Yaroslavl. Ivan would place another seal on the document once it got back to Moscow. It would then be placed in the care of the Metropolitan, the church being the repository for all official documents of the Rus.

To be sure that Von Markenburg would not denigrate Rainey in front of Ivan over the events in Yaroslavl, he rode back to Moscow with him. He sent the rest of his entourage home, keeping only Krasenoff with him. Along the way, the two slept in shifts at night, just to be on the safe side. But Von Markenburg did not try anything untoward.

Once in Moscow, Ivan met privately with Rainey and Von Markenburg. Ivan held the scroll in his hands, a big smile on his face.

"Well done, my friends," Ivan said. "Always nice to acquire property without using my army and angering other princes in the process."

"Have you decided how you will split up the lands among your brothers?" Von Markenburg asked.

Ivan looked knowingly at Rainey. "They did nothing to acquire this land. Therefore, I see no reason for them to receive a reward. Boyar Rainey, on the other hand, will receive lands form Yaroslavl."

"My prince," Rainey responded. "I have no desire for any land that far away from Zenoplata. It would be a challenge for me to control and it would be taken from the rural boyars of Yaroslavl, of whom many were very helpful in acquiring the principality for you."

Ivan frowned. "May I remind you that if I give you nothing, it will get around court that I don't reward my boyars. Their support could be easily taken up by my many rival princes. I do not wish to find myself in Prince Brukhati's position."

"I'm sure we can come to an accommodation."

Ivan turned to Von Markenburg. "Is Dovyetsky well positioned among the Yaroslavl boyars to maintain a governorship?"

"Yes, my prince," Von Markenburg said. "The boyars will all come here during the summer to officially swear their allegiance to you."

"And some of the city's boyars are looking forward to moving to Moscow to set up their businesses here," Rainey added.

"Excellent," Ivan exclaimed. "That is all. Connor, I wish you to stay a few extra days in Moscow. I haven't had a good sword practice in months."

Rainey bowed and began to exit backwards for the door. "As you wish, my prince." Von Markenburg followed him out.

"A good day, indeed," Von Markenburg said.

Rainey stopped him in the hall. "Gunter, please note that I did not mention your attempt to add to the succession document."

"What addition?" Von Markenburg asked innocently.

Rainey smiled at him. "Exactly. We should not be at odds. Your skills managing the court are skills I do not have and do not wish to acquire. Don't ever think the grand prince doesn't appreciate those skills. I know he doesn't show it, but he does."

Von Markenburg looked shrewdly at Rainey. "What are you after?"

Rainey stepped back. "Nothing. Just that you have nothing to fear from me. We both want to protect our prince. You don't need to send someone to replace Anna. I'm sure her reports to you were rather dull."

Von Markenburg didn't even blink. "I was saddened to hear of her passing. Maria was very fond of her. She did give you a son, right?"

Rainey nodded slowly. "Yes, she did." He was not going to be able to change anything about the way Von Markenburg thought. The man was all about leverage and mentioning Ruslan was a subtle threat.

"It's good you have Ludmilla to raise the boy. I'm sure he will turn out to be strong." He slapped Rainey on the shoulder. "I must leave you. I must find out what has been happening since I left Moscow." He smiled and left.

Rainey stood there, wondering if he had just made a very big mistake.

21

"You seem to be somewhere else," Ivan said after striking Rainey across the back with his wooden sword. "You are usually not this easy to beat."

Rainey walked in a circle to come back and face Ivan. "I'm just tired. Spent too much of the winter riding around Yaroslavl."

"That would be an explanation if you were slow. It does not explain the mistakes you are making."

Rainey's mind was indeed elsewhere. Von Markenburg and his subtle threat were foremost in his mind; how to deal with it had not become apparent. He had never before had anyone who could be used against him. In the past, he could just kill anyone who would threaten him without worrying about repercussions, but that was not an option here. Apart from the threat to Ruslan, Von Markenburg was needed by Ivan to keep an eye on the court for him. And the court could easily be used to retaliate against any move Rainey made against Von Markenburg, being that many of the courtiers were no doubt leveraged by the chancellor.

Rainey raised his wooden sword for another bout. "I'll try to do better."

Ivan lowered his sword. "You are not going to be any fun. What's on your mind? And I expect an answer."

Rainey sighed and lowered his sword. "I would really like to work it out for myself."

"Is it something Gunter said?"

It never ceased to amaze Rainey how perceptive Ivan was, even at his relatively young age. "Nothing in particular . . ."

Ivan nodded. "Master of the subtle threat. I guess you had a small dispute in Yaroslavl?"

"I wasn't going to say anything, and I didn't, but Gunter sees threats everywhere."

"Mostly, he's jealous of your access to me. You not being here very often is a good thing. That's why, when he suggested we give you Zenoplata, I agreed. Mostly, I knew having you constantly around court would be dangerous. I also sensed you would not be happy just being a courtier boyar or a lowly bogatyr." He placed his sword on the table. "So what did Gunter do? I won't tell him you told me."

Rainey looked around the room. "He's probably got someone listening in."

"No, he doesn't. Igor is standing guard."

Rainey thought Igor was out in the taverns, spending his time and money as he always did when in Moscow. "You're keeping Igor away from his entertainment?"

Ivan touched his nose. "I don't fully trust anyone, including you. Gunter taught me that. But Igor is a different breed of man. He would never work for Gunter unless I ordered him to."

"And he'd probably argue with you about it, too."

Ivan laughed. "That he would. Now, what did Gunter do?"

Rainey shifted his weight from one foot to the other. "You gave me that succession document. The day before Prince Brukhati was to sign it, Gunter arrived and said you had sent him."

"Indeed, I did. Had to have a Muscovy seal on hand."

"He also said he was to start splitting up the territory into parts for boyars in Muscovy. I told him the rural boyars, whose support had gotten us to where we were, would renege on supporting us if that was part of the succession plan. We had a little standoff—until he must have concluded he hadn't brought enough of his black knights with him to push his issue."

Ivan rubbed his head. "I see. That was my fault. We had been talking about how to govern the new territory and he mentioned some of the court boyars were interested in acquiring new lands. I said we could look at that."

Rainey smiled. "I guess he was looking at it much more closely than you were."

"I had no knowledge of any deals you had made with Yaroslavl boyars. I couldn't close off any possibilities. Remember, I rule at the pleasure of my boyars. Some of them must have been whispering in Gunter's ear."

Rainey nodded. "They don't need to whisper. Gunter can read their minds. No harm, then."

"That depends. Those boyars now may not be very friendly towards you."

"That I can handle. I can always threaten to let Ludmilla loose on their sons."

Ivan let out a big bellowing laugh. "So true. How is the Kolchin girl doing?"

"She is raising little Ruslan for me."

"I never said how sorry I am about Anna Tripenskaya. Maria wondered why you never married her before the birth of the child."

I can't tell him, Rainey thought. Anna had been a lady in Ivan's wife's entourage. For the grand prince to find out she had been a spy for the chancellor would be dangerous. Von Markenburg would no doubt deny it and Ivan would have to wonder if he could believe Rainey. He had just said that he didn't fully trust anyone, including him. And then Krasenoff, too, would be in a difficult situation if put in the middle of it all.

"I'm a romantic," Rainey said. He would speak the truth to Ivan; just not the whole truth. "I wasn't sure if I loved her or not. She did seem to win over Ludmilla."

"Ludmilla. She was the talk of the court for months. Why did you teach her how to fight? So unladylike."

"After her two years with the Topoffs, I wanted her to be able to take care of herself. I don't like anyone being able to threaten someone I care for." He hoped Ivan perceived the unspoken meaning behind that statement.

Ivan nodded. "Well, no one wants to marry Ludmilla now. She's going to have to marry you."

"Me?"

"Who else will be able to handle her? And you just said you care for her."

Rainey remained silent. Ivan was right. He was the only man who gave her any sort of respect. Krasenoff respected her, too, but that wasn't the same. Rainey was fond of her, but how she felt about him was unknown after Anna had arrived at Zenoplata. And her tendency to throw knives in his direction when she got upset with him was a little disconcerting.

"I think she would make you a fine wife," Ivan said. "You said she already has fondness for your son."

"Why is everyone so interested in getting me married?"

Ivan grinned. "Personally, I don't care. But Maria does and I have to live with her." He picked up his wooden sword. "So, you think you can give me a challenge now?"

Rainey raised his sword. "You better pick up another sword."

* * *

Home. It was his home now. After all the years of travel, from Scotland to France, Italy, Constantinople and Kiev, the little town of Zenoplata felt more like home than anywhere else. Rainey's reputation now was beyond legend. No one would dare plan a raid on the town. His town. He could concentrate on living peacefully, away from the wars and sieges and slaughters of his earlier years. The grand prince might call upon him to fight in the future, but he had proven himself to be a wise ruler. Besides, Muscovy had the largest, best trained and equipped army in the Rus. Just the threat of it showing up on a battlefield was enough to deter an enemy.

The sun was warm on their faces as Rainey and Krasenoff entered the town. The many townsfolk out in Zenoplata's streets greeted their return with enthusiasm, but no one was in the courtyard. They sat on their horses, waiting.

"I guess Grigori is out somewhere," Krasenoff said.

"I suppose we could put our own horses away," Rainey replied.

The door to the house opened and Ludmilla came out with Ruslan in her arms. She looked up, surprised, and then smiled. Rainey got down off his horse.

"Put away my horse," he said.

"So now I'm a stable boy?" Krasenoff exclaimed.

"For the next ten minutes, yes." Rainey handed his reins up to Krasenoff.

Krasenoff mumbled something as he guided the horses towards the stable. Rainey went to Ludmilla.

"Welcome home, Connor," she said. "Ruslan has missed you very much."

Rainey looked into her eyes. "He's not even a year. He probably barely knows who I am." He stroked Ruslan's cheek, eliciting a smile from the child. "Did you miss me too?"

Ludmilla paused before answering. "Yes."

Rainey smiled, not knowing what to say next. There were feelings for Ludmilla, but he had never put much thought into them before his talk with Ivan. Now, seeing her there, holding his child and thinking about what Ivan had said, he was seeing her in a whole new light.

"I'm not carrying your bags," Krasenoff shouted from the stable.

The spell was broken. "Where is Grigori?" Rainey asked.

"He's out at one of the farms," she replied. "They needed some new parts from the blacksmith for their plow. It's bigger now that you gave them two horses."

"But Orina is here?"

Ludmilla stood up a little straighter. "Yes. I am not a helpless girl."

"I didn't mean . . ."

Ludmilla tilted her head to one side. "Yes, you did."

They stood in silence for a moment. "I'd better go get my bags before Igor yells at me again." Rainey turned towards the stable. As he walked, he decided he would need to go see Father Kirill.

* * *

"So, now you want to convert to our faith?"

Father Kirill seemed pleased and gave a sense that what was occurring had been inevitable. But he wasn't going to make it easy for Rainey.

"It's not like I was following another religion," Rainey said.

"You were baptised into the Latin church, were you not?"

Rainey shrugged. "Well, yes, but I'm more of an agnostic."

"You mean pagan."

"No. Pagans pray to multiple gods. I've never done that."

"Do you pray at all?"

Rainey was getting frustrated. "Let's just say I believe in the same God you do. How I relate to him is my business."

Kirill leaned back in his chair. "That statement does not encourage me to invite you into our faith."

"I . . ." Rainey stopped himself. He didn't want to get into a theological debate over the definitions of faith and religion. He had faith, but he wasn't too interested in the religion part. He'd seen way too many wars and deaths in the name of religion. "I just want to know what is involved in becoming part of your church."

"Why the sudden interest?"

Rainey was ready for that question. "Yours is the religion of the people I rule over. It is time I earned more of their respect by following their customs."

"You think our faith is a custom?"

"No, I think your religion is a custom." Almost instantly, Rainey regretted saying that. Before Kirill could respond, he put his hand up. "I don't want to debate God, Jesus, the Holy Trinity, or anything else. I want to convert. What do I do?"

Kirill's thin smile was barely discernable. "For a start, you will have to go to the monastery where the monks can teach you our faith."

"The monastery. For how long?"

"I would think two years of study should suffice."

Rainey laughed and leaned forward. "That is not going to happen. I want to join your religion, not become a priest to it."

"From what you have told me, you must be taught truths that our people learn as they grow into adulthood. That means you must also be purged of your currents truths."

Rainey stood up. "I could tell you a few truths that would curl your hair." He calmed himself down. "There must be an easier way."

Kirill smiled. "Then tell me the real reason you want to join my faith."

The sly old fox has already surmised why, Rainey thought. No point keeping it a secret. "Can you keep it to yourself for now?"

"A priest isn't much of a priest if not discreet."

Rainey nodded. "I'm thinking of marrying Ludmilla."

Kirill's smile was as wide as the room. "Has Ludmilla agreed?"

"I haven't asked her yet."

"And, since you want to join my faith, I surmise you want me to marry the two of you."

"Yes."

"Then I would say you had better get to courting her. I understand she is quite particular about her suitors."

The memory of the boy hanging from Ludmilla's window flashed through Rainey's mind. He hoped it wasn't going to be that much of a challenge.

"You were joking about the monastery, right?"

Kirill just smiled.

* * *

Ludmilla swung the wooden sword at Rainey's head. He dodged it and came around to attack her side. She shifted her swing and blocked the attack. Rainey slid his sword up and back along hers. Ludmilla followed the motion and with a flick at the end, stopped Rainey from getting inside her blade. He stepped back.

"That was excellent," Rainey said. "I don't recall teaching you that flick you did at the end."

"I can invent moves, too," she replied.

"Glad to see you're being creative. That's enough for today." Rainey sat down in the grass. "Sit with me for a while?"

Ludmilla tilted her head. They always ended their sword sessions by just riding back to the house. She stood looking at him, wondering what had changed.

Rainey tapped the ground beside him. "Sit."

Ludmilla sat down a few feet away from Rainey. He didn't seem happy about the distance, but she wasn't about to sit down right beside him, thinking he had another lesson in defense to spring on her. He sat still, looking at her, saying nothing. She didn't understand why they were sitting in the middle of a meadow.

"Was there something you wanted to discuss?"

But Rainey kept staring at her. She started to get up.

"If you're not going to say anything."

"No, please," Rainey finally said. "Just give me a minute."

Ludmilla sat back down and stared back at Rainey. He looked like a little lost boy. He had never looked lost like this before, at least not that she had ever seen. She began to fear something very bad was going to happen. Her mind tossed around thoughts about what could possibly be happening.

"Are you sending me away?" she asked quietly.

Rainey blinked. "No, no. Nothing like that. This is your home. I would never take that away from you."

"Are you dying?"

"No. Ludmilla, please, I want to get this right."

"Get what right? We're sitting here doing nothing."

Rainey shifted over to her and took her hand. Now she was really worried.

"Ludmilla," Rainey began, "I know I've been absent from Zenoplata on many occasions. I should have been here for you more often, with you looking after Ruslan. And I thank you for that from the bottom of my heart. I really do. He's not even your child, but I see how much he means to you." He paused for a second. "Now, I don't see the demands of the grand prince changing for me. He needs my counsel, often. Sometimes, I wish he'd just ask Gunter instead of making me go all the way to Moscow, or maybe let me write a letter. I spend way too much time on a horse, and . . ."

"Connor," Ludmilla said. "You're rambling." This was surprising to her. He had never rambled on like this before. "What do you want to tell me?"

Rainey was quiet again. Ludmilla was now getting angry. She didn't like being anxious.

"Just say it." She said forcefully.

"I want to marry you." The words spilled out of Rainey in a rush. He looked shocked for saying them. Ludmilla was shocked as well.

A wave of emotions flooded through her. The long-ago feelings she'd once had for him rose and faded. Thoughts of sadness, as this was supposed to be Anna Tripenskaya's moment. Then confusion. *Why is he asking me now?* Her thoughts raced in that direction. *Was he afraid I might stop taking care of Ruslan? Does he feel his age and decided to settle for me? Why was it so hard for him to ask?*

Her last thought was the decider. *Does he really love me?* In the end, she didn't know. Rainey had always been more of a father figure than anything else. He had never shown any desire for her, even if he did have those feelings. Her feelings for him had faded while Anna was in Zenoplata and had not really come back.

She pulled her hand away. "No." She started to get up.

"What?"

"I said no." She turned and ran for her horse. She could feel tears forming in her eyes. She didn't want to hurt Rainey, but she had no choice.

"Ludmilla!" Rainey called after her.

She almost leaped up onto her horse, grabbed the reins and pushed the horse into a full gallop.

22

Ludmilla had turned him down. Rainey was beside himself. He thought she might want to put off the decision for a while, but to say no outright to marrying him was beyond expectation. He was left speechless. He wanted to ask why, but the words never came out. After Ludmilla left the field, Rainey got on his horse and went for a long ride. He arrived at the same spot he always did, by the river upstream from the town.

He sat there, deep in his thoughts. Had the feelings he knew she'd had before Anna appeared totally turned cold? Was there someone else? No, he would have noticed that. Maybe, perhaps, it was because she didn't think she could give him children. He had told her it could have been the Topoff boy's fault, not hers, but she may still believe she is barren. Even if she was, he didn't care. The sudden realization that his love for her ran so deeply eliminated any premise for him to suppress his feelings. And his feelings were now gut-wrenchingly painful to experience when considering a life without Ludmilla in it.

He had been sitting there for what seemed hours when his senses picked up the presence of someone else. "Hello, Igor."

"Igor told me where to find you."

Rainey leaped to his feet and whirled around. Ludmilla stood before him. A strong sinking feeling in his stomach almost keeled him over. He couldn't believe she was here. He wanted to speak, but again, couldn't get any words out.

"I thought I needed to explain why I won't marry you," Ludmilla continued. "You told me I would not be forced to marry anyone I didn't want to. There was time I did want to marry you. Then Anna arrived, carrying your child. I felt broken. Perhaps betrayed. But after a while, I realized you never said anything about your feelings for me and I could see you had feelings for Anna. I don't understand why you didn't marry her. Now that she's gone, you have a son. I feel privileged that you are letting me be a part of raising him. But that is not a reason to marry me. I want to marry for love. You should, too."

Rainey stood motionless, staring at her. It felt like he was turning inside out. But still he couldn't speak. He could feel a tear forming in his right eye. He tried to blink it away.

"Are you crying?" Ludmilla asked.

Rainey wiped his eye. He looked down to hide his face from her. "No." As he looked up, Ludmilla was smiling at him. "Yes."

"Someday, you will find someone you love and all will be well," she said.

"I have."

"Who?"

"You."

Ludmilla took a step back, then turned and ran for her horse. Rainey ran after her. She swung herself into the saddle while Rainey went for the reins.

"Let me go," she pleaded. The horse started to rear, but Rainey pulled its head down.

"Ludmilla, we need to talk."

"No. I will not become a wife out of convenience."

"I love you."

"I don't believe you." She reached down and pulled the reins away from Rainey, yanked her horse around and trotted off towards Zenoplata.

Rainey was left standing alone, heart sinking ever deeper. He did love her. He knew that for sure now. He had never loved Anna. That had been just about responsibility for the child. He shook his head. He must be the only man under heaven who thought this way.

"I must say, that didn't go very well."

Rainey turned to find Krasenoff leaning against a tree. "What are doing out here?"

"I followed the girl," Krasenoff said. "Just in case she tried to kill you."

"She isn't talented enough for that."

"Oh, I know. I was more afraid you might let her succeed. Then I'd have to explain it all to the grand prince."

Rainey sank to the ground. "I don't know what to do?"

"If I may give you a little advice."

"Advice? What do you know about love?"

"I know that if you lose it, you will be in pain for the rest of your life."

Rainey looked up. Krasenoff's face was very sad. Rainey had never seen him look like this before. He had never thought of Krasenoff as a lover past his times with tavern girls. "Tell me about her."

Krasenoff crossed and sat down beside Rainey. The grave look on his face never changed. "It was many years ago. I was just becoming a bogatyr for Muscovy when I met her. It was during a raid into Rostov. We were doing the usual burning and killing in a village when I found her huddled under the floor of a house I was setting fire to. She looked up at me, the face of an angel, but with a mixture of fear and defiance. I was enchanted. I hauled her out and put her up on my horse. I whispered that she had nothing to fear.

"On the way back to Moscow, she got her hand on my knife and stabbed me in the leg. She bolted across the field. It was all I could do to keep anyone else from shooting her with their crossbows. I sent the raiders on and went after her myself. For three days, we hunted each other, she determined to kill me, me determined to have her. Then one night, as I was setting a fire to cook a rabbit I had killed, she came out of the woods, knife out in front of her. She just stood there. Her eyes were flickering back and forth between me and the rabbit on the spit. Once the food was ready, I placed some several feet away from me. She eventually sat down and ate it. After our meal, I said she didn't have anywhere to go now, so she should come back to Moscow with me. I would treat her well. But she disappeared back into the trees.

"The next morning, there she was, feeding grass to my horse. She stayed hesitant towards me for two weeks before she said a word to me. Wouldn't even tell me her name for over a month. Over time, we learned to love each other and she agreed to marry me."

Krasenoff stopped. Rainey knew the painful part of the story was next. "What was her name?"

Tears formed in Krasenoff's eyes at the memory. "Zarya."

"You don't have to continue."

"Yes, I do. A few days before our marriage, she was in the market. A thief was caught stealing some trinkets and as he ran through the market, the fool shopkeeper took out a crossbow and shot it after the man. He missed, striking Zarya in the back. She died within minutes."

"I'm sorry, Igor."

"It's been over ten years, and I still think about her every day." He turned to Rainey. "You love Ludmilla. You have for a long time now. She loves you, too. That is obvious. But you let that Tripenskaya woman come between you. You distanced yourself. Now you are on the verge of losing what could possibly be the only true love of your life."

"I didn't know you were such a romantic."

Krasenoff slapped Rainey on the side of the head.

"Ow!"

"You're a fool, Connor. Get off your ass and go after her."

"She doesn't want me."

"Yes, she does. You just have to prove you want her. Now go."

Rainey looked deep into his friend's eyes. He could see the deep pain, but also a determination not to let a friend do something he would regret. He got up off the ground and ran for his horse. He headed off at a full gallop, wanting to reach Ludmilla before she reached the town. As the minutes passed, he began to feel uneasy as she and her horse did not appear in the distance. He left the trees into and open field, then onto the dirt road leading to the distant buildings of the town. Ludmilla was nowhere to be found. He reined in his horse, looking all around.

Nothing.

I should have caught up with her by now. All sorts of frantic thoughts raced through his mind, all followed by reason. *She's gone off to kill herself. No, Ludmilla wouldn't do that. She'd be more likely to wait to kill me. Maybe she fell off her horse and is injured. No, I would have seen her along the road. Maybe someone took her. No, I wasn't that far behind her and she's quite capable of fending off an attacker for the few minutes it would have taken for me to reach her.*

There was only one thing left. She was leaving Zenoplata. His mind went back to the meadow by the river. He didn't think anything about it then, but now he remembered that her horse appeared to have been packed for travel. She was also dressed for travel. Pantaloons and boots, fur cloak. But where would she go?

That deep sinking feeling in his stomach was there again. She was gone, and he didn't know what to do.

* * *

Ludmilla arrived at the first village to the west of Zenoplata. She waited out in the trees until dark. They people in the village would know her and she didn't want word to get back to Rainey about which direction she was going. She remembered where she could find good lodgings and a meal, but a woman travelling alone would be looked upon with suspicion at best, or even downright contempt. As she waited, she cut her long hair so it reached only to her shoulders. She tied it back so she would look more like a man and practiced speaking with a lower voice. She also pulled a hood over her head to cast a shadow across her face. As night fell, she headed into the village to find the inn.

"I will need a room for the night," she said to the innkeeper.

The man looked at her with curiosity. "You're awfully young to be travelling alone. Can you pay?"

Ludmilla threw a gold coin on the table. "Yes, I can pay."

"Where did you get that?"

She leaned forward, close to the man's face. "I earned it." She tapped the hilt of her sword. That got her the reaction she hoped for: a short flash of fear.

"How do I know you didn't steal it?"

Ludmilla stepped back and pulled her sword. "Would you like a demonstration?"

The man quickly waved his hands. "No, no, no. I believe you."

"I would like a meal as well, and some ale."

The innkeeper poured her an ale. She was never fond of ale, but she felt she needed to play the part she had started here.

"What is your name, boy?" the innkeeper asked.

She hadn't thought she'd need a new name, but if she was going to play a man, she would need a man's name. One quickly came to mind.

"Ruslan Tripensky," she replied.

* * *

"It's been two weeks. She could have made it anywhere by now. She doesn't want to be found."

Rainey and Krasenoff stood in the bow of the boat as the walls of the Moscow Kremlin came into view. Ivan had requested their presence without mentioning a reason, as usual. Krasenoff had mentioned that Ivan was probably wanting to cheer Rainey up. He had been sulking since Ludmilla had left, but had also been sending out men to search for her everywhere. They had all come back with no news.

"I can't believe that," Rainey replied. "You were the one who told me to go find her."

"I thought we would have found her by now. The girl is much more resourceful than I gave her credit for."

"Yes, she is."

"Or she's . . ."

"She's not dead."

They went silent. This was becoming how many of their conversations ended as of late. It was putting a strain on their relationship. It had gotten to a point where Rainey was afraid his friend would request a reassignment somewhere else when they saw Ivan. But he didn't know how to fix it. He was too deep in his misery over Ludmilla.

No more words passed between them until they came through the Kremlin gates. Von Markenburg met them both outside the throne room.

"Good, you're both here," Von Markenburg began. "We have a problem."

"What is it this time?" Krasenoff asked.

Von Markenburg scowled at Krasenoff. "This is serious. The Great Horde is falling into civil war."

"Not surprising," Rainey observed. "But, why is that our problem? Or are we interested in who wins?"

"Not exactly. Mahmud is still in power, but his brother, Ahmed, has been raising support in the east. There was a small battle near Sarai. Mahmud drove off the rebels, but Ahmed is far from defeated. It would be in our interest to keep them fighting."

Rainey nodded. "Indeed. But why are we here? This sounds like something you could accomplish by yourself."

Von Markenburg smiled. "We don't know much about Ahmed. We need someone to go meet him, hint at support from Muscovy, and determine if he would be better or worse than Mahmud. But mostly, keep him fighting. Not to win, just to fight."

"Why don't you go?" Krasenoff asked, already knowing the answer.

Von Markenburg sighed as if talking to a child. "Ahmed would expect too much if I arrived. Connor is just a boyar. It will be easier to just trickle in support."

"You'd probably make a good prisoner, too," Krasenoff said.

"That would be a possibility."

"You afraid our grand prince wouldn't pay your ransom?"

Von Markenburg moved menacingly towards Krasenoff. Rainey stepped between them. "Igor, stop it." To Von Markenburg, he said, "Our grand prince doesn't trust any of his other boyars enough to do this right?"

The throne room door opened. "The grand prince is ready for us," Von Markenburg said. "Shall we go in?"

Ivan was sitting on his throne, a number of the members of his court in various degrees of leaving. The three newcomers approached and bowed. Ivan rose from his chair and removed his crown.

"I really hate this thing," he said. "Gunter, when is the small court crown going to be ready?" He tossed the crown onto the throne.

"Soon, my prince. It does need to reflect the respect and symbolism of the throne. We can't have you sit there with a simple ring on your head."

Ivan came down to their level. "Did Gunter inform you of what I need?" he asked Rainey.

"Yes, my prince. We are to go and assess Ahmed, and keep him in the fight for as long as possible."

Ivan nodded. "Anything he needs, within reason, send a courier to Gunter. I'm sure I can rely on you to make sure Ahmed doesn't get too much support."

"You can."

"Excellent. You three will dine with us tonight and we can discuss this more in depth." Ivan turned on his heel and disappeared through a door behind the throne. Von Markenburg stepped up to the throne and picked up the crown.

"He really should show this a little more respect," he said.

23

The meal was the best Rainey had had in several months. The venison was tender and moist, the breads sweet. And the ale was excellent. He leaned back in his chair as a servant refilled his mug.

"I've always said the food at the Moscow Kremlin is the best in all of the Rus," he exclaimed.

Krasenoff and Von Markenburg raised their mugs in unison. "Here, here."

"I am pleased you like it," Maria said. "Perhaps you should come more often."

Ivan chuckled. "She's still concerned about you not having a wife, Connor."

Maria stood gracefully. "And what would be so bad about him having a wife? He does have a child that needs raising."

Rainey felt a chill go through him as he thought of Ludmilla. He needed to deflect the conversation. "My lady, you don't seem too concerned about wives for Igor . . . or Gunter."

Von Markenburg spit his beer back into his mug.

"Interesting," Ivan said. He turned to his chancellor. "Why have you stayed unwed all these years, Gunter?"

Von Markenburg put down his mug. "I am still, foremost, a warrior monk. We remain celibate. However, our bogatyr here is not married either and he has not taken any vows of celibacy that I know of."

"Igor spends too much time entertaining the ladies of the taverns," Maria said. "No wife would put up with that for very long."

Krasenoff was ignoring the conversation.

"I will leave you to your business," Maria added as she stood to leave the room.

Rainey set down his mug. He needed to get back to business, to get Ludmilla out of his head. "Ahmed. May I speak freely, my prince?"

"Always," Ivan replied.

"I was thinking about how to approach the man. How much of a link to Muscovy should I let on? Or should I just sell my sword as a mercenary?"

Ivan nodded. "Gunter and I think it best that the link be strong. By sending you, a well-known boyar, Ahmed will feel he has strong support from me, even though he knows I cannot openly pick his side."

"Then I will need to take an armed group with me. If I go alone, I won't be able to project that idea that you're backing me."

"We can supply you with a number of bogatyrs to join you," Von Markenburg said. "I can also give you two of my black knights. That should solidify your standing with Ahmed as Muscovy's envoy."

And keep an eye on me, Rainey reminded himself. "Agreed. If it's all right, I'd like to do a little recruiting myself here in Moscow. I'll have to leave Igor back in Zenoplata to keep an eye on things."

"What?" Krasenoff cried.

"Igor, I'm going to be gone a long time."

"The town can take care of itself quite well on its own."

"I'm sorry, Igor, but I need you at home."

Krasenoff looked like he was sulking. "You're going to make me keep searching for . . ."

Rainey raised his hand to cut him off. "Can't be helped," he said firmly and turned back to Ivan. "Where can I find Ahmed?"

* * *

Novgorod.

Ludmilla had only been there once before, but it had meant salvation for her. She was saved from the Topoffs there and reunited briefly with her brother Andrey. That was also a time before she had loved Rainey. Besides all these reasons to favor Novgorod, she had nowhere else to go. She was too well known at the Moscow court after having left a trail of suitors in her wake. And Vladimir would have been like going back to Hell.

Night had fallen by the time she reached the city gates, and she was fortunate to be able to enter just as the gates were swung shut for the night. After asking at a couple of taverns, she got directions to Andrey's home. Standing across the street from a solidly built two-story house, she got the sense that he had done well in business. This pleased her. But just knocking on the broad oak door made her nervous. It had been over a year since they had seen each other. He might ask uncomfortable questions about why she was here.

Out of the darkness from up the street came four men, striding purposefully. Ludmilla glanced at them without any curiosity until she saw the weapons. Three had swords drawn. One carried a crossbow. And they were all looking at her brother's house. She felt a sudden tension in her arms and hands, her right hand instinctively reaching for her sword's hilt. The men stopped at the foot of the short staircase below her brother's front door. Then they ran up together and crashed the door open.

From inside, Ludmilla heard a woman scream. She pounded across the street, sword out and ready for use. She mounted the steps two at a time and burst through the open doorway, skewering one of the four men in the back. She pulled her sword free and saw Andrey backing up, his wife and two small children behind him, into a room to her right. All he had to defend himself with was a candlestick. The attacker with the crossbow was taking aim. He was within reach of Ludmilla's sword, which she sliced downward. That severed the man's left arm above the wrist. He screamed and his crossbow tipped upwards, its bolt lodging into the ceiling.

The last two attackers turned on her. For Ludmilla, everything seemed to slow down. Rainey's voice was in her head.

Speed is the key. Watch where your opponent's sword is headed, and don't be there. Let his forward motion move him past you. Spin quickly and slice open his back. Keep spinning and bring your sword upwards either to cut or fend off the next opponent. If you don't land a blow, jump away from his sword; get your sword free of his and swing high for his exposed throat.

When she stopped moving, the second swordsman's head had already hit the floor, the rest of his body following it down. It was safe to look again at Andrey. He now had a fireplace poker, pointing it menacingly at her. Andrey's wife cowered in the corner, holding the two little children close.

"Who are you?" Andrey demanded.

Ludmilla lowered her sword and pulled back her hood. The shock on Andrey's face was palpable.

"Ludmilla?"

"Hello, Andrey." The man with the crossbow writhed on the floor at her feet, whimpering, blood pouring from his severed wrist. "Who are these men?"

Andrey threw the poker at the fireplace and crossed to his sister. He hugged her hard. She wrapped her arms around him.

"What are you doing here?" Andrey asked. He stepped back. "Mikhail!" He picked up one of the swords that had clattered to the floor moments earlier and headed for the splintered door. Ludmilla grabbed his arm. She knew he was concerned about his partner's wellbeing.

"Stay with your family. Remind me how I get to Mikhail's house from here."

"Ludmilla, it's too dangerous."

She looked around the floor at the four bodies. "For whom?" she said. "Tell me how to get there."

It took a little more convincing, but Andrey finally agreed to stay home and let Ludmilla find out if anything bad was happening at Mikhail's home. As she approached the house, she saw smoke coming out the front windows. She ran up the stairs and through the broken door.

The fire was just getting started in the hall and on the stairs. She moved to check the rooms downstairs and found Mikhail, his wife and two children lying on the floor. Mikhail had a crossbow bolt embedded in his chest. The other three had been stabbed with swords. There was nothing she could do for them. Then she heard the cry.

A baby's cry. It was coming from the second floor. She wrapped her cloak around herself, quickly passed through the flames and ascended the stairs. Following the cries, she found the infant in a cradle. Wrapping the baby up in its blankets, she made her way back to the stairs.

The flames were higher now, engulfing the ceiling. Through a window at the top of the stairs she saw a roof about a foot down. Climbing out the window, she steadied herself and moved quickly across to a ladder. Once on the ground, she moved through a back alley and back into the street. A crowd was gathering to try and fight the fire. She faded into the shadows and made her way back to Andrey's home.

On the way, the baby had quieted down. Ludmilla's sense of despair over the tragedy she had witnessed slowly turned into a rage. As she arrived, Andrey was trying to fix his door enough to lock it. She only had one question.

"Who did this?"

* * *

"I could be gone for years. Someone has to take care of Zenoplata."

"But who will watch your back?"

Rainey gripped Krasenoff by the shoulders. "You know better than anyone that my back really doesn't need watching. I need you at Zenoplata."

"No, you want me to find the girl."

Rainey lowered his head. Krasenoff knew him too well. "That too. Bring in the harvest first, and then head over to Novgorod. She has most likely gone to her brother's home. He goes by the name of Andrey Kolochoff now. I can't think of any other place she could go"

"And what am I to say to her? Come home, but by the way, the boyar won't be home for five or six years?"

"It might not be for too . . ." Who was he kidding? Krasenoff was right. Rainey had already said he could be gone for years. So why would Ludmilla come back for that? "I'll find a way to get back for a while during the winter."

"It'd be more likely that she would go to you," Krasenoff said offhandedly.

Rainey brightened. "Yes. I can accept that. You want to watch my back? Go find Ludmilla and bring her to me."

"You would risk her life among the Great Horde?"

Rainey smiled. "You know her talents. She could watch your back."

Krasenoff paused for a beat. "You really want me to take her into the khanate?"

"I love her," Rainey replied. "If I'm going to be living down there for a long time, I want her to be by my side. And you at my back."

"You said you didn't need me at your back."

"Igor, you want to be there, whether I need you there or not."

"And Zenoplata?"

"One of us is going to need to go home every fall for the harvest."

Krasenoff nodded. "What if the girl won't come?"

"I have faith that you can persuade her."

Krasenoff huffed. "Your faith may be misplaced. But I will try."

* * *

Standing in the shadow of a building across the street, Ludmilla watched the place Andrey had described to her. He hadn't wanted her to go, but Ludmilla was insistent. He made her promise to be extra careful. Now, as she looked at the house, being extra careful gave her pause. It wasn't just a house. It had a walled courtyard similar to the house in Zenoplata. As she watched, several guards appeared along the top of the wall as well as out in the street. She figured more would be inside. This man, who had tried to kill her brother over a trade dispute, was well protected. While Rainey had taught her how to fight, he never gave her any lessons about how to infiltrate a well-guarded house.

The story Andrey told her was steeped in intrigue. He and Mikhail had made a fortune with the silk trade, but after their business was rerouted back through Moscow, their fortunes began to decline. They looked for new trade opportunities and came across metals coming in from the Baltic coast and the Hanseatic League cities. The metal trade in Novgorod was controlled by a powerful boyar named Chergin, so it was difficult to carve out a niche in the market. Andrey thought they should try another business, but Mikhail was stubborn, and with their contacts they began to build a sizable business. It was then that the true reason Chergin had full control of the metals market became apparent.

It started with customers being intimidated. Mikhail countered that by forming them into a guild for mutual protection. Then some of their metal shipments never reached Novgorod. The partners countered that by keeping their shipping schedules a secret. Chergin then started to directly target Mikhail and Andrey. One day, Natalia was roughed up in the market. On another, a fire was started on Mikhail's front steps. A storage building was set on fire. They had to hire guards for their supplies and to accompany them everywhere. They stayed the course, even as the costs of doing so continued to rise. Until tonight, that is, when Chergin made the ultimate decision to resort to murder. And Ludmilla was determined that he would pay dearly for that decision.

She pulled her cloak tighter around herself against the coolness of the night. She could see no way in without facing several men before even getting to the gate. She would have to go around and check for possible entry points that weren't so closely watched.

Just before she stepped out to scout the wall, four women sauntered down the street towards the guards. Ludmilla decided that these were the type of women Krasenoff visited in the taverns of Moscow. They seemed very friendly with the guards. A germ of an idea came to her. She went to the end of the street and crossed over to the side the house was on. She waited in the shadows until the four women moved on. Lowering her hood, she opened her cloak and her shirt to expose the tops of her breasts. She gripped her dagger in her right hand, hidden behind the cloak, and started slowly towards the gate.

"Excuse me, sir, can you help me?" she said, approaching the first guard. He turned towards her.

"How can I help such a fine young la—"

She sank the blade up to the hilt into his stomach. He started to bend over. Ludmilla helped him to the ground and looked up at the next guard.

"He's falling. I think he's ill."

The second guard came up quickly. As he reached her, she slit his throat. He fell, gasping for air. She got up quickly and ran for the third guard at the gate.

"Help me," she cried. "Someone has killed those men."

The third guard began running towards her. As he passed, Ludmilla stuck out the knife so he ran into it. As he fell over, she moved to the gate, drew her sword, pressed herself up against the wall and let out a horrifying scream.

The desired effect happened. The bolt on the gate was pulled back and several men stormed out. After the last one went by, Ludmilla slipped into the courtyard, pushed the gate shut again and bolted it. She turned into the shadows of what looked like a stable. She paused for a moment to redo up her shirt and cloak. From there, she made her way towards a window at the side of the house. The shutters were not closed, so she let herself in. She could hear the commotion outside the walls. As of yet, none of the men had attempted to come back into the courtyard.

She was in a kitchen. She pulled her cloak up tight and lifted the hood back over her head. She listened at the doorway. She could hear two people speaking through an open door farther down the hallway.

"What's all the commotion outside?"

"I don't know, father. The men haven't come back yet."

"Have we heard from the men who went to the Kolochoff home yet?"

"No. They are overdue."

Ludmilla smiled. She had found her target. She moved swiftly to the open door and stepped inside. An old man was seated by a fireplace with a younger man standing beside him. Both turned when she entered.

"Who are you?" the younger man asked, drawing his sword.

"Guards!" the older man yelled.

Ludmilla stayed silent, stepping farther into the room, watching the younger man move to intercept her. She watched his sword come up leaving himself exposed. As his sword came down, she spun to the left and brought her sword around. The man's momentum forced him to bend over. Ludmilla decapitated him.

"GUARDS!"

Ludmilla brought her sword up to the old man's chest, pressing the point into a crest on his tunic, directly over his heart.

"Who are you?" he croaked.

"I'm Ruslan Tripensky," she replied calmly, and thrust her sword forward.

24

Sitting in front of the fire, Mikhail Shermenskoff's baby in her arms, Ludmilla didn't give a second thought to the evening's events. When she'd arrived back at her brother's house, all she said was that his problem had been solved. Now she could spend time with a new baby. A little girl named Svetlana. She was an orphan, but she also now had a great protector. Ludmilla planned on caring for this child as she had Ruslan. The little girl would be part of her new life in Novgorod.

Ludmilla cooed softly. Svetlana was dozing off, as was Ludmilla. She was so tired after all that had happened. Her thoughts turned to Ruslan, Orina, Grigori, and even Rainey and Krasenoff. She missed them all. Tears started to run down her cheeks.

"I will put Svetlana down for the night," Natalia Kolochoff said as she came up bedside Ludmilla. She reached over and took the baby out of Ludmilla's arms. Ludmilla looked up.

"You've been crying, too," she said to Natalia.

"Mikhail was my brother. I mourn the loss of him and his family. We were very close. But I also thank you with all my heart for what you did here tonight. You saved us all."

"For now, perhaps," Andrey said, entering the room.

"What do you mean?" Ludmilla asked.

"This is a city full of intrigue. Chergin was high up among the boyars who wish to support Lithuania against Muscovy. They will not be pleased that he is dead."

"Why is that a concern of yours?"

Andrey hesitated. "Mikhail and I have tried to not choose a side. He had been leaning to Chergin's side while I leaned towards Muscovy. It was working, without either side spending too much time trying to ask more of us. But we were realists. Receiving support from Lithuania will mean we will feel Muscovy's wrath."

Ludmilla looked into the flames. "I don't care about the politics here. I'm just glad I arrived when I did."

"It was providence," Natalia said. "The good Lord was watching over us."

Ludmilla nodded. *The good Lord, indeed*, she thought. *Father Kirill would have some wise words to say about that.* She watched the flames flicker back and forth in the fireplace, not noticing that Natalia had left the room. She slowly closed her eyes, leaned back in the chair and fell asleep.

* * *

The winter did not seem so cold down in the Khanate compared to Zenoplata. There was less snow than regularly fell further north and the sun shone more often. Still, it would have been better living in a town as opposed to the tent camp of Ahmed bin Kuchuk. Rainey had tried to encourage him at least to conquer a town before winter set in, but Ahmed insisted the only place he wanted was Sarai, the khanate capital. His little band of rebels was growing substantially, but not enough to take the capital away from his brother.

Rainey pulled his cloak closer around his neck as he stepped outside his tent. The cold was countered by the warmth of the sun on his face. He looked around, saw that nothing had changed and went off to find his two companions, the black knights Von Markenburg had sent south with him. They would be where they always were, around the group of boyars and bogatyrs the grand prince had also sent along. The group stuck together, not associating much with Ahmed's Tartar followers. That, apparently, was Rainey's job.

"Johann, Gerhard, walk with me," he said as he approached the gathering huddled around a fire. The pungent smell of dried dung, a common fuel out on the steppe where firewood was in short supply, hung in the air. Rainey waved the knights away from the fire for both secrecy and aromatic reasons.

"Any news from Muscovy?" he asked.

"The new swords are ready," Johann said. "Designed to look like they were made in the Khanate. Also spears. We can expect them sometime in the next few weeks."

"No word from Igor Krasenoff?"

Johann shook his head. Rainey sighed. "What is taking him so long?"

Gerhard shifted in his tunic. It didn't fit him very well. For this adventure, the two knights had been obliged to leave their personal black attire back in Moscow. To blend in here, they wore more Tartar garb. Gerhard was a large man and finding anything Tartar large enough for him was a challenge.

"Our host is hoping for some crossbows," Rainey said, "and he'd like to take a look at an arquebus."

"He knows about the firearms?" Johann asked, surprised.

"He has heard hints about them. I've been telling him that such talk sounds like magic to me." Rainey had wisely left his arquebus back in Zenoplata.

Johann and Gerhard nodded together. Although Rainey knew the knights were there to keep an eye on him, he had started to develop a bit of a friendship with Gerhard. He hoped that one day, he might even talk with him about Von Markenburg, but he would not try to initiate that conversation. Eventually, he knew, most things they had in common would get discussed and perhaps the chancellor would then become a topic of conversation.

"Let's go for a ride."

Winter was always a very slow time for life in general. No farming, very little raiding, mostly everyone just holed up in a house trying to keep warm and waiting for spring to arrive. Rainey also had lots of time to think. Most of his thoughts revolved around his mission—and Ludmilla.

Ahmed was startlingly different from his brother. Unlike Mahmud, who spent his time worrying about assassins and keeping out of sight, Ahmed was gregarious. He believed he should be khan because he was better than his brother. His followers adored him. Rainey soon came to realize that Mahmud's actions were actually creating more support for Ahmed. When your leader shows fear, people generally go looking for a new leader who is more self-assured and confident. Ahmed was that and more. He proved to be more than competent as a warrior and planner. His hit-and-run raids were designed more to spread terror with minimum losses than to gain any territory. He was biding his time, confident that he would end up on the throne in Sarai in a year or two. And that worried Rainey. Ahmed had a vision that included recreating the glory days of the Golden Horde.

In his reports to the grand prince, Rainey warned that Ahmed was the type who would not stop at claiming the khanate. He would go out of his way to reclaim all of the Golden Horde's original territories and perhaps go on to conquer more. That meant Muscovy could very well be forced to meet much higher demands for tribute or even face the khanate's army. And from what Rainey had seen, keeping the khanate in civil war might not be as easy as anyone had first thought. If things continued to progress the way they had for the last six months, Ahmed could very well find himself on the throne in Sarai no matter what Muscovy did. Rainey had thought he could preach caution, but Ahmed, he was learning, was a patient man and not prone to reckless actions. He was a lot like Ivan in this respect.

About Ludmilla, Rainey's thoughts were always the same. *Where is she? What is she doing? Has Igor found her yet?* He didn't like being stuck down in the khanate with Johann and Gerhard when he should be looking for Ludmilla himself. But this mission was too important for him to neglect.

"Gentlemen," Rainey said as he and the knights rode out onto the steppe, "Your opinions on Ahmed's chances of taking Sarai this coming year."

The two knights were well experienced in military affairs, having been with Von Markenburg for over twenty years. They had followed Von Markenburg to Muscovy to put Vasily back on the throne, followed by fighting in the Polish-Teutonic War. They had been young then, but even now in their elder years were still threatening.

"He's going to need a lot more soldiers to take Sarai," Johann said. "I don't see his army growing fast enough to make his move until perhaps the following year."

"Sarai wouldn't be hard to take," Gerhard added. "He probably has support in the city that would help him. But he doesn't seem to be in a hurry. I'm thinking the following year as well."

"And I can't seem to get him to face off with Mahmud's army at all," Rainey said. "Can't very well keep them both weak if they don't go out and fight each other every now and then."

"So then, what are we doing here?" Gerhard asked, saying what all three were thinking.

Nothing, Rainey thought. He was unsuccessful at encouraging a consuming civil war between the two brothers. His entourage, including the boyars, were all anxious to go home, as was he. His next letter to the grand prince would have to clearly spell that out.

He looked at Gerhard. "I will put that to the grand prince in my next report."

* * *

Ludmilla sat at her usual business table against the tavern's back wall. A new client required her services and the money was best she had ever been offered. She contemplated that the job would require killing someone, but it wasn't like she hadn't done it before. It had never been part of a contract before, but she knew that one day it would be asked of her. She wasn't sure how she would deal with such a request. Novgorod was seething with political intrigue; some parties were hoping to distance themselves from Muscovy while others were willing to stay under the grand prince's protection. That was the main distinction. One group considered Muscovy a protector. The other, an oppressor.

It all started right after Chergin was killed. Because on that same night her brother had faced off an assassination attempt that had clearly been instigated by Chergin, everyone wanted to know who Andrey had hired to kill his enemy. Andrey stuck with the story that he didn't know who had sent the assassin; after all, many business people in Novgorod could have done so. But the inquiries persisted and people started to take note that Ludmilla had arrived in Novgorod the very night so much blood had been spilled. No one was silly enough to think she had gotten inside Chergin's house and killed him, but plenty of townspeople thought she knew who the assassin was. It was a simple step from that idea to the next question. People began asking her if she could get in touch with that mysterious man, as they required his expert services. After getting enough of these inquiries, she finally set herself up as an intermediary for the unknown enforcer. People called her the Emissary. And likewise, she gave the enforcer a name: the one she had invented during her journey to Novgorod. Ruslan Tripensky.

Most of the contracts involved thievery. If she needed to get close to someone or something without being noticed, she found no one paid much attention to a woman. Sometimes just being seen during a dangerous business deal was all that was needed, her sword and hood being her signature. There was the odd time Ludmilla had to pull her sword and deal with violence, but after a while, the Tripensky reputation kept most business deals calm. This was especially true with disputes between pro- and anti-Muscovy parties. She stayed above the political divide, confirming that by accepting contracts from both sides. Some boyars announced that "Tripensky" had been hired for some meeting when in fact she hadn't been involved. She put a stop to that by visiting those boyars, in her disguise as Tripensky, and extracting a payment. After a while, she came to consider her work a public service. In the past, business in Novgorod had never been so civil.

She kept Andrey in the dark about the services she provided, but she sensed he suspected what she was up to.

In her new career, Ludmilla had already done some killing, though it had been incidental to what she'd been hired for. She never thought of it much afterwards. If a man attacked one of her clients, she dispatched him. That was part of the job. She never felt a sense of remorse, a wish that an incident could have gone differently, not even a fear that she could have died herself. The way she permitted herself to think about it was simple and direct: be there, take care of threats, get paid, and go home. There was no satisfaction, no joy, no sense of accomplishment, no filling a hole in her soul. The work paid the bills and then some, but nothing more.

Her real life revolved around little Svetlana. Ludmilla stayed on with Andrey and Natalia, taking care of the little girl like she had with Ruslan back in Zenoplata. In doing so, she was able to shut out her life as a hired sword. To remind herself that there were joys in life. As much as she had become a mother to Ruslan when Anna died, she took on the motherly role for Svetlana. This was what she was on earth for.

Now, though, she was on the job. She scanned the crowd in the tavern. Her client was late. Apart from the usual looks she got from the men, no one approached her table. She began to tap her fingers on the scarred wood, then took a drink from the mug in front of her. She had acquired a taste for ale. In her business, men liked to drink to their deals.

"I'm looking to hire Ruslan Tripensky," said a man in the shadows to her right.

She looked over, but could not see the man's face. "I can help you," she replied. "Come, sit down. I'll order you an ale." She signalled to the bar.

"You are a hard girl to find," the man said, stepping out of the shadow.

Ludmilla sat up straight. "Igor!"

Krasenoff sat down across from her and picked up her mug, taking a long drink. Ludmilla regained her composure.

"What are you doing here?"

Krasenoff put the mug down. "Like I said, you're a hard girl to find. I've been in Novgorod for a month now. Your brother recognized me, but wouldn't tell me anything. I was going to try threatening him, but I was warned off by some locals who told me he was protected. Started to hear these wild stories about a mystery man for hire. Took a while, but I finally got a name for this man."

"Ruslan Tripensky," Ludmilla said.

Krasenoff nodded. "I knew right then it was you. Does your brother know?"

"I think he suspects."

"I've been told the story of Old Man Chergin. Tripensky got quite the reputation for that. How did you do it?"

Ludmilla smiled mischievously. "An assassin never reveals her secrets."

A brimming new mug was placed in front of Krasenoff. He raised it in a toast. Ludmilla raised hers and the clunk of the mugs meeting rang across the table.

"Never thought I'd be drinking in a tavern with you," Krasenoff remarked.

"I've never been your kind of woman," Ludmilla replied. Krasenoff grimaced. "So why are you here? I don't think you would be looking for my kind of services."

"I've come to take you home."

"I am home."

"Your real home."

"This is my real home."

Krasenoff paused. Ludmilla continued. "You thought I was waiting here for you to come and take me back to Zenoplata?"

"I was hoping."

"And why would I want to go back?"

"Because Connor loves you and wants you to."

"If he loved me, he would have come here himself."

"He can't."

Ludmilla sat back. Worry began to seep into her mind. *Why couldn't Connor come to Novgorod? Is he sick? Is he dying?* "What's happened?"

"Nothing to worry about. He's down in the khanate on the grand prince's orders. Been there since just after you left Zenoplata."

A sense of relief passed through her, followed by the thought that Rainey was never home. She looked down at her mug, trying to hide her feelings from Krasenoff, but it was too late.

"You love him, too. I know. Which is why I can't understand why you left."

"Because he chose Anna over me."

"He never chose Anna for anything."

"Yes, he did. I could see."

"Girl, he would have never chosen Anna. Christ, she was . . ."

"She was a what?'

It was Krasenoff's turn to look down into his ale. "Nothing."

Ludmilla pressed on. "You were gone much of the time Anna was in Zenoplata. I thought it was because she didn't like you. But that isn't it, is it? What were you doing then?"

Krasenoff picked up his drink, downed the ale and slammed the mug down on the table. "That is in the past. I'm here to take you home. Are you coming or not?"

Ludmilla had never seen Krasenoff like this before. He had always been friendly to her, even teased her a bit. He never seemed to be bothered by anything, taking one day at a time. She had looked on him as a friendly uncle. There could be only one reason he would act this way. "Connor told you not to tell me."

"I wasn't planning to tell him, either, once Anna died, even though he sent me to find out."

A man appeared behind Krasenoff and pulled him back by the shoulder. He looked at Ludmilla. "Is this man bothering you?"

She stood up quickly. "No, no. Just a difficult negotiation. I'm fine."

The man looked sternly at Krasenoff, who smiled back at him. "You act respectful to the Emissary," the man commanded.

Krasenoff glanced at Ludmilla, the smile still on his face. "Emissary?"

Ludmilla placed her hands on the table and leaned forward. "I am in negotiation," she told the man. "You should know not to intrude."

"I was only trying . . ." Ludmilla's glare made him back up and leave. She sat back down.

"He was scared of you," Krasenoff said.

"He was scared of Ruslan Tripensky," she replied.

"Who is you."

"He doesn't know that."

They looked each other in the eye. Ludmilla was serious; Krasenoff wore his ever-familiar grin. Neither spoke while a servant placed a fresh mug of ale in front of Krasenoff.

"So, you prefer a life of killing people to marrying Connor?" Krasenoff asked.

"I don't kill people . . ." Ludmilla looked down again with a quick sigh. ". . . every day."

They sat silently for a moment. Ludmilla started to count in her head just how many people she had killed during the last five months, since she had first drawn blood from Chergin and his guards. There had been nine just that first night. As her mental tally grew, she started to lose her composure. This was the first time she had ever evaluated the results of her new career.

"I have become death," she mumbled.

"I'm sure they all deserved it," Krasenoff said.

"How would I know that?"

Krasenoff shrugged. "Were any of them defenseless? Were any of them innocent of the business? Women? Children?"

Ludmilla quickly went back over the list in her head. "No."

"Then they deserved it."

"How can you be so sure?"

"If they come at me with a sword, they deserve it." He leaned forward. "You didn't kill anyone in their sleep, did you?"

"No."

"Then you're fine. I'm sure even Father Kirill will forgive you, assuming you have the guts to tell him." He took another drink of ale.

They went silent again, Ludmilla thinking about what she should do, Krasenoff waiting for her to make that decision. She remembered that he had told her Rainey wasn't in Zenoplata. "When is Connor coming back from the khanate?"

"I don't know. He said it could be years."

Ludmilla was exasperated. "Then what is the point of me returning to Zenoplata? He's not even there."

"Because I am supposed to take you to him in the khanate, to be together."

Something in the way Krasenoff said that didn't seem right. "You don't agree with me going to the khanate?"

"No, but considering you are Ruslan Tripensky, the most feared man in Novgorod, I am endeavouring to get past my misgivings."

Ludmilla smiled. "Good. But I can't leave Novgorod at this time. The idea of Ruslan Tripensky has given me independence. I have little Svetlana to take care of."

"Who's Svetlana?"

"Never mind. What I'm trying to say is I have a life in Novgorod now, with my brother and his family. There is nothing in Zenoplata for me anymore."

"You forget little Ruslan. He misses you."

"He's barely over a year old. He probably doesn't even remember me by now. Go back to Connor. Tell him if he really loves me, he needs to come to Novgorod. If he's too busy with the grand prince's demands, I'm not interested in marrying a man who won't ever be with me."

Krasenoff pointed his finger at her. "Girl, you have no . . ."

"And I will not tolerate you calling me girl any longer."

Krasenoff smiled. "And what will you do if I do?"

Ludmilla smiled back at him. "Do you plan on leaving this tavern alive today?" She stood up and walked away.

25

1464

It was early summer when the note arrived recalling the group from Ahmed's camp back to Moscow. It had been an arduous mission, moving frequently as Ahmed continued making his small raids and gathering support, avoiding pitched battles with Mahmud's army. The signs were there. Ahmed's patience was paying off. When he did make his move directly for the throne, no retaliation from Mahmud would be possible. There would be no civil war, just Mahmud running for his life and Ahmed walking in and taking the throne. It all rather impressed Rainey. It also made him uneasy. Ahmed was a dangerous man with ambition, talent, and a following. Once in command of the Great Horde khanate, he could also be formidable threat to Muscovy. Ivan had mentioned that he would have to make a trip to see Giray this fall to discuss what to do if and when Ahmed took the throne.

In early July, Rainey finally arrived back in Zenoplata. The town hadn't changed. No one had dared to raid it or the surrounding farms after the attack from Yaroslavl. Little Ruslan was almost two years old now, running around the courtyard, nervously approaching Rainey, not sure if he knew him or not. But eventually, Ruslan took to him again, talking a mile a minute in broken, garbled sentences.

Krasenoff reported on his trip to Novgorod to find Ludmilla. He admitted to being a little scared of her after their meeting in the tavern. He even suggested that, perhaps, Rainey might want to find himself a different woman. Rainey was surprised, having never known anything to frighten Krasenoff before. Even so, he planned on going to Novgorod. Not just to try to convince Ludmilla he loved her, but also because he'd heard the grand prince might be considering some action against the city. Ivan had discovered that Novgorod had been in contact with envoys from Lithuania. Rainey was confident Ludmilla could well protect herself from individual threats, but not from the armies of Muscovy. He had suggested that an ambassador delivering a threat would suffice, leaving the army to keep the Kazans busy. Ivan agreed it was a fine idea, and promptly named Rainey as that ambassador. Rainey's first thought was not to take the job, but by now, he knew Ivan wasn't offering. It was an order.

At the end of July, he found himself at the gates of Novgorod, riding beside Krasenoff. They paid the toll to enter the city and proceeded towards Andrey Kolochoff's home. Signs of damage to the front door remained visible, reminders of that night Ludmilla arrived. A spyhole had been bored through the center of the thick oak door at about eye level. Rainey knocked and stepped back.

The slide was pulled open and two eyes examined him for a very long time. Rainey remained silent. The slide shut with a click. It took another few seconds before he heard the clank of latches being disengaged. The door slowly creaked open, revealing Andrey Kolochoff.

"Greetings," Kolochoff said, a tremor in his voice. "Welcome to Novgorod."

"You know why I'm here?" Rainey asked.

"Ludmilla."

"Is she here or out killing someone?" Krasenoff said.

Rainey gave his companion a dirty look. "I need to speak with her," he told Andrey. "And you as well."

Hesitantly, Kolochoff stepped back. "Come in." He led them to a sitting room. "Wait here. I will fetch Ludmilla."

Krasenoff settled himself into a large comfortable chair. "Guess she's not out killing anyone."

"Igor, that is not amusing," Rainey said. "Try to behave a little."

Rainey remained standing, slowly walking around the room and examining the icons, wall hangings and furniture. It looked to him that Kolochoff was still doing well, even without the busy silk trade he used to dominate. Rainey turned when he heard a noise behind him.

Ludmilla entered the room carrying a baby. Kolochoff stood behind her. Rainey tried not to show any surprise, but he felt he'd failed to accomplish that. Ludmilla remained in the doorway, a blank look on her face. No one said a word until Krasenoff spoke up.

"You said he needed to come himself. Well, here he is."

"Igor said you could be years in the khanate," Ludmilla said.

"It wasn't working well, so the grand prince recalled us," Rainey replied. "It's good to see you."

Ludmilla floated through the room and sat in a chair by the fireplace. She shifted the baby onto her lap, smiling as she tapped the child's nose with her finger."

"Whose baby?" Krasenoff asked. Rainey wanted to know, too, but hadn't known how to ask.

"This is Svetlana. She is the daughter of my brother's partner. Her family are all dead."

"You do have a habit of collecting babies," Krasenoff said.

"Igor," Rainey retorted. "I said behave." Krasenoff shrugged.

"It's all right," Ludmilla said. "Igor will ask the questions you won't."

As if to confirm her words, Rainey stood in awkward silence. Ludmilla's attention was focussed on Svetlana. Kolochoff remained in the doorway while Krasenoff looked about the room with feigned interest. This was not how Rainey had imagined the meeting going. He praised himself for knowing or figuring out what to do and doing it in any situation, but dealing with Ludmilla, or women in general, had always baffled him. He thought he loved her, but maybe she was right. Looking at her now with Svetlana brought back his warm feelings from seeing her with Ruslan. Was that all it was? Was this really about nothing more than taking her home for Ruslan?

Ludmilla finally looked up at him. "I have a contract for tonight, so I don't have much time. You need to tell me what you want. Or should I ask Igor?"

Rainey still didn't speak. Ludmilla's words stung him and he couldn't find any words to reply. Usually, when someone spoke to him like that, he could use a little anger to bring forth a good response, but he had nothing. With a little snort of exasperation, Ludmilla turned to Krasenoff.

Krasenoff shook his head and sighed. "Two things. First, let's deal with something that has nothing to do with how you two feel about each other. Namely, the grand prince has been getting reports about some boyars in Novgorod talking with Lithuania. Talking about changing allegiance."

Kolochoff stepped into the room. "I have nothing to do with that."

Rainey broke out of his spell. "Do you know who does?"

Kolochoff bit his lip, but said nothing.

"How about how widespread this notion is among the Novgorod boyars?" Rainey asked.

"I have heard rumors," Kolochoff replied. "Because my ties to you are known, I have not been approached. But I know some of my friends have been."

"It's still a minor notion," Ludmilla said. "It's not taken seriously by most of the boyars." The three men all stared at her, their eyebrow raised. "I've been hired to watch over some meetings," she hastened to explain.

"How minor a notion?" Rainey asked.

Ludmilla shrugged. "There has always been anger over Novgorod not being a free republic as it was before. Some boyars would like to go back to that, but most believe that paying tribute to Casimir and giving some power to govern here would be no different from how things are now with Ivan. Casimir may lend them a little more independence, but that is all."

"That's good," Rainey said, "but if the notion grows, the grand prince will send his army. I don't think you or your brother and his family will want to be here with Muscovy's troops at the gate."

"What do you suggest?" Kolochoff asked.

"You could transfer your business to Muscovy."

"I am supposed to be dead to those people. Besides, my contacts with the Hanseatic League require me to be here. I can't just pack up my business and move."

Rainey thought for a moment. "No, I don't suppose you can. But since you will be staying here, can you at least become my ears in the city?"

"You want me to be a spy for you?"

"Not a spy, but keep me apprised of what's going on here. I don't expect you to start taking part in plots or anything."

Kolochoff nodded. "That I can do."

"And I will need to address the Veche. I promised the grand prince that I would leave behind a threat. I think asking what they want would be another good use of an appearance."

"Did you bring credentials?" Kolochoff asked. Rainey tapped his tunic. "Then we can approach the posadnik tomorrow about you addressing the Veche the next day."

Rainey looked over at Ludmilla. "Great. And then you can come back to Zenoplata."

"No." Ludmilla didn't even look at him.

"Why would you stay here?"

Ludmilla started rocking Svetlana in her arms. "Ruslan Tripensky's business is here."

Krasenoff chuckled. Rainey was stumped. He now knew beyond a doubt what he had created in training Ludmilla. Her skills had proven useful far beyond any need to defend herself. Like his life before Zenoplata, she was now a mercenary. A sword for hire. He had never imagined that a woman would be able to sell her sword, but she had managed to hide her womanhood behind the facade of Ruslan Tripensky.

He looked over at Kolochoff. "How strong is Tripensky's reputation?"

"Very. In his . . . her first act, she penetrated a fortress and killed a man everyone had deemed unreachable."

Rainey turned to Ludmilla. "Why would you do that?"

She didn't look up. "He killed Andrey's partner. And he tried to kill Andrey and his family."

Krasenoff spoke up. "She threatened me with a tavern full of men who were proud that Tripensky used their tavern for business. I'd say 'strong reputation' is putting it lightly."

"They were just being protective of me," Ludmilla said.

"Oh, yes. The Emissary."

"The what?" Rainey asked.

"The gir . . ." Krasenoff stopped when Ludmilla scowled at him. "Ludmilla passes herself off as the contact for people seeking Tripensky's services."

Rainey looked at his friend and was surprised to see the slight flash of fear on his face. For as long as he'd known him, he had never heard him refer to Ludmilla as anything but girl. The full extent of "Tripensky's" reputation finally came into view. If Ludmilla could scare Igor . . .

"I see. You have quite the system in place."

Ludmilla ignored him. "Andrey, I wish to stay here with you and your family."

"So you want to be a sword for hire?" Rainey asked.

Ludmilla's cold look cut deep into his soul. "Isn't that what you were? What you still are? At the beck and call of the grand prince?"

Rainey felt his stomach drop. His sense that she was lost to him was overwhelming. He had been proud of what he had created in her. Had even felt love for her. Now he realized she didn't need him and that his time with Anna may have poisoned any hope that she would love him back. There was nothing he could say, but he tried anyway.

"I love you."

The silence that followed seemed to last an eternity for Rainey. His emotions flew back and forth between despair and hope. Ludmilla had no reaction to those words, but finally spoke.

"Andrey. Igor. Would you please leave the room?"

Krasenoff shot up out of the chair and almost charged out of the room. Kolochoff slowly backed out, closing the door behind him.

"Please, Connor. Sit down."

Rainey moved to the chair Krasenoff had been sitting in. He waited patiently, not wanting to threaten any chance Ludmilla would agree to come home with him. He was prepared to accept any terms, including little Svetlana or even yearly trips to Novgorod so Ruslan Tripensky could still do business. Whatever it took.

"Have you ever been a slave?" Ludmilla began.

"Of course not," Rainey replied, not sure where this was going.

"Although I have not had that title, I have felt like one. A woman in Rus is just a possession. You know that. I will never be on an equal footing with a man, or receive his respect. When I was a child, I knew my father only viewed me as a pawn in his negotiations. In Vladimir, I learned what a pawn was worth if it didn't produce children. I will admit, when I returned to Zenoplata, I felt safe. But I didn't feel free. That is why I left. You loved Anna, whether you believe it or not. I could see it. And I worried that I would never be free. Never respected. Even a peasant's wife gets some respect from her husband. I would have gotten none."

Rainey moved to respond, but Ludmilla held up her hand.

"You taught me how to defend myself. I will be forever grateful for that because it was my means to gain my freedom. Full freedom. Even more than yours. I answer to no one but myself. I am respected. Yes, I have to pretend to be a man for that, but it turned out to be easy. And useful. No one suspects a woman as a sword for hire. It allows me to go unnoticed on my assignments. And I am paid well. I will not give up my freedom to be your wife in Zenoplata."

And there it was. Rainey understood Ludmilla's feelings and her motivation. He recognized that she was very mature for someone who had not reached her twentieth birthday. He couldn't recall such self-awareness when he was that age. He was just a cocky Scot with a sword then, off to fight in Italian wars. But here and now, Ludmilla was a woman, strong, free, independent and with skills that would allow her to stay that way.

However, reality is a different thing. He thought about how much freedom from the grand prince she really had. If Ivan were to want her dead, her freedom would not be worth much. Even Ivan was a slave to his throne, palace protocols, his boyars. In the end, no one was really free.

But first, Rainey concluded, he had to dispel Ludmilla's notion that he had loved Anna.

"Anna was a spy."

He took some satisfaction from Ludmilla's look of surprise. "What?"

"She was sent to keep an eye on me. Best way to maintain residence in Zenoplata was to get me to marry her. Getting herself pregnant almost worked."

"But you knew she was a spy."

"Actually, I couldn't confirm it until after she died."

"So that's what Igor was doing last year. He hinted that to me the last time he came to Novgorod."

"He'd gone to Pskov to learn her story. What he came back with was illuminating."

"Who was she spying for?"

"Doesn't matter. Never did. I never did anything that would be worthy of a spy's report. Not because I was careful, but because I normally stay out of politics."

Ludmilla nodded. "But I could tell you loved her."

"She was carrying my child. I was responsible for that, whether she'd planned it or not. What you saw is me caring. And Anna was a very unique woman. I did like her a lot. Once you got to know her, you liked her too, right?"

Ludmilla nodded again. "I did. She never pushed me toward any of the suitors. After a while, I think, she didn't care whether I stayed or left with a new husband."

"No, she didn't. At first, she did want to get rid of you. You were a rival. Later, I don't know."

"Were you in love with me then?"

Rainey paused. That was the big question. When had he fallen in love? Was it after Anna died? Was it before, and he just didn't realize it? He could just lie and say he'd always loved her, but she deserved the truth.

"To be honest, I'm not really sure."

"But you are now?"

"Yes."

She looked down at Svetlana. "But I can't have children."

"And I told you that could very well have been Pyotr Topoff's fault." He smiled. "Regardless, we have Ruslan to raise and now, I would think, this little one."

"I would lose my freedom."

Rainey was ready for that discussion now. The thought of the grand prince not being totally free rang in his head as a good starting point.

26

The building was dark. Ludmilla would have expected at least some light for this meeting between two boyars who competed in the grain trade. She had already done some work for one of them, so she was not expecting anything out of the ordinary. Perhaps the meeting had been cancelled. Not informing Ruslan Tripensky of the cancellation was very poor form and would require a visit to the offending party.

She had left Rainey at Andrey's without a definite answer. She was beginning to believe that he did really love her, but had to weigh this against the life she had now. A life she liked. A life of respect she had never had before. But before any decision about it could take place, she had a contract to fulfill.

She entered the building cautiously, moving down a hallway into what appeared to be a large storage room. She kept to the walls, moving along slowly towards a ladder that went up to the roof. She would get a better view from up there.

The sound came from above her. The sound she knew well. A sound that made her flash back to the field outside Zenoplata after she had killed Ilya Topoff. She had been running back towards

Rainey when she heard it. The sound was ingrained in her soul because of the pain that followed.

The sound of a crossbow being shot.

Ludmilla ducked down into a ball as the bolt smacked into the wooden wall at about the same level as her heart had been. She rolled to her right, coming up and running for the darkness just past the ladder. Two more bolts slapped into the wall behind her. She saw a large crate ahead and dived in behind it, coming up in a crouch with her back to the crate. She quickly pulled her sword, ready for anything.

"Tripensky!" someone called out.

She didn't recognize the voice. She didn't dare speak for fear it would give her position away. Her assailants had crossbows, no doubt reloaded by now. She had a sword. Not a very even match. There was at least the darkness. Until, that is, a fire was lit in the center of the room. Hiding was no longer an option.

"You are going to die tonight," the voice said.

Ludmilla knew she couldn't stay there. Looking at the walls on either side of the box, she could see shadows slowly growing. The men with crossbows were getting closer by the second. She had to do something, but would have to wait until they got closer. She took a deep breath and slowly let it out, deciding on a course of action.

There were three shadows. One was by itself on the wall to her right. She decided to go after that one first, once they all had come up beside the box. But she noticed one of the shadows hung back. Still, she had no other option.

"I have waited a long time for . . . who are you?"

The sound of clanging swords drew the crossbowmen's attention. She saw the shadows turn back towards where the voice was coming from. It was an opening and she took it. Jumping up, she turned past the corner of the crate and charged the first man. He heard her coming and turned to face her, but it was too late. Her sword sliced deep into his stomach, spinning him around as she pulled it free and went after the next man, the one who had held back. He got his crossbow up. Ludmilla's sword slapped it to her right as it discharged its bolt toward the third man, making him duck. She twisted her wrist and flicked her sword up against the man's neck, slicing it open, and finishing her move by placing herself firmly behind him and holding him up as a shield. As she'd hoped, the bolt from the third man imbedded itself in this one's chest.

Dropping the dead man, she now only had one assailant left. Frantically looking around for help that would never come, he drew his sword, clutching the crossbow in his other hand.

"Who hired you?" she asked him calmly

The distant clanging of swords had stopped. With a thud, a body fell from the scaffold to the floor. Neither she nor the man in front of her knew who had died over there. Friend or foe? But Ludmilla was betting on her known foe lying in a heap.

"Do you really want to fight Ruslan Tripensky alone?"

The fear was stark on the man's face. He took two tentative steps backwards, then turned and ran for the door. Ludmilla lowered her sword and turned to face the fire. A figure was walking towards her out of the shadows. She brought her sword back up, but then smiled.

"You followed me," she said.

Rainey came into the light, his sword already back in the scabbard on his back. "Of course I did."

"And Igor?"

Rainey gestured towards the door. Krasenoff appeared with a crossbow.

"You had a crossbow and you let three men come after me?" Ludmilla asked.

"This isn't mine," Krasenoff replied. "Took it from a fellow running for his life. Besides, you're the great Tripensky. You had it handled."

Ludmilla went over to slap him. He caught her wrist before she could make contact.

"Igor," Rainey said. "You deserve it."

Krasenoff let Ludmilla's wrist go. She stood there for a moment, anger starting to subside, and then slapped his face. Hard. She turned to Rainey.

"What about that first crossbow?"

"We weren't in the building yet."

It all came to her in a rush. She could have been killed tonight. Although it was not the first time someone had tried to kill her, it was the first organized attempt on the life of Ruslan Tripensky. She now knew, only too well, that it wouldn't be the last.

"Life is getting dangerous for me in Novgorod," she said to no one in particular.

"Time to come home, little one," Krasenoff said.

Ludmilla turned to Rainey. "I don't understand. People here respect me. I am useful. You were a sword for hire. Why would anyone want me dead?"

Rainey shook his head. "I don't know. I hired my sword out for wars. My opponents really didn't know who I was. And I kept changing wars. Italy, Constantinople, Poland and Prussia. Maybe you've just become too well known here now. Maybe someone wants to take your place."

"I will have to be more careful, then."

"No," Rainey said. "The next attempt is likely to involve kidnapping you—your real self, the Emissary—to draw Tripensky out. That would leave you no way to rescue yourself." He put his arm around her shoulders. "I think you are done in Novgorod. Let's go see if you recognize the man who led this attempt on your life."

They slowly walked over to the crumpled body. The man's face was aimed upward, an abject look of surprise permanently etched in his face.

"I don't know him," Ludmilla said. Then she saw the crest on his tunic. "He's a Chergin."

"You know who the Chergins are?" Rainey asked.

"They are the family who tried to kill Andrey."

Rainey nodded. "They want you dead. And they'll try again."

Ludmilla thought of the Topoffs. They had refused to let her go, even after Pyotr went missing. That was the way of powerful people. As Tripensky, she had thought that hiring out her sword to anyone willing to pay would keep her out of politics, but she hadn't counted on the Chergins having such long memories. Rainey was right. She had to leave Novgorod.

She sheathed her sword. "We will leave after you have addressed the Veche."

* * *

The room was full of men, Novgorod's leaders, each sitting in a heavy wooden chair. The conversations created a wall of sound throughout the large room. Rainey looked around, not recognizing any of them until his eyes fell on Andrey Kolochoff, who nodded to him. He looked back up at the place he would speak from.

His nerves were on edge. The largest group he had ever addressed had been about twenty men, and they had all been soldiers. He had only issued instructions, raised their morale, gotten their spirit up for the fight. This, however, was politics. Some of these men will not want to hear what he had to say. Some may even try to shout him down.

Why did Ivan send him for this? In his mind, Rainey could see Ivan smiling.

It's a lesson. Whether he liked it or not, the grand prince was determined to make him a politician as well as a warrior. Next step, lessons from Gunter.

Rainey shook his head to clear his mind. He looked up at the stage again. *How hard could it be?* he thought to himself. Kolochoff's words rang in his head.

The pro-Lithuanian boyars will be disrespectful to you and the grand prince. Be firm with them. He wondered what he'd meant by disrespectful, but he knew what being firm meant.

The posadnik stepped onto the stage and banged a gavel three times on the table. "I call the Veche to order!"

The crowd settled down until the only sounds were of men shifting in their chairs. The posadnik continued. "This special session has been called to hear an ambassador from Muscovy." He stepped down and motioned Rainey up to the stage.

"What's the grand prince have to say for himself this time?" someone yelled from the gathering.

"Probably needs some more furs to keep his ass warm," another replied.

The crowd started laughing. Rainey stood silently, waiting for the laughter to subside.

"Who's this *mudak*?"

"Another *chinovnik* kissing Ivan's ass."

If they were trying to intimidate Rainey, it didn't work. They just angered him. Now he knew what disrespectful meant. The meeting was getting out of hand before he had even spoken a word. In armies, this kind of disrespect was countered with fear. It was time to show his version of firm. His hand flashed up over his shoulder, grabbing his sword's hilt. In a single motion, it slid out of its scabbard and came down with a bang onto the table in front of him. The wooden tabletop split in two and collapsed to the floor. The entire room went silent.

"Now that I have your attention," Rainey began. He put his sword away. "I am here to express the grand prince's concerns about possible discussions between Novgorod's boyars and the Grand Duchy of Lithuania. According to your treaty with Muscovy, such discussions are forbidden. If they are continued, there will be consequences."

"What kind of consequences?" someone yelled.

"Ones you do not want to face," Rainey replied.

"What can he do? His army is in the Kazan khanate."

"That's a long way from here."

"A lot of good a bunch of horsemen can do against our walls."

The crowd was starting to get loud again. Rainey had hoped the sword demonstration would be enough, but it wasn't. He banged his on what was left of the table.

"Listen to me!" But the crowd was beyond control now. "Listen!" he cried.

The big doors into the room crashed open. Krasenoff stepped in, aimed his arquebus and fired. Everyone in the room jumped out of their chairs and dived for the floor, except Rainey. The city's carved wooden crest high up behind him splintered into pieces.

"The man is trying to tell you something!" Krasenoff bellowed. He raised the arquebus up above his head. "See how this small hand-held cannon spread fear among you all. Now imagine one much larger, firing a larger stone. The grand prince has many such weapons. Those weapons are not in the khanate. They can come here. Do you think your walls can withstand fifty of them? It would be in your interest to listen. You can argue about it later."

The men slowly began to regain their chairs, murmuring amongst themselves. Rainey nodded to Krasenoff. He waited until everyone was seated again and quiet. Time for the carrot.

"Now, the grand prince knows you may have some grievances that he has not effectively dealt with over the last few years. I am here to record them and take them back to Moscow. It is our grand prince's desire that this fair city may be better served. Who would like to speak first?"

* * *

The first couple of days on the road from Novgorod were quiet. Ludmilla rode alongside a wagon carrying Svetlana and her nursemaid. Rainey rode at the front of the group while Krasenoff scouted ahead. Not a word was spoken. Andrey and Natalia had agreed it would be best if Svetlana went with her to Zenoplata. Rainey knew she had a lot to work out. He agreed it wouldn't be the same back in Zenoplata, but he also knew he couldn't help her make the adjustment from sword for hire to become mother to Svetlana and Ruslan. And would she love him some day? He knew he couldn't press that point, either.

When they reached the landing near the source of the Moskva River, they had to wait two days to get passage on a river boat to Zenoplata. Moving downstream was always faster than upstream. The trip took twelve days heading upstream, but only five going down.

They were sitting in the boat's bow, sharing some bread and wine. Krasenoff was at the stern to give them some privacy. Svetlana was sleeping soundly, wrapped in a cloak, the gentle swaying of the boat helping to keep her that way. It had been several days since leaving Novgorod. Rainey hoped Ludmilla had thought through what her future held. He hoped dearly that it included him.

"Everyone will be so happy when you return," Rainey said.

Ludmilla stayed silent. Although it looked like she was ignoring him, Rainey knew she was well aware of what he was trying to initiate. He had grown anxious waiting for her to start talking, but nothing had happened. It was one thing to give her time, quite another to go days without speaking.

"Please talk to me," Rainey said, trying a more direct approach.

Ludmilla finishing chewing on a piece of bread. "Why are you so different from other men?"

It was a start. Best to find out where this was going. "What do you mean?"

She sighed. "Every man I have ever met has only considered women as possessions. We have no say in our lives. We are supposed to do as we're told. We are barely given a second look. But you. You said I could marry whomever I like. I am asked what I want. You taught me to fight."

"I'm not from the Rus."

"I know. What I want is to go where you come from. Where women are treated like they are more than just baby makers."

"Scotland isn't really like that."

Ludmilla looked at Rainey. "You mean women are no better off there than they are here?"

"I didn't say that, but it isn't the heaven on earth you seem to think it is."

"So, Scottish men do not treat their women like you do?"

Rainey grinned at that. "I am unique." He grinned a little wider. "I think you'll find that women are treated differently in different cultures, but from my experience, they never have the status men do."

"But there are places where women are treated better?"

"Yes. And one of them is Zenoplata."

Ludmilla scowled at him. "That's just because you are boyar there."

"Yes, it is. And if you want to be as free as you want, you will need a duke, or a count, or a boyar who also thinks like me. But, like I said, I'm unique."

"Why are you unique?"

Rainey had never been asked that before. He just knew he was. He thought about it for a moment and came up with an answer. "My parents raised me to be this way."

"How?"

She wasn't going to let this go, Rainey thought. "I was taught to respect my mother. That isn't out of the ordinary, but she also taught me to be respectful of other girls or I'd end up with no wife. I thought I could just pay off their fathers and take one. But then my father told me that if I wanted to be happy, I would pick one who was in love with me as much as I was in love with her.

That means she has to be smart. And then he told me something odd. He said that this girl, whoever she was, would probably hate me at first. Apparently my mother hadn't been overly fond of my father in their early days together. But they grew to love each other, respect each other. If you want to see how that works, go visit the farms around Zenoplata. When peasants marry, they become one and work together, because if they don't, no family, no farm, and they die. Peasant husbands and wives have a respect for each other. My parents weren't peasants, but they behaved with each other like they were."

"I think I would have liked your mother," Ludmilla said.

"She would have liked you, too."

"Are your parents still alive?"

"I have no idea. It's been about fifteen years since I left and I haven't been back."

"Why did you leave home?"

She wants to know more about me, Rainey thought. It was a very good sign.

"I was the one with the adventuring eye. I took to the warrior training my father gave us better than my brothers did. When I was nineteen years of age, I was given this sword and sent out to find my fortune. My fortune turned out to be Zenoplata."

"So your father undertook a similar adventure in his time?"

"Not really. My grandfather was born in Germany. He fought with Prince Edward of England in France and Spain. He found his love in Spain and his fortune in Scotland with the Earl of Orkney. My father found his love with a Scottish lass. This was before he was given this sword, so he stayed in Scotland and became a knight."

"A lass?"

"A woman."

Ludmilla nodded. "And you couldn't find . . . a lass in Scotland?"

Rainey smiled. "It wasn't that. My father went on many adventures for the earl. For me, that is what I wanted to do, too. I sailed for France, hiring myself out to the Duke of Burgundy for a while. I moved on to Italy where I joined a Genoan mercenary troop. We never lacked for work in the never-ending fights between the Italian cities. Then we went to Constantinople to help defend it against the siege. When that ended, I escaped north and found myself in Kiev. Fought for the Polish king for a while until I was pretty much done with war. I headed east to find a place to settle down. Find my fortune. And as fate would have it, I saved the grand prince's life and he gave me Zenoplata."

"Which had been in my family's possession for over a century."

"And, if you marry me, it will be again."

Ludmilla frowned.

"Too soon?" Rainey asked.

"I have mixed feelings about you. I still need to sort them out."

"Take all the time you need. I'm not going anywhere anymore."

"Until the grand prince sends for you again."

* * *

The grand prince did send for Rainey. On several occasions. He led a large counter raid into the Kazan Khanate that year. His work to convert the allegiance of some boyars in Rostov began. But he was never gone long. By the time of the harvest, Ludmilla had decided that Rainey was the best man for her and agreed to marry him. She came to the conclusion that she had always loved him. She had just been confused during Anna's time in Zenoplata. After a few months of behaving like a family and of Rainey courting her instead of staying aloof, her love for him bloomed again. It was like a flower opening after a long winter.

The wedding was the affair of the season. Of course, Father Kirill presided at the ceremony, held out in the town square so everyone could attend and see. The whole town celebrated for almost a week; it didn't hurt that the harvest festival coincided with the wedding. For the next three days, Rainey and Ludmilla never left their room. Orina had to leave food outside their door.

As the year came to an end during Christmastime, even better news spread through the town. Ludmilla was with child

27

1467

The snow was still deep. It had been a hard winter, but the sun was warming the landscape. Rainey's horse struggled through the drift, the thin ice crust collapsing under the weight. It seemed like it would take forever to get clear of the forest and find the road back to Zenoplata.

Rainey had gone out to one of the farms. Many of the farmers had come into town looking for provisions as the winter dragged on longer than usual. One farm family had not been heard from, so Rainey loaded a small wagon with supplies and set out by himself to make sure they were surviving. He found their home buried in snow. Inside, the farmer and his wife were sick in bed with their three young children struggling to take care of them. It didn't help that the oldest was only eight. They had run out of food three days before Rainey appeared like a spectre out of the darkness. He was thankful that they still had enough fuel to keep a fire burning, or they all likely would have frozen to death. He stayed with them for four days, digging out the house and teaching the eldest how to cook and nurse their parents back to health. As he stood at the door ready for the long ride back to town, the three children hugged him tightly, not wanting him to leave. From their bed, the farmer and his wife blessed him so profusely that he thought he was bound for sainthood. He smiled as he rode away. As his father had taught him, fear may be a useful tool to control people, but kindness was a much stronger force for earning loyalty. His people knew he would look out for them; hence they would be less inclined to switch allegiance to whoever came along to threaten them next. Besides, he had never been a cruel man. All the blessings he had just gotten made him feel very good about himself. Maybe he would become a saint, despite Father Kirill's suspicions that he had never really converted to the Orthodox religion.

The forest finally came to an end and he could see Zenoplata in the distance. He thought of Ludmilla, soon to be giving birth to their second child. Their first, Helena, would soon be two years of age. With Ruslan and Svetlana in the home, Ludmilla and Orina had their hands full. Grigori kept threatening to move into town to get away from the children, but these were empty threats. He loved them, too. Even Krasenoff showed a soft side when around the children. Svetlana seemed to be quite taken by the gruff bogatyr. It was beginning to be a regular occurrence to find Krasenoff sleeping in front of the fireplace with Svetlana snoozing in his lap.

Rainey lifted his face to the sun, relishing its warmth. Another year had begun. He wondered what it would bring. What would the grand prince require of him this year? Time would tell, but he would always have the peace of Zenoplata to come back to. No one had raided his lands since the Yaroslavl attack four years earlier. Reputation had its benefits. He pushed his horse forward out of the trees. The snow was shallower here and his horse, seeing the town and knowing it was home, picked up speed, anticipating a warm stable and feed. Rainey did not try to slow the horse down, also wanting to make town as soon as possible.

Many townspeople were out in the chill afternoon air, taking in the sun. Many greeted him as he rode by, asking about the farmer he had gone to visit. They were glad to hear that the family was all right. As he entered the courtyard, he could see Ludmilla standing at her window. She smiled down at him and beckoned for him to come up after he'd put away his horse. Grigori came out the front door.

"Good afternoon, Boyar Rainey," Grigori said. "Was it a good trip?"

Rainey nodded. "Petrey and his wife were pretty sick, but the children are fine. They hadn't eaten anything for three days, but I fixed that. They should all be up and about in a few days, I should think."

"Good to have you home." Grigori leaned in. "Ruslan has been a holy terror. I can't control him. He broke one of the paddock doors swinging on it. He hit me with a stick. And he was throwing his food at Orina."

Rainey laughed. "Can't control? Or not wanting to control? I know you, Grigori. You were probably encouraging him."

"I . . . I . . . I . . ." Grigori was frowning, but Rainey could see the light in his eyes. He knew the source of much of Ruslan's mischief.

"Just put my horse away," Rainey said, handing him the reins. Dropping his gloves just inside the door, he went directly up the stairs to Ludmilla's room. As he entered, Ludmilla was sitting in a big chair watching Helena on the floor, playing with some wooden blocks. A small fire in the fireplace warmed the room.

"Welcome home, husband," she said. "I hope all is well at Petrey's farm?"

"Yes. The parents were sick, but the children were just hungry. I'll have Igor pass by on his next patrol and check up on them."

"They must have been happy to see you."

"I had to dig my way in. I think the children were scared to death about who was out there making all that noise until I actually made it into the house with the food. I became a saint to them."

Ludmilla shook a finger at him. "Don't talk like that around Father Kirill. You're not allowed to call yourself a saint."

Rainey smiled. "I might just do that to keep him happy. Him giving me a lecture is the best part of his week."

"That's because you argue with him. He thinks you are still attached to your Latin church."

"He knows I was never that attached to it, as he knows I am not overly attached to his, either." He got down on the floor next to Helena. "How's my little girl?"

"Deda," Helena said without looking up from her wood blocks.

He looked up at Ludmilla. "At least she acknowledged me."

"Someday, you will be more interesting than her blocks."

"And how are you doing?"

Rainey could almost see a glow around Ludmilla's face. He loved her so much. He wondered if his love for her had always been there, even back to that first night when she'd come at him with a dagger.

"I'm ready to get this baby out of me," Ludmilla said.

"You have another month, right?"

"That is what all the women in town say. Orina is now even more sure it will be a son."

Rainey nodded. "Where are the other two?"

"Svetlana is taking a walk in town with Igor. Ruslan is no doubt planning another way to irritate Grigori."

"And Grigori will love it."

"Yes, he will."

A noise in the courtyard alerted them to a rider arriving. Rainey went to the window to find one of the black knights lowering himself from his horse.

"Looks like a message from Moscow."

Ludmilla sighed. "The grand prince wants you for something, again. I will expect you to be home for your son's birth."

"I'll do my best," Rainey said as he left the room.

Gerhard was standing at the foot of the stairs. "Gerhard, come in. What is the news from Moscow?"

They headed into the great room. Gerhard handed him a scroll. "News is not good. The grand prince wants you to return to Moscow with me."

Rainey unfurled the scroll, recognising Von Markenburg's flowing script. The concern on his face became ever darker.

"Is she still alive?" he asked.

"She was when I left, but no one knows what her affliction is."

"We'll leave first thing in the morning." Rainey looked up to see Orina and Grigori in the doorway. "I'm going to Moscow. Prepare my travel requirements. And see that Gerhard has a place to sleep tonight and provisions for the return journey."

* * *

Moscow was quiet when they arrived. It reminded Rainey of when the grand prince's father had died. A sense of despair hung over the Kremlin as he passed through the gates. He was met by Von Markenburg.

"How is she?" Rainey asked.

"She has gone to sleep and hasn't woken up for two days now," Von Markenburg replied. "The grand prince has isolated himself with her. He will talk only to you."

"Where is young Ivan?"

"I have him protected in the back courtyard, with four of my knights."

Rainey knew Von Markenburg would have immediately moved the heir to Muscovy's throne into a safe and guarded area. Now he knew where that was. Von Markenburg signaled to Gerhard.

"Take Boyar Rainey up to the royal apartment."

Rainey slowly entered the living quarters of the grand prince of Muscovy. He had never ventured into this part of the Kremlin before. On the bed, Maria of Tver lay unconscious. Ivan was kneeling at her side, her left hand encased in his, head lowered and almost touching the bed.

"My prince," Rainey said hesitantly.

Ivan slowly raised his head. "Connor, thank you for coming."

"What do the healers know?"

Ivan shook his head. "They don't know what it is, but they are sure it is a poison."

"Poison? They are sure?"

"Yes. And they have told no one else."

"So Gunter doesn't know."

"No one, just the healers, myself and you."

"He's very good at finding out things."

"Yes, he is, and I will tell him, so when the time is right he can go and find out who did this. But he will not become aware of what I want you to do until you've done it."

Rainey stayed silent. He felt a familiar twinge of discomfort, having no idea what Ivan wanted of him. Ivan stood and crossed to the fireplace, keeping his back to Rainey.

"You know where my son is?"

"He's safe in the back courtyard with four of Gunter's knights."

Ivan lowered his head. "Do you find that unusual, considering Gunter does not know Maria has been poisoned?"

Rainey was honest. "Not overly. When a royal member of the family falls ill, poisoned or not, the line of succession has to be protected. Your son is the only heir. There is no other. Considering the fight your father went through, I would have done the same as Gunter did. He was there for that."

Ivan nodded. "Do you think I'm being overly suspicious?"

Rainey smiled. "You're the grand prince of Muscovy. For you, I don't think there is such a thing as being overly suspicious. Remember, all those years ago, I found you facing down three armed men."

Ivan turned. "Should I be suspicious of you?"

"Of course," Rainey replied without hesitation. "I would expect nothing less. But I do let my history with you speak for itself."

Ivan moved back to the bed and gazed down on Maria. "I'm worried for my son. If Maria dies, there won't be anyone I can count on to be regent if I die. With Maria here to look out for him, though, I would have many choices." He looked up at Rainey. "I don't trust my brothers not to take the throne for themselves.

With Gunter in control of my son, he can determine who will be regent."

"You don't trust him to follow your wishes?"

Ivan looked at Rainey as if he had said something idiotic. "Do you?"

Rainey had to think about that for a moment. "His ways do not endear us to trust him, but he has been a loyal protector of your house for many years."

"Only because we pay him."

"And he's a mercenary. Loyalty can be bought. You might not like the power he wields in your lands, but he wields it very well and to your benefit."

"And if both Maria and I are gone, he will go to the next highest bidder. He will not care if it leads to civil war or not." Ivan looked at him curiously. "Were you bought when you were a mercenary?"

Rainey shifted uneasily. "Yes, and no. Yes, I was paid, but I tried to choose which side of a conflict to fight for. It would have been easier in the short run to fight for the highest bidder. It was my good fortune that I never really needed any payment."

"You continue to fascinate me, Connor Rainey, my great Celt." Ivan put his arm around Rainey's shoulder. He leaned into his ear and lowered his voice.

"This must not leave this room. If the time comes, I want you to take my son to Zenoplata with you. When you leave, you must do so quietly and hurriedly. I do not want him missed until it is too late to catch you from reaching your home. He will stay there with you until such time as Gunter can expose the cabal that wants me dead. Gunter will be hurt, but he won't force the issue."

"How long do you think I will have to wait here?" Rainey was concerned about not being there for Ludmilla when the baby arrived. He was in no position to turn down the grand prince of Muscovy. But even had Ivan been just a friend, Rainey would still have helped him as asked.

"I don't know," Ivan answered. "Maria may yet recover. I hope it will be before your next child is born." Ivan looked back at his wife on the bed. "Maria will be very angry with me if I keep you from that."

"I'll need an extra reason to be in Moscow. Just consoling you will only be good for a day or two."

Ivan nodded. "There is some business here that I think you would be interested in taking over. It will occupy you during your time here." Ivan paused. "I have no other demands for you beyond being here—if the time comes—for my son to leave with you."

"Thank you, my prince."

"We are alone here, Connor. You may call me Ivan."

It was hard watching his friend hurting so much. Ivan deeply loved Maria. She had been twelve and he thirteen years old when they were betrothed. It was arranged, but they learned from each other how to love. Rainey couldn't figure out what advantage, other than making Ivan very sad and even more angry, could be gained by poisoning Maria.

"I don't understand why anyone would want to poison Maria."

"No one would. But she drank some wine that was meant for me."

Rainey grimaced. That was serious treason.

* * *

Three days later, Maria died. Word came to Rainey during a meeting with two boyars who needed supplies for their metal-working business. Although iron was in good supply, other metals were not. They had recipes from the Ottomans for some new alloys but needed a source of raw materials. Rainey knew he could get supplies from Andrey Kolochoff in Novgorod. Evidently, the grand prince knew this too.

He entered the Kremlin to find Von Markenburg waiting for him.

"When did she die?" Rainey asked.

"About three hours ago," the chancellor replied. "The grand prince is in the great hall waiting for us. And just to warn you, he is very angry."

"Understandable."

"Yes, but even I don't know where he will direct that anger. I have yet to find out who killed his wife."

"Don't worry, Gunter. He knows you'll figure it out eventually like no one else can."

"Thank you for the vote of confidence. I'm glad I'm not going in there alone."

They entered the hall to find Ivan slumped on his throne. It was difficult to see whether he was mourning or seething with anger. It didn't take long to find out.

"Gunter," he said curtly. "What have you found?"

Von Markenburg stepped gingerly forward. "My prince, we have identified a possible kind of poison that was used. My people are tracing where the ingredients for it could come from. I hope to have an answer by the morning."

"Good," Ivan said. "I'll know which direction to send my armies for retribution. How is my son?"

"Safe in the Kremlin. I have assigned all my knights for duty in his defense."

"I want to see him."

"My Prince, that would not be wise. You would identify where he is being kept to our enemies."

Ivan scowled, but did not argue with Von Markenburg. "Yes, that is true." He looked to Rainey. "Connor, about our business. I think it is time."

Rainey nodded. "Yes, my prince."

Ivan got up and left through the back of the throne room.

"What business is that?" Von Markenburg asked Rainey.

Rainey had a made-up story prepared. "Preparation. I will lead his army of retribution. I'll just need you to tell me where I'm going."

28

Rainey crept along the dark hallway. As he turned the corner, he met up with Ivan.

"No one followed you?" Ivan asked.

"No."

Ivan looked over his shoulder. "They are keeping him in the north gatehouse. I have set up horses for you both, and provisions nearby, in the stables. You will be able to get into the gatehouse through the window facing the stables. I don't know what room he'll be in, but the gatehouse isn't large."

"How many black knights are there?"

"I don't know. I couldn't ask Gunter without giving him a hint I might be trying to free the boy."

Rainey gripped Ivan's shoulder. "I'll manage. If I have to kill one of them, I won't have much of a head start."

"Then don't kill one. Godspeed, my friend."

They headed off in opposite directions. Rainey made his way through the Kremlin corridors and across the courtyard to the stables by the north gate. Inside, he found his own horse was saddled and ready to go, along with a mount for the little prince.

He slowly opened the door a bit to take a look at the gatehouse. What he saw was not encouraging.

Standing in the open window that he was supposed to go through was Gerhard.

Of all the black knights, Rainey liked only one of them. And that was Gerhard. They had struck up a friendship during their time in the khanate. Rainey was never sure if that friendship had an ulterior motive or not, but the solemn German had opened up to him. He was contemplating how he could talk his way past Gerhard when a shadow passed by the stables. It caught Gerhard's attention as well.

"Who goes there?" the knight called out.

The shadow stopped. "You dare ask me that in my own Kremlin?"

The figure stepped into the light cast from the window. It was Ivan.

"My prince, I apologise," Gerhard said firmly, no sense of fear in his voice. "We are being extra careful in these dangerous times."

"You are on guard duty?"

"Yes, my prince."

"But this window looks into the courtyard. Shouldn't you be looking out from the wall?"

"There are two knights up there now."

"Then what are you doing here?"

"I am the reserve."

Ivan had drawn Gerhard's attention away from the stables. Rainey slipped out and made for a gatehouse door. He breathed a sigh of relief when he discovered it was unlocked. Now he hoped another black knight wasn't standing just inside. Opening it slowly, he saw a room with two doors at the far end. One was open. Through it he could hear Ivan and Gerhard talking.

"So, I remember you arriving with Gunter at …." Ivan's voice faded away and Rainey couldn't hear everything he was saying. ". . . you were pretty young then."

"We all were then. You were just a child."

"Yes, I was. But old enough to start training with a sword. Who was that old knight who trained me?"

Rainey smiled. Ivan had been around the black knights long enough to be able to lengthen any conversation. Hearing the ease with which the prince was talking, Rainey got the impression this wasn't the first time he reminisced with one of them.

Rainey stepped past the door through which Ivan was visible. To his relief, Gerhard was out of view.

"He was a crusty old man and I hated him," Ivan rambled on, "but he was an excellent teacher. I had dreams of having him killed when my training was finished, but when . . ."

Rainey wasn't sure, but as he went on past the open door, he thought he saw Ivan wink at him.

He crossed to a second door and slowly opened it. Inside, young Ivan, known as the Molodoy, lay sleeping on a bed. Rainey tiptoed in and clamped his hand over the boy's mouth. He awoke with surprise, fear in his eyes, but they softened when he saw Rainey's face.

"Get dressed," Rainey whispered. "We're going on an adventure."

"Where?"

"If I told you that, it wouldn't be an adventure." He placed a finger against his lips as a signal to the boy. "Now, we will play a game. Let's see if we can sneak by Gerhard without him knowing."

The boy smiled as he dressed. "Is that my father talking to him?" He was playing along, Rainey was glad to hear, whispering too.

"Yes. He is helping us with our game."

The boy smiled even bigger and hurriedly finished dressing. Rainey checked the door. Ivan and Gerhard were laughing about something. He went back to the bed and arranged pillows under the blankets to make it look like the boy was still there sleeping.

"Let's go," he said. Together they stepped out of the room.

"You are pretty loyal to Gunter," Ivan was saying.

"He brought me into the order, saved my life at least twice. Of course, I saved his three times, so he owes me one."

Ivan laughed, stealing a momentary glance at Rainey and his son as they passed out of the gatehouse. "I promise not to try and kill you, then. Can't have Gunter attacking me. It wouldn't look good at court."

The laughter died down behind them as they reached the stables. Rainey and the young prince each took their horse and guided it out of the stable, out of view from the gatehouse. They walked silently before the boy spoke.

"Where to first?"

It was still a game to him. "To the west gate. We're going for a ride. Pull up your hood. We don't want anyone to know you're leaving." Rainey pulled his up as well. As they approached the gate, he saw one guard. He stopped to help Ivan Molodoy up onto his horse. As he mounted himself, he saw the guard raise his hand in salute. *That's odd*, he thought.

He urged his horse forward until he reached the guard. The man removed his helmet.

"About time you got here," Krasenoff said.

Rainey shook his head. "Why am I not surprised?"

"You think you could just ride out of the Kremlin with the Molodoy without someone at this gate to let you out?"

"Our grand prince thinks of everything. I didn't even know you were in Moscow."

"The grand prince sent me a separate note."

"Where is the real guard?"

"He'll be back in another hour. I told him I'd stay here until he got back. Something about feeling ill. Must have been something he ate."

"Something you gave him, no doubt."

Krasenoff just grinned. "Get going. I'll catch up with you."

* * *

They rode hard through the night, alternating spells of galloping with a slower gait for the horses' benefit, and to give Rainey a chance to check up on the Molodoy. He didn't have to worry. The young prince was wide awake, not wanting to miss any part of this adventure.

As the horizon began to show signs of light behind them, they came across a farmhouse nestled in the woods. A man was outside chopping wood. When he saw them, he ran for his house and slammed the door. Rainey rode into the yard and stopped. He nodded to the Molodoy.

"You're the royal. Make a command."

The boy smiled broadly. "Peasant," he shouted. "In the name of Grand Prince Ivan of Muscovy, I command you to come out and speak with us."

"Show him your medallion," Rainey encouraged him.

He pulled at the chain around his neck to expose a large circle of gold. He held it out proudly. "I am Ivan Molodoy, son of the grand prince."

Rainey turned back towards the door, waiting for a reaction. He couldn't imagine how the conversation inside the house was going.

Finally, he heard the door being unbarred. Hesitantly, the man reappeared, his hands tightly gripping his hat to his chest. He ventured a look at the two riders in his yard and quickly lowered his eyes.

The Molodoy tucked the medallion back under his tunic. "Boyar Rainey, you may address the peasant."

Rainey had to bite back a laugh. "My good man, we need to rest ourselves and our horses. Some water as well and a bed for the Molodoy."

"You are Boyar Rainey?" the man asked, excitement in his voice.

"He seems to know of you," the Molodoy said. He turned to the man. "Tell me how you know of the boyar."

"The stories of the battle at Zenoplata. It was a great victory."

Rainey looked at the Molodoy. "It wasn't a real battle."

"You will tell me these stories once I've rested," the Molodoy said to the man.

Once inside, they ate some of their provisions, sharing them with the family. The Molodoy finally showed signs of exhaustion and dozed off in his chair. Rainey carried him to a bed and lay down on a pile of furs beside him, closing his eyes and quickly drifting off.

He dreamed of Ludmilla, surrounded by all the children. It was peaceful, but he awoke instantly when he heard the door creaking open. He reached for his sword as a silhouetted figure, backlit by the early morning sun, filled the doorway.

"You got pretty far last night," Krasenoff said. "I wasn't sure I was going to catch up with you."

Rainey relaxed. "Anyone in pursuit?"

"I didn't see anyone. No alarm went up before I left the city. I think you were good until everyone woke up this morning."

Rainey got himself up off the floor. He heard the Molodoy move behind him.

"Igor," he said groggily. "Are you part of the game too?"

Krasenoff looked at Rainey with disdain. "You told him this is a game?"

Rainey shrugged. "It was easier."

"My mother is dead, isn't she," the Molodoy said.

Rainey turned to him. He saw no tears, no anguish, just acceptance. "When did you know?"

"You seemed sad for most of the trip when we were supposed to be excited," the boy said. "Am I in danger?"

"No, but it is safer for you to be under my protection for a while."

The Molodoy nodded. "Good. Only Gerhard of the black knights would even talk to me."

"The peasant knows he's the Molodoy," Krasenoff said. "Even tried to defend him against me. I had to knock him down. You are leaving a trail."

"If they know I have him," Rainey replied, "they'll know where I'm going and that I'll have an entire town protecting him. Did you hurt the peasant?"

Krasenoff shrugged. "He got back up."

* * *

They arrived in Zenoplata late in the afternoon. Many of the townspeople smiled and waved as they rode through the streets towards the house. None seemed to recognize the Molodoy, which was fine by Rainey. They would protect him regardless of who he was because he was with their boyar. In the courtyard, they dismounted, Grigori running out to take the reins.

"Another child?" Grigori inquired. "At least he's older. More likely to behave himself."

"Do you know . . ." the Molodoy began.

Rainey cut him off. "No, he doesn't know who you are. And you're not going to tell him."

Grigori leaned towards Rainey. "Who is he?"

"Just put the horses away," Rainey snapped. "You'll find out soon enough. Igor should be along within the hour."

He led the boy to the door, which opened to reveal Orina standing inside. "Welcome home, boyar." She looked at the Molodoy. "And who is this?"

"Set an extra place for dinner," Rainey said. "All will be revealed then. Is Ludmilla upstairs?"

* * *

Ludmilla heard them coming up the stairs. She shifted a sleeping Helena from her lap onto some blankets on the floor. She struggled to stand up. It was then she noticed the wet stain on her dress.

The door opened. "How is my—"

"Get Orina, NOW!" she bellowed.

Rainey froze in the doorway, shock on his face.

"GO!" she screamed at him. At her feet, Helena woke up and started to cry.

Rainey bolted towards the stairs, leaving a frightened-looking young boy standing in the hallway.

"Who are you?" she spat.

"I . . . I . . . I'm not supposed to tell."

Ludmilla held her arm out. "Help me to the bed."

The boy ran forward, taking her arm. They moved towards the bed as the sound of several footsteps thundered up the stairs. Orina was the first one in, charging across the room like a bull.

"Out of the way, boy," she said, pushing him sideways. Ludmilla was now on her back, a short shot of pain making her cry out.

"But she isn't due . . ." she heard Rainey say.

Orina cut him off. "Tell that to the baby." She turned to Ludmilla. "You are early, so maybe the baby wants out fast."

Ludmilla gripped Orina's hand, hard. "Let's hope." Sweat was starting to form on her forehead. "Connor, get Helena out of here. She doesn't need to hear this." She was remembering how noisy and terrifying it had been when Helena herself was born. Her eyes found her daughter on the floor. The girl wasn't crying. In fact, she was wobbling on her feet, steadied by the boy who held both her hands. They were both smiling. Another contraction made her wince.

"This will be fast," Orina said. "Your pain is already coming very close together. There might not be time for the midwife to get here."

"We know what we're doing this time," Ludmilla assured her, although not so sure herself. She closed her eyes as soon as she confirmed that Rainey, the boy and Helena had left the room.

* * *

As promised, the labor was quick. Ludmilla stayed awake only long enough to find out she had a son. She fell asleep knowing Rainey would be pleased. When she awoke several hours later, she found her room was full of people. Rainey, the children, Orina, Grigori, Father Kirill, the town midwife, Krasenoff, even the boy who had helped her to the bed. They all had worried looks on their faces, but when she blinked a few times and frowned, everyone broke out in smiles. There was almost a chorus of relief sweeping through the room.

Orina and the midwife came to the bedside. "You gave us a start, girl," Orina said. "No one has ever slept like that after giving birth."

"I was tired."

"From what? You were in labor for less than an hour." Orina turned to the crowd. "She will be fine. Now, everyone out."

"I want Connor to stay."

Everyone was shuffling out of the room. Rainey appeared beside Orina. "How is my brave wife feeling?"

"Never mind me," Ludmilla retorted. "How is the baby boy?"

Rainey looked over at the midwife. "The boy was a little early," the midwife said, "so he's a little small. But he has all his parts and can scream like a devil. I think he will grow strong over the next few weeks. It's time for nursing. Would you like to feed him?"

Ludmilla brightened up. "Yes, please."

The midwife went to fetch the baby. Orina was finished fussing with the covers. "I will leave you two to name the boy." She winked at Rainey. "I expect a good, strong Rus name." She left the room.

Ludmilla began to nurse the baby as soon as the midwife returned with him. He had screamed lustily until he found Ludmilla's breast.

"He's much more aggressive than Helena was," Ludmilla said.

"He can scream like a banshee, too," Rainey replied.

"Banshee?"

"They're from Irish folklore. A rather noisy spirit."

Ludmilla looked down on her new boy. She felt herself swelling with pride to have produced a son for her husband. She imagined he would grow up and become a boyar in his own right. She assumed that Ruslan, as the first-born, would inherit Zenoplata, but there were many other opportunities. Perhaps this second son would inherit the sword and go out and do great things like Rainey had done. So many possibilities. But Rainey had said earlier that children must grow into their own destinies. All the parents should do is guide them, he insisted, and that included Helena and Svetlana.

"What should we name him? And no, not after the grand prince."

"He's going to want us to name one of our children after him."

"He can have our last one."

"And if it's a girl?"

"We'll call her Ivana."

Rainey laughed. "You really want to have me killed one day, don't you?"

Ludmilla gave him a mischievous smile. "I've been trying since the first day we met. My new method is to smother you with children until you die of exhaustion."

"Oh, so that's your plan. Well, I think I can keep baby making down to a minimum."

"Sure you can," Ludmilla teased. "All you have to do is resist me when I take all my clothes off. So far, that hasn't worked out too well for you."

Rainey let out a big laugh. "So true. Let's get back to naming the little banshee."

"We could call him Banshee."

"No, those spirits are female. Worse, they herald the death of someone in the family."

"Oh. So inappropriate. Do you have a Celtic name in mind?"

"We live in the Rus. We should keep with Rus traditions."

Ludmilla nodded and smiled. "We have to choose a name Father Kirill can pronounce."

"He's a great screamer. Although I don't think I want to name him for that."

"But he will be great. So, I would like to name him Maksim Connoryevich Raynykov."

Rainey thought for a minute. "Maksim. I like it. Maksim it is."

Maksim had finished nursing. He licked his lips, let out a gurgle and once again began to scream.

"Although he will be known as the Great Screamer in this house if he doesn't learn to sleep," Ludmilla commented. She shifted Maksim and he quieted down. "There. Now, tell me who the new boy is. I don't think I've ever seen him before. He dresses rather fine."

Rainey hesitated. "He's Ivan Molodoy."

Ludmilla's eyes widened. "The grand prince's son? What's he doing here?"

Rainey went on to explain that Maria of Tver had died of poison meant for the grand prince. It had been decided the Molodoy would be safer in Zenoplata than in Moscow while the search for the traitors was undertaken by Von Markenburg and his black knights.

"Who else knows?" Ludmilla asked.

"I plan on making it common knowledge," Rainey replied. "It will be too difficult to keep it a secret."

"But it could be dangerous for us. For the whole town."

"No one is going to come looking. Remember, no one takes on Zenoplata without an army. I don't think our traitors have one. And if an army should come calling, they'll be noticed, and the grand prince will bring his. And if anyone comes with a smaller party and tries anything, they have to get by me, Igor and you, not to mention Grigori and his pitchfork."

"Don't forget Orina and her kitchen knives."

Rainey chuckled. "Yes, her too. The whole town will be honored to protect him. Any strangers will be closely watched. So you can see, this is the safest place for him because everyone knows what a challenge it will be to get to him here."

"I agree," Ludmilla replied. But she still felt uneasy about it all.

29

The people of Zenoplata were pleased to be the Molodoy's protectors. They considered it a great honor. They also all firmly believed they were up to the task. Their loyalty to Rainey was strong because of how he had led them. He saw the same type of leadership in the grand prince, which is why he liked him. However, a good dose of fear helped reinforce the command from the throne. One cannot always be kind when hard decisions needed to be made.

By the end of the week, the townsfolk had experienced about all the excitement they could handle. There was a festival, of course, for the birth of the new baby. Father Kirill performed the christening. He seemed pleased with the name Maksim, which pleased Rainey. He knew the priest would find some way of expressing his distaste if he didn't like the name. Rainey had no desire to give him a lifelong stick to hit him with.

The festival took on a whole new meaning with the Molodoy's presence. The people showed a certain level of reverence for the boy. Rainey suggested that he allow the people to be more open to him. When he became grand prince, he would know that the people of Zenoplata would be his most loyal subjects. The

Molodoy started asking them questions, asking about their traditions, and showing curiosity about their lives. This was a major change from his life in the Kremlin, which Rainey wanted to be an especially good experience.

By the end of the week, the Molodoy found himself pushed away from center stage when Ludmilla finally came into the streets with little Maksim. At first, the young prince felt some resentment, but soon realized he was just as curious as everyone else about the new baby. He had become one with the townspeople by then. Everyone asked him what he thought about it all. He asked what life would be like for the new baby. All the while, he had a shadow. Two in fact. Krasenoff was always a discreet distance away and little Svetlana clung to the prince's side.

In the house, things also changed dramatically. The Molodoy had never had so many other children around him. Ruslan changed from finding ways to irritate Grigori to playing around the Molodoy and going on adventures in town. Ludmilla allowed Ruslan to go into town for the first time without adult supervision. She knew he wouldn't stray far from the Molodoy's side, and that Krasenoff would never be too far away.

As with everything in life, things eventually calmed down. When the newness of Zenoplata wore off, the Molodoy began to remember that his mother had died and that he was a great distance from his father. Although Rainey had always been a hero to him because of stories his father had told, he was still a substitute for his real family. Rainey took him hunting, to visit farmers, whatever he could think of to keep the boy close and know there was love for him in Zenoplata. But having no word from Moscow was not helping. The Molodoy began worry aloud that maybe his father was dead, too.

It would be two months before a message finally arrived. It told Rainey that the source of the poisons had been tracked to the Kazan khanate. The attempt on the grand prince's life was likely retaliation after the many strong raids Muscovy had undertaken into Kazan's territories. Ivan was now planning a far more massive campaign that would put the Kazans in their place once and for all.

Rainey well remembered the events of two years ago. Ahmed had finally driven Mahmud out of Sarai and taken control of the Great Horde. His first act as khan had been to raise his army and march towards Muscovy for no apparent reason. By the time Muscovy heard about this expedition, Haci Giray had routed and dispersed it. After that, Ahmed settled for his regular tribute, expending his military might to the south on the Crimean khanate. Ivan was looking forward to the day he could pitch aside his vassalage to the khan. But for now, with Ahmed's attention elsewhere, it was safe to assume he wouldn't interfere with Muscovy's vengeance on the Kazans.

The note from Moscow continued by directing that by the following spring, Rainey would lead the excursion into Kazan territory. Rainey would be required to raise forces for this army from his people. The note concluded by saying it was time for the Molodoy to experience how warfare was carried out, under the tutelage of someone who knew what he was doing. Perhaps some training for the boy would be appropriate.

Rainey rolled up the scroll. Another war. He didn't want to embroil himself in another war. At least he would be in command, so perhaps he could keep the fighting to a minimum. But the chance to keep the Molodoy's mind off his family by beginning his military training struck Rainey as a great idea. Ludmilla agreed and wanted to participate. The two of them would show the boy how moves worked in both offense and defense, allowing the training sessions to move along quickly. Even as a young boy, the Molodoy would be able to defend himself when they headed into Kazan territory.

Preparations for the expedition continued all through the summer and into the fall. A pause took place so the harvest could be completed before the first snow. All was well, but Rainey lived with an uneasy feeling. Ludmilla began to notice his customary outings to his favorite thinking spot were becoming more frequent. She decided to follow him out one day and found him sitting by the river.

"Something is bothering you, husband," she began. "It has been bothering you for a while. Tell me what it is and perhaps I can help."

"That's the problem," Rainey replied. "Something doesn't feel right and I don't know what it is."

"Is it the training for the men?"

"No. Igor has that well in hand."

"Is it about the khanate you are going to attack?"

Rainey didn't answer. Ludmilla knew she was close to the answer.

"You don't believe the khanate is responsible for the death of the grand prince's consort."

"I don't know," Rainey replied. "I'm sure the poisons came from there. Gunter doesn't make those kinds of mistakes. But what would be the advantage to the Kazans? They don't have an army big enough to attack Muscovy. And changing grand princes wouldn't deflect Muscovy's course of action for at least a few more years. The army would still be well led."

Ludmilla sat down beside him. "If the grand prince is dead, what happens then?"

"A regency would be set up to guide Ivan Molodoy as grand prince."

"Who would be the regent?"

"One of the grand prince's brothers, I suppose, depending on who he had chosen. Considering the old rules of succession, it would be the next oldest brother, the one who would succeed to the throne. Ivan's father, Vasily, fought a long civil war to bypass those rules, but . . ."

"Perhaps one of the brothers poisoned Maria?"

"That's what I thought at first, but there would still be too many obstacles between him and the throne. The grand prince is well liked by the boyars. They are not so fond of the others. The army would be more likely to follow me than any of them. And they would need to get Gunter on their side because of his influence with the court. But there is no way any of the brothers could pay Gunter enough to give up the grand prince."

"So, who else is there?"

"I don't know. Regardless, it would take someone inside the Kremlin to make such an attempt possible. I can't think of any group that would have those kind of inside contacts and still gain any advantage from the grand prince's death."

Ludmilla sat in deep thought. She remembered how her father had attempted to kill the grand prince. "My father tried to kill him. Did you ever figure out why?"

"No. That was a mystery that hasn't been solved."

"Could they be connected?"

"It was seven years ago."

"Still."

She watched Rainey as he looked up at the sky, a now familiar trait when he went into deep thought. She knew he was looking at the problem from this new perspective. He suddenly looked at her.

"Seven years ago, what city was causing the grand prince the most problems?" Rainey asked.

"I was fifteen. I didn't concern myself with politics."

"But your father did. And he had a deal with the Topoffs to route the silk trade around Moscow to Novgorod. If the grand prince had died then, the turmoil that followed could have given Novgorod a chance to break from its vassalage to Muscovy."

"What has that to do with what is happening now?"

"Your brother mentioned to me during my last visit to Novgorod that a movement has been growing to seek Lithuania's protection against Muscovy. Something like that was taking place seven years ago."

"Novgorod is behind the assassination attempt?"

"It makes sense. For now, the Molodoy would still need a regency. But if they wait too long, he would inherit the throne with the same council of advisors, namely me, Gunter and a few of the other boyars. Nothing would change. But in a regency, there could be a fight."

"Giving Novgorod a chance to break away," Ludmilla said.

"Same plan as seven years ago," Rainey said. "But that still doesn't tell us who was the inside man in the Kremlin."

"You should send a message to the grand prince; tell him to stop his preparations to fight the Kazans."

Rainey thought about that for a minute. "No, the Kazans have been a thorn in the grand prince's side for years now. This gives him an excuse to do something about it. I don't think he'll let the truth get in the way of that plan. But still, he must be warned. A message to Gunter would be the best way. Anyway, Gunter is already in charge of finding that inside man. That's what he's good at."

* * *

Winter had set in. Everything slowly ground to a halt. In Zenoplata, business was wrapping up as the river, the main source of commerce, froze over. The crops were in, food and drink for the winter put in place. Nothing was left to do but await the arrival of spring. Rainey continued his trips to Rostov to meet with boyars who were interested in giving their allegiance directly to Muscovy. But most of the time he spent at home with his growing family.

Christmas was a joyous time, but the freezing temperatures kept most activities indoors. Rainey, Ludmilla and the rest of the household attended services in the town church on Christmas Eve. On their return, the children were allowed to finally open their presents. The Molodoy got a present from his father. A new sword, perfectly balanced for him. He took it outside and swung it back and forth as Rainey had taught him. It was easy for him after training so long with the heavier wooden swords. He didn't stay out long as temperatures dipped well below freezing. With the excitement dying down, the adults put all the children to bed and got ready for bed themselves.

Somewhere during the night, Ludmilla awoke. She didn't know why, but she got up and went down into the kitchen for a drink. When she got back to her room, she saw the door slightly ajar. She was sure she had closed it when she left. As she pushed it open, she saw a hooded figure standing over Rainey, sword in its hand.

Her sword was where it always hung, just inside the door. She grabbed the hilt and heard the familiar scrape as it left its scabbard. She swung it high, waiting to see what the figure would do. The intruder turned, bring its sword up. The blades connected. Ludmilla spun to get behind the figure and brought her sword around to strike. Another clang occurred. She found herself facing the figure. In the dim light, she could make out a pair of eyes, wide open in surprise.

"Hold it right there," Rainey said from the bed. Ludmilla glanced over to see Raney aiming his arquebus, the firing cloth lit and ready to fire.

The figure slowly lowered its sword and turned to face Rainey.

"Hello, Connor."

It was the voice of a woman. Ludmilla's mouth dropped. Who could this woman be? She found out in the next second when Rainey spoke.

"Aunshaunie?"

30

Rainey quickly pulled the firing cloth from the arquebus. "What are you doing here?"

The loud clomp of footsteps pounded out in the hall. Krasenoff appeared in the doorway, sword at the ready. Ludmilla had yet to lower her sword, so Krasenoff charged forward at the figure he didn't know. Aunshaunie made a quick side step, redirected Krasenoff's sword away from her and threw her foot out into Krasenoff's feet. Krasenoff fell forward and slammed into the wall.

"Igor, she's a friend," Rainey said as Krasenoff struggled to recover. He sat up, leaning against the wall.

"Friend?" Krasenoff looked up at Aunshaunie. "How many women have you trained to beat up men?"

Ludmilla had to laugh, in spite of her concern about how Aunshaunie had gotten into the house—and why she was holding a sword.

"Ludmilla," Rainey said. He signaled her to lower her blade. She did so, slowly. Another set of footsteps announced a new arrival. This time, it was the Molodoy, his new sword in his hand.

"It's all right," Rainey announced, loudly enough to be heard throughout the house. He got up and stuck his head out the door. More people were hurrying up the stairs. "All of you, go back to bed." He turned back into the room. "Everyone, please sit down. Swords away."

Krasenoff stayed on the floor where he was. Ludmilla moved to the bed. The Molodoy sat in a chair by the door. Aunshaunie took a seat by the window. She pulled back her hood to expose her face and hair.

"Zarya," Krasenoff murmured.

Aunshaunie looked at him. "Who?"

Krasenoff shook his head.

"It's good to see you, Aunshaunie," Rainey said. "Why did you feel you had to break into my house?"

"I was sent to kill you," she answered calmly. "I didn't know you were the boyar of Zenoplata until I got in this room."

"You were sent to kill me? Not the grand prince's son?"

"I didn't know the grand prince's son was here."

"Who sent you?" Ludmilla demanded, trying to hide the anger in her voice, but failing.

"I don't know. I never do. I get my contracts through an intermediary."

"Is he known as the Emissary?" Krasenoff asked offhandedly.

Aunshaunie looked at him. "Why would you ask that? I'm not Ruslan Tripensky."

"You've heard of Tripensky," Ludmilla said.

"Everyone has. The protector of business in Novgorod. Someone tried to kill him three years ago and failed, but he and his emissary disappeared. Not sure if he was a myth or not."

"She was real," Rainey said, raising his hand towards Ludmilla.

"You?" Aunshaunie exclaimed. "Well, that would explain quite a lot. You were the Emissary as well?" Ludmilla nodded. "Impressive."

"Do you have a trade name yourself?" Rainey asked

Aunshaunie nodded. "The Ghost."

"I've heard whispers of an assassin called the Ghost," Krasenoff said.

"Do you know where your intermediary met your client?" Rainey asked.

"Novgorod."

Ludmilla stiffened. She looked at Rainey, whose gaze was fixed on her. They both nodded at each other.

"That confirms it," Rainey said.

"But why kill you?" Ludmilla asked. "I would think they would come after the Molodoy."

"Me?" the Molodoy exclaimed.

"A child on the throne is more easily controlled," Rainey replied. "They would want him alive. Now, if I'm dead, where does he go?"

Ludmilla realized where this was going. "Back to Moscow."

"He's the grand prince's son?" Aunshaunie asked.

Ludmilla fully realized the implications. "When he goes back to Moscow, he will be within reach of whoever inside the Kremlin is planning to murder the grand prince."

"And the plan can go forward," Rainey said. "Without anyone like me to interfere with it."

"Wait a minute," Krasenoff said. "Someone is trying to kill the grand prince?"

"Yes, Igor," Ludmilla told him. "They've been trying for years. But they won't try again if the Molodoy stays here."

"Then perhaps I should pretend to die," Rainey said.

Everyone went silent. The full intent of what Rainey had said sank into Ludmilla's mind. It was Krasenoff who put it into words.

"You want to smoke the bastards out."

* * *

Ludmilla insisted on going along to Moscow. The children would all be fine. Maksim was old enough for Orina to care for him for a time. Nothing would be threatening them with the Molodoy gone. Surprisingly, Rainey agreed with her. Also, he acknowledged, it would make for a better story if it came from both her and the Molodoy. The trip to Moscow took longer than normal because of the snow. Krasenoff and Grigori had covered the sleigh and filled it with blankets and furs for Ludmilla, Aunshaunie and the Molodoy. Krasenoff rode alongside with one of his patrol parties. It all looked proper and important as they reached Moscow's gates. Looking back into the wilderness they had just passed through, Ludmilla wondered where Rainey was. He was to make his own way into Moscow, staying hidden from sight. For reassurance, Ludmilla gripped the hilt of her sword.

"Now it begins," she said. "Remember, it is important that no one knows Boyar Rainey is alive. Especially not your father. Understood?"

The Molodoy nodded. Ludmilla wondered if bringing a nine-year old boy into this deception was wise, but the young prince had shown an advanced level of maturity over the time he spent in Zenoplata. In any case, it was critical that everyone believed Rainey was dead. The best advantage they had was for the Molodoy to convince his father of this.

She glanced at Aunshaunie, wrapped in fur and dressed as a servant. She had assured everyone that no one in Moscow would know what the Ghost looked like. During the trip, they had talked about their pasts. Ludmilla learned that Aunshaunie's transformation into the Ghost had been very similar to hers into Ruslan Tripensky. Much the same way Ludmilla had operated in Novgorod, she even used her womanhood as a way to gain access where a male assassin could not go.

"I was all set to marry a fine young man in Kiev," Aunshaunie told her. "His name was Aleksei. Connor had met him and approved of the marriage before he left Kiev. He had only been gone about a month when we were set upon while out walking. It was men sent by a boyar who was a rival of Aleksei's father. Aleksei fought them off bravely, but he was killed. I picked up his sword and dispatched the rest of them. I cried all night, cradling Aleksei in my arms.

"The next morning, I was found by another boyar who took me to his home. When I told him what had happened, he realized I had killed most of the attackers. He then assigned me my first assassination. I was more than happy to take on the task; my target was the boyar who had ordered our deaths. From then on, I was the Ghost. The boyar who first hired me became my intermediary, contracting me across Poland, Lithuania and once even into Novgorod. I was there during Tripensky's time. Your time. I had heard stories about you and wanted to meet you. I went to the tavern every night for two weeks, but the Emissary never appeared. Then I heard that Tripensky had been attacked and had likely been killed, but not before killing his assailants."

"I had help that night from Connor and Igor," Ludmilla explained. "What happened that night told me it was time to retire the Tripensky legend."

"It still lives on, you know. Whenever an evil man meets a mysterious death in Novgorod, Tripensky is given the credit. It's as if your legend has become the wrathful hand of God."

Ludmilla had smiled at that. She wondered if her brother had a hand in perpetuating the myth. That would be to his advantage, since he had been the first benefactor of the Tripensky legend. Keeping it alive could be useful to keep his family safe in the turbulent world of Novgorod business, especially in these times where the city's politics were so divisive.

After exhausting the topic of their respective careers as swords for hire, the two women fell silent for a time. Then Aunshaunie leaned close and lowered her voice. "Do you know why that Igor fellow keeps staring at me?" she asked. "And who is Zarya?"

"I don't know. When this is all over, we'll have to ask him."

As they stepped down from the sleigh inside the Kremlin walls, Ludmilla looked back at Aunshaunie. "I am going to treat you badly. Stay subservient. It will establish you as my servant and hide your true purpose."

Aunshaunie nodded. Ludmilla strode up the steps to the grand prince's palace with the Molodoy. Aunshaunie came up behind them carrying three sacks. She tripped on the steps. Ludmilla turned and slapped her across the face.

"Are you totally inept, girl?" she screamed into Aunshaunie's face. Grabbing her by the chin, Ludmilla winked. Aunshaunie winked back.

The doors opened and Von Markenburg emerged. "What is this? You have brought back the grand prince's son. Why?"

Ludmilla scrunched up her face. She needed a tear or two here. "My husband has been murdered in the night. I feared the

Molodoy was no longer safe in Zenoplata. I had nowhere to take him but back here."

Von Markenburg looked up at Krasenoff, who nodded. Ludmilla made herself sob. The Molodoy took her by the arm.

"Chancellor, let us pass and go find my father. I have much to tell him."

Von Markenburg stared at the boy for a moment, then turned to a couple of his knights in the doorway. "You, go fetch the prince to the great hall. You, take these people there. I will be along shortly. Igor, I will need you to tell me the story."

Ludmilla watched Krasenoff follow Von Markenburg down a long corridor. So far, everything was going well. She looked at the black knight with her. "Where will I stay while I'm here? I want to send my servant to prepare the room."

The knight signalled another servant to take Aunshaunie to a room. Rainey had given them both a detailed description of the palace's interior. Once Aunshaunie was alone, she was to disappear into the building and keep an eye on the grand prince. Ludmilla's job was to keep the Molodoy from falling under the control of anyone, including the chancellor. If he was taken away from her, she was to find out where. The Molodoy would also insist on keeping Ludmilla with him, so hopefully if he was taken away, it would be with Ludmilla in tow. Krasenoff was to be their link to Rainey, who would be hiding somewhere in the city. No one knew how long it would take for the traitor to make his move, but the little party from Zenoplata could at least settle in for the rest of the winter without suspicion.

Ludmilla was astonished by the great hall. Although she had been to Moscow years before, she had never been inside the Kremlin. The high ceiling, the torches along the walls, the throne sitting at the top of three wide steps: it was all awe inspiring. She twirled around, taking in its size. The Molodoy took her hand.

"Yes, it's a big room," he said. "My father will come out from behind the throne."

Almost on cue, the grand prince entered. He strode across the room and embraced his son. "Why are you here? You are safer in Zenoplata."

The Molodoy stepped back from his father. "Boyar Rainey is dead. Killed by an assassin. I am no longer safe there."

"There is no guarantee you are safe here, either," Ivan replied.

The Molodoy gripped his sword's hilt. "Boyar Rainey trained me. And you gave me this sword. I can protect myself."

Ivan looked on his son with what Ludmilla thought was pride. The Molodoy was acting all grown up, which must be pleasing for Ivan.

"That's good," Ivan said. "But this man was able to kill Boyar Rainey. I fear no one is going to be good enough against him. I will post guards with you at all times."

"Yes, Father."

Ivan looked over at Ludmilla. "And who is this?"

"May I present the widow of Boyar Rainey. Ludmilla Raynykova."

Ivan took her hand. "I am sorry for your loss. I feel it, too. He was a great man and a great friend to me."

"Thank you, my prince," Ludmilla replied. She faked a small sob and sniffed loudly.

"You are as beautiful as Connor described you."

Ludmilla lowered her eyes. She wasn't sure how to take that comment. "Thank you, my prince," she said again.

"You may call me Ivan. In private, your late husband was allowed that privilege." He turned and put his arm around his son's shoulder. Turning to the knight, he asked, "Where is Gunter?"

"He is getting a report from Igor Krasenoff," the knight said.

"Good. Tell him I want to see him here in an hour." Leading the Molodoy away, he looked over his shoulder. "And find Ludmilla a room."

"Father," the Molodoy said. "I would like to have Ludmilla stay close. We have become close friends during my stay in Zenoplata."

"Very well. Knight, put her in the room next to my son's. And I want two guards outside each of their doors."

Ludmilla turned to the knight. "You can leave my servant in whatever room you left her in. I won't need her until the morning. Bring her to me then."

That should give Aunshaunie plenty of time to scout around.

* * *

Rainey sat in the back of the tavern, his hood pulled up, his face cast downward to avoid recognition. Rainey had been in this particular tavern before, but it had been at least a year. Krasenoff, however, was well known in most of Moscow's taverns. This would be a safe place to meet, but not to acknowledge each other.

Krasenoff entered and went to the bar. After he'd gotten a mug of ale, two girls approached him as they always did.

"Igor, we never thought we'd see you here in the winter. What a wonderful surprise."

"I'm here on the grand prince's business." He took a seat on a vacant bench. "I might be here for a while."

One of the girls sat on his lap. "How long is a while?" she said seductively.

Krasenoff pushed her off. "Not tonight, girls. I'm tired. I just want to have an ale and go to sleep."

"You can sleep with us," the other girl said.

"I said no!"

The girls got up. "What's the matter with you? You've always enjoyed our company."

"I'm sorry. Just not tonight. I'll come back tomorrow for you, all right."

They smiled. "We'll be waiting," they said in unison. They turned and left, looking for more agreeable customers.

Krasenoff rapidly downed his ale and walked out. After a minute had passed, Rainey got up and followed him out. They met in a stable down the street from the tavern.

"That was unusual," Rainey said. "You attracted unwanted attention by not acting your normal self in there."

Krasenoff stood quietly, saying nothing.

"What is it?" Rainey demanded.

Krasenoff rubbed his face. "Remember when I told you about Zarya?"

"Yes." Then the realization hit Rainey. "You called Aunshaunie 'Zarya.'"

"Your friend is almost the spitting image of her. A little older, a lot darker, but it's her. And it's driving me to distraction."

Rainey could see the war going on in his friend's mind. He had only seen him like this once before. That was by the river, when he told the story of Zarya, inspiring Rainey to propose to Ludmilla. He took Krasenoff by the shoulders and shook him.

"You have to concentrate. What do you have to report?"

Krasenoff took a deep breath. He was coming back from wherever he had drifted off to. "Ludmilla has a room next to the boy's. Your Ghost is spending the night in another room, although she didn't want to stay there long. It's where they wanted to send Ludmilla first. She told me she's found secret ways to move around the palace. She can stay in touch with Ludmilla and keep an eye out for the grand prince and the chancellor."

"Watch Gunter? Why?"

"She says she doesn't like him."

"Neither do a lot of people. When you see her next, tell her to stay on the grand prince." He thought for a moment. Perhaps seeing what Gunter was up to would help them expose the traitor more quickly. "Never mind. Have her watch Gunter, too. You never know what he might turn up, and that will be good to know in advance."

Krasenoff's face remained full of sorrow. "She'll be in danger."

Rainey patted his friend's cheeks. "Igor, she's the Ghost. THE Ghost. I think anyone who gets in her way is in much more danger than she is."

"I suppose."

Damn, he's in love with her, Rainey thought to himself. "Tell you what, my friend. When all this is over, I will give you a proper introduction to her. But I can't guarantee she will stay around Zenoplata for you. She has a life. You will have to convince her that a life with you will be better."

Krasenoff scoffed. "What, you think I want to marry an assassin?"

There is the old Igor I need, Rainey reassured himself. "I did," he said jovially. "Why not you?"

31

1468

Two months had passed. Spring was trying to push winter out of its way and that was the only obvious struggle taking place in Muscovy. Preparations for the next campaign into Kazan were well under way, but Rainey was no closer to determining who inside the Kremlin was willing to kill the grand prince. His friends continued their vigil. Ludmilla stayed close to the Molodoy. Aunshaunie kept an eye on the grand prince and continued spying on Von Markenburg while Krasenoff kept his ears open at court. He reported regularly to Rainey at various taverns around Moscow. But nothing stood out. No one seemed to have a hidden agenda. Although Rainey knew Von Markenburg would continue his own inquiries, he didn't seem to be finding out anything, either.

He met with Krasenoff in the back of another tavern, expecting another nothing report. He was getting restless.

"I don't know, Igor. Maybe we should just go home."

"You'd have to reveal you're not dead," Krasenoff replied. "The grand prince will want to know what you've been up to."

"I'm not worried about that. I'm more concerned about revealing myself to the traitor. He should have made a move by now."

"Maybe he's waiting for Gunter to stop looking for him. That could take a year."

"Have we heard anything from Kolochoff in Novgorod?"

"Not as of yet. I'm not sure I trust him anyway."

Rainey sighed. "He's Ludmilla's brother. He's alive and pretty rich in Novgorod because of me. I think he's trustworthy. It's probably just taking him time to find out who's behind this treason. So, anything new in the Kremlin?"

"Still nothing. The grand prince is leaving in two days to see his army on the Kazan frontier. Gerhard told me Gunter and all twenty-four black knights are going with him for protection."

Rainey had told Krasenoff to befriend Gerhard. The man was the only link into the brotherhood that was the black knights. Rainey never expected Gerhard to give up any secrets, but a little information here and there was worth it.

"How is Gerhard doing?"

"He's not mourning you, if that's what you think."

Rainey laughed. "Didn't think he would be. So, the grand prince is going on an excursion. No doubt our traitor will be aware of it, though getting past twenty-four knights would be tricky. Still, it is an opportunity."

"Perhaps we should get out of Moscow and shadow them," Krasenoff said.

"I need you to keep searching here," Rainey replied. "I'll follow the grand prince and take Aunshaunie with me."

"I'm bored out of my mind here. I can't stand all those courtiers whispering to each other about each other."

Rainey felt sorry for his friend, but he needed him to stay in Moscow. Then something else occurred to him.

"If Gunter is taking all his knights, who will be guarding the Molodoy?"

"I don't know," Krasenoff said. "Most of the court is afraid of your wife. Maybe Gunter figures she can handle it for a few days."

"Or Gunter has figured out that the Molodoy is not under any threat unless the grand prince dies. So for him, taking all his knights makes sense."

Krasenoff nodded. "The chancellor is smart."

"Then you'll go with me and Aunshaunie. I'll head out ahead of the grand prince to check the road. You and Aunshaunie wait a few hours and follow. I would suggest you leave by the west gate and take your time coming around so people will think you are returning to Zenoplata. Maybe even mention it at court. You can catch up with me at their first stop for the night."

"And your wife?"

"She stays here with the Molodoy."

Krasenoff rubbed his chin. "I don't relish that conversation."

"She'll understand. The Molodoy can't be left alone. There's a good chance there will be an attempt to take him if we fail. She can pretend she's Ruslan Tripensky again."

* * *

"I have to stay here?"

Ludmilla was not happy. Krasenoff continued his explanation.

"You have to stay with the Molodoy. You can pretend to be Ruslan Tripensky again, guarding his life."

"Did Connor tell you to say that?"

Krasenoff lowered his eyes. "Yes."

"And did he say anything about how I might get away with guarding him? No one in Moscow knows who Ruslan Tripensky is."

"Actually, the legend has . . ."

"Igor. It won't be safe."

Krasenoff sat down. "You are but a woman. If the traitor strikes, it will be with only a few men, expecting just to kill you and take the boy. But they will be in for a surprise when they try. That will also give you the best lead to who the traitor is. Then you can 'Ruslan Tripensky' him."

Ludmilla sat in thought. It did sound like a good strategy to make the traitor expose himself, but the odds did not seem in her favor. Yes, she was skilled and could fend off any small attempt to take control over the Molodoy. But there would be no one she could tell about the attack. All the black knights would be gone. Von Markenburg, too. No Aunshaunie or Igor. And no Connor. A second attack would be imminent, with the plotters armed with full knowledge that she would be a formidable obstacle to overcome. She remembered the night that she had been ambushed in Novgorod. She had survived that only because Rainey and Krasenoff were there. She didn't want to argue the point with Krasenoff, but just to plan an alternative.

"Very well," she told him. "I will stay here and protect the boy."

"Good," Krasenoff replied. "He will be in good hands."

After Krasenoff left, Ludmilla went to see the Molodoy. "Who would I talk to about provisions for a five- or six-day journey?"

"Are you returning to Zenoplata?" the boy asked.

"No," she said in a near-whisper. She stepped in close to his ear. "You and I are going to follow your father east."

* * *

Rainey had left Moscow several hours before the grand prince's party started its journey. He took his time, looking along the roadsides for any signs of an ambush. He found no one on the road or in the forests, all the way to the lodge where the group would spend its first night on the road. Perched in a tree, he watched as the black knight scouts arrived just before dusk. The rest would not be more than a quarter of an hour behind. The two knights did a search of the place and spoke with the owner of the lodge about who else was staying there that night. Rainey had already scouted out the area and knew a small caravan of seven men was already there for the night. They were questioned and told to keep to their rooms for the night.

The rest of the party soon arrived. The grand prince was led into the lodge. Once the horses had been stabled and fed, all went quiet. Five of the knights emerged and took positions where they could keep watch. Rainey knew that every three hours, the guard would change, with new knights relieving those on watch. The lodge was secure. Rainey quietly descended from the tree and crept into the woods to where he had set up camp.

It was Aunshaunie who found him first. She came out of the night so silently that Rainey noticed her only when she sat down beside him. He reached for his sword, but stopped when he saw it was her.

"How did you do that?" he asked.

"Do what?"

"I didn't sense you at all until you sat down."

"I mastered a few more talents after you left Kiev."

"Where's Igor?"

"He's circling around the long way." She gave Rainey a quizzical look. "Why does he keep calling me Zarya?"

"You'll have to ask him that."

"He makes me uncomfortable. He kept staring at me on the road. I threatened to slit his throat, but he wouldn't stop."

Rainey smiled. "Did you talk with him?"

"About what? We are on a mission. We only spoke when we had to."

"You need to speak with him. Tonight. Ask him about Zarya."

"Why?"

Rainey put his hand on her arm. "Just talk to him. For me."

He stared into her eyes, trying to find the fun loving little girl he'd left behind in Kiev. And for a moment, he thought he saw a flicker of her childhood behind the cold, all-business facade Aunshaunie had been showing for the past two months. Her hardness had even disturbed Ludmilla, according to Krasenoff. Rainey looked away, thinking of Ludmilla. He missed her so much. Missed her touch, her mischievous smile, the way she was with the children. He had spent the last two months in the same city with her and never once had seen her.

"What is it?" Aunshaunie asked.

"I was thinking of Ludmilla."

"You love her."

Rainey turned back to Aunshaunie. "Of course."

She gazed into the flames of the small fire. There was a sadness in her face now.

"You were in love once," Rainey said. "I remember that young boy. He always made you smile."

"I don't smile anymore."

A tiny crackle of footsteps on twigs behind them signalled Krasenoff's arrival. They turned, but were surprised at who was there.

"Hello, my husband."

Rainey leaped to his feet. "Ludmilla, what are you doing here? You were supposed to stay with the Molodoy."

"And I am." She raised her hand towards the darkness behind her and the Molodoy stepped into the light, sword in hand. "There is no place safer for him than here, where no one knows where he is. We brought our own food and water. Now, if you don't mind, can you welcome us to your fire to keep warm?"

Rainey hesitated for a moment, then signalled for them to sit. "He was safe in Moscow."

"Only if you came back with a live grand prince. I would not have been able to defend him by myself."

He had to admit, Ludmilla was right. The Molodoy would be much safer out here with them than back in the city. As they all found seats around the fire, Krasenoff came out of the woods. He looked around at everyone.

"Did I miss something? There should only be three of us."

Rainey glanced at Aunshaunie and raised his eyebrows. Aunshaunie nodded and got up.

"You, me, over there," she said to Krasenoff.

Krasenoff turned to Rainey, who just nodded in return. He followed Aunshaunie into the darkness. Rainey looked up at the sky, studying the stars, listening to the flickering flames.

"What are those two talking about?" Ludmilla asked.

"Igor's obsession," Rainey replied. He reached over and touched her hand. "I missed you."

"I missed you, too."

Rainey got up. "I'll take the first watch. You and the Molodoy get some sleep. Bundle up; it'll be cold tonight."

32

They were up and moving before the black knights assembled outside the lodge. Rainey, Ludmilla and the Molodoy hung back to watch while Aunshaunie and Krasenoff went on ahead to scout the road. The first set of four knights left first. As soon as the main party got on the road, the three watchers mounted up to follow at a discreet distance. They saw no signs of anything out of the ordinary. The grand prince did not appear to be disturbed.

The grand prince's party moved quickly along the road for the first two hours. Rainey and his group had difficulty keeping up without being detected by the rearguard of black knights riding a hundred yards behind the main party. He knew it would soon be even more difficult, once they cleared the forest into open fields.

As they reached the edge of the forest, Rainey stopped and watched the rearguard carry on. The main group appeared to have stopped about five hundred yards ahead. Farther on, he could see the knights in the vanguard. With nothing but empty fields in all directions, Rainey realized, this was not a necessary or even an appropriate place to stop and rest. No one had dismounted.

"Why are they stopping?" Ludmilla asked.

Rainey began to get an uneasy feeling. "I don't know and I don't like it."

A horse and rider bolted from the group, heading out across a field. He was cut off by the vanguard riders and turned back towards the road. The rearguard knights moved to cut off his escape back towards the forest. The rider pulled out two swords, one in each hand.

The rider was the grand prince.

"How could I have been so stupid?" Rainey muttered to himself. It all fell into place in an instant. Von Markenburg couldn't find the traitor because he was the traitor. He had been all along. It was why Alexander Kolchin knew which room in the Kremlin palace Rainey had been staying in that night seven years ago. It was why Von Markenburg had Kolchin's family slaughtered: to protect himself and pass it off as a conspiracy to treason. And perhaps Anna's role had been to kill Rainey in his sleep when the time came. With Anna gone, however, he had resorted to hiring the Ghost, Aunshaunie, to murder Rainey and force the Molodoy to return to the Kremlin. There the young prince could be kept under Von Markenburg's control. But why did it take seven years?

There was no time to ponder that point now.

"Stay here!" Rainey yelled, spurring his horse into a full gallop. As he came near, he could see the grand prince's horse had been shot with an arrow, forcing Ivan to the ground. The black knights had dismounted and were walking towards him. They stopped when they heard Rainey's horse galloping across the frozen field. He reached back and pulled his sword free of its scabbard, charging into the group of knights who scattered out of his way.

He yanked the reins hard and wheeled his horse around to where the grand prince was standing.

Ivan was looking up at him, shock and confusion on face. "They told me you were dead."

"That was the plan," Rainey said. The knight nearest to him, he realized, was Von Markenburg, still mounted. His face also showed shock, mixed with dismay. "Gunter, you look like you've seen a ghost."

"How . . . ?"

"The ghost you sent to kill me is an old friend of mine. Maybe you can tell us who hired you to kill the grand prince. Someone from Novgorod? One who favors Lithuania, perhaps?"

Regaining his composure, Von Markenburg pulled out his sword. "It was only because of you that I failed to kill him seven years ago. It took this long for those boyars to get up the nerve to have me attempt it again."

That explains the seven years, Rainey thought.

"Novgorod?" Ivan howled.

The black knights had formed a circle around Rainey and the grand prince, their master just outside it. They all had their swords drawn.

"So, kill the grand prince, and then what?"

Von Markenburg shrugged. "I'm sure they have a plan. I am to keep my position in Muscovy and encourage Novgorod's independence. The prospect will be much easier with the young Molodoy and one of his uncles as regent."

"So, this is just business."

"I am a mercenary. Does that surprise you?"

"No, and you will fail again."

Von Markenburg laughed. "Now, I know the two of you are formidable warriors, but against all my knights, I like my chances." He looked to his men. "Kill them both."

The knights slowly began to close the circle. Rainey dismounted and slapped his horse's rump to move it out of the narrowing circle. He stood back to back with Ivan.

"Just two of us," Ivan said. "I don't like these odds."

"We're not alone," Rainey said softly, his eyes falling on Gerhard. The man looked distressed. Rainey thought that perhaps he wasn't comfortable with regicide, even if he was being paid for it.

"And perhaps a knight or two are not comfortable with this." He centered his gaze of Gerhard. "Gerhard, my friend, you can't possibly be all right with this. Being paid for guarding and war is one thing, but assassination?"

"He is loyal to me," Von Markenburg said forcefully. "They all are."

The circle was closing. "Do you have a target?" Rainey asked.

"Yes," Ivan said, "and I'll be going right from there."

Rainey gripped his sword a little harder. "On—"

He was cut off by a terrific howl from the field. Krasenoff was up and charging, reaching the first knight before he could turn around. The distraction was enough.

"Now!" Rainey yelled. He charged the knight he had chosen. From the corner of his eye, he saw Gerhard slicing the sword hand of the knight on his left and then turning on the man to his right. Rainey returned his attention on his own target, blocking a downward thrust of his sword, spinning and slicing at the man's exposed midsection. He continued his spin to take on the next knight. His sword thrust was blocked. He stepped back to avoid the slicing motion of his opponent's sword and thrust his own blade directly into the man's midsection. Pulling it out, he kicked the man aside and charged at the next man. It was then that he saw Von Markenburg, still on his horse, charging at him. He had to block a sword and couldn't get out of the way. Before he could move he saw a blur of clothing leaping up and knocking Von Markenburg out of his saddle. Rainey leaned away from the horse as it made contact. He was knocked sideways, turning his body to go into a roll and coming up quickly to find himself at the mercy of a knight with his sword up. The man's head suddenly left his body as a charging horse thundered past. A quick look at the rider was enough. The hooded figure was Ludmilla.

* * *

Ludmilla turned her horse, but the field was too crowded to fight mounted. A knight grabbed her leg, pulling her off. She forced her body to slide on top of him, grabbed her dagger and thrust it into the man's neck. As he fell away, she hit the ground in a roll and came up facing another knight. She charged her target, aiming herself to his right. As he turned to swing at her, Ludmilla planted her foot, sprung up to her left and slashed open the man's side. Her sword continued across to clang loudly against another blade, blocking a downward swing at her head. She dropped into a crouch and swung her sword back across the man's boots. He screamed and toppled over. Ludmilla rolled again and came up against two more knights. They came at her together, swords held high. She moved at them, putting her sword up to block both blades. Then, arching her back, she ran between them. As her sword released, she slashed at one man's side and then spun quickly to slice at the other man's back. She had turned to take on the next knight when Rainey came to her side.

"Your left," Rainey said. A knight was coming at her. She raised her sword, let out a terrifying scream and stepped inside the man's thrust. She thrust her sword right through his chest. It was exhilarating. She placed her foot on the man's belly and pushed him off her sword. She screamed again and charged the next knight she saw. This one dropped his sword and ran.

She stopped, breathing heavily, spinning around looking for another knight to impale. None remained standing. Black knights lay scattered on the snowy ground, some dead, some groaning. Ivan was standing over one, the Molodoy at his back, his head shifting back and forth looking for any threat to his father. Krasenoff was standing by himself, breathing heavy just as Ludmilla was. He caught her eye and grinned.

"Well done, girl." He winked.

Turning again, Ludmilla saw Rainey, standing like she was, surveying the carnage around them. She charged at him, dropping her sword, and swung her fist at his head. Rainey wasn't ready for this; it knocked him to the ground. Ludmilla jumped down on him and pounded her fists against his chest.

"How dare you!" she screamed. "How dare you!"

Rainey finally got a hold of her wrists and stopped the deluge of blows. He sat up and hugged her as she began to cry. Her voice became that of a child.

"How dare you. You would have left me alone. Our children would have been without a father."

Rainey held her tight. He pulled the hood from her head and kissed her on the forehead. "I'm sorry. I had no choice."

Ludmilla opened her eyes to see Ivan and the Molodoy standing there watching her. She tapped on Rainey's back to get his attention.

"You train your women to fight?" Ivan asked.

The two helped each other to their feet. "I don't have to worry about her," Rainey replied. "All of Zenoplata have been taught skills so they can take care of themselves."

Ivan nodded. "And where did you find this one?" he pointed at Aunshaunie, who was standing over Von Markenburg, her sword at his throat.

"Would you believe Constantinople?"

"Connor . . ." Ludmilla turned to see Krasenoff fall to his knees. Everyone rushed to him. Three streaks of blood stained his clothing. One on his chest, one on his left side and a very bad one on his right leg. Ludmilla helped him lie down.

Rainey checked his wounds. "You'll live. Only the leg wound is deep enough to be a concern."

"The blood on my chest is someone else's," Krasenoff said, struggling to rise.

"I will tend to him," said Ludmilla, gently pressing on his chest to stop him. He relaxed and lay quietly.

Rainey nodded and stood up. "Come, my prince. Let's hear what Gunter can tell us."

As they left, Krasenoff took Ludmilla's hand. "He is a good man. Try not to kill him."

She smiled. "I'm more concerned about you at this moment." With her dagger, she started to tear a strip of cloth from her cloak. "I'll need your belt to stop the bleeding on your leg. So remember to hold up your britches when you stand."

* * *

Rainey found Gerhard on one knee, his sword point in the ground, his forehead resting on his sword's pommel, eyes closed.

"Gerhard?"

He looked up at Rainey, tears in his eyes. "I've betrayed my brothers. Betrayed my oath to the Teutonic Order. My soul will be damned."

Rainey knelt down beside him. "Your Teutonic oath is not betrayed. It was Gunter who has betrayed you all by leading you down this path of treachery." He looked across the field. "Some of your brothers have survived. Help them find the way back to your true oath."

"The grand prince will execute them for treason."

"I'll see what I can do about that." Rainey wasn't sure he could do anything, but he could at least ask. Ivan had always considered Gunter's knights a necessary evil. He got up and walked over to where Von Markenburg lay. Ivan was questioning him, his sword hovering inches above his chancellor's chest.

"I want names," Ivan demanded. "All of them."

"If I am about to die," Von Markenburg replied, "what would be the point of telling you anything?"

Ivan pushed his sword slowly into Von Markenburg's shoulder, eliciting a gasp of pain. "It depends on how fast or how painfully you want to die."

"I am a Teutonic Knight. I have no fear of pain or death."

"You were a Teutonic Knight," Rainey replied. "You stopped being one when you became a duplicitous mercenary." He looked at Ivan. "My prince, you need to ask the right question."

"And what is that?"

Rainey looked into Von Markenburg's face. "Why?"

Von Markenburg stared blankly up at Rainey. "As you said, I am a mercenary. I was paid."

"But you had position and power in Muscovy. Why would you risk that for money?"

Von Markenburg smiled. "You still do not fully understand the politics in the Rus, Connor."

"Explain it to me."

Von Markenburg paused for a moment, then looked at Ivan, who relaxed the pressure from his sword. "This adventure started long ago. Your father did not send for me and my men. I sent a note offering our services for the protection of Muscovy's throne. I did this at the behest of a cabal of boyars in Novgorod. They knew I had helped to restore your father to the throne back in the 1440's. But as a mercenary and skilled in the art of politics, they assumed correctly that I could be bought, and that I could ensure a weak succession to the throne. That would allow them to break free from their ties to Muscovy."

"They are mostly free of Muscovy," Rainey said. "Freer than they would be with any other ruler."

"No, they're not." Von Markenburg looked at Ivan. "Care to explain?"

Rainey turned his attention to Ivan, who shrugged.

"I have a say in how the riches of the Dvina district are handled."

"And . . ." Von Markenburg encouraged him.

"And they need my approval of any dictates from their Veche. And when they appoint their prince."

"Continue."

Ivan scowled at Von Markenburg. "Their archbishop is appointed by me and consecrated in Moscow."

"So they're not free," Rainey said.

"Freer than Yaroslavl and Vladimir."

"They still like to call their city Novgorod the Great," Von Markenburg remarked. "Although the sentiment has risen and subsided through the years, some do want to relive those days when they answered to no one. They got a taste of this during the civil wars of Ivan's father, when they were allowed to do as they pleased."

"So, they want to plunge Muscovy into civil war again?" Rainey asked.

Von Markenburg shook his head. "That would be too difficult. Too many Muscovy boyars support the current grand prince over any of his brothers."

"Who were you going to make regent?" Ivan asked.

Rainey realized now where all this was going. It wouldn't have ended with Ivan's death. There was more to Von Markenburg's blood money than just a payment from Novgorod.

"I was thinking Andrey Bolshoy would suit the Novgorodians the best," Von Markenburg said.

"With you in control," Rainey stated.

"But my father made you chancellor," Ivan said. "We treated you well."

Von Markenburg spat. "There are no chancellors in the Rus. Your father asked me what title I would like and I chose it. After that, I was just a necessary minion. Trusted, but mostly ignored. It suited me very well; that let my intrigues go unnoticed."

"I still want names," Ivan said.

"And you will get none."

Ivan turned to Rainey with a tiny nod of his head, then thrust his sword through Von Markenburg's heart. With only a small grunt, Von Markenburg squirmed momentarily and went still.

"Time to go," Ivan said. "I have an army to inspect."

"You're still going to attack the Kazans?" Rainey asked.

"The army is already there."

"What about Novgorod?"

"The traitors will go into hiding for a while once they discover Gunter is dead, but they won't go anywhere. In a few years, they will arise again and I can deal with them then."

* * *

The Muscovite army was impressive. Mostly on horseback, it included a good-sized contingent armed with arquebuses. But this was a fight with the khanate. This war would be a series of raids and, if the khanate came out in force, an open cavalry fight on the steppe. The arquebuses and a handful of cannon were mostly for defending camps.

Rainey was nodding to himself. His assistance in building a double-style army for Muscovy was about to bear fruit. Against the khanates, the old style was deployed, with some improvements in discipline and weapons. Against enemies to the west, these same men would form into infantry companies and regiments with arquebuses and cannons, more suitable for the siege warfare common in Europe.

"You look pleased, Connor," Ivan said.

"They are impressive. And their leaders are skilled. They will do well."

"I will be sending my son out with them. I would feel more comfortable if you went along. This is almost as much your army as mine."

Rainey shook his head and gave a look to where Ludmilla was standing. "If I do that, my wife will kill me in my sleep."

Ivan laughed. "That's what you get for teaching women things they should not know. Go to her. We will leave for Moscow in the morning."

Rainey joined Ludmilla and placed his arm around her waist. "We head home in the morning."

"Good," she replied. "I miss my children."

They turned towards their tent. "The threat to the throne is not over," Rainey said.

"But the plotters will stay hidden for some time. You can spend more time at home."

"One never knows when the grand prince will need me. But he knows I'm not inclined to go to war anymore and he is fine with that."

"But you will still train soldiers."

"Yes. We will be building a training academy in Zenoplata."

"Not in Moscow?" Ludmilla said, surprised.

"No. The grand prince knows it will be more efficient to send recruits to me. He knows you won't like me moving to Moscow."

"And he would be right."

Rainey kissed her on the top of the head.

Ludmilla had a new thought. "Igor and Aunshaunie seem to be getting along well," she said.

Rainey turned to see the two of them sitting on a log, deep in conversation. "She appears to have bewitched Igor."

"It helps that she looks like his lost love. It still remains to be seen if she can keep him out of the arms of the tavern girls."

"She is capable of slitting his throat without him ever being aware she was coming for him. He'll behave." As he looked at Aunshaunie, he thought he saw something new: what could only be described as a smile.

They stopped as he pulled aside the tent flap. "So, what shall we do until our next meal?" Ludmilla asked with a mischievous smile.

"Oh, we can think of something," Rainey said. He swept her up in his arms, kissed her deeply, and carried her into the tent.

33

1471

Rainey stayed to the shadows, his hat pulled down over his eyes. He scanned the street as well as he could in the dark. A lone figure was barely noticeable down by the cross street. That was Krasenoff. Rainey looked up the other way. He couldn't see Gerhard at all, but knew he was watching the next cross street. He didn't even try to spot where Aunshaunie was watching from.

He was getting cold and impatient. He pulled his furs closer about his neck. Ludmilla had gone into her brother's house almost an hour earlier. The object was to get in and out of Novgorod as fast as possible. Times were getting very bad. The city's rival factions were virtually in a state of war with each other. The trouble had begun with the death of Archbishop Ioan back last November and the election—with Ivan's approval— of Feofil to replace him. But then the Novgorod Veche not only pushed for Feofil to be consecrated by the Metropolitan of Kiev instead of Moscow, but began discussions with the Polish king about changing the city's allegiance from Ivan to Casimir. The pro-Lithuanian faction had gained the upper hand. Casimir gladly sent

Mikhail Olekovich to be Novgorod's prince. The stage was set for war.

Ivan had sent an ambassador to Pskov ordering the city to raise troops for a war with Novgorod. As things escalated, Rainey thought it would be a good time to find out who among the pro-Lithuanian faction had been trying to assassinate the grand prince for all these years. No doubt culprits would come out of hiding under these circumstances. He hoped they would expose themselves, and their deeds of the previous eleven years, to Andrey Kolochoff.

Rainey heard a commotion from Gerhard's direction. A light was growing from around the corner, along with the noise of a crowd moving through the street. A crush of men carrying torches turned the corner and marched up the street Rainey tried to count, figuring there were at least fifty people. He backed into the shadows a little more. From the conversations he overheard from the crowd, he determined it was pro-Lithuanian. The torch-lit mass stopped in front of Andrey's house.

"Andrey Kolochoff!" someone yelled from the front of the crowd. "You have been found guilty of supporting the evil from Muscovy. Come out or we will burn you out."

Rainey scanned the crowd, spotting Gerhard in the back. His sword was hidden under his cloak. Rainey looked down to where Krasenoff had been. He was slowly moving up the street towards the house.

"Kolochoff. Come out!"

There was a pause, after which the mob's leader took a torch. As he raised it, ready to throw, the door to the house opened. Ludmilla stepped out, hood up and sword in hand. There was an audible gasp.

"Yes," she announced to the crowd. "I am Ruslan Tripensky. I am alive. And know this: this house is under my protection."

The crowd fell silent. No one moved except Gerhard, slowly making his way towards the leader.

Still clutching a torch, the leader broke the silence. "Even Tripensky couldn't take on a crowd this size."

"Are you sure?" Ludmilla replied. Her low voice was almost a growl.

The leader raised the torch again, but before he could throw it, a crossbow bolt struck his chest. The force knocked him over, making him fling the torch back into the crowd. People scurried out of the way before settling down into silence again, looking around to determine where the bolt had come from.

Thank you Aunshaunie, thought Rainey.

"Anyone else?" Ludmilla asked. When no one replied, she said, "Go back to your homes. Your families. There will be no more killing here tonight."

No one moved. Ludmilla pointed her sword directly at them. They started to move back to where they had come from. Gerhard eased himself into the crowd and went along. When they rounded the corner, Ludmilla looked over her shoulder and nodded. Andrey, in the window, nodded back. She moved down the steps and crossed to where Rainey was hiding.

"I had to give Andrey time to get his family out," Ludmilla said. "From what Andrey told me, supporters of Muscovy are being terrorized all over the city."

"Do they have a safe place to go?"

"Yes. There's a place in the city where other supporters of the grand prince can go." She touched his arm. "He has told me a very interesting story."

"Then we should head to a quiet place, out of the way. You know the city. Lead on."

Ludmilla led Rainey and Krasenoff through the streets to the city's north wall. There stood an abandoned building. The doorway gaped open and the windows had no shutters. A large hole yawned in the roof.

"I used to hide my weapons here," Ludmilla said. "No one comes around."

They stepped through the doorway and into the darkness. She led them to a back room, pitch black except for a little pile of coals glowing in the corner. Rainey and Krasenoff waited by the door until the light from a candle lit the room.

The candle's glow rose to illuminate the whole room. A table stood in the middle with a single chair. Ludmilla sat down and pulled seven scrolls from her cloak.

"These are notes Andrey made since you asked him to look into the Lithuanian faction two years ago. Certain boyars slipped out of society for a while after the last attempt on the grand prince's life failed. From the list, the most prominent are the Boretskys. Another family, familiar to me, are the Chergins."

"Your first kill," Krasenoff said.

"No. He was my ninth."

"Ninth?"

Rainey needed the conversation to get back on track. "What was Chergin's business?"

"Metals. Iron, gold, silver, copper. Back when Andrey was first doing the silk trade, the Topoffs requested a fair amount of silver."

"Explains Vladimir's currency," Krasenoff noted.

"Andrey feels that the Chergins would be the family to go to if you wanted to hire assassins," Ludmilla said. "He knows firsthand that they do make use of them. The Boretskys are too involved in the Veche to risk the scandal of hiring an assassin directly."

"Have all the families on the list made their presence known again recently?" Rainey asked.

"Yes."

"So, most likely, they're once again moving towards their goals. Explains both the new Lithuanian prince and the attempt to consecrate their archbishop in Kiev."

"So, another attempt on the grand prince is likely in progress," Krasenoff said.

Aunshaunie's voice was heard from outside the doorway. "We have company."

Ludmilla blew out the candle. They made their way to the doorway to find ten men standing in the street, swords drawn.

"How did they find us?" Ludmilla asked quietly.

"Probably followed us. Do we know who they are?" Raney whispered.

"Does it matter?" she replied.

"Yes. If we don't know, we need to keep one alive. Let them come into the house. The darkness will be to our advantage."

The men slowly began to move towards the house. Rainey unslung his arquebus and moved back to the room where the coals smoldered. He got his firing cloth glowing and moved back into a hallway. He heard a clash of swords. Two shadows appeared. He slapped the wall to get their attention. They turned towards him, swords up. From the way they were approaching him, Rainey was sure they weren't part of his group. He raised his arquebus and squeezed the lever.

The noise was amplified inside the hallway. The two shadows crumpled to the floor, disappearing into the darkness. While Rainey began reloading, a task he had learned to do without looking, he stepped over the two dead men on the floor.

He heard the twang of a crossbow. More swords clanged together. Rainey moved to the doorway and down the steps, taking a position against the wall. After a moment, three men bolted down the stairs and into the street. As they ran, Rainey stepped forward and fired at their legs. All three went down, but one got up and limped quickly on. Rainey heard another crossbow shot. The bolt hit the limping man square in the back. He fell to the ground and didn't move.

Rainey looked up the steps to see Aunshaunie reloading her crossbow. Krasenoff and Ludmilla came out of the doorway. The two men who'd been shot in the legs were groaning.

"Didn't trust us to keep one alive?" Krasenoff asked.

"In the dark, no." Rainey replied.

"Probably a good assumption," Krasenoff said.

"Ludmilla, do you have another safe place or two we can make use of?" Rainey asked. "We'll need some time to get these two to talk."

* * *

"You think you're going to die," Rainey said to the man tied to the chair in front of him. "But, if we like what we hear, death isn't your only way out."

He stepped behind the chair and got close to the captive's ear. "However, if you resist, I won't be able to stop Ruslan Tripensky from using his many talents to extract the information we want. You'll be begging us to kill you after that."

Another man's scream echoed down the hall from the next room.

"Your friend appears to have chosen the hard route," Rainey said softly. "He will die. What you have to ask yourself is this. Is protecting the man who hired you worth your life and the pain that will go into ending it?"

Another scream pierced the gloom. The man in the chair began to shudder. Rainey walked back around to face him. When the man didn't speak, Rainey shrugged.

"You had the choice." He stepped back while a hooded Ludmilla stepped forward, sword drawn.

"Wait!"

Rainey turned and waited.

'Chergin! Feodor Chergin. He hired us."

Ludmilla lowered her sword. Rainey stepped forward. "How many Chergins are there?"

The man shook his head. "I don't understand."

"How many people are in Feodor's family?"

"I don't know."

"Is he the head of the family?"

"Yes."

Another scream rang down the hall.

"I know he has two brothers left," the man said quickly.

"Left?"

"One died with the old man, years ago. Another was killed six months later when they tried to kill him." He cocked his head towards Ludmilla. "Kill Tripensky."

Rainey stepped back to Ludmilla. "I don't think the Chergins like you very much."

"Why did you follow us here?" Ludmilla asked.

The man hesitated. Ludmilla took a menacing step towards him.

"We . . . we have a standing order to kill anyone claiming to be Tripensky. When you came out of Kolochoff's house, we knew you were the real Tripensky."

"Men have pretended to be me?"

"Yes, ever since you and your emissary disappeared; right after Kostya Chergin tried to kill you."

Ludmilla looked at Rainey, who shrugged. "People like to perpetuate a legend," he said. He saw the flash of intensity in her eyes.

"Is that everything we need to know?" she asked.

"Yes, I think so."

She spun so quickly that Rainey couldn't stop her. The man in the chair knew what was coming.

"You said—"

His sentence was cut off. Just like his head.

Rainey watched Ludmilla, waiting for the tension in her muscles to start relaxing. He stepped forward and put his arm on the wrist of her sword hand.

"I promised him he would live," he said.

"I didn't," was all she said. She shook off his hand and left the room. Rainey followed her to the other room. She swept past Aunshaunie and thrust her sword into the other prisoner's heart.

"Ludmilla!" Rainey shouted. "You have to stop."

"Not until every Chergin and the men working for them are dead. I will go alone if you refuse to help."

No one spoke. Ludmilla looked at each of them one at a time, seeking a response.

"Are the Chergins the family that hired me to kill Conner?" Aunshaunie finally asked.

"Very likely," Ludmilla replied.

"Do you know where they are?"

"Yes."

Aunshaunie looked up at Rainey. "Then I'm with you."

"Ladies—" Rainey began.

Aunshaunie cut him off. "Igor?"

Krasenoff looked sadly at Rainey. "If she's going, I have to go. And if the Chergins are the family that does the assassinating for the pro-Lithuanian Novgorodians, my vote is kill them all, too."

Rainey sighed. "Fine, but we need a plan. How are we going to get in?"

Ludmilla was already through the door. "Same way I got in last time. Follow my lead."

* * *

They stood down the street from the walls of the Chergin compound. More men were posted on the walls than when Ludmilla first intruded a little over six years ago. Five men stood outside at the gate. Word of the real Ruslan Tripensky's return had no doubt reached the Chergins. They were not taking any chances.

Ludmilla turned to Rainey. "My plan won't work. They are watching for me this time. One of them may know what the Emissary looks like." She and Aunshaunie had put on long skirts, hoping to get close as women, but there were too many guards to get past.

"Then perhaps we should just leave the Chergins be," Rainey said. "They can be dealt with when the grand prince arrives with his army."

"That could be months away," Krasenoff said. "They may have another plot in play."

"I can get in," Aunshaunie said.

Everyone turned to her. "There's a blind spot over by the guardhouse on the south wall," she explained. "We can get up on the wall there, silently clear a few guards and be on the ground and into the house before anyone notices."

"We don't know how they're patrolling the courtyard inside the wall," Rainey said.

"We can find that out once we're up on the wall." Aunshaunie began moving down the street towards the guardhouse.

"And how do we . . ." Rainey began.

"Scale the wall?" Krasenoff smiled. "I think she has that figured out." He turned to follow Aunshaunie. "Damn, I love that woman."

Rainey looked at Ludmilla. She grinned back at him. "Coming?"

They arrived at the point of the wall where they would scale it. Aunshaunie handed her crossbow to Rainey. "Watch for the guard to reach the corner, then signal me. If he hears my hook hit the wall, shoot him."

Ludmilla was fascinated by Aunshaunie's equipment. Both shed their skirts, Aunshaunie picking up her hook and rope. On Rainey's signal, she threw the hook up and over the wall. After a quick jerk to ensure it was secure, she scaled the wall in a matter of seconds.

"Guess she's done this before," Krasenoff said. He started to climb, much more slowly. Ludmilla turned to see Rainey tracking the guard as he made his way back towards the guardhouse. The man had just reached the corner and turned to track back when

Aunshaunie jumped him from behind and slit his throat. A few seconds later, Krasenoff was over the wall. A few seconds after that, he appeared wearing the dead man's cloak and slowly making his way to the corner.

"You're next," Rainey said to Ludmilla.

She had never climbed a rope like this before. Watching Aunshaunie and Krasenoff, she had figured out the technique, placing her foot up against the wall and pulling herself up with her arms. Those years of swinging the heavy wooden swords with Rainey paid off in a new way; she found that her upper-body strength made the climb easy. Reaching the top and climbed over, she looked down to find Rainey already on his way up.

Aunshaunie tapped Ludmilla's shoulder. "Come into the guardhouse." Once inside, she asked, "What do you remember about the inside of the house?"

* * *

Rainey came over the wall and pressed himself against the guardhouse. He surveyed the courtyard to see only two men. Most of the guards were on the wall. Krasenoff was making his way back from the nearest corner.

"My next pass I can time with the guard coming along the other side," he said. "Crouch down and stay behind my cloak. I'll get you there and you can replace him."

Rainey nodded. He unslung his crossbow and left it by the guardhouse door where Aunshaunie could find it. He slipped under the cloak and followed Krasenoff. As they reached the corner, he heard Krasenoff speak to the other guard.

"Cold night."

"Who are—ugh."

Rainey slipped out from behind Krasenoff, who was withdrawing his sword from the man's gut. Rainey quickly pulled off the man's cloak and threw it over himself.

"He goes about half way to the gate and returns," Krasenoff said. Rainey nodded and started his walk. As he reached his point, he turned to look out over the street. On the way back, he glanced back to the guardhouse. The crossbow was gone. He turned and was sauntering back towards the corner when he saw Ludmilla and Aunshaunie rush out behind one of the men in the courtyard. He shifted his attention to the men on the wall. They were all turning outward around the same time and failed to notice anything untoward behind them. Rainey looked back into the courtyard. Ludmilla was lowering the guard to the ground while Aunshaunie let fly at the second man with the crossbow bolt. He went down with hardly a sound. The two women then made a dash for the house.

Rainey gripped his arquebus and brought it up. He blew on the firing cloth to liven the coals and assessed the range to the men in front of him. From this distance, he thought he should be able to get both of them with one shot.

The sound of wood breaking brought the attention of the wall guards to the house. A woman screamed. Rainey raised his arquebus and fired. The two men in his range crumpled to the ground. Rainey threw off the extra cloak, began reloading and made for the steps. As he reached the ground, he saw Krasenoff dispatching another wall guard and scrambling down off the wall. Rainey turned to see two men coming at him with swords. The arquebus roared again, sending both men backwards to the ground. Rainey swung the arquebus onto his back, pulled his sword and made for the house. He reached the door at the same time as Krasenoff. The sounds of swords meeting rang from the house.

"You go in. I'll keep any more guards out here from getting in."

Krasenoff ran past him. "Aunshaunie!"

"I'm fine," Aunshaunie announced from the first floor. "Go upstairs and help Ludmilla."

34

Ludmilla ran down the hallway. Three dead men sprawled across the floor. She wondered who had killed them, being that she was the first to reach the second floor. An open door revealed a study with two men inside. Both had their swords drawn.

"Which one of you is Feodor?" she demanded.

"I am," said the man on her right, "and I will send you right to hell."

"Perhaps you can show me the way," Ludmilla responded.

Feodor came around a heavy desk and raised his sword. Ludmilla took one step towards him then sprang to her left up onto a large chair as Feodor brought his sword down. Ludmilla leaped from the chair and stuck her sword deep into his neck. He gasped, his free hand coming up to try and hold his blood from pouring out. He failed. Blood spurted out of his wound. Ludmilla landed on the desk, her feet scattering papers and an ink bottle. She pointed her sword at the second man, who dropped his weapon, fear consuming his face. She glanced over at Feodor. He was still standing, gripping his neck. He tried to raise his sword, but it fell from his hand. He sank to his knees and then toppled to the floor.

Ludmilla turned her attention to the other man. "And who are you?"

"No one. I just . . ."

Ludmilla noticed a crest on his tunic. She'd seen it before. She looked down at Feodor. He wore the same crest over his heart.

"You are a Chergin." Before the man could deny it, her sword pierced his heart, right though the crest. She pulled the blade free, allowing the man to collapse onto the floorboards. She jumped down and headed for the door.

Two Chergins dead. One to go.

She moved to the next room and kicked open the door. A guard quickly came at her. Ducking under his swing, she sliced at his feet. He yelled in pain and began to fall over. Ludmilla pointed her sword upwards; the man impaled himself on it to the hilt. She pushed him over and extracted her sword from his gut. Standing up, she found three women and eight children huddled on the floor in a corner. The children were screaming in terror, the women clutching them tightly. Ludmilla paused for a moment. She knew instinctively that these were the wives and children of the Chergin brothers. She raised her sword. *All Chergins must be killed.*

As she took a step towards them, a hand grabbed her wrist. She quickly spun, drawing a dagger from her belt with her free hand. She stopped when she saw the man's face.

It was Gerhard.

"You're here," she said to him.

"Yes."

"How?"

"When they heard that Ruslan Tripensky was back, they hired extra men. I signed on."

Ludmilla looked back at the women and children in the corner. "They are Chergins."

"Yes, but you do not kill helpless people."

She turned back to Gerhard. "They kill helpless people all the time"

"No, their husbands did. They are dead now. You don't want to go down that road. Do you want to join them in that special place in Hell for people who kill women and children?"

Ludmilla glared at Gerhard, but his sad features reduced the hatred in her heart.

"You have killed women and children," she said.

"And I live with that shame every day," he replied. "It's why I couldn't participate in killing the grand prince. It was wrong and I knew it. You slaughter these innocents, you will live with regret for the rest of your life."

Gerhard let go of her wrist. Ludmilla looked at her sword, blood still trickling down its blade. She lowered it and turned to the people in the corner. They cowered silently, all eyes on her. She could feel their fear. Sounds from elsewhere in the house had ceased. She turned back to Gerhard.

"There's still one more Chergin."

"He was downstairs," he replied. "I'm sure Aunshaunie took care of him."

Ludmilla passed him out into the hallway. Behind her, Gerhard told the women, "Stay here until after we leave and you will not be harmed."

* * *

"We have to leave now," Rainey said. "No telling who may send the Chergins help."

He had found Ludmilla standing over a dead man on the main floor.

"Ludmilla," Rainey repeated.

She pointed her sword at a crest on the man's chest. "This is the third Chergin brother. They're all dead now. I had to see for myself."

Rainey wrapped his arms around her and whispered in her ear. "Doesn't really make you feel better, does it?"

Ludmilla turned to face him. "It should. Why doesn't it?"

"Vengeance is like that. It consumes you. It becomes the biggest part of your life. You think it gives your life meaning. Then, when you've achieved it, it just leaves you empty. You don't know what your meaning is anymore."

"I have to find a new meaning,"

"Yes. May I suggest you consider me and our children?"

Ludmilla smiled. "I miss them."

"I do, too. Let's say we go home to them."

* * *

"There are a lot of them."

Ivan sat on his horse behind his five thousand-man army at the Shelon River. It was summer, four months after Rainey had returned from Novgorod. Rainey was at his left and Daniil Kolmsky, his general, on his right.

"If what Kolochoff told me was true," Rainey said, "the archbishop's cavalry will only attack the Pskov troops."

"That's why I placed them way over there," Kolmsky said. "They aren't as useful as our own men, anyway."

"He's playing it safe," Ivan said. "When they lose, he can say he really hadn't attacked my army."

"Are you sure those are mostly citizens of the city?" Kolmsky asked.

"Yes," Rainey said. "Gorbaty-Shuysky is up in the Dvina region with their main army. These men are not well trained and will not be well led."

"Then I leave you to defeat them easily," Ivan said. He turned his horse around and trotted back to his camp.

"Anything you'd like me to do?" Rainey asked the general.

Kolmsky nodded. "Perhaps you can help the Pskovs not to get overrun by the archbishop's horses."

"My pleasure."

35

1478

Ludmilla rocked back and forth, her new baby in her arms. It was another boy, taking her brood to six children. Add in Ruslan and Svetlana and the household now included eight children.

She thought about all her children while nursing the new one. Ruslan had grown into a fine young man, sixteen years of age and already thinking about marriage to his love. His love, of course, was Svetlana, one year younger. He absolutely adored her. Svetlana was turning into a real beauty. She loved him, too, and they were becoming inseparable. It had gotten so hard to get them to do their chores that Rainey had finally reorganized their duties so they would work together. Chores were still done slowly, but at least they were getting done.

In a few more years, Svetlana would inherit her father's part of the business in Novgorod, something Ludmilla's brother Andrey had kept separate for her. Ruslan spent many hours with his father and Father Kirill learning the skills of commerce, planning to go to Novgorod with Svetlana when she got her inheritance and work with his uncle Andrey and his son. Father

Kirill kept offering to marry the two young lovers, but Rainey insisted that they wait until they were ready to leave and start their new life.

Helena was growing up fast, too. Ludmilla's oldest daughter looked a bit like a Scottish lass, according to Rainey, clearly exotic by Rus standards. At thirteen years, she was attracting offers of marriage, with political ties in the bargain. But Rainey, as he had with Ludmilla, wanted Helena to marry who she wanted. If a political gain could be had from her choice, so be it, but it would be her choice. She did not seem in any hurry to take an interest in boys. She was more interested in her father's training exercises, which he taught at the army school in Zenoplata. Rainey already felt sorry for any suitor who came calling.

Maksim was in line to become the next boyar of Zenoplata. He showed signs of being a good and smart young man and spent his time learning as much as he could about the lands and the business he would inherit one day. He was followed by three girls: Alexandria, Oksana and Tatyana.

And now, finally, the newborn was in her arms. Ludmilla's thoughts were interrupted when Rainey entered the room.

"How is the little one doing?" he asked.

"He's stubborn, like you," she replied. "How is Novgorod?"

Rainey had just returned from the city with the Muscovy army. "I don't think they will be searching for allies any longer. This time, the grand prince fully annexed all their lands. He's forcing many of the boyars to move to Moscow and other cities in his realm. The most treacherous ones he had killed or imprisoned. I am constantly impressed by the way he works slowly and successfully to build his country.

"And my brother?"

"His loyalty has earned him a seat on the new council. The Veche has been disbanded. He will report directly to the governor."

Ludmilla looked up at him. "The grand prince didn't make you governor, did he?"

Rainey grinned. "No. Never even came up."

"Good. Who do you think you'll have to fight next?"

"My guess is Ahmed. Since the grand prince cut off his tribute a couple of years ago, it's only a matter of time before he comes calling."

"Nice of him to wait until the grand prince finished with Novgorod."

"Yes, it is. No doubt he'll regret waiting."

Rainey had always wanted to be present at his children's births, but the grand prince couldn't be refused. Alexandria had been born while he was in Rome with Ivan Fryazin in 1469, negotiating the betrothal of Zoe Palaiologina, niece of the last real Byzantine emperor, to Ivan. Rainey had been sent along because of his knowledge of the Latins. Rainey was called to go back to Rome to escort Zoe to Moscow. This was in 1472, causing him to miss Oksana's birth. When Tatyana was born in 1474, Rainey was in Rostov completing the grand prince's outright purchase of that city. All Rainey's work with the Rostov boyars finally forced their prince to offer to sell his dominions, not wanting to end up like Brukhati of Yaroslavl.

But he had made it home for the new baby's birth, barely. As he rode into the courtyard, he could hear Ludmilla screaming from her room. He bolted up the stairs and was present when the baby was born ten minutes later.

"I received a letter from Gerhard," Rainey said.

"Really. Where has he gotten to?" Ludmilla asked.

"He's married into a Von Dietrich family in Istria."

"Where's Istria?"

"It's part of the Hapsburg lands southeast of Venice. He says he's very happy."

"Excellent. He deserves it."

They sat quietly for a moment, marvelling in their new son.

"So, what shall we call him?" Ludmilla finally asked.

"Well," Rainey began, "the grand prince has mentioned a few times that he would be pleased if one of my sons were named after him."

"No."

"Ludmilla, he's the grand prince. I couldn't say no."

"Then tell him you had another girl."

Rainey sighed. "And if he comes to visit, are you going to put him in a dress?"

Ludmilla looked down at the baby. "He doesn't come often."

They sat together silently, the only sound coming from the rocking chair and the baby gurgling.

"Ivan," Ludmilla said quietly.

"It's a good strong name. Igor named his first boy Ivan."

It had taken three years, but Krasenoff had behaved himself and devoted all his free time to Aunshaunie. She only agreed to marry him after her agent showed up in Zenoplata one day demanding that she come back into service to him. He had threatened her with exposure to kings and dukes who wanted retribution for some of her past assassinations if she refused. Krasenoff split the man's head open with an axe. And that was it for the legend of the Ghost. They now had two children of their own.

"Very well," Ludmilla conceded. "His name will be Ivan Connoryevich Raynykov."

36

2007

"So, your family began with this Scottish soldier who wandered into Russia and saved Ivan the Great from being assassinated."

Evgenia was tired. It had been a long night listening to her father-in-law talk about his family's origins. It was quite the epic tale to be passed down from generation to generation.

"That is correct," Dmitri said.

"Then why is there nothing about him in the history books? A lone Scot being so important should have gotten some press."

"No one remembers Von Markenburg, either, and he was the chancellor," Sasha said.

"It was almost six hundred years ago," Dmitri added. "Records weren't that common back then. Central government administrations in Russia weren't established for almost another century under Ivan the Terrible. And apart from some key players like Ivan and Von Markenburg, no one would have known where Rainey had come from."

"And you would be descended from which son?"

"Maksim, whose line eventually became the Counts of Zenoplata."

Evgenia nodded. "Ok, let's go back to your great-grandfather and his rescue of the Romanov kids."

Dmitri breathed in deeply. "Alexis couldn't move because of his bleeding condition, but Anastasia could be sent out of Russia. A team was put together to get her out through the West. But they ran into a patrol somewhere along the way and Anastasia was killed. Her body was brought back and buried near her family."

"And Alexis?"

"My great-grandfather couldn't be found with the Tsarovich, so he passed him off to British agents. Turns out the British couldn't move him safely either, so they passed Alexis off to another party. Turned out to be an American industrialist who had organized a small army to get the boy out."

"And that small army was led by a man with the sword of the Great Celt," Sasha said excitedly.

"So what happened to Alexis?" Evgenia asked.

"Their train was caught in an artillery barrage in Siberia and Alexis was killed," Dmitri said. "Vasili brought his body back and buried him with his sister."

"What about the man with the sword?"

"He returned to America, I guess."

"And he would have been a descendant of . . ."

"Ivan, the Great Celt's youngest son."

Evgenia noticed a slight smile on her father-in-law's face. She felt he knew more about this American than he was telling. "There's more to this story, isn't there?"

"Of course. There's six hundred years of it I could tell you about."

"No, I mean since 1919."

Dmitri's smile disappeared in an instant. Evgenia felt a pang of nervousness creep into her body. Dmitri had never looked at her like that before.

What did happen after 1919?

Author's Notes

When I looked at where the second novel in the Rainey Chronicles should go, I was torn between writing a sequel to The Locket or going back to an earlier time. I had left hints in The Locket about where the sword had been before. If I just wrote a sequel, all the ideas I had for placing a Rainey and his sword into key times in history would be hard to get back to.

So, after talking with my editor, it was decided to make use of the reference to "The Great Celt" in The Locket as the theme for Book 2. And I'm so glad I did.

Ivan III, known as Ivan the Great, was a fascinating historical figure. A man who multiplied his holding considerably with only minimal use of his army. He had access to modern firearms with Moscow being generally isolated from the inventors of them. He sat on his throne for over forty years and only because his nobility let him. He was what I call an anomaly in history and it is these anomalies that history turns on. Wiithout Ivan, there may never have been a Russia,

My research sources again began with Google and Wikipedia. There isn't a lot of material to find on mid 15th century Russia that isn't in Russian, but the book "Ivan the Great of Russia" by James Fennell is an excellent biography of Ivan, enabling me to keep straight the dates and chronology of events in the novel. It also reinforced how I viewed Ivan as a character. He was smart, cautious, and only used his army when he knew he could win. A truly rennaissance man on the fringes of Europe.

I'd like to acknowledge my editor, John Meyer from Cape Fear Publishing for another excellent job bringing my book up to professional standards; another great cover by Alisha at Damonza; my beta readers and fans for their enthusiasm; and the gang at

ARWA for the support and the wealth of writing and marketing tips I've received over the last year. After all my searching for how to market my books, I'd like to also thank Mark Dawson and Nick Stephenson for seminars and access to writer's groups for joint promotions. The internet can be a scary place. And Stacey Kondla and Nicole Haugen at Indigo have been so supportive for my book signings down at the Signal Hill store in Calgary.

Writing is a very solitary endeavour. My only companion while writing tends to be my dog, Piper, who comes to distract me every few hours so I don't totally ruin my eyes from staring at my laptop screen. Keeping me from going down the rabbit hole entirely are my brethryn at St. Mark's Masonic Lodge #118 and my lovely wife, Carmen. I know Carmen would like me to get a real job some day, but I thank her greatly for her support as I express my imagination in writing.

B.G. Cousins
Calgary, Alberta

Coming in 2018
Book 3 of the Rainey Chronicles

Dark Before Light

The adventure of the children of Robert and Elizabeth Rainey through the dark days of the Second World War.

Follow the Rainey Clan and the sword that defines their destinies.

Book 1 of the Rainey Chronicles

Available through Amazon or
through our website at:

www.glenkeltybooks.com

A Woman in Search of her Father
A Soldier in Search of a Future
A Journey Through the Maelstrom of the Russian Revolution

"An exciting and unpredictable tale of espionage and adventure in the early 20th century." *Kirkus Reviews*

"…the lives of the three primary characters make for great reading. Each individual is alive on the page complete with flesh and blood emotions and the descriptive battle scenes do their part in adding to the adventure." *Red Rock Bookworm*

"The locket is a beautiful blend of war story and love story with a strong heroine to top it all off." *Books & Life*

"I actually learned quite a bit while reading the book. It held my interest the entire time. I recommend this book to anyone who enjoys, history, war, romance and a good book." *Goodreads*

"This is an excellent piece of historical fiction that I would recommend to anyone who enjoys this genre." *NetGalley*